The Prince Madoc Secret

The Prince Madoc Secret

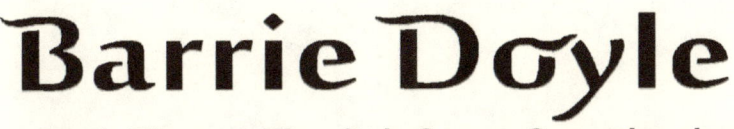

Barrie Doyle

Book Three - The Oak Grove Conspiracies

THE PRINCE MADOC SECRET
Copyright © 2018 by Barrie Doyle

ISBN: 978-1-4866-1588-9

Word Alive Press
119 De Baets Street, Winnipeg, MB R2J 3R9
www.wordalivepress.ca

WORD ALIVE
—PRESS—

Cataloguing in Publication may be obtained through Library and Archives Canada

For Kathy, my love, my friend, my muse, my strength

GLOSSARY OF NAMES AND PLACES

A

Aberystwyth	Ab-er-ist-with; seaside university town in mid wales
Ap	"son of"

B

Bach	As in the composer; literally 'small'; term of affection
Blimey	Blie-me; Slang word expressing surprise' short for "blind me"
Bore Da	Boor-eh-da; good day
Borth	seaside village on Cardigan Bay; north of Aberystwyth
Borth-y-gest	fishing village in North Wales, near Porthmadog
Bwylch-y-de	boolk-ee -dee; damn in mid Wales

C

Carriad	carry- ad; term of endearment; darling, dear
Castell	pronounced as written; castle
Conwy	Con-way; town in North Wales
Crikey	pronounced as written; slang expression or surprise or shock

D

Dafydd	Daff-ith; David
Dai	dah-y; short form of David, or Dafydd
Dew dew	pronounced as written; similar to English 'goodness gracious'
Diolch	Dee-ol-k; Thank you
Dolwyddelan	Dol-with-e-lan; Owain Gwynedd's castle e in North Wales
Dyfed	Di-feth; county in Wales

G

Gorbals	former slum district in Gasgow,Scotland
Gorsedd	Gore-seth; council of Druids

Grassed	slang criminal expression for informing on gang members
Guvnor	Boss

H

Hendre-y-derwen	Hen-druh ee der-wen; Oak woods
HRH	His Royal Highness
Hwyl	Hoo-will; man's name

I

Idrith	Pronounced as written; man's name
Iechyd da	yekky-da; Cheers!
Iolo Morganwyg	eye-o-lo Mor-gan-wig; fictional college named after late 17th poet and cultural druid
Iowan	eye-o-wan; man's name
Iowerth	eye-o-worth; man's name

L

Llan	thlan; small enclosure, usually a church yard/graveyard; prefix for many town names in Wales
Llanfrothen	thlan-froth-en; village in Snowden Mountain region, North Wales
Llanidloes	thlan-id-lows; market town in mid Wales
LLyn Clywedeg	th-lin clew-ed-eg; reservoir near Llanidloes, mid Wales
Lummox	teasing slang expression meaning 'dummy'
Lundy Island	island in Bristol Channel, near Devon's north coast

M

Menai Strait	divides the mainland of Wales from Anglesey Island
My patch	slang for 'my territory' or 'my responsibility'; used often by police

N

Nick	slang for steal; also for police station

O

Ogma	Celtic god
Old Bill	slang for police; reportedly named after King William IV because the Metropolitan Police in London came into being during his reign
Old College	Victorian building on the Aberystwyth seafront; site of the first University in Wales

P

Penmon Priory	located on Anglesey Island
Powys	county in Wales

R

Rhossili	village on the Gower Peninsula, west of Swansea in South Wales

T

Telly	slang for television

U

Uni	slang for university

W

Worms head	headland outcrop separated from mainland by tides daily; at Rhossili

CAST OF CHARACTERS

UNITED KINGDOM

Stone Wallace	American journalist
Myfanwy "Mandy" Griffiths	History professor, Huw's daughter
Huw Griffiths	Professor, historian and archaeologist
Sir Giles Broadbent	Director, Crown Security Bureau
Freddy Garrett	Assistant Director, Crown Security Bureau
Lord Edward Greyfell	Director of Druid research centre, Greyfell Abbey
Lady Nees Greyfell	wife and co-director
Greg Maddox	Crown Security agent
Gregory Belmont	Minister of Security and Policing; Druid
Fiona Moffatt	Secretary to Minister
Dr. Richard Evans	Dean, Iolo Morganwyg College; Dragon Master
Dafydd "Badger" Morgan	professor, IMC, Druid
Hamish McLeod	Druid killer
Bob "Marsh" Mello	BBC producer
Maggie Railstone	BBC director
Adam Carswell	Police Detective Chief Inspector; Crown Security agent
Nathan Griffiths	Researcher, National Library of Wales
Evan Thomas Evan ("ET")	ex history professor; Bed and Breakfast operator
Dilys Evan	ET's wife and B&B operator
Ioan Parry	Druid
Martin Bryn	Druid
Sir Michael Donovan	financier; Druid
John Beauchamp	Templar Master
Gilbert Fitzsimmons	Templar knight
Henry Syme	Templar knight
Anna Grindell	Greyfell contact and informant
Mavis Green	Evans' housekeeper, Llanidloes
Ifor Beynon	Druid; Evans' groundskeeper, Llanidloes

UNITED STATES

Chad Lawson	SID agent
Oscar "Wiz" Zanelli	SID agent
Calvin Tyler	Director, Security Investigation Division
Liam Murphy	Druid; ex-presidential candidate and Raven Master
Bethan Price	Druid; Raven Master
David Price	Druid; Raven Master's son
Dexter Armitage	Druid; Chief of Staff to the President
Gen. R.G. Wells	Druid; Serpent Master
Malcolm Coughlin	Oilman; friend of Bethan Price
Cliff Ronson	ex-Army soldier; drifter
Lee Schumacher	ex-Army sniper

Madoc, I am the sonne of Owen Gwynedd

With stature large and comely grace adorned

No lands at home, nor store of wealth me please

My minde was whole to search the Ocean seas

Meredith ap Rhys, 1477

Alone with none but thee, my God

I journey on my way

What need I fear, when thou are near O king of night

and day

More safe am I within thy hand

Than if a host did round me stand

Columba, (circa 52-597)

There is a seed of courage hidden...waiting for some final

and desperate danger to make it grow

Lord of the Rings, J.R.R. Tolkien

Author's Note

I would like to acknowledge the many readers who have commented in person or in writing about my two previous books, *The Excalibur Parchment* and *The Lucifer Scroll*. Your appreciation and rave reviews are extremely encouraging (and a lot make me blush), so I am over the moon when you pass along your kind thoughts.

Each of the books is a stand-alone story, although obviously they and **The Prince Madoc Secret** form an ongoing series. While they are fiction, I strive for as much precision and historical accuracy as possible. Any mistakes are my own, created by my own carelessness or stupidity. History is a story. It is the story of people. As that story is recorded (whether verbal or written) it changes based upon the perspectives of the individual telling the story. History is always open to interpretation. Out of the repeated tellings and re-tellings of a historical event, legends and myths are created. So, in the modern era, my protagonists see historical situations and artifacts through the prism of time and previous interpretations.

J.R.R. Tolkien said, "*I believe that legends and myths are largely made of 'truth' and indeed present aspects of it that can only be received in this mode.*" By extension, the kernels of truth contained in legends and myths reveal truth and reality in a profound way. If Tolkien is correct, then it is also the way truth is conveyed to mere mortals.

In a day when society is in such a tumult, I try to show the personal development of my characters as they struggle with the challenges set before them. Some are weighed down by previous disappointments and loses. Others are meeting real challenges for the first time. How they cope—whether it is anger, fear or faith—is a key developmental factor in the story. I have met great challenges in my life—personal as well as professional. Faith in God is the one constant I have and has led me through and blessed me each time. For others, that is not a factor, and I respect that. Some have great internal strength that takes them through. Others do not and drop into shells, reluctant to face the challenges life throws at them. Yet others react by building a sense of rage and revenge against those who laid the challenges before them. Each reacts in their own way, and I have tried to reflect that myriad of responses in the books.

I am also amazed at the way today's news reflects and often jumps ahead of my stories. I say that because when I first started writing *Excalibur* I thought I had created a thoroughly unprincipled and evil set of zealots as my villains. Then along came ISIS who did more depraved things to humanity than I could ever have imagined. I have tried to explore the supernatural world and evil as it hovers around modern society, especially in *Lucifer*. Certainly, modern culture wants to explore the supernatural and wicked world, particularly in movies and television. Then I see the news headlines and read about man's inhumanity to man on an individual as well as mass basis so, again, I am trumped by reality.

Some have asked why my antagonists are Druids. The answer is both complex and simple. First, I was sick and tired of reading novels where the villains were always the same generic groupings—corrupt businessmen, politicians or church leaders; Nazis; neo-Nazis; Russian mafia, communists or post-communists. I wanted a 'new' group of villains that fit into the framework of the stories. Second, in any religious teaching, there always seem to be those who become brutal zealots violently and cruelly demanding obedience and "their way or the highway." Since I wanted to explore the supernatural and issues of faith in challenging times, the Druids seemed to fit. I made them a zealous, violent branch of Celtic society where things like the supernatural world are, well, natural. The beliefs in fairies, leprechauns, and the thinning veil between the underworld and the current world (especially at Halloween) fit with the themes I was developing and are still a part of modern Celtic culture and thinking. Druids in ancient times (pre-Roman) were their society's priests, philosophers, historians, judges, wisdom and bards, or storytellers. Today, in Wales, they are the poets and musicians that keep Welsh culture alive at Eisteffodds (cultural gatherings). But there has always been a malevolent side to the Druids, including human sacrifice and a belief in terrifying and cruel multiple pantheistic gods rather than a monotheistic God.

Having or searching for a faith to believe in is an essential component of the motivations of many of my characters. How they make the search and how successful they are reflects, I believe, the modern search for spirituality in a secular world. For my main protagonists, faith is a critical part of who they are or who they are becoming.

Why have I set so much of all the books in Wales? Again, several reasons. Wales is a beautiful but little known country, especially in North America where, if you think of Celtic nations, Ireland and Scotland come to mind immediately. Wales, not so much. Which is unfortunate because of all six Celtic nation—Wales (Cymru), Scotland (Alba), Ireland (Eire), Cornwall (Kernow), Brittany (Breizh), Isle of Man (Mannin)—Wales is closest to the original Celtic standards of any. (It is indeed little known. Look at any guided tour of Britain and you'll hit England and Scotland and Ireland, but very few spend any time in Wales.) Yet, it is a land of mystery, myths and legends (the year 2017 was labelled by the Welsh government as 'Year of the Legend'). Music and the arts are a core value. Castles and history ooze out of the ground (there are seven castles within a 15-mile radius of my hometown); more than any other nation in the world. History. Legends. Myths. I can think of no better, fresh setting for a novel than this proud nation that, like my protagonists, faces every challenge with courage, conviction and pride. Perhaps I might intrigue you enough to entice you to visit this marvelous land. I appreciate the ones who have joined me in tours of some of the key sites in the books.

When I started writing The Prince Madoc Secret, I planned it as the third in the trilogy, The Oak Grove Conspiracies. My characters, however, tell the story; I am the mere recorder. They decided that while the story is complete as its stands, it is not finished. What happens with the legend of Madoc in the United States? Did he, in fact, travel into the interior? Did his people integrate with the indigenous peoples? Were they the ones who constructed stone fortifications and towns? If I listen to my characters, they still have more to tell.

I would be remiss if I did not also express appreciation to close friends like Doug Davis, Gordon Bucek, Jean Legg and many others—you know who you are—who have encouraged, criticized, helped and supported the development of these stories. To all of you, I am eternally grateful.

—Barrie Doyle, 2018

Prologue

Temple Mount, Jerusalem 1122 AD

Flames flickered against the roughhewn stone walls as the knight, fully clad in chainmail and wearing his Order's distinctive white mantle surcoat, hurried down the myriad of tunnels beneath the hill men of all religions called Temple Mount. Hugh de Payns, founder and Grand Master of the Poor Fellow-Soldiers of Christ of the Temple of Solomon, now known simply as Templars, struggled over the rubble and rock on the tunnel floors, eagerly anxious to look at the find his men had just reported.

Together, nine of them had formed their Order as armed and trained monks dedicated to the protection of pilgrims visiting the holy city of Jerusalem. Early in the year 1118, Baldwin, the Crusader King of Jerusalem moved his palace from the old al-Asqua mosque on the top of the hill to a new, more luxurious, building west of the old site. Sir Hugh and his second in command, Sir Godfrey of Saint-Omer pounced on the King's decision to move, supporting it and begging for the old palace and its environs as the Order's new home.

Pleased with the new Order's piety and determination to build a mighty fighting force to protect the Holy Land, Baldwin agreed and the knights moved in immediately. They lived there and began recruiting as well, building up their stores—arms, clothing and food.

His years in the Holy Land meant Hugh was at first familiar then obsessed by the stories passed down by generations of inhabitants, of treasures hidden under Temple Mount. Using the stories as a guide he soon found a huge underground vault in the southeast corner of Temple Mount. Convinced this vault was the remnant of Solomon's vast stables he immediately used it for the Order's own horses. It was all the proof he needed that the stories were true.

Consumed with the stories of treasure, Hugh directed the search personally. Especially after he and Godfrey wrenched confessions out of a prisoner years earlier, that the Seljuk Turks too had searched for Solomon's treasure under Temple Mount.

For three years they'd steadily built their Order and it grew in numbers and reputation. But as they organized and trained, Hugh also drove the core founding knights—most of them his relatives—into probing the secrets of the underground spaces. Much of the time their excavations had proved fruitless. Now that effort was beginning to bear fruit.

Six months ago, they'd stumbled upon a large chamber. Chipping away at the sides of the room, a hole soon emerged. They hewed away at it for days, steadily enlarging it. Soon they realized they'd opened a smaller chamber with rough stone shelves around it. As they peered in, they saw piles of dried old scrolls of parchment. Flushed with excitement, they removed the scrolls and showed small portions to scholars among the city's remaining Jews. Cowed though they were by their Christian overlords, the scholars could not contain their excitement, confirming the scrolls were ancient copies of the Old Testament scriptures.

The discovery invigorated the Templar leaders. They arranged quietly for two Jewish scholars to move into the temple area under guard and translate the scrolls into Latin while they renewed their excavations.

Now, this day's news drew Hugh running and stumbling through the dank, dark mustiness to the site of their latest discovery. As he got closer, the tunnel became narrower and smaller. He motioned the knight with the flaming torch ahead of him as they slowed their pace to a crawl.

"Just ahead, Grand Master."

Hugh peered into the barely lit darkness, then saw more light coming from the burning torch of the man left guarding the find. Apart from the heavy breathing of the knight in front of him, there was no sound in the stygian darkness. Suddenly the tunnel opened into a chamber large enough for him to stand.

"There!" The knight pointed the torch to the right. A square wooden chest lay on its side, its dust covered exterior littered with stone debris and even the bones of small animals.

Godfrey and two other knights crowded into the small chamber.

"We have not touched it since we found it, Grand Master," the knight holding the torch murmured reverently as Sir Hugh knelt before the chest and straightened it. The overwhelming stench of decay created a burning sensation in his nose and throat. Once the chest was upright he saw there was no lock. Hugh reached up and seized the torch from his knight's hands, breathed slowly and paused in prayer. He slowly and carefully opened it and stared inside.

Gently, Hugh moved some of the items aside and picked up a ragged parchment. Surprisingly, it was in Latin. He began to read, his finger following slowly as he struggled with the words in the dim, flickering light. The chamber was silent except for the quiet anticipatory breathing of the knights as they stared at their Grand Master. Finally, his fingers stopped briefly then ran back across one word. He repeated the movement twice, his lips moving slightly each time before he quietly breathed one word, "Jesus."

He painfully squinted at the parchment again, gesturing the man above him to lower the torch so he could see. Holding the fragment in his left hand, his right forefinger slowly moving under each word, Hugh struggled to read the document. Finally, he had seen enough.

"Praise God that we have been privileged to find this," he muttered, then began praying aloud as his fellow knights, also knelt. When he was finished, he rose.

"God has given us great mercy. He has allowed us, of all his people, to discover this magnificent reminder of his constant presence and love for us and also of the continuous threat to our faith. Jesu be praised!" He paused and looked each knight in firmly the eye. "This find is for our Order alone, until I decide how we will deal with it. Until then, we keep this secret amongst ourselves. Nobody, not even our recruits, must know."

He looked around at each of them again. "We will pray and ask God what he would have us do. He has given us this incredible responsibility. We are his to use as he directs. We must be patient and obedient, brothers."

Slowly he left the chamber trailed by his fellow knights, cradling the chest tightly in his massive arms.

Chapter One

Gwynedd, North Wales 1171

A cold morning mist clung to the shore. Although it was near the longest day, cool winds and rains had marked the past week. The shriek of gulls at first masked the sound of galloping horses splashing through the waters and clacking against the rocks of the shallow stream that tumbled down from a trickle in the mighty peaks of Snowdon to its wide but shallow mouth near Borth-y-gest.

Inside the crude but sturdy hut two men heard the approaching horsemen. A skeletally thin and unshaven Idrith ap Gruffyd pushed himself painfully to a sitting position on his makeshift bed and signaled to his servant to find out who was visiting their unlikely shelter so early in the morning.

Hardly had his young serving lad opened the hide that served for a door, before a stocky man strode through and into the dark interior. Only the flickering flames of the breakfast fire the boy had tended provided light. The visitor was clad in muddy boots and an equally muddied black cloth vest bearing no coat of arms or identification and covering heavy chain mail. He pushed the chain mail off his grizzled head, dark eyes lurking under thick black eyebrows.

"Idrith ap Gruffyd". The man spat the name out coldly. "You are commanded to reveal the hiding place of the Prince Madoc."

"And who commands it?" Idrith struggled to stand, leaning heavily on the rough wooden shelf that served as his sleeping place. As he moved, the man's hand swung swiftly to the massive sword hanging from his left side.

Idrith raised his shaky hand. "I can do you no harm. As you can see, my body can barely fend for itself."

The knight dismissed his words with an angry wave of his hand. "Madoc. Where is he?"

"Again, Sir Knight. Who are you and who commands me."

The knight glowered then answered harshly. "Who I am matters not. You are commanded by the Lord Dafydd ap Owain."

Standing stiffly, Idrith carefully scanned his visitor. "Aye," he said softly, "Madoc warned me your vermin kind would soon appear."

With one step, the knight delivered a vicious backhand that smacked Idrith against the shaky wall of the hut. As he collapsed onto the ground, the man used his other hand to block Idrith's servant from rushing to his aid.

"My lord," the boy, barely twelve summers, sputtered "My master is ill with the fever. His right arm was shattered and now he is crippled. He has barely enough strength for the day."

Ignoring the servant and pushing him roughly outside, he leaned down to Idrith. "Where is Madoc? His brother the Lord Dafydd wants him."

Spitting blood from his mouth, Idrith looked up. "I do not know." Before he could say more the knight reached down and grabbed his remaining good arm and dragged Idrith across the dirt floor and out into the still and misty morning.

"Get him on a horse and take him," he grunted at his three companions. He pulled the remaining two to him and jerked his head towards the servant cringing against the hut walls. "Kill him. Then search the hut and the area completely. If you find anything bring it to me at Dolwyddelan. Then burn the place," he whispered. Without another word he swung onto his horse, waited briefly while his men lashed Idrith into place on another horse and without looking back galloped west across the stream.

A mile from the hut and high above, hidden by the trees that tumbled down the hills to the shore, a solitary monk dressed in his stained black habit knelt in prayer, tears flowing down his cheeks unchecked as he saw the slaughter of the young servant lad and the burning of the hut.

If only he had not stopped last night at Castell Llanfrothen. He railed against himself, beating his fists against his body and crying out silently against himself. His journey from Penmon Priory on Anglesey had been hard; he pushed himself and his companion monk as they strode the rugged paths from the priory and across Menai and the lower passes of the mighty crags of Snowdon. He had been desperate to get back to the seashore at Borth-y-Gest. But the capricious early spring weather made it very difficult. Weary and, almost dropping after three body-numbing days, they'd accepted the welcome at Llanfrothen where Lord Rhys ap Cadwaladr urged them to stay and eat.

As they feasted, Rhys probed for information on the rapidly unravelling state of the succession to the king. As one of Owain's minor stead holders, Rhys' concern about the squabble for supremacy between Owain's four oldest sons was palpable. All four —by three different women—Dafydd, Rhodri, Iowerth and Hwyl were considered legitimate heirs to the King whether base born or not. Of the four, Dafydd and Rhodri seemed to be the strongest; Iowerth, also known as Trwyndwn or broken-nosed, was considered 'unprincely' and therefore unqualified because of his disfigurement. Hwyl, on the other hand, was known as the Poet Prince for his bardic skills. Military skills notwithstanding, the common belief was that while he might be a good man, he could not withstand the fury and hatred of his half-brothers Dafydd and Rhodri. No, the battle for kingship would likely be between those two evils who hated each other with hellish fury even though they were full brothers, sons of Owain's second wife Cristin.

For his own protection, Rhys sought information from all who passed his castle; information that would help him choose wisely which side to support, however unwillingly. Especially, he wanted to know if Owain's popular and respected son Madoc had any aspirations to the throne.

Brother Padraig was no different from any other traveller. He was persuaded to enter, rest and eat.

A full night he'd delayed, answering Rhys' questions and assuring him that Madoc, though a bastard and potential heir, had no yearnings in that area. He was known as 'Madoc of the ships' for good reason. An earlier voyage of discovery across the western seas captured his mind and heart. Madoc's desires lay in places other than the crown, Padraig assured Lord Rhys. After hours of interrogation weakly disguised as hospitality, Padraig was anxious to move on, Finally, he persuaded Rhys to let him leave but he left alone, moved by companion, Brother Phillip's pleading of exhaustion and severe ague due to the harshness of the weather.

Hours later he'd arrived at Borth-y-gest only to be told that Madoc's fleet of ships had left three days earlier. All the terrified villagers would tell him was that one of Madoc's close companions, Idrith, had crushed his arm in an accident aboard ship. That and the resulting fever forced Madoc to reluctantly leave his friend behind. The superstitious Borth villagers banished the ailing Idrith to a small hut several miles away, where his fever could not infect them. It was this hut Padraig now saw in flames with riders riding hard to the north.

He flayed himself mentally for his delay but then reminded himself of God's goodness. Had it not been for that stop he undoubtedly would have been at the hut when the murderers appeared. He'd missed death by minutes. Surely God had a reason for his survival.

Waiting no longer, he rose and wiped his tears with his sleeve as he ran and slid down the hillside and along the beach to the still burning hut. He pulled up short, appalled at the crumpled, broken bleeding figure of the young boy. He knelt beside him, praying the last rites as he pulled the boy's body to himself. The eyes fluttered open and he gasped unintelligible words to the priest before him.

Padraig leaned in. "Are you giving your confession? Who did this, boy?" He listened carefully to the mumbled gurgling reply. All he could decipher were the words "Druids" and "Dafydd" before the lad expired in his arms. Tears flowed down his cheeks once again as he quietly and reverently laid the body down. "I accept that you made a full confession to me and in God's name I ask mercy on your soul."

Two hours later Padraig stood silent before the rough grave he'd dug for the boy. As he'd worked he'd mentally grappled with the dilemma before him. Idrith he could only commend to God's love and care. He knew Idrith would never betray Madoc and his secret. Nor would he succumb to Prince Dafydd's Druid's savagery. If God truly had mercy on Idrith, the man would die from the fever or his injuries before Dafydd could even question him.

For now, he decided, it was essential that he return as quickly as possible to the Priory. He considered it likely that Madoc heard Dafydd's men were coming for him and left hurriedly before Padraig could return. He suspected Madoc was even now sailing for Lundy Island, the Templar stronghold in the Bristol Channel.

He sighed and stood. With a sign of the cross and another brief prayer over the small grave, Padraig turned and began retracing his steps back to Penmon Priory. As he walked he prayed and considered what he should do. He could, of course, report the boy's murder and Idrith's kidnapping. But to whom? Owain was on his deathbed. His sons cared more about succession and seizing Madoc—particularly if they had any inkling of his secret—than anything else. His own Prior? He would certainly pray and perhaps even condemn the sins of the unknown men who committed the murder, but would he take it further? Likely not, Padraig decided, because the Prior's main concern would be his own and the priory's safety in this time of uncertainty.

The more he thought and walked and prayed, the more Padraig became convinced the best thing he could now do was finish the journals of Madoc. He'd started them at the Prince's request. From the time Madoc returned from his voyage to the far western lands two years ago, he'd been gripped with the idea of returning to what he called the warm and beautiful land. And he wanted to take a larger number of people and ships with him. There, he'd declared joyfully, they could live free of the bloody battles and wars between the various Welsh princes, and between the Welsh and England's Henry II.

At Borth-y-Gest, Madoc had taken Padraig aside and asked him to be his man of letters, recording his preparations and vision for all time. But Madoc was too open with his thoughts and plans, speaking excitedly with anyone who would listen to his tales of the seas. The stories reached the ears of the king himself. Owain sent strong messages demanding that Madoc fulfil his duties as Prince of the realm rather than dream about new worlds. One voyage to the new world was enough, Owain grumbled. Despite Madoc's enthusiastic and compelling stories of the beauty and green warmth of the new land, Owain was unmoved. To him, Madoc's duty lay in Wales and Wales alone.

Word about Madoc's vision went beyond the high snow capped and wind-swept peaks of north Wales.

Two months ago, while he supervised the building of his newest and largest ship, Madoc bubbled with the idea of defying his father and sailing away from the internecine warfare that was his family legacy. *Marcwr Ton.* the Wave Rider, would be bigger, sturdier and carry more people and supplies than his earlier vessel *Gwennan Gorm*. In that ship he'd crossed the western sea and met his dream. Together, he and Padraig talked about the men and women they would take on the next voyage. As Madoc spoke he stopped suddenly, aware that two men approached them. Padraig swiveled around and saw their measured steps aimed directly at them. The men stopped and one spoke in French directly to Madoc.

"You are the Prince Madoc who seeks to voyage across the western sea?"

Warily, Madoc, fluent in a number of languages, nodded, his hand resting casually on the sword ever at his side. Ignoring the gesture, the man turned to Padraig. "And you are the Irish monk Padraig who is companion to the Lord Madoc?" Padraig nodded.

"My name is Guillaume de Troyes of the Order of The Poor Fellow-Soldiers of Christ and of the Temple of Solomon. This is Robert de Rennes," he said simply. "May we sit? We have much to discuss with you."

"And what would Knights Templar want with a prince of Wales?" Madoc grabbed Padraig's arm to stop him from leaving. "Anything you wish to say to me you say in front of Padraig," he told the Templars in explanation. They nodded. After a brief pause, Madoc softly hissed. "You say you are Templars, but you do not dress like Templars."

Both men stood so that they faced Madoc, looked warily around and then unfolded the long black woolen cloaks that covered them head to foot. As the robes parted both Madoc and Padraig saw the white mantle with the unique blood-red cross that covered their chests. Quickly the men pulled cloaks together again and, at Madoc's nod, sat carefully on the grassy tufts that lined the pebbly beach. "Our men-at-arms are hidden in a small valley just north of this place. All our weapons save for our small daggers are with them. So, we are as you see us, unarmed and coming in peace, but truly Knights Templar."

"I had to be sure."

"*Bien certainmant!*" Guillaume responded. "We understand your caution."

For more than an hour the four sat quietly on the shore watching the work continue on Madoc's great ship. Madoc and Padraig listened as Guillaume explained their need for Madoc's ship.

"You say the Grand Master himself has blessed this request?"

"Blessed it? My lord prince, he commands it in the name of Christ and of the Holy Father," Robert sputtered. "By all that is holy and in the name of the blessed Virgin herself, this is a vital task you are asked to undertake."

Sir Guillaume calmed his companion down. "My Lord Prince, here is a letter from the hand of the Grand Master, Philip de Nablus himself." He reached into his pouch and drew out the parchment, handing it silently to Madoc who carefully read the missive, looked up startled, and read it again.

"Our Order is prepared to fund your voyage to the Western Seas, including supplying more vessels and manpower, and a squadron of knights and men-at-arms. These will meet you at our Lundy Island base."

Madoc pursed his lips at this. "I thought the de Marisco family controlled Lundy in defiance of King Henry's gift of the island to you Templars."

A slight grin appeared on Sir Guillaume's face. "Certainly, that is true. But as Templars we have access to funds and trade without which the de Mariscos could not stand against Henry." He shrugged. "Let's just say our Order and Lord de Marisco have an understanding about certain uses of the island at times." He grew serious. "And this is one of those times, my Lord."

The discussion continued but Padraig saw the die was cast. Something in the Templar's words and the letter combined with his fears of bloodshed over the succession, had stiffened Madoc's resolve. He would go on this voyage and carry whatever secret the Templars bade.

"You understand all of this must be kept secret, even from your followers. But especially from your brothers Dafydd and Rhodri."

Madoc jumped up in anger. "For all his outward piety, understand this, Sir Templar. My brother Dafydd is more closely tied to the Druids than he is to the church. Oh yes, he mouths the words and attends the services, but his black heart has been sold to the devil and the cursed Druids. They are the driving force behind him. My brother Rhodri is no better. Their hatred for me is very real and dangerous. You will not find me conspiring with them."

The decision made, the two Templars nodded and, with assurances they would meet nine weeks hence on Lundy, they strode away.

Madoc wrapped his arm around Padraig's shoulder as they walked to the edge of the water. Madoc smiled as he took in the sight of his new vessel, its high prow and tall mast seemingly ready to leap into the fiercest waves at his command. Together the two stopped and looked at the flurry of work as men struggled to finish her.

Madoc turned towards Padraig and made his request.

"This matter has changed my plans," he said quietly and slowly. "I'd planned to ask your Prior to release you from your service there and be our spiritual guide and counsellor as we sail. But I cannot do that now." He sighed and paused before continuing. "You now know I will carry Templars and their secret, though at this point even I do not know what that is. It changes things for both of us, Padraig. If I do not come back it will be essential that someone remain behind to remind the Templars that I did what they wanted but also, I expect them to keep the rest of the promises including payments for the families of those I take with me. I need someone here in Wales who has knowledge of all this. It is a surety for me and a protection for those families that there's someone still here who knows the truth of our voyage."

Madoc looked at the fallen, disappointed face of his companion. He gripped Padraig's shoulder. "I ask a lot, I know. But it is essential. I just have a feeling—mayhap you could consider it a message from the Lord Jesu himself—that someone trustworthy and honorable must remain in these islands; someone who has faithfully recorded these events for future generations."

Madoc turned gloomy. "I fear for the nation, Padraig. Once the king is gone, I dread what Dafydd and his Druid followers will do. I can only pray as I go. But you, my friend," he smiled, "will be my witness here should I need one, that I was obedient to God above all kings and princes."

He slapped Padraig on the back. "Go to your Priory and then return here quickly my friend. Tell my Lord Prior that Prince Madoc commands it. We will then sail together to Lundy and see what this great secret is."

Despite the speed of his trip to Penmon and return to Borth, Padraig had missed him. Madoc was gone. The task now was clear. Return to Penmon and retrieve the parchments he'd already written. Then, with or without the Prior's permission, sail immediately on one of the many Irish traders to Dublin and thence to Lundy. It would take Madoc at least four more days to reach Lundy. With God's blessing, Padraig estimated he could be on Lundy himself in less than two weeks. Pray God it would be in time.

And, as he hurried on, new realities weighed on his soul. Now he had to keep to himself, watching carefully who he spoke to and mingled with. He was already known as Madoc's boon companion and priest. If Dafydd had come for Idrith, he would surely come for Padraig. And there was also now the added burden of Madoc's parchment to be kept from the prying eyes of Dafydd.

It was a duty he owed to Madoc. And, to Idrith and the young lad as well.

Chapter Two

London, Hampstead Heath

For a late January day, it was surprisingly warm and sunny. Indeed, there'd been several summer days last year he remembered that were both colder and rainier. Nevertheless, don't complain, Stone Wallace told himself as he walked down through Hampstead Heath park towards South End Road and the railway station.

At Keats Grove he crossed over South End. He knew he had almost forty minutes before the next train. Still time to dawdle and think, which is why he'd come to his favorite London park.

Since Christmas he'd struggled with 'what next' in his life. His successful—until now—career as a travel writer and broadcaster for various American media clashed with the harsh realities of the past two years. Exciting though travel was, none of it compared with the incredible adrenalin rushes and outright terror he'd been exposed to. Plus, he acknowledged, he'd done very little writing the past six or seven months. Money was drying up rapidly. Fortunately, Sir Giles and the Crown Security Bureau provided a small flat in Belgravia as well as what Sir Giles called an 'honorarium' for cleanup research he was doing. But that couldn't last forever. No, he had to make a final decision sooner rather than later. Was he staying in the UK or returning Stateside to resume his career?

On that side of the Atlantic he should be able to pick up new work; there was a vague offer for a travel series. Then there was the offer to join the Security Intelligence Directorate in recognition of his service and skills. Not a likely choice, he ruefully admitted, reckoning he was no debonair and jaunty James Bond type. It just wasn't him. Sure, he needed work but not that, he told himself as he walked briskly along.

Then there was the United Kingdom. Leaving Britain would mean leaving Mandy. His feelings for her had not diminished and he assumed, or perhaps just hoped, that her attitude toward him was masked by the trauma she'd endured. Huw Griffiths, her father and his friend, cautioned him to go slow and let her crystalize her feelings at her own pace. Her wounds at the hands of the Druids were severe and the recovery slow. A transfer from hospital to Crown Security's safe house, The Grange, had helped but there was still a way to go. The doctors considered the main problem now was psychological rather than physical and that a change of scenery might do a world of good. As he considered, he realized increasingly that he couldn't leave until she was well and they'd sorted out their relationship—a subject both had so far avoided.

He ran his hand through his wavy light brown hair and saw the reflection of his six foot solidly muscled frame in a shop window as he passed. On a whim, he turned in to the bookstore on South End Road. One thing Mandy cherished was her beloved books. One more to cheer her up and help the recuperation would never be amiss, he decided.

Twenty minutes later, a bag of four books in hand, he left the store, checked the busy traffic and quickly scurried across, through the perennial collection of parked cars. He dodged both a van and motorcycle carrying a helmeted passenger with an umbrella held in a stiff awkward upright position. He chuckled at the odd sight, though he nodded ruefully that carrying an umbrella this time of year was probably wise.

Stone moved faster, determined to give himself plenty of time to catch the train to Willesden Junction. He stopped suddenly on the pavement to check his watch and switch the books to his free hand.

A sudden stab in the fleshy part of his upper thigh was followed by sharp pain and then a rapidly increasing numbness. "Hey!" Stone's agonized shout of pain and the sudden cries from other passersby startled the helmeted man about to take another stab. He dropped the umbrella and ran back to the motorcycle which suddenly roared off southwards through a red traffic light, narrowly missing a collision with a small blue car.

Stone sank to the ground, a numbing paralysis sweeping from his extremities into his core. His eyes began to droop. Suddenly a man dropped beside him. "Stay awake man. Where does it hurt?"

"Legs...whole body...no feeling..." The words were slurred and disjointed.

"It's all right. I'm a doctor at Royal Free hospital just down the road," the stranger said, quickly and expertly checking Stone's body and at the same time shouting for someone to call for help. As one of the passersby stooped to remove the umbrella, the doctor grabbed his wrist firmly. "Drop it. The police will want to see that."

In the background Stone could vaguely hear the mee-maw of emergency vehicles. His mind was muddled; his vision blurred.

"Stay with us mate. We'll have you at the hospital in a tick."

Stone could keep his eyes open no longer. His last coherent thought was a silent plea to God to receive him mercifully even though he had rejected God all those years.

Carreg Cennan Castle, Carmarthenshire, Wales

Amidst the few visitors strolling casually up the steep hill towards the castle, a short stocky man in a heavy grey wool sweater and jeans stood out as he half-walked, half-ran from the parking lot to the farm outbuilding that served as ticket counter, souvenir shop and small café. He paused at the door frantically looking around, scanning faces before plunging in through the door. Inside he spied one of the team sipping a large cup of tea. He ran over and whispered in his ear. The man listened quietly then whispered back, pointing up the hill towards the ruins.

Ten hard slogging minutes later at the top of the long steep hill path, he was among the gaunt, broken grey stone walls of the castle. Breathing hard, he looked around and saw his target standing on the remains of a battlement looking out from the high limestone crag and over the green valley spread below him. He scrambled up the steep wooden staircase provided for tourists and approached the stubby but immaculate man. As he did, without turning around, the man put up his hand to stop any discussion. The man stood motionless, a raincoat folded neatly over his left arm showing off his dark blue blazer and neatly pleated grey slacks to advantage.

Although the sun was bright there was a crispness to the air. Strong breezes, cold with the dampness of salty sea air, blew up the valley and swirled around. None of it seemed to affect the man as he stood immobile and silent.

"It was up there," he said finally, pointing up the small valley that lay to the northwest of the tiny village of Trapp towards the market town of

Llandeilo. "The great Druid center of Llanmerddyn. Nothing left now. Abandoned and falling to pieces. Rhiannon's body lies somewhere under there along with who knows what else and who else. They dug and shifted the rubble but could not find her body. Even now our people watch the area carefully. And we know the authorities do as well. This is as close as I dare come." He fell silent.

Finally, he turned around and looked carefully at his visitor, peering at him from under large untidily bushy beetle black eyebrows. His eyes a deep brown. His crisp tidy clothing was a distinct contrast to the eyebrows and thin wisps of longish, untamed greying hair flying in the breeze, that framed his face. "I saw you running and scrambling up the path from the farmyard below. What's so urgent you couldn't wait for my return?"

"Sir. Someone made an attempt on Stone Wallace's life this morning."

"Successful?"

"We don't know. He was taken to hospital but so far no update. We don't seem to have anyone on the inside of the hospital who can give us news." He shifted uncomfortably at his questioner's cold penetrating stare. The silence continued as the man stared at him.

Finally, he pulled all his five feet seven-inch wiry frame together, rubbed his chin then pointed directly at the jean clad man. His voice was icy as he spat out his words.

"In future, address me as Dragon Master. Now. What happened. Was it one of ours?

"Not sure, Dragon Master. It is possibly a rogue Druid, but not one of ours."

The man swore in fluent Welsh and English then gestured the still panting messenger closer. Fifteen minutes later, he sent the messenger stumbling and scrambling down the path as fast as he could without falling, leaving the Dragon Master still in his spot on the castle walls.

High above them, the Dragon Master watched the car spin out of the small parking lot and race down the narrow lanes, finally disappearing amongst the huge hedgerows that even in January towered their massive branches and leafless shrubbery over the road.

Despite his apparent calmness, he seethed inside.

Incompetent, bungling, disobedient fools, he muttered to himself. Against all his instructions, there were obviously those who'd taken decisions on their own. His hold as the new leader was not as tight as previous

Dragon Masters. Where before they'd feared the Dragon Master, now many just ignored him. He punched his fist against the unyielding eight-hundred-year-old wall. Ignoring the stab of pain in his wrist and knuckles, the Dragon Master swore. They would soon learn to fear him too. And obey.

"By the gods and all their power. This is intolerable." He swung around swiftly to make sure no tourists were near and overheard. He put the raincoat on to cut some of the cold breeze, but remained on the battement leaning against the walls and staring towards Llanmerddyn, almost willing the spirits to visit him and give him insights. After several more minutes he started back down to the car park deep in contemplation.

Word was that even the Master—the mysterious, elusive overseer of the Druid clans—had disappeared. Killed, some suggested, in the strange explosion that destroyed the previous Dragon Master and his brother. Without their spirit guide, the remaining Druid leaders simply voted for a new Dragon Master and Dr. Richard Evans, won an admittedly tight vote. The closeness meant his election was still not accepted by all. But who? And how could he identify them swiftly and destroy them?

His specific orders were to keep a tight watch on their enemies Stone Wallace and Huw Griffiths, but take no action against them. In the meantime, he had to consider how he would harness the power and cooperation of the subordinate national leaders, called Raven Masters, in France, Spain, Canada and America. They and their top security people, termed Serpent Masters, would be essential if they were to breathe fresh life into the despondent moribund mess that he'd inherited.

Stealth and intelligence would be used to gain what they wanted, not brute force. When action was finally needed, it would be done fiercely in great secret and with utmost pain and destruction. That, he argued to his fellow leaders would gain more than the brute force used previously. The ham-handedness of previous Dragon Masters, he bluntly told the other leaders, had led to the debacles in the Breton forest and the various useless bloody attacks at churches across Britain. Rather than unsettling the authorities and rattling the church, they'd only stiffened resolve and solidified opposition to the Druids.

His path was now clear. First, he had to handle this latest fiasco firmly. Disobeying the Dragon Master was punishable by death. Second, he needed alternate plans to crush western democracies and return to the true Celtic heritage. Third, the matter of their connections with the Druids in the United States might prove problematic. Once strong, they were now a shambles, and Liam Murphy, the former presidential candidate and Raven Master was in American custody.

Evans resented the fact that the previous Dragon Master, Diarmuid Callaghan, had done nothing to help Murphy. There were no clear successors to Murphy's leadership, especially if he was not freed soon. His moles in America reported a dispute growing between potential successors. Chaos reigned in that country.

Evans had coveted the Dragon Master title, lusted after it, schemed for it and reveled in his victory. Now it was his. Even so, he demanded absolute secrecy as to his identity. Apart from those leaders representing the seven Celtic nations and a few carefully screened and chosen subordinates, no one would know Evans was Dragon Master until he himself declared it.

But, three months in, the realities of the role and the challenges he now faced were beginning to dawn upon him. He needed supernatural powers and needed them now. It was time to visit his oak grove and invoke the powers of the underworld.

He stared out at the former Druid stronghold and whispered, "Arawn. Great God of the Underworld. Feed your power into me. I commit myself afresh to you."

Greyfell Abbey, Lake District, England

Lady Greyfell, known to her intimates by her nickname Nees, put the telephone down and spoke to her husband who was sitting at his desk staring at the computer, studying something intently.

"Eddie. That was Giles. He wants to know if we could handle a house guest for a while." She turned to face him. "It's Myfanwy Griffiths. The doctors feel she's had all the medical attention she needs and physically she's well on the way to recovery. Giles is concerned that she now needs a place to recuperate mentally, away from London and still out of the way so those Druids can't get to her. She's had such an awful trauma, poor girl."

"Well, that's good news. She can visit as long as she likes. It will be delightful to see her again. Hopefully it also means Huw and Stone will visit and stay longer as well."

He removed his large black-framed glasses and laid them on the desk. "By the way, I just got an email from our contact Anna Grindell in South

Wales. The Druids are stirring yet again, but the new Dragon Master is having troubles. He shrugged his shoulders. "So how long he lasts, well…. we can only wait and see."

"Who is it?"

"That, my love, is something Anna doesn't know. Whoever it is, he or she is keeping a very low profile. Apparently only a few know who it is and they're sworn to secrecy."

He eased himself away from the desk. "They may be a modern perversion of Druidism but they still cling to their Celtic history and nature." He smiled at her. "There's always in-fighting and jostling for position. When not fighting a common enemy, historically they turned on themselves. It will be the same this time. Sooner rather than later, someone will crack and we'll know who the new Dragon Master is."

He stood and looked out the library window, taking in the muted green meadows and earthy brown peaks that marked the Lake District in winter. Luckily it was a bright afternoon, unlike the normal cold, misty, drizzly days that marked the season. Down the sloping lawns of the great house he could see the shimmering sparkle of Buttermere, one of the many lakes that gave the area its name. His wife moved quietly beside him and put her arms around his waist, holding him tight. In the distance, the crisp clear air sharply defined distant Scafell Pike to the south. To the Northeast he could make out the dusk beginning to settle down over Skiddaw in the northern Fells.

She spoke quietly as she hugged him and lay her silver head against his shoulder. "Will it ever be over, do you think?"

He shook his head no. "Sorry Nees, I think this is a situation that is far more dangerous than the normal political and economic frenzy of modern today." He paused and frowned before facing her. "It is deeper than that. Much deeper. There are forces at work here that even we do not yet comprehend."

He turned and faced her. "All these years Nees, we've studied these Druids perhaps better than anyone else on these islands. We know they're not the Druids most people see; the 'cultural druids' if you will, who hark back to their past and take pride in their music and poetry. No, these are more sinister. Their blood lust and zeal for domination is frightening. That's what worries me. They're not done. They're not going away."

He paused then turned, kissed her and wrapped her in his huge arms. "But for now, we'll just keep on keeping on." His big grin broke the solemnity of the moment. "You go put the kettle on. I think a good cuppa is in order."

He was just about to settle down at his desk when the telephone rang again. No peace for the wicked he muttered as he picked it up. He listened intently and quietly hung up just as Nees was rounding the corner into the room with the tea and biscuits.

"Who was it. Eddie?" She caught the anger and concern playing out on his face.

"Giles's assistant, Freddy Garret. Stone Wallace was attacked this morning. He's in critical condition in hospital." He slammed his massive fist down on the desk causing papers and books to crash to the floor.

"Bloody Druids. What do we have to do to destroy them before they destroy us?"

SID offices. Chantilly, Virginia

A chill soaked into Chad Lawson's bones. He walked rapidly across the parking lot, desperate to get inside and get warm. To the west, he could see storms building, with dark rolling clouds. Freezing rain, the forecasts said.

He'd hardly thrown his jacket over his office chair before a gruff voice shouted out. "You're late. Get in here!"

"Nice to see you too Chief. Having a bad day?" He strode into the SID Chief's office and took a seat. Calvin Tyler sat behind the massive mahogany desk that was devoid of everything except a telephone and a single thick file folder. Behind him, a closed laptop sat on an equally massive mahogany credenza. Above that was a portrait of the current President. In the corner, beside a reinforced window able to withstand an explosion stood an American flag, sitting in its metal holder and draped appropriately. Tyler was flipping through the file and, without looking up, barked "Sit down."

Chad smiled. "Already sitting, Chief!" Tyler looked up, grunted, and went back to the file.

"Liam Murphy."

Chad grimaced. "You are having a bad day. Thanks. Now I am too!"

The former Senator had been moved from a facility in Truth or Consequences, New Mexico, to an even more remote location in a small valley high in Wyoming's Wind River Mountain range.

"I need you to get up to Wyoming right away and interview Murphy again. Try the 'good cop' routine on him. The legal beagles are putting the final push on. They're pulling all kinds of arguments out and it's a full court press. They want Murphy released; being held illegally and without charges they claim. If he's guilty of anything, charge him, they say", he kept muttering in a falsetto voice mimicking the latest functionary who'd been pressing him. "Violation of his rights they claim." He stopped, then threw the file down violently on the desk.

"Until now, all this has been kept quiet, but unless he is freed soon they're going to go public and make a real stink. It's becoming a major embarrassment for the President, so he's not happy. And because he's not happy, he's making me very unhappy. And if I'm not happy you know what that means for you, right?"

Chad exploded in anger. "He's a traitor Chief. Plain and simple. He was plotting a takeover of this country and using the presidency to blow up the constitution and turn us into a virtual dictatorship. Plus, he was culpable in the attacks on our ally, Britain! Letting him walk is a travesty of justice!"

"Chad, you, as a former cop, should know that without rock solid evidence even the guiltiest can walk. You know and I know he's guilty as hell, but we have little or no irrefutable proof. I like it even less than you do. And we know that if he goes free, it will kick start his horde again." Tyler grimaced. "If he redevelops any kind of following and power, you and I and the rest of SID will be history. Literally as well as figuratively."

"But all those congressmen and bureaucrats all over D.C. who worked with him to disrupt out nation and then confessed all! What about them?" Chad sputtered angrily. "They confessed it willingly; even proudly!"

"Retracted. Claimed they were given under duress. Apparently, they even have an FBI guy who sat in on one of the interrogations saying they were sleep deprived and had food and water denied them until they confessed. His word is packing a lot of weight around Washington right now. There's a secret Senate Intelligence Committee hearing scheduled for next week. And frankly, it's not looking good for us good guys."

Raising his hand to stifle further debate on the issue, Tyler leaned forward. "Just get up to Wyoming as fast as possible and milk him as much as you can. I want facts, names, places. Take Wiz with you. He's still on the payroll, I haven't authorized his second retirement yet.

Chad grinned at the thought of being reunited with his friend and mentor Oscar Zanelli, known throughout the agency as The Wizard or Wiz because of his initials, OZ. His grin lasted a moment then turned into a frown. "We're not going to get anything from Murphy, Chief. Better interrogators than I have tried. He'll have his mouth clamped up tight. Especially if he thinks he's close to being released."

"He doesn't know that," Tyler growled. "He's been kept in total isolation. No contact with anyone outside the house. Push him. He might just let something slip." He handed the file over to Chad. "It's a long shot, I know. But at this point, it's all we have left."

He nodded to the file. "That's a duplicate. But protect it like it's your life. If that gets into the wrong hands..." his voice trailed off.

Resigned to what he considered a waste of time, Chad stood up. "Okay Chief. I'll get off to New Mexico and pick Wiz up then head to Wyoming."

"Why go to New Mexico? He's in the cafeteria downstairs waiting for you. Get going!"

Chapter Three

Llanidloes, Wales

Traffic was relatively heavy heading into the quaint mid-Wales market town of Llanidloes. Even in winter, tourists added to the normal traffic on market day. He picked up a bit of speed as he moved past the routes into the town along the A470, skirting the market-goers as they peeled off. After the main junction, he turned left and made his way through more traffic until he reached the bridge. Not too bad, he thought. He should be at his renovated farmhouse 'Hendre Y Derwen'—Home of the Oak Trees—within fifteen minutes.

He loved the gated property that stood hidden from view up the slopes of the hills overlooking the Llyn Clywedog reservoir. It was ideal for his needs, isolated yet not remote. He could get to Aberystwyth and the university in about an hour and from there it was only four and a half hours to London. It also satisfied his need as a Druid to have water close at hand. The veneration of water, particularly streams, lakes and wells fit with the ancient Druid worship he was working hard to instill in modern Druids. Now, they seemed to care more for war and revenge. He was, he often acknowledged, a throwback to an older form of Druidry. But that was where the power came from, he believed, and that was where he was going to draw his strength.

Most of the time he used the Llanidloes property as a study retreat. His small flat in Aberystwyth fitted his lifestyle as a university professor much better, giving him ready access to everything at his own Iolo Morganwg College, known to all as IMC but, because it was an affiliate college of Aberystwyth University, it allowed him to use their facilities and the National Library of Wales as well.

Evans was frustrated. The Master had simply disappeared and not anointed a new Dragon Master. Without that official 'blessing' his opponents saw him merely as a stopgap political selection. He was vulnerable, subject to all the politics and maneuvering endemic in any organization. He mentally shrugged. At least he was used to that sort of nonsense at the college. And, he had a good idea who his main rival was and who'd probably ordered the attack on Wallace, an upstart, preening politician named Belmont. He seethed with anger at the transparent disrespect and disobedience Belmont regularly showed in word and deed. A reckoning was coming, Evans promised himself.

All the way from Aberystwyth he'd churned various scenarios around in his mind. His position at IMC gave him unhampered access to all kinds of information, personnel and, most importantly, money. That was a critical need these days as the cash flow was tight ever since the disappearance and probable death, of the movement's key financier Damien Wyndham.

The movement had lost a number of key people in the last few years including Wyndham, the two Dragon Masters Rhiannon and Diarmuid Callaghan and the Breton leader Andre Tonnerre. Not to mention the Master himself. Gods, what a mess it all was. But, he told himself as he turned his car up the long, gravelled driveway to the house, he really was the best man to pull the mess together again. His brain, intellect, contacts and drive were more than enough.

At the house, he tucked the vehicle behind a small wall of trees, out of sight from the minor road far below. He stepped out and stood for a while, taking in the brisk cold breeze. Far below, past the wintery brown-green pastures and meadows of his property, he could see small whitecaps blowing across the reservoir.

He turned towards the house. Outside, it was a large whitewashed stone two-storey building with Welsh slate roof. It was what real estate brochures described as a "quaint", "historic" and "chocolate box" building "brimming with character". Inside, it was all mod cons. Nothing but the best and most luxurious for the esteemed Dr. Evans. Discreetly placed dishes on the equally quaint barn ensured the finest available television service as well as the fastest satellite internet available. Inside the barn he'd insisted on an up-to-date technological setup, but still craved a system that allowed immediate communications access, both audio and video, with his key personnel. That, however, had to wait until funding improved drastically.

He reached into the passenger side of the car and pulled out a worn but serviceable satchel and a more up to date black nylon laptop case before heading leisurely to the front door. Inside, he called for his housekeeper who came bustling out of the kitchen, wiping her hands on a white pinafore.

Without looking at her or acknowledging her cheery welcome he simply barked "Tea and sandwiches now, Mavis. I'll take them in the study. There will be some others coming later this afternoon. Until then I don't want to be disturbed." He stalked into the study and shut the door behind him.

At the desk he quickly pulled out the laptop, fired it up and made sure the internet connection was good. As he waited he pulled some files out of the leather satchel and placed them beside the computer. He finished sorting them out when Mavis entered with a tray full of sandwiches and biscuits along with a large pot of steaming hot tea, milk and sugar. At a wave of his hand she disappeared back into the depths of the kitchen.

Muttering to himself he waited for a page to finish loading on the computer then plunged in to finishing his latest research paper. His only break was the hour or so when his visitors appeared. After questioning and listening to them he dismissed them to the various tasks he'd assigned, then settled back to a quick supper prepared by the indomitable Mavis.

While there was still some light he went outside and into the woods. There with a small axe he cut a young branch from one of the new oak saplings, wrapped it carefully in a white cloth. At the same time, he gathered some dried, fallen branches and added dried tinder to the pile. As he worked he heard the raucous cawing of his ravens, flapping around in circles over his head, demanding his attention. And his food.

"Alright my sacred beauties, you shall have it." He reached into his pocket and drew out some of the food he specially prepared for them. His hand squished the bag of rat entrails so that it squeezed them out onto the grass in front of him. Once that was done he added in some of the hard dog food he gave them as a special treat and scattered it over the meat. "There you are my messengers of the god. Enjoy these, the remnants of lesser creatures."

He stepped away, pleased to see the birds soaring and gliding above him. Ravens were incredible birds and were messengers between this world and the next; they were legendary beings in druid lore, symbols of healing and protection and sacred to the movement. Such was their symbolism that an earlier Dragon Master dubbed his subordinate leaders Raven Masters to emphasize their critical role. That same Dragon Master gave the name Serpent Master to the leaders of the movement's protective forces. They were titles still rigidly enforced today.

As darkness descended he hustled back to his study. There he began his preparations, carefully taking his sacred robe and small golden sickle out of their secret hiding place and placing them on his desk.

Midnight arrived. Mavis had bustled around about an hour ago, turning off lights and preparing the house for nighttime. Aware that her boss often worked well into the night she'd simply knocked on his study door and wished him good night. He heard her clomp up the wooden stairs to her room at the front of the house, overlooking the reservoir. He allowed the hour to pass. He got up from his desk quietly, even though he knew that if he stopped outside her door he would hear Mavis snoring blissfully, oblivious to any noises or movement around the house.

Now was the time. He gathered his robe and artifacts and quietly left the house, walking swiftly across the driveway, stepping carefully so he did not crunch the gravel too loudly. Seconds later he was onto the grassy verge, turned left and followed a faint path up the hill towards a copse of trees. As he entered the woods, out of sight of the house, he stopped and carefully robed himself. He picked up a small wooden stick wrapped in an oil-soaked cloth and lit it. His white robe shimmered in the flickering light as he stooped to pick up the wrapped oak branch and moved into the middle of a very precisely planned and planted oak grove.

Evans took a small knife out of his pocket and cut off each leaf singly, slowly and carefully placing each one into a growing circular pattern around the dead wood he'd piled up. On top of the wood he piled green saplings. Satisfied with the circle, he then arranged the final leaves so that the tips of five leaves touched the circle. He smiled as he looked down, admiring his natural pentagram. Using his sacred golden sickle, he then climbed into one of the larger oaks in the circle and cut down some of the mistletoe he'd spent years cultivating, sprinkling them over the other leaves and wood. At last, he was ready.

He touched the flaming torch to the kindling and dried wood, waiting and watching as it caught and then waiting as the young green saplings and leaves began to smoulder and smoke.

Standing, he raised his arms high above his head.

"Ta muid anseo leis na dieth a adhradh. I come to honor the gods. I bring sacrifices. May the smoke of these sacred green creations please you."

Arms still upraised, he slowly circled the smoky fire, chanting as he did. Effortlessly he switched between Welsh and English, weaving his chant in his musical Welsh accent and repeating the pattern precisely so that his chant ended precisely as he finished each circuit.

> *"Green of earth, black of night*
> *With this fire take them*
> *Open now the screen between us*
> *Green of trees, black of earth, pillar of smoke*
> *Together yoke us*
> *Corn and grain, oxen and blood*
> *Together are yours, together yoke us*
> *Green of earth, black of night*
> *Open now the veil before us."*

After his fifth circuit around the smouldering heap he took a bottle of water out of a pocket under his robe and poured it slowly and carefully over the fire, wafting the resulting smoke into his face with his left hand even as he poured, then circled the fire once again. His eyes stung and began to tear but he continued.

Finally, as the fire died and the smoke dissipated, he stepped back. He would have vengeance on Huw Griffiths—he bitterly considered the professor nothing less than a traitor to his Welsh and Celtic heritage—and that puffed up American writer. Yes, he would have vengeance, but it would be carefully and deliciously served at a time and place of his choosing.

And, more importantly, the old gods would be avenged and brought back to their rightful place in the pantheon of gods. No more would the Christians force their beliefs on people. Nor the Jews. Nor the Muslims for that matter. None of the monotheistic religions would survive. The Mother goddess would have her way; Arawn, god of the dead and the underworld, would lead them and Cernunnos, the Horned One, would rejoice.

Hampstead, London

Freddy Garret slipped quietly into the private waiting room, mugs of tea in hand. He gave one to Huw Griffiths and sat. "News?"

"Nothing yet Frederick." He slumped over, sipping unconsciously at the tea while he stared at the floor. "It's been over two days now and Bradstone's been in a coma since they got him here."

Freddy smiled at Huw's refusal at any to use anything other than full given names. "He was lucky he was attacked so close to the hospital and that doctor just happened to be passing by. A massive dose of ricin like he got, can kill if immediate action is not taken. You heard the doctors say that. There is no cure or antidote for ricin poisoning. Only quick action and a lot of luck..." he looked at Huw's drooping figure and added quietly "...and of course, prayer."

Huw sighed. "Yes, but action was taken, lots of prayers offered and he still isn't out of it."

Freddy nodded. "Don't forget he also had a suspected concussion when his head hit the pavement. That certainly complicated things."

A gloomy silence dropped over the spartan room as both men contemplated their own beleaguered thoughts. "Was it the Druids?" Huw lifted his head and looked keenly at Freddy.

The Crown Security Bureau's second in command eyed the professor carefully, not wanting to add to his misery. "Frankly Huw, we don't know. Sir Giles is working closely with the Metropolitan Police but the investigation is in their hands, not ours." Before Huw could comment, Freddy held up his hand. "That's the official line, of course. We're using all our resources and manpower as well, but we have to be circumspect about it. Police noses are still out of joint over the Hyde Park attack last summer because we exposed it and they didn't. They don't want to hear about Druids. To them, the attack on Stone was merely an unprovoked random criminal act; a robbery gone wrong.

"With ricin?" Huw broke in, agitated. "What other street robberies do you know that involve the use of ricin?"

Freddy accepted the impassioned interruption calmly. "That's what they're claiming Huw. They've shown us the street videos of the attack and there's nothing on it that we can latch onto. The attacker was wearing a helmet with darkened visor as was the motorcycle driver. The license plate was obscured but they tracked the bike, camera by camera up the Heath Road and into a residential area. The bike was later found abandoned in a laneway, wiped clean and stripped of its plates."

Freddy shrugged his shoulders and took another sip. "So, we at Crown Security are not allowed to actively look for Stone's assailant. But, the Guvnor believes finding the source of the attack is the key. And yes, therefore, we believe it was the Druids."

He began to count off his points on his fingers. "One, it was Stone Wallace that was attacked. Random? Possible, but highly unlikely. Two, the poison used was ricin. We know the Druids had a supply of ricin and were planning to use it in that aborted attack on the Queen. Three, while we cleared out one nest of Druids, Lord Greyfell has kept a pretty tight watch on them. He and Nees have detected more movement and increased communication recently. A new Dragon Master has apparently been chosen. Who? We don't know yet. Did he or she order the attack? Again, we don't know but given their history of revenge, highly probable."

Before he could expand on the points, a doctor pushed through the door. "I think you'd better come. It looks like your friend is coming out of it."

For ten minutes they sat quietly at Stone's bedside, seeing the myriad of tubes running into every visible orifice of his body except the ears, along with more tubes and monitors attached to his arms and legs. Multi-colored lights flashed on and off in seemingly haphazard patterns while computer screens above and beside the bed beeped and blipped. Although his eyes were still closed, Huw and Freddy could see he was breathing easier and the few monitors they could understand, like blood pressure and heart rate, seemed stronger and more regular.

"Look!" Huw suddenly gestured to Stone's fluttering eyelids. They watched as slowly Stone's eyes opened and gazed around unfocused at first then gradually seeming to focus in on the people in the room. He tried to speak, but the doctor shook his head. "Don't try to speak, Mr. Wallace. Your voice will be very rough and your throat very sore."

Stone stubbornly glared at the doctor, then switched his eyes towards Huw. "Where am I? How long" he rasped, ignoring the doctor's frantic admonitions.

Huw reached over and touched his shoulder lightly. "You're at the Royal Free Hospital in Hampstead, Bradstone. You've been here almost three days."

Stone closed his eyes. "Confused. Voices. Groggy. Bright lights."

Quietly and as calmly as he could, Huw told Stone what had happened, interrupted occasionally by Freddy. Neither mentioned their suspicions about the attacker's identity and both shook their heads when Stone croaked one word "who?" at them. Thankfully, drugged or not, he understood and asked about Mandy.

Another five minutes passed before the doctor ushered them out with assurances that Stone was on the way to full recovery and needed more rest of a physical rather than drugged nature.

Once back in the waiting room, Freddy phoned the news to Sir Giles. It was agreed that Huw would continue to monitor Stone until the evening. If he felt secure enough, Huw could reveal a little of Crown Security's thinking. Just as they were finishing the quick briefing, a familiar face burst through the door, his huge bulk bearing down on both of them.

"Lord Greyfell," Freddy blurted.

"Edward, it's good to see you again. It's a long way for you to come," Huw quickly added.

"Gentlemen, I've done some more research for Sir Giles. Not much, but it may help. Before I went to see him, I thought I'd look in and see how Stone was doing.

"Well, Edward, it seems Bradstone may be coming out of his coma now and, hopefully, is on the way to recovery." Despite his friendships with them all, Huw could never bring himself to call any of them by their shortened nicknames. He preferred the formality of what he called "the full names given before God at their christening". The three caught up on each other's activities and concerns and Lord Greyfell and Huw finalized the details of Mandy's transfer from the safe house to Greyfell Abbey.

As they headed out the door, Lord Greyfell stopped and turned. "You know, gentlemen, it might be a good idea to consider transferring Stone up to Greyfell as well. I've got it on very good authority from a close friend of mine, who also happens to be the Queen's personal physician, that once the crisis is passed in ricin poisoning, recovery can be quite rapid. Something to think on."

He smiled and walked out the door.

Rock Springs, Wyoming

For the umpteenth time since leaving the Salt Lake City airport, Chad ragged on his partner and driver Wiz. "This is even more bleak and god-forsaken than your area of New Mexico, Wiz. I don't think even you could stand to live out here."

"You're just jealous."

"No, I'm serious Wiz. Look at it," he gestured at the passing scenery. "Brown, interspersed with light brown, sandy-stony color and chalky white.

The only color around here is the scrungy green of what might laughingly be called grass fighting for survival on the side of the interstate!"

"And the deep blue of the sky. Don't forget that. Oh, and how about the tufts of white clouds dotting the sky. And those gorgeous grey-blue mountain peaks in the distance."

Chad grunted disgustedly and pushed his sunglasses back up his nose. The flight from Washington to Salt Lake City had been uneventful. They'd picked up a rental car at the airport and hit I-80 east. At first, they'd driven through the green mountains and valleys of eastern Utah but the scenery changed as they crossed the state line into Wyoming just west of Evanston an hour and a half later. It had gotten bleaker by the mile since then.

"We're booked at a motel in Rock Springs. Tomorrow morning, we'll visit our old friend Murphy."

Chad nodded. "I still don't see why we're wasting our time. We've pumped him for months, isolated him and still he gives us nothing. I just don't understand why the Chief thinks he's going to crack now? Especially when Murphy's people are pushing for his release ASAP."

They were pulling into the motel parking lot when Chad's cellphone rang. He glanced at the screen and quickly answered it. As he listened, a curse slipped through his lips. He held up his hand to forestall questions from Wiz while he listened intently and pushed the speaker button.

"....and there's crap all we can do about it!" Tyler's voice boomed into the car as Chad increased the volume. "...so stand down. You and Wiz can return. I have a meeting with the President tomorrow morning. I'll see you when I see you." He hung up without another word.

"What the hell was all that about." Wiz shouted the question even as he turned the vehicle off.

Chad stared at him, a blank look on his face. "Murphy has been freed by presidential order. He will be released late this afternoon. Some of his people are apparently in Rock Springs right now and the man himself will be brought to the county court house while custody is transferred. We're done here. Let's get back to Washington."

Wiz stared ahead at the motel wall. "No so fast junior. You know Tyler doesn't give up that easily. You also know he's not stupid. He knew this order was coming down today. He wanted us here, on site. He told us to return to the office and that he would see us when he saw us, right? He didn't order us home. He said, if I recall correctly, we 'can' return, not 'must' return.

Chad eyed his partner shrewdly. "You've got something up your sleeve."

Wiz grinned. "The Chief doesn't do anything off the cuff. We're right here right now because he wanted us here. You saw how he literally pushed us out the door to get here. Now he tells us we 'can' return? He's subtle. He wants us to watch what happens when Murphy is released; see who picks him up and, if possible, follow. Remember, he said he'll see us when he sees us. He's giving us some latitude; some freedom."

Gloomily, Chad nodded agreement. "Sure hope you're right. My guess is the Chief knows he's finished. The President was pushing him for results but Murphy wouldn't crack, so Tyler takes the fall. Our 'esteemed' President is nothing if not self-protective. He'll sacrifice anyone and everyone to save his skin. And where does that leave us when we do get back to Chantilly?"

"Where indeed," a thoughtful Wiz replied.

Chapter Four

Hampstead, London

In the hours since Stone recovered consciousness, Huw and the medical team had seen rapid improvement. The once comatose body hooked by multiple tubes to various machines and monitors, was now sitting up and attached only to one IV bag and two monitors.

"So. How long before I can get out of here?" Stone looked belligerently at the doctor hovering around the bed.

The doctor raised his eyes skyward in exasperation. "You have just survived a massive dose of ricin poisoning plus you gave your head a tremendous crack. You've been in a coma for over forty-eight hours. You can't just walk out of here like nothing has happened. You need to be monitored in case there are any after effects, for God's sake."

Silenced, Stone looked pleadingly at both Huw and Freddy who sat patiently by his side while the doctors and nurses bustled about. "The food here is awful, anyway."

"And how would you know?" the doctor shot back. "You've been on medication since you got here, dosed up with morphine, antibiotics and other drugs to keep you alive while we flushed your stomach and your whole system several times to get rid of the poison."

"Everyone knows hospital food is atrocious," Stone defended himself. "Can I have a plate of fish and chips?" The doctor merely glared at him. "Didn't think so," was Stone's quiet response.

Freddy looked at Huw then at Stone and finally at the doctor. "The issue is continued medical monitoring while he recovers. Is that correct, Doctor Brownslee?"

Seeing the doctor's cautious nod of agreement, Freddy continued. "Supposing we could guarantee the finest medical supervision and service. Would you authorize his release then?"

Dr. Brownslee snorted. "Nobody but the Queen herself could give that guarantee and even then, it probably wouldn't be enough. Mr. Wallace is my patient and I, and I alone, will make all medical decisions."

Freddy looked meaningfully at both Huw and Stone, then stood quietly. He pulled a small wallet out of his suit jacket and approached the doctor, opening the wallet so he could see the ID enclosed. "Could I speak to you privately outside, Dr. Brownslee?" Without waiting for an answer, he guided the man out of the room.

Fifteen minutes later they returned. "Dr. Brownslee wishes to apologize for his recalcitrance, understandable though it is because of his great and professional concern for you Stone. Nevertheless, I have assured him that you will have the finest medical supervision and that he will be kept informed as to your progress while you are in our care. If you regress in any way, you will be brought back and Dr. Brownslee will again be your primary care doctor."

A subdued Dr. Brownslee merely nodded and quietly told Stone he had already signed the necessary papers and that as soon as the approved medical staff arrived, Stone would be handed over. He quietly left the room.

"Hate to be heavy on the poor doctor who, after all, was just doing his professional best. But he cannot guarantee your security here and neither can we. So, you're back in our hands again Stone. We're sending you back to Greyfell Abbey."

A grin cracked Stone's face. "If you can handle it, I can Freddy."

Rock Springs, Wyoming

Wiz crumpled his empty bag of potato chips and slurped the last of his drink before dumping the containers in the back of the SUV. He and Chad had sat for more than two hours in their car, scrutinizing each vehicle that came and went. They were interrupted by a county deputy sheriff at one point, who, politely but firmly, asked them to explain why they were sitting opposite the court house in a primarily residential neighborhood. Identities and credentials established, he moved on and left the pair alone.

The sun was beginning to set behind them. Across the street and past the court house they could see a children's playground. Beyond that there was a thick scrub line of dense trees and thick bushes. Shadows began to lengthen across the playground and courthouse parking lot. There was a brief flurry of activity as two police officers ran out of the courthouse door just as an unmarked black Suburban raced down C Street and turned left into the parking lot.

Chad and Wiz sat upright. Chad began taking photos with his newly purchased camera and zoom lens. It was the first vehicle's occupant that grabbed Wiz's attention.

"Holy Crap! That's Dexter Armitage, the President's Chief of Staff." Chad kept clicking away as the man stood patiently waiting outside the building's main entrance. Minutes later another black Suburban pulled up and Chad kept clicking as Liam Murphy exited the car, quickly climbed the few steps and warmly shook hands with Armitage before disappearing inside.

Fifteen minutes later there was another flurry of activity as a third, less obtrusive dark blue sedan pulled into the parking lot and just ahead of the first Suburban. Seconds later, Murphy and Armitage walked through the door and shook hands again. Armitage stepped back and Murphy headed towards the sedan when there was a sudden splash of red around his head.

Murphy crumpled to the ground. What had been a relatively calm and common place situation became a scene of frenzied activity. Guns drawn, police and court security people cautiously peered around the cars, weapons raised, looking for the source of the single shot. Hands grabbed Armitage and bodily threw him to the ground and dragged him inside. Apart from the sudden clamor of sirens, nothing seemed to be happening. As they leaped out of their own car, Chad and Wiz saw one deputy race across to the downed Murphy.

"Silencer," Chad said. "Must have come from over there, the trees." He began to run towards the scene but Wiz grabbed his arm and stopped him. "We can't do anything now. I don't think the Chief would want us involved in this."

As others raced to help Murphy, other officers pointed in the direction of the trees. A sheriff's pickup raced past them and lurched right into the lane that paralleled the tree line. Just as quickly, another deputy suddenly appeared at Chad's back, pistol drawn, and began questioning them. Again, ID's were exchanged and Wiz explained they were present to watch the handover of one of their detainees.

"Didn't do a good job of protecting him, did ya?" the deputy said bluntly, "Shot right in the head as he stood there." With orders that they were not to move from their vehicle, he moved on as paramedics lifted Murphy's limp body onto a gurney. Chad noticed fleetingly that the furor had drawn a sizeable crowd, most with their cellphones out, taking videos and stills of the scene.

It was more than two hours before Chad and Wiz were finally allowed to leave after being taken into the courthouse building itself. The Sheriff was not happy with their presence but, without orders to the contrary, unable to do anything about it. They told their story several times to various authorities and heard the discussions and debates. They'd been unable to add anything to the cumulation of evidence but got confirmation that the assassin had hidden in a laneway behind the trees and used a silencer. In the confusion, he'd escaped, ditching his stolen car in at the railway freight yard and then disappeared completely.

Exhausted, the two pulled into their motel just past midnight. As they sat in Chad's room downing the burnt, cooling take-out coffee and burritos that amounted to supper, they looked grimly at each other. In the background, an all news station breathlessly blared the news of Murphy's assassination. The Sheriff, the Mayor and other officials were interviewed and shown ad nauseum. Washington-based politicians droned on with their condolences while others pontificated on Murphy's strange recent history; almost President then invisible non-entity. While the talking heads shrieked and the stark news was repeated interminably, Chad and Wiz debriefed.

"Not a good day, partner. Not a good day at all."

Chad took another bite of his burrito. "The question is, why kill Murphy? Who gains by his death? The Druids? Maybe, but how? What about the government? Again, possible, but how do they benefit and who would sanction an assassination anyway?" The questions poured out of him, but neither he nor Wiz could find any answers.

"It's definitely back to the drawing board on this one. And it's back to Chantilly for us. Tyler will want a complete report. I doubt the President will meet with him in the morning with this news going on."

Chad grunted agreement. "The question I have is what was the Chief of Staff doing here in the first place? Did the President send him, or was he doing a lone ranger? Is Armitage a Druid? You noticed that he was completely absent during our questioning in the courthouse? Was he even in the building or had he been moved out?"

He nodded to the television. "And note that nobody—not the sheriff, the mayor or the Washington talking heads—even mentioned him." He rummaged around in the pack he'd brought in from the car. "If I hadn't seen it, I'd doubt it myself." He pulled out his camera and fired it up, flicked through a few shots then held it up for Wiz to look at. "Either that's Dexter Armitage or a freekingly good double. So where is he now and what was he doing here?"

Wiz flicked through the photo series again. "Questions. Questions. Tons of questions and no answers. This is going to be a long, messy investigation. And our necks might be on the chopping block as well as the Chief's."

"Yeah, but at least you've got your retirement hideout back in New Mexico. You're just along for the ride." Despondently he glanced up at Wiz. "Me? I've got nothing. Only my police pension and I'll have to wait years for that."

"You'll survive junior. You always have," Wiz commented as he grabbed his jacket and coffee and headed for the door. "Sleep tight. Early start tomorrow!"

Greyfell Abbey, Lake District, England

It was remarkable, this transformation in his body, Stone reflected. A day and a half ago in a coma in a London hospital. Today, he felt as weak as the thin, wintery sun he saw out the window, but he was up and walking, however gingerly. He felt strangely invigorated. It was good to be back at Greyfell Abbey. This was a haven of warmth, hospitality and friendship. At the same time, it was a unique place of knowledge all encapsulated in a zone of tight security.

The last time he was here, he'd asked Lord Greyfell about security. They were walking high up on the fells. From the heights, Greyfell Abbey seemed so open, plopped into beautiful but seemingly unsecured countryside. He saw no fences or gates protecting the property and as far as he could determine there was just Lord Greyfell, Nees and a few staff, none of whom seemed to carry weapons of any kind.

"The Druids must know you're scrutinizing their every move and they must surely know where this place is," Stone had asked. "They don't shy away from killing and destroying their enemies, so how do you survive?"

"Lots of reasons, I think." A pensive Lord Greyfell leaned against a tree he'd stopped at when Stone posed the question. "We have an excellent intelligence operation within the Druid movement itself. Remember, our Druids are a violent offshoot merely using the name to hide under. Despite the seeming solidarity, it's actually a fractured community much as the old Celtic tribes were. Our safety comes partly from a carefully cultivated a wide number of informants in Wales and Ireland particularly. None known to the others. And all with different ways of passing information to us."

He waved his walking stick over the fells, adding that their very remoteness was protection. Years of carefully cultivating excellent relationships was also key. "We're known and appreciated throughout the entire District. If anyone—even an individual or a couple—moves in our direction, we'd be informed by an army of shopkeepers, farmers, shepherds, pub owners and tour guides. Our net watches over us carefully, Stone. Very carefully.

"Then there's the isolation itself. The fact is there's only one way in, along that road down there. Then there's the fells themselves," he used his stick pointing to the bleakness of the district, particularly the high fells. "Anyone who tries that way would have to be very hardy and foolish, given the constantly changing and dangerous weather conditions up there. Too many people have been lost and killed trying to climb or hike across the fells. It's dangerous any time of year."

He gave Stone a penetrating glance. "Perhaps more importantly, we have a greater protection." He searched Stone's face for any sign of skepticism or scoffing. "I firmly believe we're protected by prayer. I told you we are engaged in a spiritual battle, dealing with supernatural forces beyond our ken. There are people all over the world, friends and supporters praying for us. That, quite frankly, is our biggest protection, I think. Unseen but infinitely more powerful than any technological gizmos I could muster."

Stone had stared at him. "You really believe this stuff, don't you?"

Lord Greyfell nodded but before he could elaborate, Stone switched the topic, asking instead about the small dots of sheep he could see high up one of the fells, at the same time suggesting they rejoin the group at the house.

That conversation flooded back into Stone's memory as he gazed out the window. The whole thing puzzled him. As a consummate pragmatist, religious faith was just so much mumbo jumbo; fine for those who didn't have the confidence in their own abilities and intelligence he' believed. But in times of danger and stress for Huw and even Mandy in particular, faith was far from a crutch. Instead it seemed to be a calming, empowering facet of their very being. That realization was a small shaft of light in the deepening gloom of cloud and darkness surrounding him. He remembered just before passing out on the street in Hampstead, grasping at that shaft and just calling out 'help me'.

Now that he was recovering, Lord Greyfell gave him a pleasant surprise less than an hour ago when he casually mentioned Mandy would be joining him in convalescence at the Abbey. "Might as well have both of you here," he'd grinned. "Saves on medical expenses for Her Majesty's government."

Stone smiled at the news, but inside, his heart jumped. Perhaps now he could grab a moment, take her aside and bare his heart.

Waves of rain drummed against the window. Typical Lake District in the winter, he thought as he watched it lashing down. Sunny one moment, then suddenly clouding over, fells disappearing into the mist and rain or freezing drizzle dumping down. Even though a warm fire crackled in the fireplace, Stone shivered. Premonition or just simply cold? He didn't stop to analyze.

Stone looked out the window again. Watching for the car that would bring her.

Chapter Five

Sausalito, California

The view from the ferry landing was spectacular. Sun sparkled off both the water and the myriad of boats large and small scurrying in and out of the huge marinas up and down the bay. The area bustled with activity; people going in and coming out of the restaurant down the pier and bikes in bike racks awaiting their 'green' owners who eschewed gas-guzzling cars and were even now hustling off the inbound ferry.

At a slightly shaded bench facing the water on the grass verge surrounding the parking lot, a young man sat quietly eating a burger and fries. Brown lensed gold-trimmed aviator glasses concealed his eyes. Although you couldn't tell when he was seated, the man was very tall, not so much in body as in long legs. He arrived an hour ahead of time just in case his passenger caught the earlier ferry. Between ferries he grabbed his snack from one of the small cafes on Bridgeway, the main street that ran the length of the Sausalito waterfront.

He wiped his face with a crumpled napkin and spotted a garishly dressed, squat man exit the boat and begin moving towards him. The man was just as described; stocky, florid face topped by a floppy Panama-style hat, and colourful Hawaiian shirt and white slacks. Black sunglasses perched on a bulbous nose, the most prominent feature on his pudgy face. A black laptop case hung from his right shoulder.

The man raised his six foot-six-inch frame and had barely dropped the remains of his lunch into the metal disposal container when the stocky one stopped in front of him. "She will see me?" he asked quietly in a harsh Midwest twang.

"Yes. I am to drive you to her."

Not another word passed between them as they walked to the white Lexus SUV. The visitor got in the back while the driver eased his frame behind the wheel. After a few furtive efforts to converse with his driver, the florid, sweating man finally gave up. Thirty minutes later they passed through Mill Valley and were working their way up a switchback road cut through the ancient mountainside forests and lined with expensive residences. They drove up a smaller side canyon and finally, as they skirted the top of the smaller mountain framing the canyon, pulled into a short driveway blocked by a massive wrought iron gate.

They paused briefly while the driver spoke into an intercom placed inconspicuously amongst the shrubs on the left side of the driveway. Seconds later the gates quietly opened and they purred up to the main door. A white coated butler stood with the door already opened and quickly reached forward to open the SUV's passenger door, escorting the man inside.

The vehicle pulled away. "Stuffed up little turd," the driver muttered as he pulled into the huge three car garage.

Inside the house the man was swept through the entrance hall and living room onto the back patio and pool area with its stunning views of the rich green forested mountains behind and to the sides. The statuesque woman in her Armani blouse and slacks put her drink down as he approached, hand extended.

"Thank you for seeing me Mrs. Price."

"Please. Call me Bethan," she waved her hand lazily, not getting up and not accepting the proffered handshake. "Drink?" Without waiting for an answer, she gestured to the white-coated servant. "You flew in from Washington this morning?" she continued, using her manicured finger to stir the remnants of her ice-clogged whiskey. "I trust you had a good trip, but why the ferry from the city instead of renting a car and coming across the Bay on the Golden Gate Bridge?"

"No cross-country flight is a good one and I hate driving in San Francisco and particularly dislike high bridges," the man grumbled. "Add to that the fact that stick of a driver you sent didn't even have the courtesy to speak to me. It's been a crappy day so far, I don't mind telling you Mrs...er...Bethan."

Just then the tall driver walked across the patio. Bethan looked up at him and smiled, then turned with a cold look on her face. "Oh, you mean my son David? I gave him specific instructions not to engage you in conversation until we find out exactly what you want."

The color drained out of the man's face as he began sputtering apologies. She scowled at him for several minutes.

"Your name is Dexter Armitage. You are the President's Chief of Staff. Now, why would a man like you be so determined and push so hard for a meeting, even to the extent of rushing across the continent to get that meeting done, I ask myself? Oh, and does the President know?" She leaned back in her chair languidly, keeping a cold smile on him. He knew too that beneath the dark sunglasses her unblinking gaze was on him. "I am merely the widow of a very successful oil man. So, am I under investigation for something? If so, what? And if not, why are you here?"

Armitage sputtered again, taking a handkerchief out of his pocket and dabbing his now profusely sweating face. Normally a man well in control, he was completely flummoxed by the woman and her constantly shifting personas. "Again, I am so sorry for my thoughtless words, Mrs. Price. I can only plead exhaustion and stress for my blustering introduction to you."

She waved her hand nonchalantly, never looking away from him, her face expressionless as she waited for his response.

"No, you are not under investigation in any way, Bethan. This has nothing to do with the government." He was unsure how to handle the woman. Normally, people complied with his every whim and word and never challenged him. He looked around at her son who was pulling up a chair to the table. "I would prefer, if you don't mind, that our conversation be strictly between us."

Bethan slammed down her now empty glass and stood with such ferocity that her chair tipped backwards and clattered against the stone tiles. "Anything you say to me you say to David. That's the second time in a minute you've insulted me and my family. Get out!"

Armitage jumped up wringing his hands and apologizing profusely yet again. "Please, Mrs. Price, my only concern is security of the information I am about to share with you. I meant no offence." The handkerchief was again scrunched up and wiped over his face.

His pathetic plea stopped her. She turned and faced him. "Obviously, Mr. Armitage, your trip has indeed affected you and stripped you of basic civilities. You may go inside. Raul will show you where you can freshen up. We will eat an early dinner. Then perhaps you will be in a more pleasant and courteous mood." The butler had just stepped onto the patio, drink tray in hand, as she exploded. Used to his employer's ways, he waited quietly.

Before Armitage could move, the butler stepped up, put the drinks down and held Armitage by the elbow, leading him into the house as the stumbling man continued apologizing all the way.

Bethan pulled the chair up, sat down and picked up her drink again. David reached over and took the second glass. "Nicely played Mother. You certainly unsettled him."

She smiled richly at him. "Of course, Davey darling. Can't let a pumped-up toad like that get the upper hand. Especially when we already know what he's up to and why he's here." She paused. "Give him a quick rest, then we'll see how he handles everything."

They smiled and toasted each other. "Down the hatch, my love."

Llanidloes, Wales

"Dead?"

Evans slumped back in his chair, right hand rubbing his brow while his left pushed the phone harder into his ear as if that would somehow change the message. "What happened? Where?" He listened intently then hung up. He paused, breathing deeply. The news startled him and now left him anxious. Questions about culprits and motives swirled in a chaotic pattern in his mind. He shook his head violently as if that would shake his thoughts into a rational series of answers. It didn't help.

He paced the room. This always happened to him when major events impacted his life—good or bad. He had a sense of chaotic panic that could only be soothed by walking. Then a cool calmness would envelop him and a path would reveal itself. He grabbed his cap and coat, shouted to Mavis that he was out walking, then strode purposefully across the yard and into the grove. This would be a long, tiring but invigorating walk.

Three hours later, soaked by rain the last thirty minutes, he stomped into the house, shouted for drinks and food and retired into his study. He waited calmly while the ever-efficient Mavis rushed in with biscuits, sandwiches and tea and as soon as she left, grabbed the phone.

Less than an hour later he'd set preliminary plans in motion. He dedicated the afternoon to his work as a professor even though, as Dragon Master, his mind raced and spun in psychedelic circles, plotting, wondering, flitting from subject to subject. Several times, the phone rang and new information was transmitted to him. Each fragment began to build the picture in his mind.

By early evening the rain stopped. He slipped out of the house and entered a small shed beside the double car garage. He unlocked it and entered. Inside, he reached into a cage and retrieved a rabbit. Outside was craggy, tough, Ifor Beynon's kingdom. His groundskeeper and gardener had long ago shifted his loyalties and beliefs to the Druid cause and become Evans' trusted confidant. As such, he watched over the property ensuring Evans's security remained strong. Happy unthinking Mavis was left alone to cook and clean inside. Other than Evans himself, only Beynon had keys to the shed, the garage and the main outbuildings. Beynon's other task was to ensure a regular supply of animals, particularly rabbits, for the inside pen and to care for them until needed.

Holding the squealing rabbit tightly by the scruff of its neck, Evans stalked determinedly to his oak grove. This time he merely lit a small fire and stood gazing at the smoke until it reached the proper density. Holding the rabbit at the fullest extent of his arm he reached into his pocket with his other hand and withdrew a sharp knife.

With one quick slash he cut across the rabbit's throat then held it so the blood poured down on the smouldering fire. As the blood drained from the animal's body he began to chant.

Evans repeated his chant three times while the blood drained out of the rabbit. He slashed its body each time he chanted, ensuring that most of the blood flowed out. He began chanting again as he threw the lifeless carcass into the trees.

With the last words of the ritual and the smouldering fire almost doused with the blood, he kicked some dirt over it to fully snuff it and walked back to the house, energised. Above him, the sacred ravens cawed and soared in a cacophony.

The whole mess—Murphy's killing included—was going to consolidate and strengthen his power. He was sure of it.

Sausalito, California

Dex Armitage stormed into the monotoned living room, ignoring the all white chairs and couches, carpets and walls. His already red face was nearly turning purple in anger. "Where the hell are my cellphones and communication devices. Somebody came into my room while I was in the shower and took them." He glared meaningfully at David then at Bethan and let loose another florid round of curses. "I'm Chief of Staff to the President for god's sake. I must have immediate and constant communication with my office. Return my property immediately or I can and will have charges laid against you."

Mother and son let him bluster a bit more. "Relax, Dex. This is a place where you are to kick back and leave your worries behind. Cells and their instant access only add to your high stress and it would seem, judging from your very red face, your blood pressure as well." She gestured at the chair beside her. "Sit down, enjoy the views and tell us why you're here, why don't you. Besides, this is a secret trip. Am I right? You didn't let people know where you were going or who you were meeting with."

David thought Armitage would burst with fury. As the man shouted and threatened, David was unsure which made Armitage angrier—the fact that his devices had been taken or that Bethan was completely unfazed and unmoved by his threats. Certainly she exhibited a calm that made it quite clear she was uncowed and unimpressed by him.

"Quite simply, my dear Dex, you have no position in this house other than that of honored guest. Your devices will be returned when you leave and I promise you, they are even now locked away securely in a safe. I'm as aware of security as you are. It's just that you don't need them here. This is obviously not government business so I didn't want you distracted." She flashed a brilliant smile at him and gestured for him to sit.

"You wanted this meeting. Speak."

The choleric Armitage finally stumbled into the chair. He glared at Bethan, his eyes conveying both threat and surprise that she was unmoved and unthreatened. He glanced at David but, loath to reignite Bethan, swallowed and looked back at her.

"I am here on behalf of...of...the movement." He shot a quick glance at David.

"He's fully aware of who and what you're talking about. You can say Druids if you like Dex."

"Very well. We had a Gorsedd."

"I didn't know you could hold such a meeting unless the Raven Master convened it," Bethan interrupted. "Liam Murphy holds that position."

Armitage had the grace to blush slightly before pressing on. "Murphy was killed last night after his release from detention. We have no functioning Raven Master at this time."

Bethan lit a cigarette, drew on it and exhaled slowly. "You're the President's Chief of Staff. You have access to government forces. Find his killer."

"People are working on that. Murphy was a spent force. His credibility was gone. With the public, and the vast majority of Druids."

"You seem sure of that."

He nodded.

"So again, why are you here?"

"The Gorsedd wants a new Raven Master. We are in a bit of a chaotic state. There's a new Dragon Master in Wales but we don't know who. It's being kept secret at this point. Damien Wyndham, our key link with the Dragon Master, is also most likely dead." Armitage relaxed as he delved into recent Druid history, feeling comfortable with his information. "I had my people do a quiet but thorough investigation on Wyndham. He's not in custody in any of our facilities nor is he any facility in the UK. No question about it, Wyndham is dead."

"What happened to his funds?" David, ever practical, suddenly burst in. "He owned that airline, Air Celtica, and lots of other businesses besides. That's what was largely funding the movement and Murphy's presidential campaign."

Before Armitage could answer, Bethan pointed her cigarette at her son. "But Davey dear, it was all basically a shell. Wyndham's empire existed only due to the force of his own will." She flashed a quick glance at Armitage. "And the power of the gods, of course."

"Yes, well at any rate, the Gorsedd asked me to meet with you urgently. The Gorsedd wants you as the new Raven Master." Before she could respond, he hurriedly continued, "They want a dynamic leader, one who can pull the movement back together again and one who has credibility in both the business and political communities, but not active in government or politics. We sought the gods' favor and the signs were strong. The goddess Brigid marked you for her own and now she, and we, are asking you to step forward. We need you Bethan."

"Her money, you mean," David said drily. Before Armitage could respond, Bethan whipped around and demanded an apology. "This man came across country to ask this very important question. How dare you insult him like that!" Her son quickly apologized, but could see he'd scored a hit.

"And what about our dear friend Liam? Not hours in his grave and you're already replacing him? The Gorsedd has absorbed the news of his death, had time to gather, meet, discuss and choose a successor then select you to fly out all the way from Washington? All within a matter of hours? Not to mention flight time."

Armitage had the grace to look embarrassed. "Liam's time was over. We knew he was close to being released, but he could never again command the attention or respect of the public or the movement. We had a meeting four days ago and agreed he needed to be replaced. It was our intention to take care of him, but you were the Gorsedd's choice to replace him."

She stood and stretched, then paced the room. She had a severe look on her face as she stood in front of the still-seated Armitage, towering above the stubby man. She instructed David to retrieve the man's equipment and return them to him.

She glared at the squat little man. "Be clear about one thing. If Liam's murder was your doing, or if it was someone else in the Gorsedd, I will find out. As Raven Master, I will brook no opposition. I will not tolerate treachery amongst any of you or any of the followers. I will be obeyed without question.

"Did you think I would be so stupid as to agree to a meeting with you and not know why you were coming? My sources in the Gorsedd told me exactly why you were coming. They told me you boasted about your plans to 'retire' Liam—I think that was the word you used was it not, dear Dex?"

David walked into the room with Armitage's devices and placed them on the table in front of him as she spoke.

"Understand this Dex Armitage. Your position in government means nothing to me. I can have you removed at any time. I have done my homework, little man, and have a dossier on you that the President, the FBI, the media and many others would be delighted to get their hands on. Can we talk about bank accounts in the Cayman Islands and laundered funds out of Homeland' Security's budget 're-allocated' to offshore security companies? Can we talk about ritual sacrifices? Oh, I know they were animals. But would others? Especially if there were hints or questions about missing children."

Horrified, Armitage jumped to his feet. "Bethan…I…I…" he stuttered apoplectically.

"I just want you to know where I stand. I accepted the role of Raven Master early this morning and conveyed that to my contact. You need to know that I am ready, willing and able to move on anyone who stands in my way. Whether they are an enemy, or a Druid."

A cold-blooded reptilian smile creased her face. "So, we understand each other, right?"

Without waiting for a response, she turned to David. "Mr. Armitage is leaving now. He has urgent government business in Washington. I've already arranged for his return flight. Have Raul drive him to the ferry in Sausalito.

"Have a nice flight Dex, and pleasant dreams. I do believe you're on the red-eye."

They watched from the main windows as Armitage was hustled out of the house and into the car. "That man is dangerous, mother." David calmly faced his mother. "And he does want your money."

"Of course he's dangerous. He didn't get to be the President's Chief of Staff because he's meek and mild. He's a cobra." She swept back through the room to her chair, and perched on the arm. "And yes, he wants our money. Funding has dried up since Wyndham's disappearance and Murphy's arrest. He and the Gorsedd are desperate. Paying for operations against the state can be very expensive." She glanced up at him. "Sorry I spoke so severely, but it was for show. Good cop, bad cop, you know."

David laughed. "Mother you're incorrigible. You had Armitage eating out of your hands after you'd turned him upside down and inside out. You bundled him out of here and he still doesn't know what happened. He came offering a position you already knew about and accepted. His macho posture was emasculated before his eyes and he's gone before he even comprehends what happened. I could almost feel sorry for him." He smiled again. "But I don't."

Bethan bowed in acceptance of her son's praise. "Thank you, Davey. I do my best."

She slipped down into her chair and became more businesslike. "Raul downloaded everything from Armitage's devices. I want you to take a good look at everything. If you can't make out what it is, bring in one of our experts and have them decipher it. Tomorrow I want you on a plane to New York and meet with Serpent Master. He's holding some meetings with his counterparts at the United Nations, but I've already messaged him to expect you. He will send you details of where and when. Try to find out where else he goes and who else he meets with. Then I want you in Washington. Stay at a hotel, not our apartment. I don't want you visible yet. Wait until I contact you."

"What do you want me to do there?"

"I don't quite know yet." She stretched her arms. "It depends. I'll wait and see if anything interesting comes off his devices; if I get useful information about Murphy's killing, and where Armitage has been and who he met. Until then…" she shrugged.

She looked up at his puzzled face.

"Oh yes, Davey dear, I will have him tracked. He will be under constant surveillance because he is indeed a dangerous cobra and I want to see how and where he will strike. Ta muid anseo—as the Master wills."

Chapter Six

Chantilly, Virginia

"You want what?" Chad exploded with frustration and anger.

"I want your resignation on my desk in ten minutes. The order is surely clear enough in plain English." Tyler blasted the demand at full volume, oblivious to his door that was slightly ajar.

"But Chief…"

"No buts!" Tyler interrupted. "Your resignation on my desk. Ten minutes." He looked up at Wiz. "No need for yours. You retired a couple of years ago. You were just along for the ride." He waved dismissal.

Silenced, a fuming Chad and pensive Wiz left the office. The door slammed shut behind them. In the outer office, secretaries and other agents kept their heads down, embarrassed for the two men who'd just been fired. Everyone had heard the angry exchanges and the Chief's demands. Silence enveloped the room as Chad went over to his desk, sat down and began to compose his letter. Wiz quietly took up a cardboard box sitting on another desk and began filling it with Chad's personal belongings. Every so often Chad muttered an angry stream of invective, as he worked away at the computer.

In less than the allowed time he stormed back into Tyler's office and slammed the required letter on the chief's desk. Just as he was leaving, Tyler barked. "Wait." A little softer he continued, "I want you and Wiz downstairs in the underground garage immediately. Get into a dark green Ford Edge—the one nearest the elevator. Go with the driver."

Chad hesitated, looked at Tyler, nodded and closed the door quietly. In the office, he signaled to Wiz and the two walked out of the office and into the hall towards the elevators without a word or glance backwards. As they walked down the hall Chad repeated the Chief's last words. All he got from Wiz was a grunt and a questioning glance.

In the basement they spotted the car immediately and got in. The driver said nothing.

As they emerged onto the street Chad noticed the light sensitive windows darken down immediately. Nobody could see in and, in the dreary drizzly skies, Chad could see very little out either. He glanced at Wiz who merely looked over and put a finger to his mouth in the universal sign for quiet.

The silent drive took them down I 66, across the Potomac River and into the District of Columbia. After a short drive down Constitution Avenue, the driver made a left turn onto 18th Street past the Department of the Interior building and Constitution Hall. A couple of blocks later he made a turn onto New York Avenue, then almost immediately turned again into the entrance to an underground parking garage.

Once in the garage, the driver kept driving down into the bowels of the garage until he finally arrived at a concrete barrier tucked away out of sight from the main garage lanes. At the barrier, he waited while a wide red laser beam travelled slowly over, under and around the vehicle. Fascinated, Chad watched as the beam suddenly switched off and the barrier dropped suddenly into the floor. An entrance slid open in the wall.

The car stopped beside a small door and the driver got out, opening the passenger door for the pair to exit. He still said nothing. As soon as they were out, a bearded man in a nondescript navy blue suit looked them over carefully, checking them against whatever information was in his handheld iPad-like device. Back in his little glass-enclosed booth Chad could see his lips moving. A moment later, satisfied, he gestured them through the door. It closed behind them, leaving the silent guard alone in a small booth. He pointed down a short corridor to another door at the end.

Shrugging, Chad looked at Wiz and began walking. At the door, he knocked then pulled the handle. As he knocked, both men flattened themselves against the walls. Not that it would do any good, a chagrined Chad briefly acknowledged to himself, since neither was armed or capable of any defense in this fortress-like set up.

The door opened on a small boardroom. There was a familiar looking man sitting at the far end, waiting silently alone in the room. Wiz grinned. Chad gulped.

"Mr. President?"

New York City

Davey Price followed the directions carefully after memorizing them and deleting the text from his cellphone. Two days had passed since he arrived in the city, waiting for the Serpent Master to contact him. Finally, this morning, the brusque command to meet came through.

The mid day traffic in Manhattan was as slow, noisy and chaotic as ever as the cab worked its way slowly up Fifth Avenue from the hotel. At Price's direction, the cab stopped in front of the Metropolitan Museum of Art. Price crossed over Fifth avenue quickly, dodging cabs and buses as he did.

Turning right he walked down Fifth Avenue, picking up the pace as he came to the south end of the Museum and entered Central Park. By the time he got through the convoluted winding pathways to Central Park West he regretted not bringing a warmer coat. A sharp chill wind whistled down the street as he crossed it just in front of the Museum of Natural History. He sped up his pace, striding quickly up to the corner of West 83rd Street, then turned left. The red-brick brownstone building was on the north side of the street about half way down the block as his text had indicated.

He casually scanned the street as he'd done all morning. He was so tall, he knew he couldn't easily disappear into the crowds as others could. No matter where he was or what he was doing, he couldn't help standing out, and therefore tracked. It was why he hated all cloak and dagger stuff and wished his mother wouldn't send him on such errands.

On the third floor he quickly found suite 3A and knocked. At the vocal command 'come', he pushed the door open. The man he'd come to see gestured for him to sit. Although he was out of uniform, wearing a dark grey suit, white shirt and muted red tie, there was no mistaking the military bearing and prominent bald head of General Ronald G. Wells known to his face by equals and politicians as 'RG' and, behind his back--especially by those under his command--as 'Old Stoneface' or 'Iceberg'.

Price nodded, and sat down on the black leather couch. He scanned the room quickly, taking in the stark modernist furnishings and décor devoid of any warmth or hospitality. Much like the man himself, he considered.

Wells stared coldly at him unblinking for several moments before sitting down stiffly in a plain black leather armchair across from him. The chair was specially constructed for Wells' shortened frame.

"Raven Master says you will be my sole contact with her." It was a statement, not a question. Price waited. "I prefer not to deal with subordinates and lackeys, but the Raven Master commands. I will obey." His clipped icy tone was meant to intimidate those he considered inferior. Price returned Wells' unblinking stare and deliberately relaxed his body, crossing his legs and letting one of his patent leather loafers flop idly against his heel.

Irritated, Wells reached into a briefcase beside him and pulled out a thick wad of paper. He thrust them across to Price. "This is the report I received on the killing of Liam Murphy." As Price picked them up, Wells added. "you can read them, even memorize them if you can, and pass the contents on to the Raven Master, but under no circumstances are these documents to leave this room. I will only allow her to have the actual documents and I will give them to her personally. Not to you." Abruptly he got up and disappeared into the kitchen.

As he read, Price whistled a few times, surprised by what he read.

Wells returned to the living room almost an hour later holding a glass of whiskey in one hand and the quarter full bottle in the other. He placed the bottle on a small sideboard then snapped his fingers and held out his hand to take back the documents, placing them carefully back into the briefcase. "Not what you expected, Mr. Price?"

Suspecting he'd been under surveillance the entire time, Price leaned back casually, smiled an insincere smile and paused before replying. "No, not at all. You have confidence in this information?"

"Tell the Raven Master that this information was dug out by my best people, including some very highly placed at the National Security Agency. Some are part of us, others are on my staff or beholden to me."

Price leaned back into an even more relaxed posture. Wells remained sitting ramrod straight in his chair. Another look of annoyance crossed his face as the civilian did what no subordinate would dare in his presence; take a casual approach to his presence and authority.

"So, let me understand this fully, General…"

Before he could continue, Wells snarled at him. "I am Serpent Master! You will not use my name or rank in any way, shape or form when we are together. Remember who I am. Your situation as son of the Raven Master has no place or authority here. I am Serpent Master, responsible for the movement's senior personnel and security. You, Price, are a nobody; a mere messenger. Got it?"

Recognizing that Wells was using his own mother's favorite strategy to unsettle people, Price looked back, smiled tightly and murmured an apology. "Of course, Serpent Master. It shall be as you wish." Better to give Old Stoneface a small victory at this point, he decided.

"So, you're saying Armitage had nothing to do with Murphy's assassination?"

Wells snorted. "He was visiting your mother in San Francisco, as you well know."

"He arrived at our house after the killing," Price reminded Wells. "Of course, he could have ordered it prior to leaving Washington. Very easy to do. Verbal. No paper trails." He paused a moment. "Did your operatives check out that possibility, Serpent Master?"

Wells was apoplectic. His faced reddened as he jumped up. "You think we're amateurs at this?" he raged. "You think my men have never conducted deep surveillance or intelligence gathering you little piece of arse-wipe." He continued to rage, swearing and using all the derogatory terms a career in the Marine Corps had taught him, plus others he'd picked up from the other branches of the military and other parts of the world.

Price stood, pulling his gangly full 6-foot 6 inch frame to its fullest extremity and looking down on the furious man, holding his palm up to stop the flood of invective.

"Serpent Master, you misunderstand. I'm not questioning your operatives' account, merely confirming their work so that I can report this to her." Price sat down once again and continued. "Now, according to this report, Dex Armitage was pushing for Murphy's release. It also states it was Armitage's idea to remove Murphy as Raven Master in North America. To do what? Take the top spot himself? A bit ambitious and transparent, don't you think?"

Wells prided himself on his ability to fly into sudden violent rages and then turn the tap off as quickly as he turned it on. His icy stare did not waver, even as he reached over and topped up his glass without once taking his eyes off Price. "No way on earth that little moron could assume the role of Raven Master. He hasn't got the guts or the stamina for the job. No sir, he sees himself as the power behind the throne. He had plans for another to become Raven Master." He paused. "And for damn sure it was not your mother."

Price nodded. "Figured that out ourselves." He pointed to the closed briefcase. "The report also indicates that POTUS might have had a role in the assassination, correct?"

Wells paced the floor, downing the whiskey in one gulp and just as quickly refilling the glass as he paced. "It's a possibility. Gets rid of a major embarrassment before there's any real damage. Remember, he's in the top slot only because Murphy was removed just before the election. It's possible the President was behind it. If so, it's a highly dangerous game he's playing. We could bring him down."

The two continued to discuss the report, a slight thaw developing between them as both silently acknowledged their first impressions did not do justice to the reality of the intelligence and determination of the other.

Finally, Price stood. "Thank you for this, Serpent Master." As he turned to leave, he stopped in his tracks. "One more thing. Your report indicated that there is a new Dragon Master. Do you know who it is?"

Wells shook his head and shrugged. "Not yet, but I will. That information came from my counterpart in the British military. He got it from a highly-placed politician but apparently, that's all they know. The identity is closely-guarded." He smiled coldly. "Understandable really, considering the very short life span of Dragon Masters over there."

With assurances that Wells would continue to probe for the identity, Price left the building. Though he didn't let on, the news that the new Dragon Master had not only been chosen but was kept under wraps, was certainly something Mother needed to know immediately. That plus the fact that it seemed the movement also now had someone back inside Parliament, meant he had some juicy news to import to her.

It almost made it worthwhile, putting up with that dictatorial little jerk, Old Stoneface, he supposed.

Whitehall, London

Gregory Belmont was a non-descript man by any standards.

He stood barely five feet six, his thinning hair had more wisps of grey than brown, and a large bald spot in the middle, leaving a huge forehead mottled by freckles. His face was unremarkable except for his small pinched chin, while his watery brown eyes and wrinkled bags underneath were partially covered by thick lensed black hornrims that seemed leftover from the seventies. A slightly tight-fitting grey suit pulled across his belly—the one prominent feature in his whole body—and crumpled over his shoes. Even his walk was more shamble and stutter than it was walk.

Nevertheless, he was one of the most powerful men in government, a fast-rising star known for his bellicose and pugnacious nature. His breeding in the Gorbals, the old lower working-class areas of Glasgow south of the Clyde River—he refused to call them slums—had hardened his unforgiving approach to friend and foe alike. But today he was in an effusive mood. A quick smile crossed his face as he walked down Whitehall towards his office in the Houses of Parliament.

The summons to meet the Prime Minister had made his day. His hard work of quietly building coalitions across party lines and across government departments had paid off. Since the election he'd been Parliamentary Secretary to the Secretary of State for Culture, but now the PM had offered him a major jump in job and status. He looked at the hundreds passing him on the street or in the double deck buses plying their way up Whitehall. You may not realize it, he preened to himself, but all of you are now looking at the newly minted Minister for Policing and Internal Security, a key member of the Home Office and well-positioned to take a run eventually at even higher power positions in government.

He turned towards Westminster Bridge, aiming at a quiet little pub, The Wig and Robe, tucked into a small side street off the Victoria Embankment. Inside the dark, noisy crush around the bar, he spotted, as expected, his long-time assistant Fiona Moffatt holding down a pair of seats at a small table in the darker recesses of the pub.

He rarely grinned. But this time he did. And it intrigued Fiona. "Well?"

He settled himself on the chair, juggling a pint of Guinness in the process. With a satisfied smile he told her the news. He looked carefully around, checking out those closest to him. "The PM even said there's a knighthood in it for me in the next honours list." He preened himself, oblivious to her delighted reaction. "Sir Gregory. I like the sound of that, don't you Fiona?"

She congratulated him and they talked quietly and strategized his next moves. "You will, of course, join me at the Home Office. I need your steady hand and wisdom, Fiona." She was the one person in the world he appreciated, but she was part of his public world and had no idea of his second life. They were in the middle of planning his first moves as Minister when he noticed a man enter the pub; a man he had texted to meet him there.

"Would you excuse me for a wee while, Fiona. There's a man I must talk to."

Without waiting for an answer, he jumped up from the table, pushed through the crowd, grabbed the man's arm and pulled him out onto the street. He led his man up onto Westminster Bridge. Halfway across they stopped and leaned on the stone parapet, seemingly watching the busy river traffic. As a crowded tour boat left the pier, Belmont and the man spoke without looking at each other.

"Whatever else happens, Bryn, I want a close eye kept on Evans and his minions. I want to know what he does, where he goes and who he contacts. Whatever it takes, do it." They discussed options to keep surveillance on the professor. "He looks harmless, but he's a wily old bugger. I'll set up a special contact system for you, and I expect at least weekly updates; daily or even hourly if things start happening. Under no circumstances must you try to reach me through my office or staff. Understand?" The man nodded slightly, pointing aimlessly at the London Eye as if indicating some feature of interest.

Belmont reached into his suit jacket and pulled out a small box. Inside was a mobile phone. "Keep this secure. Do not use it under any circumstances for any other use. If I need you, I will ring you on it, so have it with you at all times. At all times, d'ye ken?" Another nod.

He was just moving away when Belmont stopped him. "Have you found where that idiot McLeod is hiding away?" Receiving a negative response, Belmont barked harshly. "Find him and eliminate him. He bungled the attack on that American and must pay the price of failure. Then offer the Badger more money. I want to know every move Evans makes. I'll call you next week and expect you to report that McLeod is history."

Belmont left abruptly without another word, shambling back to the pub. I should be Dragon Master, he muttered to himself. Not that sad incompetent Evans. The thought of his rival's success soured the excitement and pleasure of the Prime Minister's decision. What really galled him was that now, in his ministerial position, he could actually do more to move the Druid agenda along than anyone else—including that damned Welshman. He consoled himself with the thought that his control of police and internal security might actually help him undermine Evans and grease his own rise to Dragon Master. Sir Gregory; Dragon Master. They had a nice ring. He didn't know yet which he preferred, so he smiled to himself and mused, I'll just have to get used to both.

Placated inside himself, he pushed his way back into the pub. Now the real work could begin.

Chapter Seven

Greyfell Abbey, Lake District, England

The reunion had been a happy, though restrained, one. Both Mandy and Stone commiserated with each other on the circumstances that enveloped them. Both tried to show the other care and compassion, Mandy more so than Stone since he was the one most recently hospitalized. Their hugs had been sincere and heartfelt, of that Stone was sure. And the way she smiled at him with genuine pleasure gave him hope. But, he sensed, there was still restraint; still a barrier.

Huw arrived with her, along with Freddy, so the reunion and good times were spread around, not just concentrated on Mandy, even though Stone deeply wanted to take her aside for a long, quiet talk. It had not been possible in the hospital, nor at The Grange, with nurses and staff constantly in and out of her room, checking on her regularly.

He put a smile on and supressed his frustration. Maybe tomorrow, he told himself.

Stone was just settling down to a good long conversation with everyone when the doctor who'd accompanied him to Greyfell interrupted and told him that he still needed lots of rest, urging him to retire early for the night. He protested vehemently but when the others agreed and began to break up the gathering, he mentally admitted his weariness and succumbed to the pressure, wishing everyone a good night and traipsing off to bed like a good boy.

Once in the massive four-poster though, he could not sleep. His mind raced from one topic to the next. From Mandy to finances; from work needs to those bloody Druids. He tossed and turned. He dropped off, only to wake what seemed moments later. It was still pitch dark and drumming rain on the windows. His mind wandered again, wondering what had happened to Chad, then concerned about his unresolved situation with Mandy. He tried listening to the music he'd loaded on his iPhone. The strains of Strass and Bach were followed by Mozart and Elgar. None helped. Not even the pastoral bliss of Smetana's *Moldau*, brought him peace.

As he listened, he rewound his relationship with Mandy from their stress-filled, antagonistic and adversarial beginning, through a slowly growing appreciation and teamwork which morphed into liking, and the beginnings of love. As he struggled with sleep, Stone replayed moments, especially after they'd both admitted romantic interest in each other. He recalled conversations about taking the relationship to a new level and they wondered about the impact on both their careers. Neither was willing to bend on their career aspirations; stubbornness on both sides set in.

Finally, Mandy precipitously accepted a professorship at the University of The Marches in Herefordshire. Miffed, Stone prepared to return to the USA. The mental gymnastics he'd played for the past few months—to return to the US or stay in the UK—came back with a vengeance. It increased the tossing and turning, as he sought to both erase his thoughts and find a comfortable position. Then the London attack happened.

He recalled how bamboozled Mandy was by Nigel Pitt, an imposter who turned out to be a murderous Druid. Suddenly, his mind filled with the horrific scene in the hotel room, where he thought she'd been killed by Pitt.

The flashback jarred him wide awake. It was no good. His weariness was gone. He could not sleep. His anger and frustration boiled over into a depressing round of self-pity and self-blame. If only he had been willing to give up his career. If only he had not got involved in the Druid mess. If only he could muster the same kind of strength and faith that Huw possessed. If only…if only…if only.

He tried listening to Elgar's *Nimrod*, but even its soaring notes could not drown his thoughts. He quietly got up. The beside clock said 4:53 a.m. He dressed quickly, figuring he could shower later when everyone else was up. He quietly crossed the hallway and down the back stairs into the kitchen. With only one light over the sink turned on, he was just putting milk in his freshly made cup of coffee when he heard a discreet cough behind him.

"Couldn't sleep either, I see." Huw was still in a robe and pajamas, his feet in a pair of too large slippers causing him to shuffle across the flagstone floor.

Stone said nothing. Huw helped himself to the kettle and grabbed a tea bag out of the nearby container. "Never could stand tea bags," he said nonchalantly. "When you pull them out they always look like drowned rats. Give me proper tea leaves in a proper tea caddy any time." He playfully held his nose while dunking the tea bag in the boiling water. With a nod towards the small wooden kitchen table, Huw led the way and seated himself. Stone pulled up the chair opposite him and sipped.

"You're looking good Bradstone. Better than when I saw you last at the hospital. The last couple of days here seems to have been a tonic for you." Stone mumbled agreement. For several minutes, the two men sat quietly, each lost in his own thoughts and each sipping occasionally from their steaming mugs. Huw got up and went to the kitchen cupboards, opening each one until he finally found what he was looking for.

"Milk chocolate digestive biscuits, Bradstone. Nothing better than these to supplement a hot drink." As he moved, Huw winced and clutched his side. Realizing Stone had seen him, Huw shrugged. "Every once in a while, those injuries from Washington keep popping up at inopportune times."

The awkward silence between them continued, broken only by the steady pounding of the heavy rains on the windows and by the occasional gust of winds creaking branches and blowing debris around outside the solid stone house.

Huw took another drink. "She does love you, you know."

For the first time, Stone pulled himself out of his funk and glanced up. "I'm not so sure about that, Huw. She is very kind and considerate and obviously willing to be friendly with me. But love? I've seen nothing to convince me of that."

"Rubbish, my boy.

"I wish."

"Dew, Dew, boy. She cares very deeply for you. All those hours I sat beside her in the hospital, worrying if she would survive and then, if she did, would she be the same Myfanwy. It draws you deeper into your faith. Thank the Lord, my prayers were answered. She and I talked a lot, about what happened and more besides. I will not betray her trust of confidence, except to say that I am convinced she loves you."

Stone reached out and took a biscuit off the plate Huw offered. "The thing is, Huw, I love her and realize what an idiot I was worrying about my television career in the States when I was letting the best thing that ever happened to me, slip away."

"To be fair, my boy, she was just as stubborn about her career as you were about yours." His cherubic face broke into a warm smile. "I just hope both of you have learned a lesson about life priorities."

Huw warmed to his topic, but Stone raised his hand and interrupted. "Please Huw. No lectures. Not now."

"Of course, Bradstone, of course." The silence renewed briefly. "You know, my boy, mostly right now she is embarrassed but doesn't quite know how to deal with it. Until she does, she won't be able to properly and openly acknowledge her feelings for you."

"What on earth does she have to be embarrassed about, for heaven's sake?"

"She was taken in by a very slick and evil man. She bought his lies, his smooth lines, his phoney romancing, his fake concern and compassion. And in that hotel at Hyde Park, it almost cost her her life." Huw thought for a moment, torn between the urge to reassure Stone and still retaining Mandy's confidentiality. "She's struggling with feelings of guilt and has pulled back inside her emotional self, afraid to take chances with feelings once again."

Stone considered Huw's words. Stone trusted him as a friend and mentor. At the same time, Huw's words hit home. Stone knew only too well how he himself struggled with opening up to others in deep and personal ways.

"Should I talk to her about it? Tell her it's okay and that I understand?"

"No, my boy. she'd know immediately that you and I have talked and that would probably drive her deeper into her self." He shook his head. "No, you two need to start fresh. You both need something to unite around, to redevelop your relationship. And I don't mean another bout with the Druids. We've all had enough of that mess. It's time for Sir Giles and his mob to deal with them now."

Huw put his cup down and grinned. "We have a saying in Wales: '*Daw eto haul ar fryn*' or in English, 'the sun will shine on the hill again'. In other words, things will get better soon."

Stone nodded thoughtfully. "Sounds good, Huw, but the trouble is, there's nothing even remotely like that on the horizon."

Even with only the single light in the dark room, Stone could see a twinkle in Huw's eyes.

"Maybe. Maybe not." He sipped from his cup. "Tell me Bradstone, what do you know about Prince Madoc of Gwynedd?"

Sausalito, California

Bethan Price hung up her cellphone. The call from David was interesting, and most of it expected. But two pieces of information stuck out for her. First, according to the report, Dex Armitage was not involved in the Murphy assassination. That baffled her. She was sure he'd played a part in it. Second, there was a potential new mole high in the British parliamentary structure.

On the first item, she was not convinced. The fact that a physical copy of the report was withheld from Davey and, therefore, by extension from her—no matter what Wells said—sparked her suspicion. Was it, in fact, legitimate? It was cobbled together very quickly yet Wells claimed it was both accurate and comprehensive. Which raised yet another question. What game was the Serpent Master playing, if at all? Was he the loyal security scourge he portrayed, or did he have a different agenda? She thought about it for the next couple of hours, turning various scenarios over in her mind. Nothing jumped out at her, but she was uneasy.

Better safe than sorry she thought as she dialed an old comrade. Malcom Coughlin was a hard shelled, immensely intelligent, well connected executive in her holding company. He'd come up the ranks with her late husband, both starting as roughnecks in the South American oilfields, then slowly rising in position and taking control of operations of the small company they ostensibly worked for. Complex and corrupt deals with authorities in Venezuela soon had the pair controlling a sizeable chunk of the Venezuelan oil industry and pocketing millions to boot.

When the government nationalized the industry, driving Coughlin and her husband Tom out of the country, the pair merely set up shop in neighbouring Guyana. Tom moved on with his accumulated wealth and invested in his own oil company. As agreed, Coughlin stayed in Guyana directing exploration and tapping new oil deposits, ensuring that a steady flow of funds went to Tom with healthy amounts making it into Coughlin's own shell companies and laundered bank accounts.

Bethan knew the two old rogues aided and abetted each other's borderline legal schemes as well as their more illicit ones. She knew too that while she and Tom moved more and more into the heart of the Druid movement, Coughlin had no such interest. To each his own, he'd told them, preferring to reject their new-found beliefs in favor of something much more solid; cold, hard cash. Nevertheless, though he remained on the outside, his loyalty to the Prices continued even after Tom's massive heart attack. It was trumped only by his loyalty to cash. She knew she could count on him for both intelligence and muscle at any time. As long as she was willing to pay.

To her, his value was tripled simply because he was an outsider and therefore she made fastidious efforts to keep Coughlin isolated from, and invisible to, her Druid partners. It was always good to keep something surprising in the back pocket, Tom had always told her. She agreed. She and her son were the only ones who had Coughlin's ultra-secure satellite voice link. She used it.

Bethan reached him at his luxurious ocean-side mansion near Victoria, south east of the capital, Georgetown. Without telling him why, she asked him to accumulate as much information as he could on US Marine General R.G. Wells and, further, to send a couple of his well-trained security operatives to tail Wells. Coughlin whistled when she outlined her request, then laughed out loud.

"You aren't serious love! Information on the guy is easy. But tailing a high-ranking US military guy like that? You're joking! He'll be protected and his rear end under protective surveillance from his own people. Won't stand a chance."

"Oh, come on, Malcom," she cajoled, "I didn't say it would be easy. But you've done similar operations on other high-ranking officials in any number of countries." The persuading and negotiating went on for several minutes before she got his agreement, as she knew she would. It cost her more than she expected, but a price she was willing to pay. If only for the security of knowing which way the Serpent Master was bending in the winds that were beginning to blow.

That settled, Bethan turned her mind to the second bit of news Davey shared. The idea of a new, highly placed source in the heart of Britain's government intrigued her. If true, it was an immensely important asset. But things were murky over there. A new Dragon Master was in place, she knew, but as yet nobody knew who it was.

She picked up her phone again. This time, she called her old friend Richard Evans. It was late evening when she reached him in Aberystwyth. Once the pleasantries were finished she bluntly asked him who the new Dragon Master was. He delicately slipped around the issue each time she broached it.

"You're being deliberately cagey, Richard. And for a reason, I know. Tell me, would you be as slippery if I were to ask you the same questions face to face?"

Five minutes later, she disconnected and just as quickly called her son in New York. As she waited for him, she beckoned to Raul. "Book me first class on the next available flight to London."

One thing she was sure of, whatever it took and however she did it, she would wring the information out of Evans and then demand a face-to-face meeting with the new Dragon Master. She had plans, big plans, and she was going to persuade the new leader to support them. There'd been too much failure, too much fumbling around. Now was the time to act.

Washington, D.C.

The President smiled and waved both Chad and Wiz to seats around the table.

"Please be seated, Mr. Lawson and Mr. Zanelli. I'm expecting one more person and then we can proceed."

Chad and Wiz took their seats as ordered. Chad was baffled by the topsy-turvy pattern his life had taken in the past two hours. He looked over at Wiz who had a bemused smile playing across his face. Wiz caught him looking and simply shrugged. The President said nothing but simply looked at the door.

Moments later, it opened. Chad's jaw dropped. Wiz nodded. Calvin Tyler walked into the room and took a seat opposite the President.

The President smiled. "Good to see you Cal. You made good time."

He chuckled at the look of bewilderment on Chad's face. "You're probably wondering why I called this little meeting." He leaned back in his chair and laughed out loud at his own joke. "This room and this building are connected by a very secure underground corridor to the White House. Security is extremely tight and only a few key people are aware of its existence."

His face and voice turned serious. "Last night, I accepted Cal's resignation as Chief of the SID and I believe he accepted your resignations this morning." Without waiting for a response, he continued. "Director Tyler and I were afraid this moment would come; that the whole Druid mess would begin to unravel despite our attempts to stop it. The final push for Liam Murphy's release was the last straw." He gestured at Tyler. "You explain from here, Cal."

"The President knew it would become politically impossible to keep Murphy under wraps, particularly since he was so, shall we say, uncooperative. Keeping him in custody was a very short-term probability. That, in turn, would undermine our ability to further investigate and block any other Druid attempts on our government."

The President nodded and interrupted. "It would also destabilize our government—particularly the judicial and investigative arms—and weaken the political ability of my administration to act. The situation could not be allowed to continue."

Tyler picked up the thread. "It was essential that the Security Investigative Directorate have the political and administrative ability to continue its other investigations and prosecutions, so we had to separate SID from the Druid investigation."

He looked at both Chad and Wiz. "You two, and I, were the obvious bad guys, pursuing the issue and drilling deeper and deeper into the activities of the Druids They wanted us stopped and emasculated."

"So, I did it for them," the President spoke up. His deep brown eyes, crinkled on the corners as a small smile creased his usually stern looking face. As Chad gazed back at the President his mind flitted to the most innocuous topics, something he often did in times of stress. My God, he thought, the President's hair has really turned grey over the past few months. It's true, the Presidency ages a man well beyond his years. He jerked back to the present.

"Cal's resignation and yours will be announced," he looked at his wristwatch, "right about now in the White House press room. None of us predicted Murphy's killing, but it came, if I can be so crassly insensitive, at the right time. Our statement will point out that you three bungled the enquiry from start to finish and that I demanded your resignations. We will announce a full-bore investigation of Murphy's death but to all intents and purposes, the government's inquiries into the Druid movement is closed." The President leaned back and stretched his arms. "Which brings us to now."

The room fell silent as the President carefully looked both Wiz and Chad up and down. "Cal tells me that you two are the best he's got. Further, you both, particularly you Mr. Lawson, are very familiar with the Druids and their plots. He briefed me on your activities in London and the way you and the broadcaster Stone Wallace, thwarted the attack on Queen Elizabeth."

"That being the case, and because I will not abide treason against this great nation of ours, means I have to find another way to root out these snakes and destroy them once and for all."

He stood and began pacing the small area behind his chair. "So, I am creating a new investigative unit, lets call it Committee D, for Druid, with full authority and total autonomy to investigate and destroy any Druid threat against the United States."

For the next half hour, he outlined his plans. Tyler would be in charge and would operate from a small non-descript property near the Rappahannock River south east of Fredericksburg.

"My so-called retirement home," Tyler explained. The President nodded and added "and he will not leave there, except to shop, golf or pursue other retirement activities. He will not accept or attend Washington social events, but simply disappear off the radar."

Chad and Wiz meanwhile were to be a two-man team. If they needed anything, they got it from Tyler—weapons, funds, equipment, whatever they needed. All this would be underwritten from a special government account that was for the President's use only and not reportable to any audit by either the government or Congress. "It's a blank check, gentlemen, but don't waste it."

Contact would be with Tyler. The Chief, in return, was accountable only to the President. Lines of communication were tight. Only four men knew of the existence of Committee D. "Not even my Chief of Staff knows about this," the President declared as he eased himself out of his chair and began walking to the door. Chad and Wiz glanced at each other, eyebrows raised. "Nor Homeland Security."

When the President finally left the room to attend other appointments, the three got down to business.

Chapter Eight

Greyfell Abbey, Lake District

Huw's enigmatic question was left hanging, as the Abbey's housekeeper came into the kitchen. She said good morning to the men at the table, flicked all the main lights on and asked them what they wanted for breakfast.

As they were responding, Lord Greyfell entered. "What a night, eh? Going to have to take a quick look around the house and make sure there's no damage. Same with the outbuildings." He plopped himself down and gratefully accepted the hot cup of tea and plate of shortbread biscuits placed before him by the housekeeper. "Thanks Mrs. Dowell. Sausage and eggs for me, beans, mushrooms and some black pudding."

Stone grimaced at what he considered one of the most odious parts of an English breakfast: black pudding, a sausage crammed with dried and curdled animal blood mixed with oatmeal, suet and a bit of meat. Black indeed, he thought, his stomach churning. Huw meanwhile asked for the other thing Stone considered equally revolting for breakfast, the smoked fish called kippers.

They exchanged pleasantries and discussed the still raging storm. "Typical for this time of year," Lord Greyfell said, "but I confess that was one big blow!" As they talked, Stone asked if he could pop into the study and use the laptop. He was determined not to be trapped into a guessing game with Huw about this Prince Madoc. The last time Huw sprung a name out of the clear blue sky at him, it was that of King Arthur. That had got him embroiled in the whole perilous Druid conspiracy in the first place.

Huw's eyes sparkled. He knew what Stone was about to do.

One by one, others appeared in the kitchen until Mrs. Dowell shooed them out so she could prepare the meal. Half an hour later they all gathered in the dining room and dove into the breakfast. Amused, Stone noted that only three people reached for the black pudding. The rest assiduously left it alone.

Breakfast finished, the doctor took a few moments to check Stone over, indicating his pleasure that for the first time, Stone had eaten a reasonably full meal. An excellent result meaning the worst was over, he pronounced, adding that if the next day went as well, he saw no need to remain.

Armed with that good news, Stone sought out Huw. He found him in a smaller cozy sitting room the Greyfells called "the snug" sitting with Mandy. They all smiled at each other and both Mandy and Huw were delighted with the doctor's report.

"Now Huw, what's this Prince Madoc question all about?"

Huw leaned forward on the small sofa. Mandy looked at him speculatively. "What have you got up your sleeve now, Da?"

"I know you popped off into the study to look up Madoc on the internet, Bradstone. Why don't you tell us what you found out?"

"Obviously nothing you don't already know," he glanced over at Mandy and grinned, "or you either, Mandy. Madoc was a Prince of Gwynedd in the twelfth century. It seems he was one of several illegitimate sons of Owain, the King, and a potential heir to the throne."

"Correct. Legitimacy of birth was not an issue for succession in those days," Huw interjected, "so long as the King himself acknowledged the child as his own."

Before he could continue, Mandy interrupted. "No lectures, Da. Let Stone tell us what he's found out. Then you can tell both of us why you're so mysterious about it all."

Stone continued. "It seems Madoc had little interest in the crown. Historians disagree as to whether he really didn't care for it or if he was simply realistic about his chances against his more powerful brothers. If indeed he even existed. Either way, his main interest was in ships and the sea. I didn't get very much further than that before the breakfast bell, but it seems there's a vociferous number of researchers who claim he actually landed on American shores around 1170, more than 400 years before Columbus. But there's no conclusive proof, no written records and, so far as we know, Madoc never came back to Wales to claim the credit."

"Well done Bradstone. Not bad for a quick internet search." Huw beamed at them both.

"I know you too well, Da. You're holding something back," Mandy chided, "so why don't you stop playing games and tell us what you've got up your sleeve." She paused for a moment. "And please, please tell me it has nothing to do with and will not involve, Druids!"

"Amen to that, Mandy." Stone added.

Huw pulled a paper out of his pocket and unfolded it. "I had a phone call just before coming up here with Mandy and then I got this follow-up email. It's from the BBC. They are interested in doing a documentary on Prince Madoc and want me to be the head researcher and presenter.

Mandy jumped up and hugged her father, "Brilliant!"

Stone rushed forward to add his own congratulations, grabbing Huw by the hand and shaking it vigorously. "That's great, Huw, it really is. Much deserved."

Huw, however, pulled back a bit. "Wait, wait. I haven't said yes yet."

"But Da, you're going to, yes?"

"What's the delay? If you need my help haggling over money and details for a TV documentary, no problem. I'm here," Stone added.

"No, wait you two. I haven't decided to do it. In fact, I probably won't."

He quelled the outbursts. "Look, it's very simple. I've had a really long think about this but it's just not the kind of thing that I would do well. I'm flattered of course. But the truth is, I don't think I'm up to it. Not my cup of tea, if you will."

He looked from one to the other. "My joy and expertise is in either one of two things: sifting through dusty, dank volumes of obscure written documents, or else on my hands and knees digging around in the dirt. I'm not so sure that doing the research, writing a script and then standing up in front of a camera would be either enjoyable or even satisfying." He held up his hand to forestall further protests.

"I do, however, think this is a splendid concept and I want to see it move forward.'

He stood up and began to pace around the room, his usual preferred stance when he was lecturing or explaining something. "I think that rather than Huw Griffiths moving this thing forward, it would be much better, much more professionally done and much more interesting if Myfanwy Griffiths and Bradstone Wallace did it."

They both objected, loudly, as he'd expected.

"Look you, it makes perfect sense. You are both young and have more stamina than I do. Myfanwy, you are a cracking good researcher, better even, I must admit, than I. You have more stick-to-it-ivness than I do. And you, Bradstone? Who better to take her research, turn it into a vibrant, compelling script and then present it on air, than an experienced scriptwriter and presenter like yourself? You have the Telly presenter look and authority. The two of you would make a splendid team."

They spent most of the morning arguing with Huw but slowly, reluctantly, they began to see the sense in his suggestion. Stone was more reluctant, remembering the early morning conversation and wondering if this was something Huw had somehow just conjured up.

"I'm sure the BBC would go for it. I broached the idea with them on the phone. This email indicates a very real interest in pursuing the project with both of you." He handed over the letter and let them both read it before glancing over at Stone meaningfully. "They are willing to pay a handsome fee to both of you. And, of course, cover all expenses and whatever travel might be involved. It has all the hallmarks of a top notch documentary from their perspective: good, interesting historical topic, top researchers and a handsome on air personality to carry it to completion."

Stone had the grace to blush at the last comment and Mandy giggled warmly. "Absolutely true, that last bit, Da."

The idea was solidified at the lunch table. Huw broached the subject and it was bandied about the table. Lord Greyfell was adamant. "You two just have to do it. Marvelous idea. Can't think of two more qualified people to do it. Brilliant. Well done, Huw."

"Wonderful. I think you would both do well. Mind you," Nees added quietly, "I do think you'd have done an excellent job Huw."

"Thank you, Denise, but while my heart is in it, my mind says no. Remember your injuries Huw, it keeps saying to me. Stick with the things you do best and let others do what you cannot."

With the blessing of Lord and Lady Greyfell the die was cast. Huw agreed to call his contacts at the BBC in the afternoon and set up a meeting as soon as possible between the producers and Stone and Mandy.

"Not here," Lord Greyfell advised. "The fewer that know about this place, the better. Set up something nearby. Down at Bowness-on-Windermere, perhaps. Small town, some nice hotels and restaurants and yet still out of the way. Plus there are tourists even at this time of year, so a few more strangers won't stick out like sore thumbs."

After lunch, he quietly pulled Huw aside. "While you're at it, I'm going to call Sir Giles at Crown Security. Have them do a check on these producer fellows. I'd hate to think this was all some Druid plot to get at the three of you."

Washington, D.C.

After the President left, the three men got down to business.

Tyler looked a bit embarrassed as he spoke. "Sorry I had to be so tough on you this morning Chad, but the people in the outer office needed to get the picture. They were informed of my resignation about ten minutes ago just before it was publicly announced and therefore after I fired you. This was the only way the President and I could think of to protect the agency itself. We had to cut loose anyone who was gunning for you, yet at the same time clear the decks for you to pursue this investigation free of any restraints."

Tyler paused a moment, then reiterated. "I mean it. You have a total free reign. Whatever you need in money or equipment, ask. I trust you both implicitly. But do not try to work your old contacts or work through existing agencies. Sorry fellas, but the price of having a free reign means you act alone and rely on just each other and myself. No one else. Not even the President."

Painstakingly they laid out protocols for contacting each other and Tyler. New identities and backgrounds would be created for both Chad and Wiz. Chad had to break his apartment lease in Alexandria and find a new location outside the capital area under a new identify. Wiz was to return to New Mexico immediately and arrange for someone to look after his property.

"Tell them you're going overseas for a vacation or whatever. Then get back up here and find a new place to live," Tyler said. "I want you on this full time with Chad." He held up his hands to forestall any protests "and yes you are on salary and yes, it's a raise. For both of you."

With the new identities came new credit cards and bank debit cards, but that would take a day or so. Tyler reached into his suit jacket and pulled out two envelopes. "There's five thousand dollars for each of you to cover initial expenses between now and the time you get the new ID's and cards. Until then, lie low and mope around. Remember, you've just been fired."

Wiz hesitated, then spoke up. "Chief, you want us to work under deep cover which is fine, but what about travel? We'll need a base of operations away from here and away from my place."

"That's what you've got unlimited expenses for. And new ID's"

"Yeah, and that's good as far as it goes."

"Meaning?"

Chad grinned then looked down at some papers to studiously examine them. He had an inkling where this conversation was going.

"Meaning," Wiz continued, "we must have ready and quick access to anywhere in the country. Scheduled airlines aren't always convenient or available. Charters require a lot of hassle and records which can be hacked into. Plus, we'll need to carry weapons which is a problem with airlines and charters, not to mention airport security. We're supposed to be invisible, remember!"

Before he could continue, Tyler blurted "No. No way. I am not authorizing a plane for you. No way!"

"But Chief, think about it rationally in the context of what you're asking the two of us—just the two of us—to do. We have to cover the whole country and who knows what leads we might have to follow and where and when. Plus, you said whatever equipment we needed!"

The argument went on for forty minutes. Chad jumped in occasionally but left most of the discussion to Wiz. Finally, Tyler began to waver.

"I still think the pair of you can do this without your own wings. But I'll ask the President."

Two hours later they were led by a security officer, via an elevator, to a side corridor on the tenth floor and instructed to go around the corner to the main bank of elevators and take one back to the ground floor. They emerged into a nondescript shiny black marble floored and walled lobby. The guard behind the desk merely nodded to them.

Out in the fresh air, the two men walked a while until they came to K Street. They turned in to a small coffee shop located in another of the office towers that crammed the street.

Sitting in a back corner and speaking softly, they began. It was critical they agreed, to determine who killed Murphy. "Find that out and we find out if the D's are still active and a case of in-fighting, or if it's a government agency taking things into their own hands."

"You think the President would call us in knowing a government agency was behind his murder?" Wiz wondered.

"He's a political animal. First and foremost, he'll protect himself. I doubt he knows anything, but he obviously trusts nobody. Not even us, I'll bet." Chad leaned back. "By the way, you seemed awfully smug back there and certainly weren't surprised by who we met."

"I was the Chief's first hire when he set up the agency. I know him. I know how he thinks probably even before he does. So, I knew this was all bluster. It was totally out of character so he was up to something, especially when he rigged up that special ride into the District. I just didn't know what."

As they worked their way through two more coffees they finalized a plan for the next few days. While Wiz sorted out his New Mexico place, Chad would relocate. They would meet in one week. At the same time, they would both prepare lists of equipment and services they needed. Leaving the coffee shop, Chad caught a cab to Alexandria while Wiz went to Reagan National to catch a flight home.

A quick discussion with his landlord plus two extra month's rent payment solved Chad\s first problem; he could leave immediately. All he needed now was a furnished condo he could move into immediately live in anonymity. By late afternoon he'd found an all-suite hotel in Woodbridge, south of the District, with easy on-off access in any direction on Interstate 95. It was, the manager assured him, an ideal spot for people who were in the area for short term business.

After he unpacked and settled in, he began writing down all he knew and remembered from his first encounters with the Druids right up to the time of Murphy's death. He considered calling Stone. He hadn't heard from him for some time. Which was worrying, but using his old cell phone was out. Until he was satisfied with security. He didn't even want to use the condo's land line. He was stumped. Until he got the new encrypted satellite cell phones he couldn't reach out to anyone. Not even his friends at Crown Security in London.

Steadily, through the evening he built up a dossier of memories and encounters. Some of the gaps could only be filled by Stone, Huw Griffiths or the British agency. But for now, it would have to do. He backed up his notes onto a flash drive and erased everything on his hard drive. At this point all he had was memories and conjecture with no way to confirm or disprove his notes.

No matter which way he turned, for now he was stymied.

Chapter Nine

Aberystwyth, Wales

"Enough of the niceties, Bethan. As I said, it's always good to see you, but why come all the way from San Francisco?"

Evans perched on the arm of the worn deep brown leather armchair, staring owlishly at Bethan Price. He had no choice, but to sit on the arm because the seat was covered by a mass of books, with odd bits of markers and paper sticking out of them. The room was a typical professor's study, small but comfortable. Crammed bookshelves covered two walls, a mismatched brown leather sofa was jammed against a third wall along with a file- and book-covered wooden desk. A decent sized window dominated the fourth, smaller wall. The window out onto the sea was one of the perks of being acting Chancellor of IMC as well as Dean of Celtic Studies. The rest of the flat was tiny but served until he could get away to Llanidloes.

Bethan waved away the offer of tea. She fixed Evans with a look that was aimed at intimidation. He waited, showing no reaction. Finally, she looked away. It was a semi-serious game they played, the few times they met; one trying to intimidate the other, each looking for a step above the other.

"I'm the new Raven Master in the States, Richard. I've know there's a new Dragon Master, and you were very guarded on the phone. Either you don't know or didn't want to discuss it. Whatever your reason, I need to know who it is. If you don't know, tell me who does and I'll talk to him. Or her."

"Bethan, my lovely, you know that I always enjoy talking to you. So, they made you Raven Master did they? And there's my dear friend Liam not days in his grave"

"Cut the crap, Richard. Liam was murdered, but it was after the Gorsedd offered it to me. There were disloyal followers trying to depose him even as others of us were trying to engineer his release from federal custody.

As Raven Master I want to know who these traitors are and I will summon the wrath of the gods upon their heads. I need to speak to the new Dragon Master. Who is it Richard? Who do I talk to? Is it you?"

Evans stood up and walked over to the window. "This is a marvelous view, Bethan. Today, the sea is relatively calm. But underneath, things are churning and when, in due course, the storms arrive, it will smash with full fury against the sea wall." He pointed down onto the street below even though he knew Bethan could not see the spot he was identifying. "You know, a couple of years ago we had a storm so savage, the waves washed up over Marine Terrace. It destroyed a number of kiosks and small buildings, not to mention washing away some of the wall itself. The sea can be very tranquil, then suddenly very harsh and destructive. Much, I would suggest, like us."

He turned his back on the window. "You say there's trouble in the movement over there. Why did you accept the position?"

"I don't need to answer to you Richard, unless you are Dragon Master. But out of friendship, I will tell you. Liam and I always had a special relationship. Days before the government moved him from New Mexico he was able to smuggle a message to me. He warned me others were trying to get him to depose him."

"Who? Did he say who?" Evans interrupted. She shook her head.

"He also said he was willing to step aside. But only if I would take his place."

She stood up, a grim look on her face as she stood nose to nose with him. "Now, for the last time, tell me who the new Dragon Master is or point me towards the one who knows. When I find out who killed Liam, my wrath will be nothing like that of your bloody seas. It will be a thousand times worse!"

She glared at him, holding his eyes in her gaze, this time refusing to look away.

He smiled and placed his right hand gently on her shoulder. "Bethan, Bethan. Allow the calmness of the goddess Bridget to infuse you and take away your anger and frustrations. I am indeed the new Dragon Master."

She stared at him for a few more seconds. "I knew it. Now will you help me root out the vipers in my nest?"

"Yes. And I need your help as well. We have traitors in our own camp here."

The tension in the room eased as they both sat. Rain hammered against the study window and dark rolling clouds swirled on the horizon. As the storm drummed incessantly against the window panes, the two briefed each other on events on both sides of the Atlantic.

Evans listened quietly, interrupting once or twice to clarify some of her comments and actions When she was done, he explained his strategy to lie low, prepare and strike only when ready.

"No more rushing into things and striking for the sake of striking," he told her. "Callaghan was driven more by personal revenge than he was by achieving the movement's goals. He paid the price for his stupidity."

Evans deliberately left unsaid some of the plans he'd set in motion. Trust was something Bethan would have to earn, he told himself, not realizing that she'd made the same decision about him and had also withheld information.

As they sat and discussed their various concerns and needs, the underlying problems of unifying a dis-unified group of egos and powerful people became rampantly clear to both of them.

Bethan nodded, pleased they were thinking along the same lines. Evans paced the room. "Part of the problem, I think, is that we have had no successes at all. We need to show those below us that while we have not forgotten our ultimate goal, but neither have we given up flexing our muscles."

"What do you have in mind?"

"Very simple. We need a very public demonstration that we are still a force to be reckoned with. I suggest one here in Britain and one in the United States. Further, in order to satisfy all our desires for blood revenge, we need to strike at those who have thwarted us in the past."

Evans had stopped pacing watching for her reaction. The strategic strikes he proposed would indeed reassure the brethren that they were not finished. And it would put the failing governments on notice as well.

He sat down next to her. An hour later they had the skeleton of a plan together. She would return to America to set her part of the plan in motion. He would develop action at home.

"Ours must be in Wales, or one of the smaller cities" he mused, "London, Manchester and the like, are sewn up tighter than a drum thanks not only to our own failures but to other terror threats as well."

Finally, she got up to leave. He ushered her to the door, knowing a hired driver waited on the Marine Terrace below the flat.

"The gods go with you Bethan. And give our cause success!"

Washington, D.C.

Davey Price was disappointed. Although he'd balked at the idea of doing what he called 'field work' instead of staying in his home office at Sausalito, he found he quite enjoyed the idea of following someone, watching from a distance, seeing where they went.

The disappointment was that the man he was following, General Wells, had so far been boring. He'd enjoyed the thrill of telling a jaded New York cabbie to "follow that car" but the excitement soon dissipated in the bumper to bumper crawl down Central Parkway, across Columbus Circle at the south end of the park and onto Broadway. It was a bigger disenchantment when the car turned off Broadway and stopped in front of a steakhouse. Wells exited and strode into the restaurant while Price's taxi continued past and dropped him off a block away. The experience was made worse when he realized it was lunch hour and, apart from the steakhouse, there were no other eateries available, not even a hot dog stand for him to grab lunch.

The other two days were similar. At the United Nations building Wells, in full uniform, was whisked through a side door. Price hung around the front of the building, near the door for most of the morning, trying to be inconspicuous in spite of his height.

Price hoped the return to Washington was more fruitful. While lurking around the lobby of Well's hotel he heard the concierge arrange for the General's car to be at the front by five o'clock to take the General to the airport for his trip back to Washington. Price checked his watch. If he rushed he could make the Amtrak express at Pennsylvania Station just a few blocks away. In just over three hours he'd be in the nation's capital and, with luck, waiting at Reagan National Airport when the General arrived back in town. His plan had the added benefit of security. Surveillance would be tighter at airports than train stations. If anyone was suspicious of him, they'd not expect someone as wealthy as him to take the train.

It hadn't worked out quite the way he planned and his frustration grew.

He'd made it to Reagan in plenty of time. In fact, he waited while three different airlines deposited their inbound New York passengers from LaGuardia and Newark. No Wells. It was only after the third flight he'd realized his mistake. As a military man, Wells would take a military flight, landing at Andrews Airbase in Maryland, not Reagan.

He pounded his fist into the armrest of the uncomfortable hard black plastic of the arrivals area chairs and swore out loud. Across from him, an elderly woman frowned at him disgustedly across her glasses then returned to her book.

Half an hour later, Price flopped down on a bed at the Ritz Carlton, desperately trying to think how he could pick up Well's trail once again. As he thought, he checked his emails and messages. Nothing from his mother since she'd told him she was heading for Britain. He'd left messages for her, complaining about his assignment, but had not heard back. He was irritated with her, the General and anyone and everyone else he could think of. This was just not his thing. Not knowing what else to do, he decided to head for the hotel's restaurant and have dinner and drinks.

He was just at the door when his phone buzzed.

"Mother, thank the gods. Where are you and why haven't you answered my messages." His sour face slowly softened and then morphed into a sly grin as he listened. "So, Uncle Malcolm is going to track him as well?"

"Yes. And I've told Malcolm to keep you fully in the loop. Particularly since you're now in DC itself."

They talked for a few more minutes. He complained yet again about his frustrations until she cut him short.

Price whistled when she told him that Williams was the new Dragon Master. "That old coot? He's a stuffy old professor locked away with his books and things. They'd have been better to choose someone like you, prepared to act and not hide away in a library."

Her stern retort silenced him.

Armed with her latest instructions, he relaxed. He placed a call for dinner from room service. Fifteen minutes later the knock on the door indicated its arrival. He swept the door open wide for the waiter to enter. Instead, two burly men burst in. Before Price could object, one raised his hand and sprayed a mist into Price's face.

The last thing he remembered was a giant black curtain rising at incredible speed from his toes until he knew nothing.

Silently the men bundled the comatose man into a wheeled laundry cart and headed for the service elevators.

Bowness-on-Windemere, England

The meeting had gone well. Stone, Huw and Mandy sat at a small table at the back of a quaint little pub just outside Bowness. Huw had moved quickly, setting up the meeting with the BBC for the following day. When morning arrived, it was a just short drive south of Greyfell Abbey down past Buttermere and through the picturesque villages of Grassmere, Ambleside and into Bowness itself.

The meeting was set for 11 am at the Old England Hotel overlooking Lake Windemere. Just as they drove into Bowness, Huw's mobile rang. After listening intently, he smiled. "Sir Giles has confirmed our BBC producers are genuine. I think we can proceed with our meeting."

After a hearty lunch and lively get-to-know you chat with the BBC crew, they began to hammer out details of the documentary. The BBC's executive producer of documentaries, Bob Mello took charge of the discussion. His assistant sat quietly beside them all, jotting notes and helping when he fished for files.

To begin with, Mello insisted that all of them—Huw included—call him Marsh. "Got hung with that nickname at school and wasn't able to shake it," he chuckled, "Schoolboy humor being what it was, I had no choice. So, I learned to embrace it and now I answer only to Marsh. Anyway, I'm certainly sweet enough".

Huw expressed his discomfort at not using the producer's given name but Marsh's ebullient nature swept aside the objections. "The only time I allow my proper name to be used is in the credits at the end of a program and on my gravestone," he boomed. "Other than that, it's Marsh or 'hey you'. Nothing else." Silently, Huw resolved to simply call him Mr. Mello, in future contacts.

Stone was surprised—and delighted—at the raging appetite he displayed as he tucked in to the rack of lamb in front of him. He was equally delighted to see Mandy break out of her shell and enjoy the meal as well. The ambience, meal, and cozy wood-burning fire as well as stunning views across the lake, all made for a special day. It was surprisingly crisp and clear. In the near distance they could see the snow-capped peak of the Old Man of Coniston. Stone was surprised to see that, even in winter, the cruise boats still plied their trade up and down the lake.

As lunch proceeded, Marsh outlined his concept for the production. "I'm delighted that you'll be fronting this piece," he told Stone. "I downloaded some of the shows you did on American television. I think you'll be perfect for this not just because of your professionalism as a broadcaster and writer," he enthused, "but also because it gives us a visual connection of the old world, Madoc, and you representing the new."

Marsh turned to Mandy. "I'm equally delighted you agreed to lead our team Mandy. You'll be our chief researcher, but I am assigning another staffer to help you."

Memories of the last time someone had helped her research came flooding back as she recalled the betrayal and her near death. He was taken aback by her vehement refusal.

Stone and Huw immediately came to her defence with Huw promising to act as her assistant, in preference to a BBC staffer. They did not explain her aversion, just supported her. After a brief but intense discussion, Marsh looked from one to the other then shrugged, "well, if it tickles your fancy to work it that way, that's fine by me."

Excitedly, he outlined his plans. "You'll have one of our finest producer/directors to work with, Stone. Maggie Railston is a cracking good creative type. You'll enjoy working with her but she'll push both of you for the very best you can produce. And we've got excellent and capable camera and sound people on the team."

As they deliberated it was clear that the budget was generous. "From initial research, Madoc apparently landed in or around the Mobile Bay area, right on the border between Alabama and Florida." His eyes twinkled. "That will mean shooting in and around that area, plus anywhere else in America that your research leads you."

Marsh was adamant about one thing. He, and he alone, would make the final decisions about the programmes. "I see this as two, maybe three, one-hour programs moving from location to location, digging out the relevant facts, circumstances, cultural nuances and historical setting. While I will value your input Stone and Mandy, I know what the audiences will want and what Auntie Beeb needs," he said, using the slang term for the BBC. "So, the final word will be mine. Agreed?" He smiled engagingly at them all.

Mandy looked at Stone and saw the big grin on his face as he nodded. She nodded as well.

Finally, they came down to the hard numbers in terms of payment for their services. Again, the producer offered generous compensation for both Mandy and Stone and added more to cover Huw's involvement. "You were the first on our list, Professor Griffiths, and I must say I was disappointed when you turned us down. So, I'm delighted you're going to be involved as well." He spun to face the other two. "Not that I think you two are second best," he protested. "In fact, I think the Professor's idea that we hire you was a dazzling stroke of genius and I'm really grateful to him."

Declaring himself pleased, Marsh and his assistant stood up and shook hands with the three. "Have a good think about the terms. I'll have a draft agreement emailed to you this evening. Make sure your lawyers look every-thing over, of course. We can meet in London, say in a week, to actually sign the contracts. Now, I'm going to hit the loo and we'll be on our way." With that, Marsh and his quiet assistant swept out of the restaurant.

Huw, Mandy and Stone sat down again and called for another round of tea. "Well, well," Huw huffed. "That man made me tired just listening to him!"

Stone merely looked across at him, a smile playing across his face. "The thing is, Huw, what have you dragged me into this time around?"

"No Druids, Stone. No Druids this time." Mandy's voice quivered slightly even though she smiled at him. "Just a nice project for us to work on. Nothing more. Nothing less."

As they headed back to the car, Stone popped into a small shop and purchased a set of earphones for his mobile. Now he could listen to his be-loved Handel and Bach in private. Once out of the shop he tested it but it was the only opportunity he had. The return to Greyfell was abuzz with ideas and strategizing and he had no time to call up music.

"National Library of Wales in Aberystwyth. That's where you should start," Huw declared. "It's Wales' national archives, so we dig there first. Hopefully you'll then get leads to other sources and information. I've got some good contacts at the Old College on the seafront. I'm sure they'll fix you up with some work space. You can get computers and whatever else you need with all the money you'll earn from this one." He smiled and leaned back contentedly in the back seat as Stone drove, Mandy beside him.

"I think this is going to be a fun project, don't you?"

Chapter Ten

Crown Security Offices, London

The office was unusually quiet. Sir Giles Broadbent stood in the doorway to his office, his perennial cup of tea in hand, sipping as he surveyed the small band of agents and support staff that helped the agency fulfill its mandate of seeking out and thwarting any and all threats against the Royal Family. In this terrorist-laden age it also meant his personnel and resources were strained so thin they were almost transparent, although he acknowledged silently, he did stretch the Bureau's mandate to its maximum. "We few, we happy few, we band of brothers," he quoted Shakespeare's Henry V as he murmured to himself.

His request to the Prime Minister about increased funding was still sitting on a desk somewhere in the morass of Whitehall's bureaucracy. The next step to jog it along was to drop a discreet word in the ear of the Queen's private secretary. It was a step he preferred not taking personally but, he admitted, it seemed things were stalled on the PM's side. Besides, he was getting quiet rumblings from his sources in Whitehall that other security agencies were annoyed and jealous; Crown Security had beaten them to the punch and twice foiled major terror attacks by the new home-grown Druids. The others had missed or ignored the signals Sir Giles had picked up on.

He had a renowned instinct for survival, and right now, the little hairs on the back of his head were standing upright and beginning to itch. While he was still standing, gazing over the main offices when Freddy Garret entered the main office, a brawny man with neatly combed rusty brown hair trailing a stride behind. One look at Freddy's face told Sir Giles it was serious. He turned back into his office, gesturing Freddy to come in and close the door behind him.

"Sir Giles, this is Detective Chief Inspector Adam Carswell from Scotland Yard. He has something he wishes to discuss with you."

Sir Giles signaled both men to sit and, as he shook hands, noticed the policeman had strong ice blue eyes that did not flinch or betray any nervousness. Rather, from the way he carried himself and held Sir Giles' own stare, he exuded confidence, strength and conviction.

"Thank you for seeing me, Sir Giles. Mr. Garret thought you would want to hear this."

He stopped as Sir Giles help up his hand. "First things first, DCI Carswell. Tea?"

Startled, the policeman looked at both then committed sacrilege as far as Sir Giles was concerned. "No thanks, but a coffee, black with sugar would go down nicely."

Freddy chuckled while a black cloud crossed Sir Giles' face and a look of consternation flashed in the policeman's eyes. "Around here, refusing a cup of tea is considered a hanging offense, DCI Carswell." He looked at Sir Giles and laughed. "I think we can let it go for this first-timer, don't you Sir Giles?"

"Hmmph." Sir Giles nodded briefly, but held up his own cup for a refill, which Freddy took care of, still laughing, reaching behind him onto a small shelf and finding the ever-present pot of tea. Sir Giles merely bobbed his head towards the visitor, indicating he should continue.

Carswell paused briefly, then plunged ahead. "Four days ago, the Essex constabulary in Southend-On-Sea found a body among some of the bathing huts on the seafront. At first, they put it down to a vagrant caught in the wrong place at the wrong time, but a mate of mine had second thoughts. I won't go into the details, but he convinced his guvnors to call us in. I was there yesterday and examined both the body and the crime scene."

Sir Giles templed his hands under his chin, "Why come to us, Mr. Carswell?"

The detective shifted in his seat and plunged ahead. "Nobody at the shop is aware I'm here. It's my day off. My guvnor would have her knickers in a knot if she knew. Probably demote me to sweeping out the nick if she ever finds out." He paused again, watching Sir Giles carefully.

"Continue. Why us? Job for the Metropolitan Police surely?" The Crown Security Bureau's head was famous for his clipped, non-sentence sentences. In his mind, extra words were superfluous. Cut to the chase, he always told his staff. Never mind the puffery.

"I saw something on the man's body that immediately seized my interest." Freddy interrupted quickly, pointing out that Carswell was one of the police officers who'd stormed the hotel room with Freddy last summer. Their timely assault resulted in the death of the Druid assassin Norris Quinn, rescued Mandy Griffiths and helped prevent heavier loss of life at a special church event in Hyde Park.

"The thing is, this body had a black dragon tattoo on his forearm, just like the bloke who fired the rocket at the Archbishops."

"You saw that slime Quinn? That miserable toe rag piece of filth?" Sir Giles boomed and jerked forward across his desk.

Carswell nodded. "I was one of the first through the door with your men. A number of my bullets hit him. I ran over immediately to check him and saw the tattoo on his arm. It was identical to the one I saw on the Southend body yesterday."

"Mention it to your guvnor?"

Carswell met Sir Giles' penetrating stare then shook his head. "No. We're not to pursue any lines of inquiry around anything to do with Druids. More especially we're to avoid all contact with your agency. Only top civil service people are to deal with you. None of the rest of us."

Carswell explained he was asked to help with the investigation because the local police did not recognize the body as "one from our patch", and assumed he was from London. When Carswell pointed out the tattoo, it got sloughed off by the local investigating officer. Many people today decorate their bodies with various exotic forms of art, he gratuitously informed Carswell. When he'd tried to take it further, he was warned off in no uncertain terms and told of the new regulations regarding the Druids.

For ten more minutes, Sir Giles and Freddy both pumped the detective for more information although there was a definite paucity of facts.

The room fell silent. Carswell stared straight at Sir Giles, unblinking. Sir Giles pursed his lips and templed his hands again. "Still haven't explained. Why us DCI Carswell? Ordered to stay away from us. Murder in Southend not our mandate. That's you and your colleagues."

"True, Sir Giles. But this is a different situation and off my patch. I know there's a Druid conspiracy. I know their goal is to disrupt society and I've seen their bloody handiwork even though I don't really know their true purpose." He paused and looked Sir Giles right in the eye. "But I do know they're malicious and must be stopped. For whatever reason, my hands and those of a lot of my colleagues are being tied down. I'm not for all show and bluster like the Americans, but I am patriotic. I love my country and I am damned sure that I will protect it. As I see it, Crown Security Bureau is the only agency in our arsenal that gives a damn about the Druids and is working to stop them. I thought you should know about this, so I came directly to you," he nodded at Freddy, "Particularly since I'd already made Mr. Garret's acquaintance."

"Well said, DCI Carswell. Wish there were more like you." Freddy Garret leaned forward and offered his hand. "Couldn't have said it better myself. Right guvnor?"

Sir Giles smiled and nodded. He stood up and shook Carswell's hand. "Delighted to meet you. Thank you for your confidence. Take your information and act on it. Keep your confidence too, by God. Need more coppers like you. Make my life a tad easier."

With Sir Giles' thanks and promises of following up, Freddy ushered Carswell out of the offices. When he returned he slipped immediately back into Sir Giles' office.

"Well, Freddy?"

"Don't know that it moves us along very much. Or anywhere in fact. But I thought you might like to know and meet Carswell. He's a good man."

"Indeed. More to it than that though."

Freddy tilted his head, waiting for the explanation he knew would come out of Sir Giles' fertile analytical brain.

"Convinced there's a link for us." He began to pace the office, from his desk to an occasional glance out his window then back again. All the time, his agile mind was rapidly examining Carswell's information. "Too coincidental. Man with dragon tattoo, not local, probably London. Murdered and dumped on that beach. Got to be a link. See what you can dig up quietly. Keep talking to Carswell. Inform me when they identify the body. Then see if you can get photo of his face. Circulate it among our sources. Might be the man who attacked Stone."

He stopped pacing. "Small piece. Still lots missing. But it might be a tiny piece that leads to a bigger picture. Get on it Freddy."

Woodbridge, Virginia

Chad had an uncomfortable feeling. He was sure he was being tailed; had been since he turned off the Capital Beltway and headed south on I-95 to his new apartment. He switched lanes, slowed down then sped up all in an effort to identify his pursuer. He saw nothing. But he couldn't shake the feeling. Rather than leave the interstate at his usual exit, he kept running south well above the speed limit to the next exit, staying in the middle lane until the last possible moment before suddenly pulling right and blasting up the exit.

Luck was with him when he reached the top of the exit. Although it was clearly marked 'right turn only' he spun his car into a tight, screeching left turn on what felt like two wheels, flying across the road and barely missing a westbound vehicle before straightening. A quick glance behind showed a large silver-grey van about to risk the same manoeuvre but slamming to a halt instead as heavy westbound traffic blocked it.

Without hesitating, Chad sped up. Less than a mile later he came to a set of traffic lights. Instead of running through, he jerked left into the parking lot of a small strip plaza and slid into the spot between two pickup truck and jumped out. He stood by one pickup's cab and watched as the van roared down the highway, hesitate at the lights, then speed through the intersection before the light change. A black Hummer trailing the van, screeched to a halt as the lights turned red. Chad ignored the Hummer and the other cars on the road, staring intently as the van disappeared into the distance. He then jumped back into his car and reversed out of the lot and headed back towards the interstate.

Breathing out for the first time in what seemed hours, he did not notice the Hummer cruise up quietly behind him. A sharp bang lurched him forward. A quick glance in the rear-view showed the Hummer dropping back slightly then race forward to slam him again. As Chad struggled to control his car, the Hummer lurched to the left and sped up again, then swinging back suddenly into the side of his car.

Around him, other vehicles were screeching to stops or frantically trying to get out of the way of the two madmen careening down the highway. Chad sped up just as the Hummer drew alongside and smashed into his door. The intensity of the collision jerked his head sideways and down just as bullets were fired into the car. Instinctively, he jammed on his brakes and wrenched the car to the right. The movement was too violent for the battered car. It began spinning clockwise, across the center lane and into the oncoming eastbound traffic. It spun and jerked as Chad tried to regain control. He fought the vehicle almost to a halt before it was hit by an eastbound pickup which smashed him into a deep ditch before flipping it onto its side.

Dimly he heard sirens in the background and sensed, rather than heard, shouting and hands pounding on the car door. Vaguely he felt wet streams running down his face. Blood, he thought idly, trying to determine how it got there. He fought against it, but slowly realized he was losing consciousness. He could fight no longer. His eyes closed.

Calvert County, Maryland

It was the sudden banging of a metal door that dragged Davey Price into consciousness. He struggled but his arms and legs were tightly bound to a hard, wooden chair. He tried to open his eyes then groggily realized his head was covered by a rough sack-like material. He shouted and screamed for whoever it was to release him. His voice echoed but no answer came. He stopped shouting and began struggling against the bonds that held him. He thrashed about so violently the chair tipped over and he slammed into the hard floor. He shouted again, this time in pain as much as fear. He lay whimpering, unable to right himself; unable to move.

A door slammed open. He heard a sharp guttural voice. "Get him up!"

He felt the chair lifted none too gently and slammed back onto the floor. "Who are you? What's going on?"

"Shut up! We ask the questions. All you do is answer."

He struggled against the wires that held him tied to the chair. "You won't get away with this."

"I said shut up!" A fist slammed against the side of his head. He almost fell over again, but an unseen hand kept the chair upright. As he tried to shake the blow off, Price heard footsteps going behind him, then suddenly felt the hood ripped off his head. It did no good. The room was pitch black. He vaguely saw a shadow off to his left and turned his head, struggling to focus his eyes even as his head pounded with what seemed like the worst hangover he'd ever suffered.

Slowly a vague figure began to form itself out of the dark and the fog of his confused mind, but he remained silent. He drew on his father's advice for tough negotiation situations—and if ever there was a tough negotiation about to happen, this was it, he thought—to remain calm and silent. Force them to make the opening gambit, he remembered the gruff advice. It gives you control.

The silence was magnified by the eeriness of his conditions. Not a shred of light penetrated the room. Even if his hands were free, he knew he would not see them in front of his face. Was the figure he saw real, or a figment of his imagination? Sweat dripped down his face and its salty trails dripped into his eyes. He blinked but it made his eyes worse. He heard a scraping sound behind him.

"Turn him around."

Hands grabbed the chair and began to turn it. As they did a blinding light suddenly flicked on, stunning him and depriving his senses yet again. Price blinked rapidly trying to get the sweat out of his eyes and at the same time block the harsh light. He said nothing. The voice spoke out from behind the light.

"Good. Mr. Price. Tell us what you know about Liam Murphy and his relationship with your mother."

Price remained silent. Another vicious blow caught the side of his face. He spit out blood and part of a tooth but said nothing. More blows followed, but still he refused to speak. Internally, he fought off the panic and fear and knew he could not keep it up; this was not like any negotiating situation his papa had ever taught him about. Finally, he broke. "I know nothing about Murphy other than he quit the presidential campaign a few weeks before the election."

"What is Bethan Price planning? Who's behind her becoming Raven Master?"

This time the blow was to his midsection. He coughed and groaned. The voice repeated the question. Each time it was asked, Price insisted he knew nothing. And each response was followed by more body and head blows. After the sixth time, a new element was introduced. This time a hard object slammed across his chest. In his pain-crazed state he felt his ribs cracking. He involuntarily spewed blood even as he heard his ribs crunching against each other.

The light suddenly went out. He heard footsteps moving away behind him; then a door open and close.

The pain and fear overwhelmed him. He fainted.

Chapter Eleven

Aberystwyth, Wales

Stone was enjoying his time in Aberystwyth, or Aber, as the locals called it. He rounded the corner, glancing at the bilingual Welsh/English street signs that fascinated him. He turned from Heol y Wig onto the narrow, dark, crowded Stryd y Brennin. Much more exotic, he decided, than pedantically turning from the English version, Pier Street onto King Street. Stone strolled down the narrow roadway, preferring it to the even narrower sidewalks on either side of the road. Although the sun was shining, the street was in dark shadow, overwhelmed by the massive stone walls of the Old College. He dodged around a parked delivery van and headed for the massive triangular red sandstone porch that covered the main entrance. Mondays were always the same on Aber's streets, as deliverymen stocked their various shop and pub clients.

He preferred the eccentric Old College to the modern facilities up at the Penglais campus in the northeast corner of the old university town. It was an eclectic, quirky collection of stairs and halls riddled with doors that led to lecture rooms, offices, study areas and who knows what all. He'd semi-mastered the intricacies and mind-boggling myriad of stairs of all shapes, sizes and construction from wood to metal to stone; from straight to circular. The quiet sanctity of the small office assigned to him and Mandy was a welcome retreat where they could get down to business.

The College's location, right on the waterfront, and status as the first university in Wales charmed him. He felt it put him into the mood, as he told Mandy, for a journey into the history of Wales.

He passed under the coat of arms carved into the stone above his head and went through the large wooden doors. With his mind drinking in the building's heritage yet again, he turned to his right, around the tall stone columns to climb the time-worn stone steps. With a sudden thump, he ploughed into a smaller man descending the stairs, arms loaded with books. Fortunately, the fellow had just stepped onto the ground floor. The books went flying while the man himself staggered across the hallway flailing his arms, banging into the wall across the corridor. A few steps further and he would have fallen through the open doors into the Seddon Room that was being set up for a recital.

"Are you bonkers, or just bloody careless!?" the man shouted as Stone, reeling from his own thump against the stone pillar, rushed to help him, apologizing as he did.

As Stone apologized again and others nearby rushed to help, the man drew himself up to his entire five-foot four height and blasted Stone yet again, cursing him for his carelessness. He accepted the wayward books from two passersby and brushed his wildly waving hair back into place. He patted it down. Stone noticed that while most of his hair was jet black, there was a significant white streak running from his left forehead down and disappearing behind his head.

Glaring at Stone, he waved off yet another apology. "From your accent, I take it you're American. That makes sense. You think you own the world and push your way around it without regard to the rest of humanity." Grabbing the last book from Stone's hand, he stormed around the pillar and down the hall.

"Don't mind him, Yank. That's Old Dai Badger. He's rude, grumpy and a thoroughly unlikeable pillock! Apart from that he's also a bloody boring lecturer." A young woman who'd helped pick up the books smiled at him.

Stone laughed. "Thanks. I wish you'd tell me how you really feel about him." As he started up the stairs he spun around and asked, "so why call him Dai Badger."

The woman grinned. "Dai is short for Dafydd or David, and Badger for the black and white hair, Mr. Yank. Check out a picture of a badger and you'll answer your own question. Same type of aggressive, nasty nature too." She disappeared into Seddon Hall.

After traipsing up the stone steps, following a short hall, taking some wooden stairs down a half level then passing through one door and up a circular steel staircase, through another door and down a small hall, he wound up outside his office door. The Old College, built as a hotel in the late 1800's and added to after becoming Wales's first college, and was truly an eclectic warren of floors, half-floors and staircases of all descriptions and construction seemingly designed to wear down even the most determined professor or student.

He opened the door and entered. Inside the cramped room, two large tables acting as desks were arranged L-shaped along one wall and around a corner. The rest of the room was largely bookshelves with some even perched precariously above one of the tables. Books and papers covered both desks and the one extra chair in the opposing corner. Just inside the door stood a small table that conveniently held an electric kettle, mugs and the necessary tea bags, biscuits, and accompaniments.

Mandy looked up as he switched the kettle on. The rule was, first to arrive in the morning, grabbed the table with the window view out onto Cardigan Bay; the second in made the tea. Stone's fruitless trip to the massive stone fortress-like National Library of Wales near the Penglais campus, meant he was last in and had lost again.

"Why do I always get the out-of-office early morning assignments?" he groused playfully, waiting for the kettle to boil.

"Just lucky I guess. Find anything interesting?" Mandy smiled up at him, large horn-rimmed glasses perched on the end of her nose and a book, inevitably, in hand. Perceiving the sour look, she added "thought not."

Mandy yawned and stretched. "We've probably hit the barrier that has stalled all the other investigations around Madoc. Lots of ifs, ands and maybes with a dollop of fiction mixed with misty wisps of legend and a modicum of fact. In short, I can't see us getting much more here at Aber. Maybe if we follow up on the plan to research in the United States we'll find some corroboration."

"Mandy, you're treating this like a research project that will fail if we don't conclusively prove Madoc was real and went to America in 1170. Remember, we're doing a documentary. The thrill of documentaries lies in the hunt, not necessarily their conclusions. If we find proof, terrific. If we don't, we present what we have found along our journey and let viewers make up their own minds. In the meantime, we'll have created a strong, interesting, thoughtful investigative television program. Either way it's an incredible story and the show is a success."

"We've got to get some breakthrough soon. We're supposed to report in to the BBC soon and update our progress. Or lack thereof!" Mandy was still not convinced.

Stone knew the perfectionist historian in her recoiled at his refusal to see their efforts as a fully academic exercise. The gloominess in her voice conveyed her frustration. It was the only wrinkle in their relationship so far. They were still at a very surface but pleasant level that he could not break through. Patience, he told himself. Patience.

As was their habit, the first job of the week was to review what they knew and what the next steps would be.

Slowly Stone ticked off their confirmed research to date. Madoc may or may not have been a son of the King of Gwynedd, Owain. The King was certainly real enough. His battles with King Henry II of England culminated in Henry's daughter Emma Plantagenet marrying Owain's son Prince Dafydd. Records showed Owain had at least nineteen children, but only fourteen were named specifically in *Chronicles of Wales*, a medieval history.

Unfortunately, Madoc was not one of them. "Not a major issue," Mandy asserted. Particularly given the fact that Madoc had allegedly taken himself out of the running as heir and disappeared into the western seas. "No need to acknowledge him historically. He'd only be recognized if he'd returned with stories of a new land," Huw observed.

Mandy discovered documents in the archives that showed Madoc was probably influenced by the sixth century poet Taliesin who spoke of a "magic country beyond the looking glass of the sea." As a man of Wales, familiar with the sea and fishermen, he would also know of the currents that swept boats and drifting materials west across the horizon and out of sight. The Taliesin story gave credence too, but didn't prove, the story of Madoc's voyage.

More research showed that people in both Britain and America, during the years of colonization and the early years of the United States, believed a tribe of Welsh-speaking Indians lived in the middle of the country. They concluded that Madoc and his descendants intermarried with the indigenous people and that they, in turn, learned from Madoc and his people. Great Indian towns and fortresses excavated over the past fifty years or so showed a degree of sophistication and European design that predated Columbus. More circumstantial evidence for the Madoc believers, but disputed by some historians and linguists.

Nevertheless, as Stone pointed out to the fastidious historians in Mandy and Huw, "it makes for a sizzling story, filled with mystery and intrigue. Perfect for a great documentary."

The trail also led them to Sir Thomas Herbert, an early Elizabethan historian and traveller, who wrote that Madoc and a fleet of ships left Lundy Island in the Bristol Channel, followed the prevailing currents and winds, landing weeks later in what is now known as Mobile Bay. That story was endorsed by various legitimate groups in the UK and US, with the Daughters of the American Revolution erecting a massive metal memorial plaque in 1953 at Fort Morgan in Mobile Bay.

Idly, Stone fingered a copy of the plaque's text: *In memory of Prince Madoc. A Welsh explorer who landed on the shores of Mobile Bay in 1170 and left behind, with the Indians, the Welsh language.*

"Obviously the DAR believed the story." Stone held the paper up. "Even though the plaque was later removed and placed in storage. Now there's talk of returning the plaque to the Fort."

He played with the paper some more, struggling with how he would raise a topic that had come up for discussion with the deputy director of the Library.

"By the way, I got a suggestion from one of the librarians at the National Library. It seems they've got an eager and very thorough young researcher on board. They suggested he might be one we bring onto our team, if only on a part time basis."

Mandy balked as he figured she might. He watched her intently. She sighed. "Are you suggesting I'm not working hard enough or finding out enough to make your script plausible?"

The prickly defensiveness surprised him. He shook his head vehemently. "Come on, Mandy. You're the finest researcher I know and I'm amazed at what you've already uncovered. The suggestion was merely that this person knows the archives better than either of us and could do some of the basic legwork up there. Nothing more."

She sighed. "Are you sure it would be wise? Especially…especially after the last time?"

Silence smothered the room. Slowly Stone explained his concern that she was working much too hard and spending too many long hours wrapped up in books and papers, particularly considering that she was still, technically, in rehab. Finally, arms spread before him helplessly, he spoke softly. "Many nights I've taken you to your flat and you've looked as white as a ghost. I'm worried about you Mandy, I really am. You're pushing yourself too hard, too fast. This is, after all, nothing more than a television documentary."

He saw the determination ebb out of her body slowly, deflating her physically. He could sense tears in her eyes.

"Look. Why don't we just call it a day and go down to that little pub on the seafront. Have some nice pub grub and then take a walk along by the sea. Maybe the weather will hold for a bit."

She pulled together a grateful smile and nodded assent, grabbing her jacket and purse and leaving her book behind. As they walked along the seafront, past the pastel painted Victorian townhouses now run as seaside hotels, they talked about anything other than the project.

They strolled casually along, enjoying the opportunity to be in the fresh air. A mini bus marked for the university, stopped across from them and waited for a taxi to discharge its passengers. Stone caught the eye of the bus driver and waved, receiving a brief unsmiling nod of the head in return.

"Who's that?"

"Oh, that's Mr. Meldrew. He drives the shuttle bus for students and faculty needing transportation between the Old College and the campus up at Penglais. Bit of a miserable man. Staunch Welsh nationalist who hates the English with a passion—always threatening death and destruction to them—and he's suspicious of me because I'm not Welsh, but not one of the marauding, destroying English either."

By now, clouds were beginning to blot out the sun. A brisk return to the Old College was in order. As they walked, Mandy herself brought up the subject of an assistant. "Who is this person the National Library is suggesting?"

Stone shrugged. "A guy named Nathan Griffiths. I was thinking about talking to him later this week. But I promise you this. Before I talk to him, I will have Crown Security vet him. If they give an all clear and I'm satisfied with what I hear from him, then I'll bring him down here to meet you."

Mandy nodded. "We could ask Da for his input as well. Don't forget, he's promised to do some of the research work as well. And, look you, we could even ask Lord Greyfell to do some background investigation on this Griffiths fellow."

"Well, he can't be too bad a guy. Look at what a great last name he has!" Stone smiled.

Mandy raised an eyebrow. "You do realize that probably more than half the population of Wales has a last name of either Griffiths, Thomas, Evans or Jones?" she teased.

They worked their way along the curve that was the town's north beach. Rain was beginning to spit down as Stone pulled Mandy across the road and into a cozy looking restaurant that had what looked like a roaring fire going in their prominent fireplace.

Orders given, Mandy sipped her tea and looked intently at Stone. "Do you really think I'm pushing myself too hard?"

"You're still recovering from major injuries and trauma so yes, you need to pace yourself. I don't think you're pushing yourself too hard yet. It's just that I'm worried that working and stressing over this project will eventually be too much for you. I'm concerned more for the future than I am for today."

She nodded silently and sipped again. "I'm trying to blot out the horror. Da told me that as well; trying to swamp it with bags and bags of reading and research. He said I'm blocking out everything, including people, in an effort to erase the memories. But I can't help it. It haunts me still."

"I know. I understand. It's hard for me to trust anyone else too. I lived and died by my work ethic. If I didn't write it, research it, or edit it, it was never good enough. I couldn't trust even the most well-meaning editor to handle my work. I alienated myself from some good people. My only real friend—other than you and Huw—was Chad and I've lost contact with him too. His phones are disconnected and his email has been closed. So, while my situation is somewhat different, the result is the same. We both have to relax, enjoy the good things in life and learn to trust people again."

Mandy smiled thinly. "You are a good man, Bradstone Wallace. I don't deserve to have you in my life."

"What utter rot," he growled, as the waitress hovered with their meals. "You deserve a whole lot better."

As they ate, Mandy relaxed and enjoyed her scampi while Stone tucked into a prime rib. Both washed down the meal with a glass of wine. In the quiet of the meal's aftermath she suddenly blurted, "Take me to the pictures tonight. A real break from research."

"Take you to the what?" a puzzled Stone asked.

"The pictures. Films. Movies."

"Ah yes, well great! Let's find out what's playing and do it."

He paid the bill and as he was putting his wallet away, he put his hand out and clasped hers. "I will promise you this. There are no Druids on the horizon, certainly not regarding Madoc. Nevertheless, we'll get the necessary background checks on everyone we're dealing with here including this Nathan Griffiths."

They walked down the street, chatting happily. As they walked along the side of the Old College approaching the main entrance, one of the college porters came running up, calling his name. Stone stopped as the man handed him a sheet of paper. He read it, blanched and crumpled it into a ball.

"What is it Stone?" Mandy was terrified, watching Stone's reaction. "Tell me what it is. What's in the note?"

Tears rolled down his cheeks as he looked into her face then grasped her in a tight embrace. "It's Chad. Huw just phoned the College. Sir Giles got word this morning that Chad was killed in a car accident the day before yesterday."

Sausalito, California

Bethan tried to remain calm as she spoke on the phone, but it was difficult. Her voice was close to cracking. "Malcolm, none of my people have been able to trace David. He disappeared a week ago in Washington. He checked into a hotel but never checked out. She listened to the response. "Yes, I've tried that. I even called our movement's security people and asked them to investigate. Nothing yet. That's why I'm turning to you."

She poured out her doubts and worries. Never before had she hit such a blank wall. Always there'd been a way out; she was always in command of every situation. Now, she was in the middle of a dark fog of fear and uncertainty. Malcolm's cool, calm voice settled her down. His promise, to put his resources and personnel into the search for Davey, was enough for her. She'd leave the details to him.

Nevertheless, it was time for the Raven Master to act. Her call to General Wells reinforced her earlier demands for his assistance. "If it was the government, I want to know who and where he is being held. If it was not, I want all your contacts working on the situation. This is a matter of highest importance. He was on a mission for the movement."

Wells weighed his next words carefully. "Have you considered the possibility that you son is in the hands of dissident members of our movement who oppose you as Raven Master?"

"Yes," she spat coldly. "And if that's the case I want them found and totally eliminated. No mercy." She paused. "And if you are the creature behind this, I will destroy you too. Make no mistake about that, Serpent Master."

"Understood," the equally cold and calm voice responded.

There was little more to say. They agreed to talk regularly, with Wells urging her to remain in California rather than head to Washington. "Your presence here would only cloud the issue. This is a security matter and you must trust me to handle it, as I now trust you to lead us to our ultimate goal."

There was nothing more she could do. Normally, she relied on Davey to do a lot of the drudge work. He did not have the intelligence to think strategically and long range, she'd acknowledged that fact long ago. But Davey was loyal and could be relied upon to carry out her wishes. In his absence, she needed someone totally reliable but unknown within the American Druid community.

The answer lay in Wales. A quick call to Evans elicited his support and one of his key aides who'd fly immediately to San Francisco and take over as her lieutenant until Davey was found. "You'll find that Ioan is highly intelligent and totally dedicated to the cause. He'll be a good intermediary between us as well."

With the promise the man would arrive in the next day or so, Bethan Price left the house and went to a quiet and secluded part of the property to prepare. In many ways she preferred her larger estate on the shores of Lake Tahoe, but the massive property there did not have an oak grove. This small acreage did. At midnight she donned her robes and headed back to the oaks. The stars were prominent, she saw, and the new moon barely visible. Perfect conditions for the rituals she was about to engage in.

In the heart of the grove she began to chant, dropping into a trance as she did so. The entire ritual took more than two hours. When she finished, she returned to the house, convinced the gods had given her direction.

A vision floated in her mind. It was a monument. She'd found the target for her planned day of destruction.

Chapter Twelve

Calvert County, Maryland

Pain wracked his body. His mind was nearly shattered. Incessant questions followed by physical pain, from beatings to electric shocks. Was it a day or a week he'd been there in this dark hell hole of a room? Why didn't the gods answer? He'd called on them often enough. He'd threatened his tormentors with the fury of the gods.

"Bethan Price ordered Murphy killed didn't she." The same question over and over. The same answer over and over. "No."

Even when food or drink was brought to him, the room was in stygian blackness relieved only by the blindingly bright light that accompanied each sparse meal and each time of questioning. His chair faced the dark walls. When he had to relieve himself, he was dragged in the blackness to a small washroom, also kept in total darkness. The only thing he knew for certain was that his captors entered and left the room by a door behind him. A door he was never allowed to see. Despite his confused mental state, he realized he was in some underground bunker that daylight could not penetrate. Otherwise he'd have seen glimmers of daylight.

He screamed. He cried. His mind was broken, but there was no relief. During the torture sessions, his arms and legs were unbound. Sometimes he was forced to stand only to be whipped or shocked into collapse. The last session had been particularly intense. The pain of the electric shocks even more abrupt and of higher intensity. His groggy mind realized his captors were losing patience. He had given them nothing because he had nothing to give. They just didn't seem to understand that. Like too many people, he realized, they wanted to hear what they wanted to hear. Truth did not really play a part. Now, even death would be preferable.

They strapped him to the chair again. The light went out and his captors began to move out of the room. Their victim was such a destroyed, whimpering shell they forgot to keep their voices low as they left. And they were slow closing the door.

He briefly heard one of his abductors speak. He couldn't comprehend what he was saying, but the strong nasal voice pulled at a string in his distant memory. He grappled with the memory, trying to identify the voice. He could hear the voices dying away and the door closing when he suddenly blurted out loud "Armitage!"

The voices went silent. He heard the footsteps as more than one of them returned. The light flashed on and was aimed down, spotlighting the broken, crying man curled up and rocking in pain on the floor.

"What did you say?" a guttural voice penetrated his fogged mind.

"Armitage," he panted, "I heard Armitage speak just now. He is behind this. Let me talk to him."

A well aimed kick slammed into his head. His world went blank.

Dex Armitage led the two other men out of Price's cell, and up the stairs into the main living area of the small riverside house. Rage and frustration flushed his already reddened face as he whirled around and stormed at his subordinates.

Armitage had played a delicate game. He needed to get a confession that Bethan Price was behind Murphy's assassination. Her son, he considered, was her weak link. Arrogant, wealthy, spoiled, hanging onto his mother's apron strings but lacking in guts and strength. He didn't seem too bright either. Carefully screened background checks showed that Price had never progressed beyond junior college, and then only in an obscure major. He was more playboy than warrior and therefore useable and disposable. Break him, get his confession recorded and he could destroy the woman.

For Armitage, the selection of Bethan Price as Raven Master was a shock. He was convinced his own choice, a malleable former Congressman, would be the one. The gods, he was sure, had decreed it. Suddenly, out of left field, the Gorsedd selected her. A total nobody whose only attribute was money. No ties to the world of government or indeed power of any kind, like the Congressman or Wells. Or even himself.

He snorted at their argument that she was untainted and unknown by the federal powers. His quick investigation turned up nothing on her though her husband and partner were suspected of a myriad of unsavory activities, none of which could be proved.

Rubbing salt in the wound, the Gorsedd ordered him to convey their message to Price. The insufferable rudeness and treatment he received at her house only cemented his hatred. He was sure he could wring a confession from the son and get the ammunition he needed to destroy her. Now he'd have to find another way.

As his men watched him, he raged around the house slamming his fist on tables and counters and throwing whatever came to hand against the wall. They were used to his furies, although this was more powerful than his normal tantrums.

Armitage finally calmed down. He wiped his sweating face and forehead with a handkerchief. Staring intently at his men, he snapped "He knows who I am. Eliminate him. Make sure it can't be traced back to me."

Without another word, he stormed out of the building.

Whitehall, London

To say the atmosphere in the room was frigid would be an understatement, Sir Giles thought idly as he listened to the new Minister of Policing rant about "unfettered and unauthorized investigations".

Furious, the Minister threw unopened files on his desk. Gregory Belmont was in fine fettle, Sir Giles conceded, although he had not yet given a reason for his verbal assault.

Showing his disdain, Belmont had not even shown the minor courtesy of donning his suit jacket. Instead he shouted invective in a crumpled long-sleeved blue shirt and loosened tie. It was Belmont's juvenile way of saying that Sir Giles was not worth even tidying up for.

As Belmont spewed his invective, it slowly became clear the attack on Sir Giles was in fact an attack on the existence of his bureau. He tossed a file, clearly marked Crown Security, across the desk at Sir Giles.

"In the weeks I've been in this office, I've had your bureau's work carefully reviewed. You can see for yourself how egregious your actions have been. You and your wee people have ignored the police forces, MI5 and MI6 and refused to yield to their expertise in matters of national security. Indeed, I would say you have interfered with all their efforts, withholding information and generally trying to grab the glory for yourselves while others were doing the dirty work."

The diatribe continued as Belmont worked himself into a higher rage, ignited by Sir Giles' refusal to get drawn into the battle. Instead, Sir Giles merely looked through the dossier, perturbed by the one-sidedness and inaccuracies but refusing to show any reaction to the blustering Minister. Finally, Belmont barked that he was shutting the Bureau down, removing all funding and ordering the dispersal of all Bureau personnel and assets.

When he finished, Belmont glared at Sir Giles looking for shock or anger, but seeing only a calm, unruffled Sir Giles staring right back at him, eyes unwavering as he stared. At least, Sir Giles thought to himself, the enemy has been unmasked. Now he knew where the orders to Carswell and others came from. It would make his Bureau's activities more difficult, but would not stop them.

"Well?" Belmont finally demanded. "Do you get it, or are you too stupid or arrogant to realize, you're finished! You and your merry band of renegades are history. I warn you, you will be personally investigated. I will see that you are prosecuted to the utmost for the damage you have done to our national security."

Sir Giles pursed his lips and tented his fingers beneath his chin. Calmly, he gazed back at Belmont. He allowed a number of long seconds to pass before blandly responding. The only sound was the loud ticking of the old-fashioned clock sitting on Belmont's credenza.

"Very interesting, but with respect Minister, the continuation and funding of the Crown Security Bureau is not within your mandate. You may not like our existence. You may indeed despise it. But we are an independent unit, part of the Royal Household. We exist at the pleasure of Her Majesty. Our funding is within the Household's greater budget and is only reviewed by the Prime Minister's Office, and therefore not subject to political wrangling. So, Minister, if you want to shut us down you will have to take up that issue personally with Her Majesty." He paused. "Frankly, I don't think she'll agree with you." Sir Giles could be quite eloquent, dropping the half-sentences and chopped utterances, when needed.

"Furthermore, Minister, I would welcome an investigation on me personally because, I assure you, you will find nothing. I, on the other hand, will be forced to expose the incompetence of tower-building politicians and bureaucrats who've handcuffed the very fine and competent investigative staff below them in the police forces and security establishment."

Apoplectic, Belmont swore.

Undeterred, Sir Giles continued.

"Minister, you really should have been briefed on the Bureau's structure and operations before requesting my presence here. When your staff prepared this dossier," Sir Giles disdainfully tossed it back on Belmont's desk, "they should have explained this agency was set up by Queen Victoria herself. Nothing has changed. Not under the reigns of King Edward VII or King Georges V and VI, or indeed right up to our present gracious monarch. Lots of politicians and enemies have tried to eliminate us and failed over the decades.

"I assure you Minister, Her Majesty is pleased with our work so far and given no indication that she wishes to 'shut us down', as you so eloquently put it. Until that time, Minister, I am pleased to say that we will continue to do our job, investigating any and all threats against the Crown. No matter where our investigations take us. And no matter whose knickers get in a knot over it."

He calmly stood, and brushed his elegant grey Saville Row suit as if to rid himself of dirt and filth. "So, Minister, if you are done…" and headed towards the door. As he did, Belmont's curses and shouts followed him. As he walked towards the door and out of the massive office he heard Belmont shouting "…and destroy you, by all the gods…" A tight smile crossed Sir Giles' lips. "Ah," he breathed.

At the door he turned and faced Belmont. "Minister, I wonder if you would indulge a whim." As Belmont sputtered into a quizzical silence, Sir Giles pointed at his right arm. "Would you unbutton your shirt sleeve and raise it for me."

A fresh round of screaming and swearing followed him out the door. "I thought not," Sir Giles chuckled, as he passed the horrified Fiona. He nodded in her direction. "Good day, Miss Moffat. Your Minister has quite the temper." and jauntily walked out of the offices.

On his return, he quickly signaled Freddy to join him. Quickly he brought Freddy up to speed on the fractious meeting.

"He's a bloody Druid, Freddy. Right here in Westminster! Cancer in the heart of the nation!"

As Sir Giles let out his pent-up anger and disgust, he calmed down quickly, his fertile mind already planning strategy to deal with this new threat. While not a fatal risk to Crown Security, certainly he knew the Minister could make things decidedly unpleasant and possibly clip their wings a bit.

"Maddox. Where is he?"

"You sent him on a well-deserved holiday. I think he's hiking somewhere in the Highlands."

"Get him back here. Today. Top priority. Want him looking into Belmont." He fired more orders at Freddy, then suddenly returned his attention to Maddox. "Maddox to Glasgow instead. Belmont is Scottish. Glasgow boy. Start there. Link him to Druids."

Less than an hour later, Freddy had indeed found Colin Maddox and cut short his holiday, delivering Sir Giles' orders. Assured by Maddox that he was "getting bored walking around all the heather anyway", he turned to his next call. In short order he briefed Lord Greyfell and set him on the same quest. "Whatever you can find out about Belmont and any ties to Druidry, Eddie. We would be most grateful."

Next, he called DCI Carswell to find out if the Southend body had been identified and asked the policeman to meet with him as soon as he was off duty.

Inside his office, Sir Giles was also on the phone. "Prime Minister? I wonder if you would be so kind as to spare me some moments of your time. Today, if possible, please." He listened carefully and nodded. "Tonight, at six it is then. At Number Ten. Thank you, Prime Minister."

Next, he dialed the Queen's Private Secretary. Fortunately, Col. Montague Frawley was also a very good old friend from Army days, having both graduated from the military college at Sandhurst all too many years ago. A quick chat around old reminisces swiftly led to agreement on drinks later in the evening at The Army and Navy Club on Pall Mall.

With Hurricane Belmont now blowing hard, it was time to put the protections in place, Sir Giles realized. Especially now, since it seemed Belmont was also a Druid.

Patuxent River, Maryland

Early morning was the best time to be fishing. It was peaceful, devoid of the noise of motorboats and jet skis that raced up and down the river. The sun, rising in the east, cast a warm, soft light over the fisherman's shoulder and onto the river. In the near distance he could see the power plant and knew that the warmer waters attracted the bigger fish. He'd been there barely thirty minutes when he felt the tug of a fish on his hook.

He played the line, pulled, and felt resistance. But it didn't feel or fight like a fish. He reeled the line again, feeling it tug against him and yet, he sensed movement. Whatever it was, it was heavy but drifting in the river rather than stuck in the muddy bottom. Fifteen minutes later he caught his first glimpse of his catch. And blanched. A ghostly white face bobbed in the water in front of him. He dropped the rod in fright and watched as the face dipped back under the surface and began to float away. The current this morning was strong. The tidal flow up river was ebbing back towards Chesapeake Bay again as the tide raced out.

Frantically, he swallowed the bile in his mouth and grabbed at the rod as it almost slipped into the water. He tugged and pulled until finally, some ten hard minutes later, he was able to step off the bank and into the river. As the water lapped against his knees and thighs, he shivered as he reached under the body's armpit and dragged it ashore.

He vomited violently and dialed 911.

Aberystwyth, Wales

Try as he might, Stone could not erase the sharp memories of Chad. His easy-going nature that concealed an analytical mind; his flippant attitude that helped him handle whatever life threw his way. He also remembered the solid bulldog methodology he used once he had a job in his sights.

Mandy tried to console him as she too processed her own grief. Chad had saved Huw's life and been instrumental in their battle against the Druids. She would forever be grateful to him and would miss him and his free and easy approach to life. He'd been one of the few men in her life—Stone included—who'd refused to take life seriously, no matter how dire the circumstances. His sense of humor and lighthearted manner had been a complement to Stone's more serious and crusading nature.

A series of quick phone calls to Huw and Crown Security revealed very little new information. Chad was fired from his job at SID and disappeared several weeks earlier. There were even hints, Huw hesitated to tell Stone, that the accident might have been suicide; the act of a despondent mind.

Angrily, Stone rejected that thesis. Chad would never have done that. He was a fighter and would never succumb to self-pity and suicide. At the same time, there was no evidence or hints that the accident was anything but that. An accident. A capricious event that took the life of a dear friend, but apparently held no sinister aspects.

The last few nights had been agony. With the help of Sir Giles, he obtained the phone number for SID only to be shocked when told that along with Chad, Calvin Tyler had also been fired in disgrace. No, the officious voice had told him, they did not have contact information for the former chief. Sir Giles had also tried. Only to meet the same blank wall.

As he heard the story of Murphy's murder, Stone refused to believe that Chad and Tyler were fired for incompetence in the incarceration and handling of the ex-presidential candidate.

"It was a setup. They took the fall for someone else," he told Mandy. "Perhaps I can look into that aspect and at least restore his good name."

There wasn't even an opportunity to attend Chad's funeral. A brief cremation service was held in accordance with the deceased's wishes, he was told.

Stone toyed with the idea of returning Stateside. That was part of the nightly struggle to come to grips with everything. Last night he'd even tried a halting prayer to a God he'd too often ignored. His wordless thought-prayer drifted and stumbled all over the map. All he knew was, he needed help to get his mind back on track. He knew Mandy was anxious that he might pack everything in and return home. She was leaning on him again and was still vulnerable. Could he help Chad by returning? How would he finance any investigation into Chad's firing? His only source of income right now was the BBC documentary. He'd burned or severely damaged media bridges back home, so it would be tough breaking in again. All this came tumbling out in halting phrases murmured silently to God, reminding him that Huw and Mandy were believers even if he, Stone, was not sure.

The grief still clung, but somehow that morning, as he'd walked into the College and up the stairs, his mind felt strangely lighter. A clarity infused his mind. He could not leave Mandy and he couldn't help Chad right now, anyway. Nor would Chad approve of Stone's walking out on a job or contract.

He walked into the office and smiled at Mandy before plopping his laptop satchel onto the desk and sitting down. Before he could move a cup of tea was pushed in front of him.

"*Bore Da*, Mr. Wallace. Drink this." Stone looked up. "I'm really very sorry about your friend, Mr. Wallace."

A young man, stocky and with penetrating eyes, wearing grey slacks and dark blue sweater over a lighter blue shirt, handed over a small bottle of milk. Nathan Griffiths, their newly-hired assistant was not his usual bubbly, friendly self. Where there was typically a fun spark in his eyes and a somewhat cheeky nature, now he looked pensive and worried.

"I've been up at the archives and haven't had a chance to speak to you before this." He paused momentarily before asking warily, "Tell me, Mr. Wallace. Are you going to shut down the project now?"

Mandy leaned forward, interested in Stone's response.

Stone poured the milk into his cup and sipped gratefully. "No," he declared firmly. "We're not giving up on the Madoc project. Chad wouldn't have wanted that and anyway, there's still a lot of work to be done." He looked over at Mandy. "I told you that this would be a good way to take your mind off things past." He was careful around Nathan, unsure of how much, if anything, he knew of Stone and Mandy's story.

"I've got to take my own advice. Working on this will take my mind off things. When we get back to the States to follow the American side of this story, I'll pay my respects. But until then…" His voice dropped off and left the rest unsaid.

Mandy leaned back in her chair and nodded approval. Her smile and sense of relief though, were palpable. Stone turned to Nathan. "And I've told you before, call me Stone. Nothing else. Okay?"

Nathan grinned. The spark flashed back instantaneously. "*Diolch!* I am so relieved to hear that…Stone." He jumped up and began to put his jacket on. "Well then, I think I might have something you both would be interested.in. It may put a whole new light on Prince Madoc's journey."

Chapter Thirteen

Lake Tahoe, California

The flight to Lake Tahoe on her jet, was short and silent. As was the drive from the Lake Tahoe airport up state route 89 to the house. She saw, but did not see, the picturesque turquoise lake unfolding before her as her limousine climbed out of the town and up the rocky treed shore. She saw but did not see the exquisite clarity across the lake to the Nevada shores. Nor did she see or even acknowledge the many twists and turns as the car made its way past Emerald Bay and into the private drive of her retreat.

She was alone. Deliberately. Ioan Parry, the Dragon Master's assistant and liaison from Wales, remained in Sausalito, ordered take care of everything. Until Davey was returned to her, the orders were specific. Only General Wells and Malcolm Coughlin were allowed phone or personal access. Nobody else.

She got out of the car numbly and entered the house. She walked numbly through and into the living room saying not a word. The driver took her bags into her living room, then quietly said goodbye, closed the door and drove off. Bethan neither saw him nor heard him.

She could not believe Davey was dead. Worse, that he was murdered. A phone call from the Maryland State Police broke the news that his body was pulled from the Patuxent River Wednesday morning. It was followed almost immediately by one from Dex Armitage expressing shock and condolences. He promised her that he would take a close interest in the Maryland investigation.

In a stupor, she contacted her lawyers and a funeral home and made arrangements for Davey's remains to be shipped to her once it was released. He'd be brought to the estate at Lake Tahoe. There, in the privacy of her massive domain, hidden from public view, Davey would receive a Druid funeral and cremation. He would be sent home to the gods.

Five minutes after Armitage hung up, Malcolm Coughlin phoned.

His call was the longest and most comforting to the grieving woman. She'd never told him, but Davey was actually his son—the result of a short-lived affair when the situation in Venezuela was incredibly stressful. Her husband Tom was off for months on end trying to salvage the business. She'd simply let her husband believe she'd become pregnant during one of his brief visits home.

But she guessed Coughlin suspected the truth from the way he'd always fawned over her son. From the time Davey was a little boy, he'd remembered birthdays and other celebrations with a generosity that went above and beyond the normal attention of good friends.

Now, in her hour of need, Malcolm had come through again.

At the end of the call, he told her he was coming to see her immediately. There was, he said, some interesting and disturbing information he wanted to share. But not over the phone. She made arrangements to meet him at Tahoe rather than the main house.

He would join her Wednesday after he'd tied up a few more details, he said.

She stared out the massive windows overlooking Emerald Bay, grappling with the realities of what had happened. A rage began to build inside her; an incandescent, blazing, blistering hot rage.

She fell on her knees first, then prostate on the floor. She mumbled curses and chants, calling on the gods to give her revenge on those who'd tortured and murdered her boy. She called upon the powers of the underworld to feed her quest for vengeance and help her torment and destroy them.

Darkness fell. She was still prostate. The burning anger was slowly melding into an icy determination. None, she promised, would ever forget her final act of vengeance upon Davey's killers; those who did the deed and those who ordered it.

Tomorrow she would begin. The plan to create a Druid statement with an act of revenge would be enhanced. But for now, it was secondary. Her priority was to draw Davey's killers into her web and destroy them.

Tonight however, she would suffer in the darkness and alone.

Old College, Aberystwyth

Professor Dafydd Morgan was proud of himself. His anger still seethed as he watched the clumsy American disappear up the main staircase. Putting his books back into their correct order, he stalked over to the front security desk and asked who the man was. He was surprised at the porter's response "an American broadcaster named Stone Wallace." He remembered hearing the name from other Druids but tried to maintain a neutral face.

"And what would he be doing here at the university?"

"None of my business."

Morgan thought he'd asked himself the question silently. He was startled when the porter answered gruffly, so he flashed an angry, demeaning look across at the man.

"Well, you did ask!" the porter responded. He was tempted to add "Badger" but refrained, knowing Morgan hated the nickname and would likely report him for lack of respect towards academic staff in retaliation.

A dark look passed over Morgan's face. He struggled with a snippy reply then, unable to think of one, stormed off and out the main doors. Ten minutes later he was on the telephone to Richard Evans.

"You're sure it was him?" Evans barked into the phone, annoyed at the interruption at first, then intrigued. He listened to the detailed response, pleased at the information his contact was providing. It was the second shock of his day. "This might work out very well, Dai Badger. Very well indeed."

Usually he just indulged his sycophantic, bad-tempered colleague. Even though Morgan was a less than stellar professor at IMC, Evans had kept him on as an informant and suffered his attempts to ingratiate himself into the new Druid movement. But it was getting harder to keep him around, given his repeatedly poor reviews by IMC students, staff and professors. His student-given nickname, Dai Badger, certainly suited his looks and personality, and it amused Evans to needle the man by using his nickname. But Morgan's usefulness and days at IMC were numbered. All Evans needed was an excuse to remove him, tenure be damned. He sighed silently. Regretfully. Badger had just bought himself a temporary reprieve.

Startled by the news that one of the Druids' nemeses was actually at the Old College, Evans considered his other adversary Huw Griffiths would not be far away either. Like a fly into my trap, he smiled as he listened to

Badger's hugely enhanced tale of literally bumping into the American and how he'd brilliantly worked out who he was.

When Morgan finished, Evans allowed a moment of silence, as if he were pondering the revelation. "Badger, go and apologize to the American immediately." He waited while Morgan fumed and swore. "Never speak to me like that again, Badger, or you will be gone. Finished." He switched instantly from anger to cajoling. "Now, obey your orders. Find Wallace and apologize. Grovel if you must. Worm your way into his confidence. Stay close to him. Do whatever you have to, short of violence, to find out what he's up to and why he's at the university. Is he alone or are others working with him? What is he looking for? Report to me daily. Especially find out where Huw Griffiths is." He hung up abruptly.

Back at the Old College, Badger fumed. Then immediately placed another call to London.

Morgan's revelations raised more questions than answers. Why indeed was Wallace at the university, he mused. He assumed the man had fled back to America after his brush with death in London. Certainly, that was the impression Bethan Price had given him. She would take care of Wallace, in America, leaving Griffiths to him.

He pondered some more, wondering if he should let Bethan know that Wallace was still in Britain. Finally, he decided to wait. After all, he preened, I am the Dragon Master. She reports to me, not me to her. Plus, it would be a test of her loyalty to find out if she indeed knew where Wallace was and told him. To hedge his bets, however, he placed a call to Ioan, asking him to surreptitiously find out what Bethan knew about Wallace.

The first shock had come when he heard the news of her son's murder. Her enemies had struck faster than either had expected. A string of further urgent instructions to Ioan followed before he ended the call.

He sipped a fine Bordeaux wine as he contemplated his next actions. If Price was killed by Druids, this really was proof they were in disarray and battling themselves. He was under no illusion; a similar revolt might be imminent for him. He needed a win now more than ever.

With Badger assigned to Wallace and Griffiths, he turned his attention to the plans for major demonstration of Druid power.

The timetable had to be moved up.

Two hours later, after another visit to the sacred grove and another sacrifice, Evans returned to the house. The previous Dragon Master had given him a clue—attack the heart of the Christian church—but had failed miserably.

But now, the new Dragon Master, Richard Evans, would not be foiled.

His target symbolized everything he hated. It would take careful planning and commitment, but he would do it.

He would succeed where others failed. He would lead the renaissance of the sacred oak grove and its powers.

Borough Market, London

DCI Carswell was pleased by the summons to meet Freddy Garrett, but surprised by the choice of a small pub in Southwark, near the Borough Market, but on reflection, agreed with it. He didn't think he personally was under surveillance but accepted the possibility that someone might be watching the Crown Security offices. It wouldn't be his people. The Met was always crying poor on budget and staffing. But, Special Branch might be assigned the job.

Better safe than sorry he agreed, as he took the Tube to London Bridge Station. Outside the station he crossed the road, passed the bulk of Southwark Cathedral and walked down the shallow ramp under the massive railway bridge and into the Market itself. A block further along, he crossed out of the Market premises, and strolled down a small side street into the pub.

The after-work lingerers were thinning out when he arrived and the early evening crowd had not yet begun to flood in. Even so, it was a lively spot, bustling and noisy. He picked up a pint of ale and selected a booth at the back of the pub where he could carefully watch the pub crowd while staying relatively invisible.

Ten minutes later Freddy walked in, stopped for his own pint, and made his way back to Carswell's booth. They exchanged pleasantries and Carswell noted Freddy automatically chose a position where he could keep an eye on the comings and goings at the pub.

Freddy got right to the point. "Things are heating up. Sir Giles just had a fiery meeting with the new Minister, Gregory Belmont. Belmont is the source of the orders forbidding contact with us. He also found out that there's a very strong likelihood that Belmont is a Druid." Carswell swore quietly.

"Has the Met identified the Southend body yet?"

"Just came through as I was leaving the nick. A copper over in Whitechapel remembered our lad. He did a bit of checking. Seems it's Hamish

McLeod, a small-time thug in one of the east end gangs. The interesting thing is, a couple of years ago, one of the gang members grassed on him over some stolen goods. Before McLeod went to trial, a top-level barrister suddenly turned up representing him. The case was settled privately—probably the victims got paid off—and McLeod disappeared. I should have more on my desk tomorrow morning. Frankly, now they've identified the body, the file will be closed at our end. Essex will keep it open, of course, until they solve the case, but basically we're out now."

Freddy carefully wrote the name down. "Scottish, I don't doubt. Might just tie in with Belmont." He saw Carswell's quizzical raised eyebrow. "Belmont is from Glasgow. He represents Glasgow West Central constituency." He thought for a moment. "When you get the material on McLeod, I need his background, particularly where he's from. And I need to know if there'll be an autopsy and, if so, who's conducting it."

They both drank their pints and Carswell went for seconds. When he returned, Freddy explained why he'd requested the sudden meeting. "We need someone to check the Met's files and see if there's any background information on Belmont. There were rumblings a few years ago that the Minister was under investigation for some financial finagling, but we can't find any resolution to that case from any of our regular sources. Plus, we need to find out where he was on the day of the Hyde Park attack."

Carswell whistled. "Blimey! Don't bloody well want much, do you!" He played with the nearly full pint in his hands, ignoring the cold wet condensation on the glass.

"I'm not going to lie to you, Mr. Carswell. We know it will be difficult. We don't in any way want to compromise your position in the police force. But we are hampered by the new rules. Not surprising really. If Belmont is a Druid, then he can block nearly every area of investigation for us, and that gives the whole Druid movement a clear road to success."

He grimaced as he considered one aspect he'd not mentioned to the detective: it would be a thousand times worse if Belmont was, in fact, the new Dragon Master.

Carswell wiped his wet hands on a crumpled handkerchief he pulled out of his pocket. "Even if I say yes, I'm not sure I can give you all that information. It should be easy enough to get the autopsy gen. But the stuff on Belmont...." He stopped speaking and shook his head. "There will be layers upon layers of permissions to delve into his background, I'm sure. Way above my pay grade."

"I understand. But you did say there were others in the Met who are unhappy with the way things are being dealt with. I assume these are people who have the same level of commitment to the nation as you?"

Carswell nodded agreement. "I want to help. I really do. I just don't know if I can access that level of information." He took a long drink. "Don't think for one second that I'm afraid. I'm a bloody good copper and the Met knows it. But, if push comes to shove, the job will lose every time. Tell that to Sir Giles if he's wondering about my loyalty."

Freddy smiled and shook his head. "Neither I nor Sir Giles have any doubt on that regard, Mr. Carswell. We really do recognize the enormity of what we are asking."

The two talked for another hour. Freddy, whose background included time in MI6 before moving to Crown Security, explained that he was quietly asking the same of former colleagues who also indicated disgust with blindness to the Druid threat.

At the end of the evening, they exchanged mobile phone numbers and a series of coded messages to be used if one or the other could not speak or meet. Carswell left first, reversing his route past the cathedral and into the Tube station.

Freddy casually walked past the bar, scrutinizing the patrons carefully, then went past the kitchen door and into the manager's office. A quiet nod to the man behind the desk, he passed through the office and out another door, down a narrow ill lit hallway. He paused at the door at the end of the hallway, opened it and quickly nipped outside. The alleyway was clear. In short order he was striding down Borough High Street where he caught a number 40 double-decker.

Alexandria, Virginia

Calvin Tyler was one of the few government officials present.

He looked around the small crematorium chapel. A few long-standing SID staffers shuffled into a pew near the front. There were no family members that Tyler was aware of. He'd asked his former secretary to dig out the Lawson personnel file, but found nobody.

The small congregation was largely composed of Chad's friends from both the SID and his police days. Tyler's sharp, ever roving eyes noted the presence of two former Congressional aides and made a note to check out who they were. Harder, now he was no longer in office, he admitted, but he knew Wiz was lurking outside the building, camera in hand, covertly taking notes and shots of attendees. There were six or seven other men and women sitting together, that he didn't recognize. From the way they chatted quietly amongst themselves he wondered if they were media. His suspicion was confirmed as a couple of them took out notebooks and surreptitiously began taking notes.

To his left he noted two rather awkwardly sitting men in civilian clothes. Their posture and haircuts gave them away instantly. Military, he thought. Interesting. Now why would they be attending? Just before the service began he caught a glimpse of three more people slip in and sit on the far right side of the chapel. He recognized them immediately as senior representatives of the Department of Homeland Security. Since they'd been the agency pushing the President and SID to release Murphy and get rid of those investigating the Druids, he was intrigued. Were they attending out of respect or, more likely, were they keeping tabs on him and whoever else attended? There were others in the place he did not recognize. Friends from Chad's civilian side, he supposed, but they too would be checked.

The service itself was short and simple. A police honor guard in full dress uniform entered with the flag and Chad's uniform cap which they placed on a small table at the front. The District's Chief of Police had insisted upon his department's participation. Whatever happened at your office is between you and the federal government, he'd boomed in a phone call to Tyler. "But he was one of ours. He was a damned good policeman and a respected detective. We will honor him."

At the end of the service, they'd left the chapel and stepped out into a light Washington drizzle. One of the reporters sidled up to Tyler and asked him for a comment. Tyler brushed him off with a curt but quiet response that he'd lost a good friend and colleague who'd done nothing but serve his country to the best of his ability. Beyond that, he told the man, he had nothing to say.

Tyler shook hands with the police chief and watched as he and the escorting officers departed. The SID staff slipped past him quietly, with a few murmuring greetings and condolences. The congressional staffers disappeared.

Alone in front of the chapel entrance, Tyler heaved a visible sigh, wrapped a light scarf around his neck and buttoned his overcoat.

He walked slowly to his car.

Chad Lawson's funeral was over.

Chapter Fourteen

Aberystwyth, Wales

Nathan refused to tell them what he'd discovered. "You have to wait," he told them, "I'd rather you see it before I talk about it."

Early on, they'd grasped that Nathan had a teasing sense of the theatrical, always preferring to bring new information to them with a sense of drama.

This time, he swore he'd be back in under thirty minutes. He had return to the archives and "borrow" the particular artifact he'd found. "It would be best if you saw it quietly and in private," he said. "It's too busy up by there; too many people nosing about. Much better down by here."

He did tell them it was a delicate bound vellum record that had been buried in unopened crates filled with other boxes and documents. "The day before yesterday, I uncovered it. What it is, is it's a remarkably preserved document. I read it briefly myself and just couldn't wait to share it." He glanced at Stone. "But I wasn't sure you were going to continue."

With that he disappeared, leaving Stone and Mandy wondering.

On his return he slipped into the tiny office and quietly shut the door. Now that he was part of the team, the room had become even more crowded. He cleared Stone's table, pushing books and files to one side. He asked Stone to move the dirty tea cup while he laid a white cotton sheet over the table. As they watched, he reached into his leather messenger bag and pulled out some white cotton gloves. He beckoned Mandy and Stone to stand beside him and with a flair, he pulled the gloves on, reaching back into what seemed his bag of tricks.

As he did so, his story spilled out rapidly. "I was down in the lower level in one of the back vaults a few days go. *Dew, dew* but it's dusty back there even though it is necessarily kept at a cool temperature." He flicked some imaginary dust off his sleeve. "There were some crates. I was going to ignore them, because I was looking for some other material related to Owain. Anyway, as I began to move the crates I noticed that they'd come from The Church in Wales."

"What church in Wales," Stone interrupted.

Nathan stopped in mid explanation. "Well, that's the official name of the Anglican Church here. Like the Church of England, but it's a separate part of the Anglican family." At Stones nod of comprehension, he continued. "So anyway, The Church in Wales apparently cleaned out their own archives and sent all these boxes along to the National Library."

He laid a dark brown leather-bound object on the table. "This was in a crate marked 'Priory of Penmon'. That priory was in the Conwy valley, not that far from Dolwyddelan Castle, one of Owain's main strongholds. I wondered if, being so close, the priory had had any contact with Owain. So, I began to scour the crate, looking at all kinds of irrelevant material, but I noticed that everything was filed simply from top to bottom; the closer I got to the bottom of the box, the closer I was getting to Owain's time period." Nathan's excitement was contagious, and when he finally stopped for breath, so did both Stone and Mandy.

"It took me almost two full days in the bowels of the building," he continued, "But finally I found this." He pointed to the object on the white cotton sheet. A big grin creased his face.

"Not to put too fine a point on it, Nathan, but, what is it?" Stone's impatience at the elongated explanation was beginning to show.

Nathan carefully and reverently opened the delicate book. "May I present to you, the work of one Padraig, a monk of the priory. It is called 'Beata vita Principis Madoc et eius navigationibus', The Blessed life and voyage of Prince Madoc."

A stunned silence enveloped the room. Nobody breathed. Mandy and Stone just stared. Stone reached out to touch it, but was stopped by Nathan. Quickly he reached into his bag and pulled out two more pairs of the white gloves. "Please don't touch anything without these gloves on," he said softly.

They both obeyed. Stone respectfully and cautiously brushed his hand gently across the heavy leather cover. Mandy could barely contain herself. The historian in her bubbled over as she too touched it. "Unbelievable. Simply unbelievable," she whispered as much to herself as her companions. "This is a breakthrough in our knowledge of Madoc. No one else has ever seen or used this source material."

"It's a very interesting record of our Prince and his activities in the days and weeks before he set out to America," Nathan breathed.

Stone was amazed how all of them had dropped their normal volume and were speaking in hushed tones, yet he continued in the same quiet voice. "You understand Latin?"

Nathan beamed. "A prime requisite if one is going to be a researcher and probe through the dust and mists of time in Wales. You have to know Welsh, of course, but you also have to have a grasp of Norman French as well as Latin, plus some Irish Gaelic to boot, if you want to rustle around in the post-Romano and early medieval periods."

Gently, he opened the book and pointed to the title page which also had the inscription

'Scriptum per Fratrem Padraid Penmon'.

"That means 'as recorded by Brother Padraig of Penmon' who seems to have been a close companion of Madoc's." Nathan explained. Then he began to slowly turn the pages so Stone and Mandy could both see it. "It's not decorated the way many monks would have done their works," he said. "It seems to be just a plain report. But what a report!"

Stone stood up. "Why didn't you tell us earlier? You've known about this for a couple of days, but said nothing."

Shamefaced, Nathan bowed his head. "You seemed so torn with grief. I thought mentioning this discovery, great as I think it is, would intrude. I knew you needed to process your grief first. Then, if you decided to pack it in and go back to America, I would mention it to your father," he nodded to Mandy. "If not, when you indicated you were ready to move ahead, I would speak up. Which you did and I did today."

Stone said nothing, not knowing whether to believe him or not. His level of trust with anyone was muted as ever. A brittleness seeped into the atmosphere.

Mandy suddenly reached out and touched the archivist's shoulder. "Thank you, Nathan. You have done good work and your kindness in letting Stone grieve is very much appreciated." She glanced up at Stone and smiled at him, willing him to agree. Cautiously, he too acknowledged his thanks, but mentally made a note to double check the researcher's background. Only a few people penetrated his shields, but once there they were cherished and, he admitted, those few were beginning to have a profound but subtle influence on how he viewed life. Nathan might be one of the good guys, he admitted, and certainly seemed that way. But Stone wanted more reassurance before he could fully trust the young researcher.

Together they pored over the document, Nathan translating roughly as they read. Mandy and Stone took notes furiously. It was a painstakingly slow process for all of Nathan's proficiency in Latin, but they made progress.

Suddenly, as Nathan verbally translated, he began reading about Idrith, Dafydd and the Druids.

"No! God, No!" Mandy shrieked and began trembling.

Stone quickly enveloped her in his arms and began consoling her, soothing her. "They are everywhere. They're out to destroy everything and everyone I know and love." She began to sob, buried in Stone's shoulders.

Nathan jerked at her first shout. He saw the color flush right out of both their faces as he stared uncomprehendingly. He was shocked and puzzled by Mandy and Stone's reactions and didn't know what to say or how to react.

As Mandy began to calm down, Stone, with his arms still carefully cradling her, looked sternly at Nathan. "Dr. Griffiths and her father have both had nasty experiences with a particularly violent sect of Druids. I must ask you to never mention this to anyone. Ever."

Nathan visibly relaxed a bit. "If it's the ones I'm thinking of—the ones that used to be down near Carreg Cennan Castle—then I fully understand her reaction. They are a vicious bunch of terrorists, in my opinion. I lost two good mates to them. One was severely beaten to the point of brain injuries. The other simply disappeared."

Stone stared at him momentarily. "You know these people?"

Nathan nodded. "Yes, and I will fight them with every fiber of my being. But," he acknowledged ruefully, "there's not a lot an archivist like me can do about it."

As Mandy grabbed some tissue, Stone looked around the room. "First off, we've got to protect this book. We must keep it out of the archives for now, where it might fall into the wrong hands. Until we fully understand what it says about both Madoc and the Druids, I'd be much more comfortable with the fewer people knowing about this, the better." He thought for a moment. "This office is not secure enough. But I don't know where to keep it safe."

"Nobody knows about it. It was buried in a crate, like I said. I never mentioned it to anyone, so nobody up at the National Library will know it's gone because they didn't even know they had it. It's never been recorded or added to the database. So, we're good there."

While they were debating the next steps, Mandy pulled herself together, apologized for her outburst and offered to make tea. Stone reluctantly released her, and she bustled around the small kettle and accoutrements.

She turned and gave a wan smile. "I may be afraid of where this is leading, Stone. In fact, I would say I am horribly terrified. But understand one thing: they have not beaten me. I will not let them. As long as I have you in my life, and Da, I will not let them. If they're back in our shadows, then so be it. They will not, must not win. I was fully prepared to die that day in London and I was not afraid. I knew that no matter whether I lived or died, God would see me through and give me strength. He'll do the same for us in the coming days."

"Thank you, God" Stone breathed to himself as he embraced her again. She's made the final breakthrough. Her strength and faith had won through. He was astonished at both her vehemence and her willingness to speak out in front of a total stranger. Moreover—he clung to the hope—he sensed that she had just declared that he was important to her. A part of her life, she'd said.

Mandy firmly pushed him away. "Now let me get the tea made while we discuss what to do next."

Stone stepped back and grinned at Nathan who smiled back. One thing was certain, Stone understood, Nathan's credentials had been verified uniquely. His doubts drained away. Nathan was another one he would let penetrate the hardened, but weakening shell.

Quantico Marine Base, Virginia

Wells stood ramrod straight, surveying the scene from his window. He preferred the office at Quantico to the one assigned at the Pentagon. It allowed him distance from the constant intrigues and pettiness of politics in both the Pentagon and the administration. Plus, he felt grounded in the Corps at Quantico.

There was a sharp knock on his door. At his command, two officers entered, carefully closing the door behind them and saluting. Returning their salute, Wells sat in the comfortable leather chair behind his desk. "Report."

As they did, Wells listened intently. He'd trained himself as a young officer to memorize the minutest details of anything and everything. He saw it as a weakness to write anything down, when listening to a report. The two men filled him in on their clandestine investigation into the Price murder. As he listened, he questioned them incessantly, sometimes harshly. Neither blinked or looked at him. They spoke straight ahead, eyes fixed on the flag and Marine Corps eagle, globe and anchor emblem framed above his head.

He knew that both officers and their men were skilled in their work. Although he didn't let on, he trusted their report implicitly. He could ask no more of them, however, because their loyalty was to the nation and the Corps in that order. They were not part of the movement; they were not ingrained in Druidry. He trusted their intelligence, their skills and their abilities, but he didn't trust them. He'd merely told them a potential national security issue impacting the Corps was under investigation.

When they left his office, he instructed his civilian secretary outside to block all calls, then sat down to reconstruct the officers' verbal report. As he always did, he used a ruler to divide an 8x10 paper in half. On the left side he noted in his precise handwriting each point they'd made, each fact they'd reported. On the right, he penned his own notes, questions and observations beside each point. When he finished, the exercise had not only recorded the report in minute detail, it had pushed him through a mental exercise of thinking through each niggling detail and each angle. He scanned the papers into his personal laptop, then shredded them.

One thing was sure, it looked unlikely the government was involved in the murder. His men's investigation had quietly penetrated government data bases, emails and computers, from the White House through Congress, to both the FBI and CIA. They'd even hacked the Defense Intelligence Agency which had tenant status at Quantico itself.

Well and his officers, prided themselves on the fact that their activities were invisible, operating under even the tightest electronic security parameters. The men and their small team were highly classified.

He had no proof yet, but it smelled like retaliation against the selection of Bethan Price as Raven Master. Much as he despised the woman, as Serpent Master he had no option but to investigate.

He cancelled or rearranged his schedule for the next three days and ordered a flight from Quantico's airstrip to Stewart International airport, the joint military-public airport close to the Army's West Point Academy, north of New York City. A quick call on his private cell phone arranged a limo to meet him and whisk him to his private mansion up the Hudson River near Poughkeepsie.

Word also went out to his small Serpent security team. They would gather at the house tomorrow morning.

Aberystwyth, Wales

The excitement was palpable as the three of them pored over Padraig's journal. Both Stone and Mandy made notes as Nathan translated and read.

Stone was ecstatic. "So, our Madoc was confronted by some Templars, asked to carry some kind of secret away with him, and in return got funding for his voyage. If we can find out what that secret is…. wow! What a story for our show!"

Stone beamed, the first time in months he felt really free of stress, delighted at the turn their research had made. The only problem lingering in his mind, was the reference to the Druids. He dismissed their presence as irrelevant and merely annoying, he told Mandy. "After all, it just seems his brother Dafydd wanted to eliminate him as a threat. Dafydd may have been a Druid, but it seems to be more about fratricide than a larger Druid conspiracy."

Mandy agreed. She had her own fears tucked away still, but acknowledged that the mention of Druids seemed peripheral and coincidental.

Nathan continued translating and paraphrasing. "Madoc set sail suddenly for Lundy Island in what's now the Bristol Channel. Padraig was too late to join them and had to race back to his Priory and grab his journal. He then made his own way on fishing and trading vessels to Lundy, via Dublin."

As he'd been doing, he stopped speaking, slowly reading the vellum, running his gloved fingers lightly along underneath each word, processing the words and phrases and then trying to rephrase it all in modern English.

They were startled by a knock on the office door. Fortunately, when Nathan returned with his treasure, Stone had had the foresight to lock it.

"Anyone in there," a muffled, gruff voice said as the door rattled.

"Hang on a minute," Stone shouted, as Nathan whipped the book and sheet into his case. Mandy pushed some books and papers onto the table to make it look busy, then nodded at Stone. He opened the door.

"Sorry to barge in like this," the man known as Badger stepped in, peering around the room over Stone's shoulder. He took in the room's other occupants. "If I might have a private word with you?"

Annoyed at both the interruption and the man's boorish behavior, Stone shook his head. "Anything you have to say can be said in front of my colleagues. Or not at all."

A flush came over the man's face. "Very well. I just came by to offer my sincere apologies for my behavior and words the other day. I am very sorry. My only excuse is that I was suffering an outrageous headache and was running late for an important appointment. I see now that it was an unavoidable accident. It is hard to see around that massive stone pillar, and I was more intent on my situation rather than looking where I was going. My words were hasty, and I do hope that you will accept my apology."

Stone stared at him a moment, then repeated his own apologies. "Thank you for this, professor. Now if you will excuse us, we have much work to do." He took Badger's arm and began leading him out of the room. Badger shook it off and proffered his own had towards Mandy, "Professor Dafydd Morgan." She shook his hand and introduced herself. Badger turned towards Nathan, holding his hand back, "I think I've seen you up at the Library. Part of the staff, aren't you?" His sneer was barely hidden.

He turned again to Stone. "If there's anything I could help you with, Mr. Wallace, I would certainly welcome the opportunity to make amends for my unkind words. It's not often we get a famous American television star here at the Old College, after all."

Stone gently but firmly refused the offer and, after thanking him once again, resolutely closed the door. They waited until they heard the man's footsteps retreat down the hall, then Stone quickly locked the door again.

For a few moments, silence reigned. Nathan broke it. "Don't like Dai Badger at all. He's a thoroughly obnoxious, officious twit. Don't trust him either."

"What do you mean?"

"Well, he's on the faculty at IMC, Iolo Morganwyg College. They're affiliated with the Uni but do their own thing, so to speak." Swiftly he told them the college specialized in early Celtic studies. "There's a lot of chatter about the students and faculty there. Talk about strange ideas and mysterious things going on behind closed doors. Mind you, that comes from students from the university who take a course of two there. You never hear anything from the ones registered at IMC itself."

Nathan's comments troubled Stone. His next words concerned him even more. "My own suspicion is that they are tied up in some kind of Druidry. Their academic Dean, Richard Evans is a bit of an odd bloke. Always dressed to the nines, but wild hair that looks like Gandalf's after it's been thinned seventy percent. Often has it in a ponytail. He's a prissy little man too. Always standing on formalities and insisting on proper respect for his position." He stuck his nose in the air, adopted a snobbish tone and pranced around the room. "I am the Dean, after all. I do have my doctorate in Celtic studies."

It broke the tension. In spite of their concerns, both Stone and Mandy laughed at the portrayal.

"If that's the case then," Stone was still smiling at the performance, "we'll have to double our precautions. I'll nose around and see what I can find out." He pointed at the bag. "In the meantime, we need to get this someplace much safer. At least until we've completed the translation and know exactly what Prince Madoc's secret is."

"What about Greyfell?"

Stone shook his head. "Too far away. I think we've still got some more work to do here. Nathan will have to look at the rest of those crates to see if there's anything else in them. We need a place somewhere near Aber that will be safe, that nobody knows about and yet a place we can access any time we need to.

Suddenly, Nathan snapped his fingers as his face lit up with surprise and pleasure. "I know just the place. My friend Evan Thomas Evan was a crack historian here at Aber. But he got tired of all the BS and politics, fell in love and moved with his new wife just up the coast a bit at a small seaside village called Borth. They run a small B and B there. Not many around here remember him all that well. But I do. He was my best mate, even if he was older than I am. We just hit it off and stayed in contact."

Nodding thoughtfully, Stone agreed it might be ideal if the man would agree. "I've never heard of anyone with three first names and no surname though."

Nathan and Mandy laughed. "It's a Welsh thing," Nathan said. "Everyone used to call him Evan the Book, but he's in the hospitality business, he goes by ET."

After a short discussion, the trio agreed to visit Borth the next day and see if ET would cooperate. They also agreed that Stone would take Padraig's book back to his flat, concealed with a load of other books and files. He might be succumbing to a bit of paranoia, but if anyone was indeed watching, they would just see him walking home with some extra reading.

As he flipped the office light out, he couldn't help shiver as a thought crossed his mind: what if the Druids *were* involved somehow?

Chapter Fifteen

Old College, Aberystwyth

It took a while, but his patience was rewarded.

Badger found a spot just inside Seddon Hall, facing the door that he left slightly ajar. Ostensibly, he was studying some books and taking notes, but he was watching the door like a hawk, peering up intently as people walked by. Finally, after an hour of scrutiny, he saw what he wanted. Wallace, the Griffith woman and the library staffer passed the door and headed out onto the street.

He gave it another fifteen minutes, then silently pulled his things together and quickly wound through the maze until he came to the office. He listened carefully in case somebody was still inside. He heard nothing. At the same time his ears were tuned in case somebody came up the stairs or down the hall. A door banged in the distance. But no footsteps came toward him.

He knew many people had a low estimate of his abilities and personality. He didn't care. He was being paid to crush information into uninformed skulls. What they did with it afterwards was their problem, not his. So long as he got his money he was happy; he just hated the nickname those stupid students gave him. That, more than anything, angered him.

But he had other skills that lay outside the academic. Most were learned on the hard streets of the slums of Swansea with swarms of other unrestrained and unsupervised kids. One of those skills was his innate ability to pick locks, honed on the doors of local shops at one or two o'clock in the morning. He would silently slip out of his house and meet his mates. With them acting as lookouts in case the local bobbies came, they would rummage through the area. Sweet shops and grocers were his main target. He was careful not to damage anything going in or out, and he judicious about what and how many sweets to take. That way, he told his mates, the shop owners would never really know anything had been taken. Then they could return and hit the same shop again a few weeks later.

He'd never forgotten his lockpicking ability. It was a skill he planned to use this evening.

The lock was old and, in his mind, a piece of cake. In less than two minutes he was in.

He flipped on the overhead light and began rummaging around. The files and books indicated a deep interest in the Welsh Prince Madoc. Nothing fascinating there. Certainly nothing that would be of interest to Evans. What he really needed was a location for Huw Griffiths.

He shuffled through some papers and picked up a notebook with handwritten notes. As he read one of the pages the word Druid jumped out at him. Repeatedly. He scanned it quickly. It was obviously a summary of some book they'd been looking at. No wonder they were all so uncomfortable when he'd dropped by to apologize as ordered. He'd sensed at the time that he'd broken in on something important; something they wanted to keep secret. That whelp of a library staffer had obviously found an item in the collection. But why the secrecy? And what was it? He tried to read more but realized he could not stay in the office much longer.

He picked up the handwritten notes again and, from the different spelling of some words, supposed the American had written them. Well, he'd lost them now. Badger was not sure if his find was important or not, but it was certainly something to show Evans. And he would pass the information along to Belmont as well. The small stipend the politician gave him was a pittance to what he would demand for this information.

He hustled out as quickly as he could, pausing only to switch off the light and close the door again. Smoothly, he made sure that door was relocked. Just like the sweet shops, he thought, but this time with a potentially bigger payoff.

Winchester, Virginia

"You're dead and by God, you're going to stay dead Junior. Deal with it."

Wiz handed him a large coffee, laden with the three creams and three sugars Chad always requested. "The Chief told me to keep you under wraps here and that's where you're staying until that doctor clears you."

Chad remembered little about the crash itself. He knew bystanders had pulled him from the wreckage before it burst into flame. Wiz told him the Hummer was found hours later in the parking lot of the Potomac Mills shopping center with no plates. Forensics found nothing in the vehicle, not even prints.

Chad's argument for the past few days was that he was well on the road to recovery and wanted to get back into harness. "I've got to find out who tried to finish me off. And then finish them off," he repeatedly told Wiz. So far, it had gotten him nowhere.

"It was only thanks to a friendly Virginia state trooper who recognized you as a former Washington detective and SID agent, that we got word you were hurt," Wiz explained. "We needed to protect you. They troopers found a tracking device on your car. You were targeted.

Within minutes of hearing about the accident, Tyler assessed the situation and pulled a little subterfuge. "As soon as you were stable," Wiz told Chad, "the Chief pulled strings to remove you from hospital. At the same time, an announcement was made that you'd been killed in a traffic accident. He thought it best if we hid out here in Winchester. He figures that while it's tucked away in the countryside near Shenandoah, it's still accessible to Washington." Wiz left no uncertainty. They were to remain there until Chad was recovered sufficiently.

Chad confessed he was still creeped out about his so-called death.

"Look, the Chief decided, for your own safety, to give you the best cover possible; your death in the accident. Anyway, it was a nice respectful service. You should have been there," Wiz grinned.

"The Chief thinks that's going to stop them?"

"He thinks they'll stop looking for you and trying to kill you. That gives us an edge we weren't expecting. So, the sooner you get in tip top condition, the sooner we take advantage. Mind you, we'll have to change your appearance a bit too. How do you feel about a beard?"

Chad snorted and immediately regretted it as a jolt of pain shot through his face.

Despite the ghoulishness of the idea, he was beginning to accept the premise behind his death. "We do need a fresh start. We're just spinning our wheels. So maybe a new angle will help."

The normally confident and optimistic Wiz heaved a sigh. "It's frustrating. No matter how you cut it, we're the scapegoats Chad. *IF* we succeed, great. The President will take the credit for his brilliant strategy. If we don't…well, we were just a pair of rogue agents anyway."

Chad agreed with the pessimistic assessment. "We might get more information on the Druids, if we could get to Britain. I think Stone and Huw could help, as would Crown Security. But how to get there without drawing attention. Can't fly out through Dulles or even the New York airports. Might have to slip back across the border into Canada and fly from there."

Wiz smiled. "You won't have to do that. I was going to suggest we go back out West and dig around Wyoming and New Mexico. But that's not a bad idea you just had, junior. If we split up with you in the UK and me out west, we double our chances of getting useful information. And, at the same time, we'll be places where the opposition won't expect us. Especially you, since you're technically not around at all."

"So how do we do this? You got something like a magic carpet up your sleeve?"

"Better than a carpet, junior. We've got wings! Remember I pushed the Chief on this? The President agreed to provide us with a small jet. There's a 'redundant to requirements' C-38A that the Air Force is getting rid of. Basically, it's a Gulfstream G-100, more than capable of taking us to Europe. It's gassing up at Andrews Airforce Base even as we speak and will be at the Winchester airport within the next hour or so. Take a couple of days while you recuperate and change your look. Meantime, I'll familiarize myself with the plane. Then we'll hightail it across to the UK and drop you off. No airport security. No records kept by airlines. Find a nice airport outside London to drop you off so you can contact your buddies. I'll turn it around almost immediately and head back west to do my enquiries."

Protesting that Wiz could not fly a jet solo across the Atlantic, Chad was shot down. "Normally a two-man crew would be best, sure. But we don't have that luxury. Anyway, I did longer flights in the left seat in my air force days, so if I don't push it and take all the required rest breaks, I'll be okay."

The more he talked, the more enthused he became.

"We've got to use what little we've been given and make it work for us. You're a smart agent, one of the best the agency has. I've got a track record as well. We can do this and we do it by truly disappearing, peering under rocks and places the Druids don't expect." Wiz slapped his hand against the coffee table. "They all—including the President—think we're either already failures or will be. He was just grasping at straws to save his administration's bacon when he called us in. Basically, he said so himself. Well, we're gonna throw them all a little curve. Those damned Druids won't expect this. You in Britain. Me in Wyoming. Gives us an edge."

For the first time since the scene in Tyler's office, Chad felt encouraged. Faced with their mammoth task—to root out a massive conspiracy and solve a political assassination—he'd been thwarted by the shackles put on them. He shifted position on the less than comfortable couch.

"Okay. It just might work. One thing we really do need to find out, is what Armitage was doing in Wyoming. Neither the Chief nor POTUS mentioned him in our meeting, and I completely blanked out about it. I was still trying to wrap my head around being fired then suddenly thrown back into the field. It would go a long way to finding out if we're really the scapegoats, or if Armitage is running his own game with or without the President's knowledge."

"You still got those shots?"

Chad nodded. He walked over to his baggage and pulled out the camera. As Wiz watched he transferred the photo file to his computer. They carefully scrutinized each shot, toying with it zooming in and out on various portions of each, trying to find clues—no matter how small.

"It's definitely him."

They studied the photos for twenty minutes, raising questions but answering none. Chad rubbed his eyes from the strain of peering intently at the screen. "I'll transfer these onto a couple of flash drives. You take one, I'll take another. We should store the third some place safe." He paused momentarily. "I don't think we should mention this to the Chief yet. Not until we have some answers.

"Another thing. I don't think we need to tell either the Chief or the President that I'm going across the pond. Not yet, anyway."

Borth, Wales

There was no ignoring the raucous cries of the gulls as they swooped and swirled over the waterfront. Stone watched as one gull dive-bombed a small child tightly gripping her newly-bought fish and chips. She cried as the gull succeeded and flapped away, a fat juicy chip in its beak. As annoying as it was to the little child, to Stone it seemed the aerial bobbing and crying of the gulls was actually a wonderfully noisy, hectic welcome to the seaside.

Yesterday's discovery had invigorated all of them. This morning they'd piled into Nathan's old Mini for the drive to Borth. None of them noticed the careful scrutiny given them by two men sitting in a parked car outside Stone's flat. Nor did they see it pull out immediately after they passed.

The day was glorious and the drive up the coast towards Borth was pleasant. Stone enjoyed the narrow road as it wound across the rolling green countryside. Already, daffodils and other spring flowers were appearing. Before too long, they were easing their way into the tiny village until they rounded a curve and the seafront, and a magnificent long beach opened up before them, looking across the bay towards the town of Aberdovey. Far off in the distance he could just see the Lleyn Peninsula of North Wales, and peeking over the horizon slightly inland, the peaks of Snowdonia.

Nathan turned left and drove slowly along Cliff Road, past a series of connected multi-colored pastel houses. Some, he explained, were holiday flats—rented for a week or two at a time during the high season, while others were private homes. The road climbed slowly towards the headland and they could see everything was becoming more modern. Nathan pulled into the gravel drive of a well-maintained brick house with a magnificent, large picture window overlooking the sea.

Before they could even get the car doors open, a massively built man with wild, unruly red hair and flowing rusty beard, burst out of the door and headed towards them. Right behind was a tiny, elfin-like raven haired woman with a baby in her arms.

Grinning, the man grabbed Nathan in a bear hug, lifting him off the ground. When he could breathe again, Nathan introduced Stone and Mandy.

"Pleased to meet you both. Nathan says you're two of the good ones. Before we go any further, just call me ET. Everyone does." Quickly he introduced his wife Dilys and baby Samantha. Stone had to turn away to smother a smile as he saw the two and mentally pictured Gandalf and a hobbit standing side by side. ET ushered them all inside and seated them in a side conservatory that, like the large window they'd noticed outside, overlooked the sea. ET gently held the baby while Dilys rushed off to fetch the tea.

"Wait till you try her Welsh Cakes," Nathan whispered. "They're to die for." As he spoke, Dilys reappeared with a large tray and set it down, a plate of the small round cookie-like cakes set prominently in the middle.

While they sipped and munched, Stone explained the reason for intruding. At his nod, Nathan produced the book and several pairs of gloves, laying them on the small coffee table in front of ET. With a whistle of surprise, ET suddenly handed the baby over to an astonished Nathan, grabbed a pair of white gloves, pulled them on, and caressed the book.

Without taking his eyes off the book, he softly turned the pages over, one by one, taking in their significance.

"I wish I'd known about this when I was doing my own thesis." He looked up at Stone. "I did a stunningly brilliant paper on the early Celtic church in North Wales, if I do say so myself." He paused briefly. "And I do. Frequently." As he chuckled heartily, his eyes embraced the pages.

When he finished reading, he leaned back. "Remarkable find. Absolutely remarkable." He pointed at Nathan, then at both Stone and Mandy. "You do realize, boyos, this will significantly alter the perception of Madoc and gives huge credence to the story of him discovering America."

Stone explained their cinematic interest in Madoc's story to the delighted man. "Well then, Stone, you'd best get yourself and your film team down to Lundy Island, hadn't you?"

Stone looked quizzically at him. ET opened the book towards the back.

"Look by'ere. Padraig says Madoc put a small chest into a grave. Padraig doesn't know what was in the chest, just that Madoc used the grave of one of his men who died of fever." He straightened up. "It seems to me, if you can get down there, you might just find what that secret thing was."

Nathan muttered to himself. "Missed that part. I was just skimming and translating on the go."

Dilys rushed to put away the tray, flipping her hair away from her two rosy cheeks. On her return to the conservatory, she invited them to stay for lunch. "We've no guests here at the moment, so it would just be us." She smiled and led them into the beautifully appointed dining room with the huge window as its main feature.

As they dove into the magnificent meal, they filled ET in on their research and activities to date. They also mentioned peripherally, their involvement with the Druids only to be surprised when ET interrupted. "Yes, heard a bit about you. Thwarted those damned evil people in London last year, didn't you?" He laughed out loud at Stone and Mandy's flabbergasted looks. "This may be a small place in far west Wales, but we're not cut off from civilization, you know."

Dilys gave him sharp poke on his arm and he grinned again, "well alright love! Dilys won't let me away with it, will you old girl?" He raised his hands in surrender and, with a somewhat sheepish, look admitted he'd been in London attending a conference at the time of the attack. "All over the papers, it was boyo. Read your name there. Unusual name and I wondered if it was you when Nathan called last night." He turned serious. "Don't you worry. Nothing will pass my lips. Your secrets are safe with me. Iechyd da, boyo. This has made my day!"

By the time they finished their discussion with ET, he'd agreed to not only keep the book safe, but do an English translation as well.

"We'll pay you for both the translation and hanging on to the book." Stone insisted, pushing aside ET's protestations. "Look, the BBC has a big budget for this documentary, so paying is no problem." Finally, ET accepted, admitting that running a seaside B and B in winter often meant things were tight.

Throughout the meal, large dark clouds had accumulated, and it was, as Dilys said, "lashing down" when they scurried back to Nathan's car.

As Nathan pulled out of the driveway, none of them noticed a small black Peugeot parked a hundred yards away on the cliff side of the road.

Lake Tahoe, California

It was a Bethan Price Malcolm Coughlin had never seen before. And it was one he was not sure he liked.

When he arrived, she was still in deepest mourning, grieving Davey's murder and unable to think or act. She was alone and had not cared for herself at all. The vibrant, well-groomed woman he knew, was gone. In her place was a gaunt, unkempt robot who'd not eaten for days.

By the time he finished reporting his preliminary findings however, a massive change had come over her.

It was a change he'd never seen before in a person, no matter how horrific their circumstances. Her face darkened. Her eyes narrowed. Fury shook her body. It was a cold rage that lashed out at him as much as anyone. As she stood, physically shaking, she glared at him with a palpable hatred for being the messenger of bad news. It reminded him of a Hollywood movie depicting someone possessed, except this was real. He was seeing it live and in person and was sure he'd seen evil personified.

"I will destroy them. Every last one of them. I will rid the world of them and, the gods will be with me, I will cleanse the body from within and, by the

Horned One, Cernunnos, they will pay—all of them—for their betrayal." Without another word, she flung her wine glass furiously over his head to shatter against the wall, then stormed into her bedroom.

Stunned, Coughlin contemplated his next move. He'd never bought into the whole Druid nonsense that Bethan and Tom embraced so fully. "To each his own," he'd told them lightly. "The only person or thing I believe in is me. And I'm quite happy with that." He'd resisted all their efforts to draw him in. Thankfully, he'd been an important asset as well as friend, so they allowed him what they considered his idiosyncrasies, and continued to use him and pay him well.

This time, he was flummoxed. He had no answers. He had no strategy for dealing with Bethan and helping her through the grief. Sighing, he picked up his cell phone and punched the number for her Sausalito residence. He knew there was some new assistant there, sent by one of her British friends to help her. He spoke quietly to the man and persuaded him to get to Lake Tahoe as quickly as possible, promising to meet him at the airport.

The next day, when Ioan Parry arrived, they had an energetic debate as Coughlin filled him in on the circumstances. Without fully explaining his role, Coughlin reported on his own investigation into the younger Price's murder.

"He was snatched from the hotel itself. I had to pay handsomely but was able to obtain copies of the hotel security videos. I won't go into the details, but we matched up timelines of people going up on the elevator around the time Price disappeared. We know he ordered room service at 7:25—I got that from the hotel records, for even more money—and we know that when the waiter arrived at the room, the door was open and Price was nowhere to be found."

He pulled the car over at a small scenic viewpoint overlooking Emerald Bay. "My people were able to identify two men who went into the lobby and up on the elevators around 7:30. But they never came back down again. So, we concentrated on those two. As I told Bethan, it took a while, but we think we identified our boys. Not by name, but we know that they were very familiar with a government guy named Dexter Armitage. They were on his personal house staff as a chauffeur and as a gardener."

Parry, familiar with Armitage's position as one of the nation's leading Druids, raised an eyebrow, but said nothing.

"I'll be frank. I'm not a Druid and not into all the mumbo-jumbo you guys are. I'm just a longtime friend of the Price's and do security type work for the company from time to time. I was very fond of Davey and want to see his killers taken down. But Bethan went around the bend when I told her all this." He shook his head disbelievingly.

"I figured she might want a fellow believer around to help her—that's what religious groups do for each other, right? —while I get back to Washington and find out more."

He pulled out onto the highway again. The rest of the drive was done in silence.

Inside, Parry and Coughlin were bombarded with Bethan's vitriol. Parry especially, for disobeying her order to remain in Sausalito. She raged and fumed. In her anger, a vase joined last night's wine glass in shards on the dark hardwood floor.

Bethan rained down invective on them. She was Raven Master, she reminded Parry, and expected total obedience. He icily reminded her that he obeyed the Dragon Master himself, not her, and that while he was asked to help her momentarily, his primary function was to ascertain the situation in North America.

"A spy," she screeched. "You're nothing but a bloody spy for Richard bloody Evans." Her invective turned up a notch as new oaths and curses crossed her lips. They ended when Parry was ordered out and told to return to his master, "or I'll kill you myself with my bare hands, by Cernunnos." Parry stared defiantly at her and merely said, "I will leave and report to the Dragon Master." He stalked out of the house.

Coughlin tried pouring oil on the troubled waters and only barely managed to calm her down slightly. He promised to remove Parry and return to Washington himself to verify Armitage's involvement in the murder.

She looked daggers at him. "You should never have summoned him here, Malcolm. He is as much an enemy as Armitage. I will stay here until Davey's body comes home. Find out exactly who was involved; Armitage, his men, that slippery, slimy toad Wells, all of them. Find out Malcolm. Then tell me. Wipe them all out but do not harm Armitage or Wells. I want that pleasure myself."

With that, she threw him out too.

Chapter Sixteen

Whitehall, London

It was surprisingly sunny and relatively warm. A pleasant change from the incessant drizzle and cold winds of the past few days. The weather matched Belmont's mood as he strolled out of the Home Office. His protection detail repeatedly argued with him about his penchant for unescorted strolls, but he always blew them off. They wanted him in their sights at all times. What they didn't realize was that there were times he didn't want to be seen. Besides, they didn't realize it, but he was always protected. His private force of Druid 'soldiers' constantly monitored him and ensured his safety. A coded message before one of his jaunts was sufficient to make sure they were on duty.

He passed under the multi-colored transparent roof covering the building's portico and its sculptured steel lattice facade. At Horseferry Road he nonchalantly turned left and walked down the road, stopping in front of a newsagent's shop. As he did, one of the ubiquitous black London taxicabs glided up to the edge of the pavement. Belmont stepped forward, opened the door and entered. The cab pulled out and instantly executed one of the tight turns the cabs are famous for, reversing direction and speeding back along Horseferry. In a quick succession of turns and reverses, the cab wound its way through Pimlico and Chelsea. When the driver was satisfied he was not being followed, he made his way onto Kings Road. At the famous World's End Pub, he turned again. Five minutes later he purred to a stop in front of a series of elegant white Portland stone townhouses. Not a word had passed the entire journey nor did it now, as Belmont leaped out of the cab and bounded up the stairs into the house.

Inside, he swept into a stylishly furnished and decorated reception room. Flopping into an easy chair he smiled at the man waiting patiently for him.

"My man Morgan just called me a wee while ago. Our nemesis, Wallace, is in Aberystwyth along with Huw Griffiths and he's discovered that our predecessors were actively involved in hunting down Prince Madoc." His excitement, as always, drew out the strong Glasgow accent, honed on the streets of Gorbals.

The man shifted in his own seat and peered at Belmont with a critical eye. "Interesting perhaps, but hardly worth insisting I drop everything and rush to hear that less than astounding news! And who, by the gods, is this Madoc anyway."

Sir Michael Donovan, one of London's successful financiers, rubbed a finger along his jaw as Belmont waved his hands in both excitement and irritation at the interruption.

"Aye. As a Scot I dinna ken either, until Badger explained. Madoc was a Welsh prince. Supposedly he sailed to America hundreds of years before Columbus and never came back. But here's the thing. Apparently, his voyage was funded by the Templar Knights in return for Madoc taking some secret item away from Europe and to the new world. Our predecessors were anxious to get their hands on whatever it was. It must be a significant item—perhaps the Ark of the Covenant, the Holy Grail or something like that—that's sacred to our enemies. If we can get hold of it before them, we could use it to destroy them."

"Again, interesting perhaps, but very vague. You still haven't explained why I had to rush here. I was in the middle of setting up a very complex deal with the Saudis. I've heard nothing that justifies my coming." He began to rise.

"Wait a wee moment Sir Michael. Let me continue." Without waiting for a response, Belmont plunged ahead. When he finished, a calmer Donovan nodded carefully. "So, you think that if we—meaning you—move quickly to find out what's going on and then seize this secret whatsit, you can undermine Evans as Dragon Master, leaving the field open for you. Is that basically it?"

Belmont nodded his head. "It's a chance to remove Evans. Badger had to report to him, but I pay him well to keep me informed as well. Plus, he hates Evans too. Evans though, won't move quickly. He's pedantic. He overthinks everything. We need action and we need it now. Find whatever it is and use it." His eyes lit up and he leaned forward conspiratorially towards the financier. "If I can finish Evans and his wishy-washy methods, and if I become Dragon Master there's no end to what we can do between us. You would have access to all kinds of power. A deal with the Saudis would be small pickings compared to what I could open up for you. As it stands, I already have the power to thwart or undermine any government moves against us. It's in our grasp, Sir Michael. Just a wee matter of eliminating Evans and his clan."

He leaned back, expectantly, waiting while the financier assimilated everything he'd been told.

"You may indeed be right, Gregory, but I fail to see how you want me involved. You didn't drag me to Chelsea just to hear an interesting story about the old days, Templars and ocean voyages."

"Verra true, Sir Michael. With my current position and responsibilities, I cannae be seen to be active in investigating all this. Frankly, I need financing. I want to put some loyal people in the field to work on this full time; our own people who will determine if there's any truth to this find."

A clock chimed on the mantle behind Donovan. Muted street noise outside was the only other sound permeating the room. Belmont suspected Donovan had the house wired for recordings; there were probably hidden video cameras covering every aspect of the building outside and in. It was what he would have done if the house was his. But it wasn't.

Donovan drummed his fingers against the arm of the chair, staring intently at Belmont. "If this is a false trail or goes bums up, you'll be the one destroyed, not Evans. And I will personally lead the charge against you." He paused, then stood up. "Very well. I'll underwrite your little research venture. But deliver results Belmont, or, Minister of the Crown or not, I will bring you down."

Belmont agreed quickly, seething inwardly at the threat but outwardly grinning. He too stood. Donovan began walking towards another room.

"See yourself out."

Broadcast House, London

Mello was delighted with Huw's news. He called Maggie Railston to join them and when she did, insisted that Huw repeat the latest discovery.

"Of course, look you, this is just preliminary. And it's just on the basis of one unauthenticated document. Stone and Mandy have a lot of work to do first, Mr. Mello."

"Good grief man, of course we understand that. But whether it's true or not, this is an unexpected twist in the saga that will bring the film alive. We'll be forging into new, unexplored territory with our friend Madoc."

Maggie Railston could barely keep still. "Awesome! Marsh, this might be one of the biggest discoveries in British history. And we'll have it on film." She wrung her hands in anticipation then grabbed her ever present notebook and pen and began jotting notes.

When he was finished Huw was exhausted by the excitement and barely subdued energy both Mello and Maggie exhibited. The two broadcasters fired volley after volley of ideas at each other as to how they would bring the story to life cinematically. Huw rapidly became a bystander in the discussion. Give me the quiet academic hall rather than this maelstrom of half-formed ideas being trumped by even more half-baked ideas, he told himself as he watched the frenzy of their creative process progress.

Finally, Mello calmed down and Maggie left for her own office to call Stone. As she left, Mello sternly reminded the director that none of this was to leak out around Broadcast House. "Nobody must know beyond us two, until we have everything in the can and ready for editing. Then we can look at a real PR launch with Huw, Mandy and Stone before we go to air."

When Marsh realized Huw intended to spend time in London doing research at the British Library, he stepped in. "I'll arrange a room for you at the Sheraton Park Lane. Nice place. Grand, old fashioned type hotel. Stay as long as you need." He waved off Huw's protestations as he walked the professor out to the building's lobby. At the entrance, he waved Huw off. On his way back, he saw an acquaintance step out of the lifts. He waved, and the smiling man stopped.

"How are you Marsh? You look even more harried than you were when you were producing that business documentary last year."

Marsh grinned. John Beauchamp, a prominent London businessman, had been one of his favorite interviews on an award-winning production. They'd taken a long serious look at the complex and fascinating economic history of London and its multifaceted financial trails back to the early medieval period. They reminisced about the program for a few moments. Beauchamp was just about to move on when Mello stopped him short.

"John, you remember we discussed the role of the Templar Knights as Medieval bankers on the show?" Beauchamp nodded. "I'm working on a new project now, and damn it all, don't the Templars show up again!"

Beauchamp looked thoughtfully at the BBC man. "Sound's interesting Marsh. You seem really excited about it. I'd love to hear more. Why don't we pop over to that coffee shop and you can fill me in. You know I'm fascinated with the Templars too."

March checked his watch. "Not all that much to tell, really, but I've got a few moments and a latte would go down well. Mind you, I must swear you to secrecy, I don't want anyone at Auntie Beeb to know anything about this for now. Don't tell anyone at Broadcast House. Or the competition networks," he smiled. With Beauchamp's agreement, they walked over to the café and ordered.

Fifteen minutes later, Marsh left the Pret a Manger, waved a cheery goodbye and headed back into Broadcast House. Beauchamp remained where he was for a few moments while Marsh disappeared, then took out his mobile phone.

Speaking quietly so the other café patrons could not overhear, he spoke rapidly to the person on the other end.

"Set up a meeting for this evening. We have a situation." His thumb hit the cancel button and he stalked out of the restaurant, signaling for a cab.

Aberystwyth, Wales

Stone was upset.

"Somebody broke in. My notes are gone. I left them right on the desk here. No way the cleaner would have put them out in the rubbish," he added, in response to Mandy's first suggestion.

She examined the door itself. "There's no sign of a break in. It's certainly doesn't seem like someone tried to force it. Don't forget, the porter said we were the only ones with keys to this office, other than those at the front desk. And, the night porter would have had to hand it to someone, which he swears he didn't."

Stone nodded but added stubbornly, "I know all that. But the notes are gone. I left them right here. There must be a lock picking expert at the College who let himself in when we were gone and took them." He saw her about to ask another question but blurted "and no, I did not take them to Borth. I tell you, I left them on this desk. Nowhere else."

"But who here would be a burglar with that kind of expertise? Mandy was slowly giving in to Stone's adamancy. "Assuming you're right, it would have to be someone who knew about Nathan's find and grasped the importance of your notes. Otherwise, why not steal my laptop, which by the way, I realize I shouldn't have left in the office. I was just so flustered and we were in such a rush to leave and study the book."

Stone plopped on his chair, baffled. Not that he was overly worried about their loss from a research point of view, he acknowledged, since Mandy took equally good notes and still had them. But they were *his* notes; notes he needed for when he began scripting and it troubled him that they were gone.

"It was just the three of us, Stone. Did you tuck them into Padraig's book, or stuff them in a jacket pocket or something? Maybe they're back at your flat."

Stone shook his head no. He'd already checked everything in his flat, including his clothes, in his panic when he discovered they were missing. A sinking feeling settled in his stomach. He tried to ignore it; tried to wish it away. He didn't want to go down that path, but it kept returning to his thoughts.

"It was just the three of us, mainly. But don't forget the interruption by that Badger guy," Stone said, cautiously watching for Mandy's reaction. "He seemed pretty nosy. And I didn't quite buy his apology and remorse."

"You think he stole the notes then? We were all watching him, and you hustled him out pretty quickly. Besides how would he know to take only them and where, specifically, to find them in all the clutter?"

Stone agreed, acknowledging the soundness of her arguments, but kept pressing the idea that somehow the famously nasty professor "finding religion" as Stone put it, and abjectly apologizing was a huge anomaly given his character. "I think he saw or suspected something. And came back to find out what." But, Stone admitted, he had no idea how the man gained entry. "I know I locked the door behind us. I tried it twice to be sure."

Returning to his suspicions, he reminded Mandy that Nathan pinpointed Badger's connection with IMC, and its highly suspect reputation among students and staff.

He delicately broached the subject with Mandy. "It probably is all speculation—adding two plus two and coming up with nine—but in case there's a remote connection with the Druids, I want to know. I'm going to call Sir Giles and ask him to check on our Badger boy."

He saw tears glistening in the corners of her eyes. He began to try and comfort her and explain, but she waved it away. "I told you, if they are involved in this, I will deal with it. *We* will deal with it. I will not let them win. I know I said I wanted to do this project free of them, but if it's not to be, well then, so be it. They almost killed me, but they didn't. God saw me through then and he'll do so again."

He stood up and hugged her. "I thought this was all something you didn't want to talk or think about. That the memories of what they did to you, were somehow haunting you," he whispered to her as she laid her head on his shoulder.

There was a long silence. She sighed. "The reason I didn't want to talk to you about what happened is that I was ashamed. I let that worm Nigel blind me to everything. I was taken in by him and I almost lost you." She pushed away from him, looking deeply at him. "I thought you'd never want to talk to me again; never want anything to do with me. Then, at Greyfell and even here, I realized that the only one doing the pushing away and re-fusing to talk, was me.

"*Cariad*, you are the most important person in my life, other than Da. You two and my faith mean everything to me. I could not stand to lose you. So, Druids or not, I will stand with you and fight them to the core. They are evil, power-mad terrorists. Nothing more. Nothing less."

They stood clinging to each other for several minutes. Stone repeatedly told her she had nothing to be ashamed of and that, further, she had become a vital part of his life. After all, he pointed out, he had chosen her over his career and returning Stateside.

For a short while, Druids, notes, Padraig and Madoc were forgotten.

A knock at the door broke them apart. The porter handed Stone an envelope simply addressed to Stone Wallace. The man explained it had been left on the porter's counter downstairs with no indication as to who left it. Thinking it might be important, he'd brought it up personally. Thanking him, Stone closed the door turning the envelope over and over in his hand, looking for some clue as to who sent it. Finally, he ripped it open and pulled out a single piece of paper with the words "*ni fyddwn yn anghofio*". Puzzled, he handed it to Mandy, who gasped.

"We will not forget," she read. Grimly she handed it back to him. "That confirms it. They're tracking us." She stiffened and pulled her phone out.

"You call Sir Giles. You know him better. I'll call Lord Greyfell. We need all the input and protection we can get."

As they made their respective calls, down on the ground floor Richard Evans walked out of the Old College. He'd surreptitiously dropped the envelope on the porter's counter. Evans acknowledged the porter with a clipped 'good morning' then stopped to read the bulletin board. He watched as the porter called to his partner, asked him to mind the desk, then proceed up the stairs towards Stone and Mandy's office.

Evans nodded to a few students he knew by sight rather than name. As he strolled out the main doors he smiled. There were times when brute force was not needed. The note was the first blow in what he perceived as a psychological war against them. Mind games, he thought. I'll play mind games with them and get them so distressed and confused, they'll make mistakes. And then I will pounce. In the meantime, he had plans to find out exactly what the medieval Druids wanted with Prince Madoc and what secrets he'd carried to America.

Ever since Badger had mentioned Wallace's presence at the university, he'd had Wallace watched and followed day and night.

The first blow would be struck that night.

Chapter
Seventeen

Crown Security offices, London

Sir Giles, for the first time in his life, was utterly speechless.

He stared at the man in front of him. Freddy Garret was equally stunned, gaping with his mouth open. The normal hustle, bustle and noise of the office died away as the rest of the staff gazed at the scene in front of them.

"But we were told...." Sir Giles struggled with the words.

".... that I was dead. I know, Sir Giles, but it was a necessary subterfuge."

Sir Giles mumbled something incomprehensible, then stuck out his hand. "Well. Good news then, isn't it?" He shook Chad's hand vigorously.

"Sir Giles is not one for show and emotions, Chad, but yes this is very good news," he said as he too shook Chad's hand enthusiastically. The guvnor harrumphed and guided them into his office with a quick "back to work" over his shoulder to the staring staff.

Inside, Chad accepted their congratulations on his new persona with beard, glasses and realistically greyed hair. "Had me quite fooled," Sir Giles said as he gestured Chad to a seat.

Both listened eagerly as Chad explained how and why he'd come to London. When he finished, Sir Giles brought him up to date including the attack on Stone and the fact that he was working on a TV documentary, only to bump up against the Druids again. "Heating up, all over. Freddy and a friendly DCI linked murder victim in Southend to Druids. Probably the one who attacked Stone. New Minister of Policing is a Druid too. Dangerous man at that level."

Freddy chimed in with his own disturbing news. "Stone rang us this morning. Seems he's got suspicions about a possible Druid connection to a professor Morgan at the university. Wants us to check him out, so I've got our team working on it."

Chad was explaining his need for information and potential leads when the phone on the guvnor's desk rang. Irritated, Sir Giles answered, listened carefully, jotted down a quick note then thanked the caller and hung up with a blistering "bloody hell!"

He turned to them both. "Lord Greyfell. Finally found out who the new Dragon Master is." He picked up the note he'd written. "Dr. Richard Evans. Dean at Iolo Morganwyg College. Part of the University of Wales in Aberystwyth." He stared at them unblinking. "Stone and Mandy. Middle of the hornet's nest and don't know it."

He fired rapid orders at Freddy to head to Aberystwyth immediately. "Take Chad. Meantime, we'll dig out whatever information you need, Chad." He told Freddy he would assemble a team to join them at the university. By the time they'd finished examining all the information and potential strategies, they were left with two primary goals, Sir Giles said: "Protect Stone, Huw and Mandy. Disrupt whatever plans the Druids have."

The discussion continued while one of the staff hastily booked seats on the next train from Euston Station.

When Chad and Freddy finally left his office, Sir Giles mused for a moment or two, then called DCI Carswell, asking to meet him at the Shakespeare pub across from Victoria railway station, as early in the afternoon as possible. A second call went to Lord Greyfell, seeking information on a Professor Dafydd Morgan and Iolo Morganwyg College as well as Evans.

Now he had a name for the Dragon Master, he also called some of his associates at MI5. He was circumspect about his queries, but confident his old contacts would slip him whatever they had while strictly disavowing any cooperation with him. After all, not even Belmont could prevent old comrades from meeting and chatting and sharing a drink or two.

Before he could make another call, his phone rang. Sir Giles listened then smiled. The news made his meeting with Carswell potentially easier. Despite Belmont's efforts, the PM's office confirmed increased funding for Crown Security in the Royal Household budget was approved.

He picked up his coat and umbrella and left the building. He didn't take any chances. It was entirely possible that Belmont would have his offices under surveillance—likely with his own Druid lackeys. No matter. Sir Giles Broadbent was a master at detecting tails and, more importantly, losing them. Within minutes he'd picked up two and chuckled as he stopped to tie his shoelace, eyes on the shop window in front of him that gave him an excellent reflection of one of the tails. The man was lounging against a lamp post smoking a ciga-rette. He gave away his colleague with a quick glance to his right. The woman was ostensibly window shopping but shared a quick glance with the man.

So, you don't know whether to follow me or not, he thought, as he straightened the coat on his arm and ambled slowly down the road. They were to watch the office, but had no orders about what to do if the guvnor left. Interesting. As he disappeared around the corner, he sped up, his long legs eating up the pavement. Halfway along, he stopped again to straighten his tie in a shop window. Neither followed yet, but they might just be getting quick instructions and could come around the corner any moment. No time to dawdle.

It was only a short four-minute walk to Victoria Station and the pub, but he flagged down a cab going in the opposite direction and hopped in. As they passed Buckingham Palace, they swung around the Victoria Monu-ment down The Mall and entered the ever hectic traffic nightmare that was Trafalgar Square. The cab dropped him on The Strand opposite Charing Cross Station. He crossed over, dodging buses and vans, flagged down an-other cab and was driven to Victoria. There he wandered through the noisy station concourse and went down into the crowded Tube station before emerging onto Buckingham Palace Road.

A minute later he was at the pub. He selected a quiet table, facing the door, and waited.

The Pentagon, Washington

"I'm intrigued Mr. Coughlin. You send me an enigmatic message demanding to see me, drop Bethan Price's name and hint at information that will help me. Help me in what, I wondered?" Wells stared coldly at the man sitting across the coffee table from him. He was in full uniform and gestured for Coughlin to sit down.

Coughlin refused, preferring to stand, realizing it allowed him to tower over the much shorter martinet in front of him.

"We are alone and, I assure you, my office is not bugged. I am not re-cording anything."

Wells waited. Finally, feeling uncomfortable at the height difference be-tween the two he sat in his office chair, leaned back and folded his arms. He had to wrestle back control.

"I've had you checked. You've been a busy boy over the years, walking a tightrope between legal and illegal deals, robbing other countries blind in their oil and energy resources, bribing all kinds of politicians and judges in countries too numerous to mention, and coming close to, but not breaking, American laws. If I am not satisfied with today's meeting, I assure you I will pass along my information on you and your activities. I'm sure Homeland Security can find a way to put you inside for a long time. Drugs, perhaps? We know South America is a hotbed of the drug trade."

He paused and leaned forward on the desk. "Look, I know you provide security services for the Price oil interests and others. You're in tight with Mrs. Price, yet not…"

Coughlin, unintimidated, interrupted equally coldly. "Not a Druid. Isn't that what you wanted to say?" He flashed a finger out, pointing at Wells, pleased that he'd shocked the old warrior into silence. "Don't threaten me, Wells. I know who you are, and I know your connections with them and with Bethan. I'm interested in none of that. Simply put, live and let live in terms of religion and stuff like that, is my motto."

"Get to the point. Why are you here?" Wells barked, annoyed that this little turd had seized the initiative from him. And in his own office, too.

"It won't take long, General." He drew some papers from his suit inside pocket and put them on the desk in front of him. "Bethan tells me everything. She's devastated by Davey's murder. She told me you were also investigating since neither of you trust the police to do a competent job." He waited, but there was no response from Wells who merely stared with barely concealed hatred. No wonder they call you Old Stoneface, Coughlin said to himself.

He pointed to the papers. "She told me you scoured the entire Patuxent area looking for clues, looking for the place he was killed and hoping to find his killers from that angle. Well, General, you missed a vital consideration. I started at the other end. Where Davey was last seen alive. This is a copy of my report to her. She already has it. I think you'll find some interesting leads in there that will pinpoint a likely suspect."

He stood up. "I'll not waste any more of your time. I don't trust the police to do the job either. With this information, I think you'll clean it up. All I want is justice for Davey." He turned and headed for the door. "I'm sure your sergeant will see me out properly."

Wells seethed, flummoxed by the audacity and confidence of the man, yet intrigued by the papers in front of him. He was undecided whether to call for Coughlin's detention or read. As Coughlin boldly stormed out the door he made his decision, reached down and grabbed the papers.

Malcom Coughlin took a cab immediately to Reagan National Airport. With luck, he'd get a quick flight to New York, then an overnight to Panama City and a connecting flight to Georgetown, Guyana. This time tomorrow he should be home. And home he would stay for a long while, isolated and protected. He wanted nothing more to do with Bethan or the Druids.

Wells too, he wanted nothing to do with. The man sickened him; paying lip service to obedience and patriotism while at the same time working to undermine the nation he claimed to love. Treachery and betrayal disgusted him. He, Malcolm Coughlin, may not be the purest man in the world, but he for damned sure was not a traitor. His word was his bond. He'd promised Bethan he'd find Davey's killers. Coughlin now had no doubts that Armitage was the culprit and passed that information along to someone who could handle it. His obligation to Bethan was finished.

But Armitage was White House. Wells was military. Coughlin's sixth sense told him to get away from the United States as quickly and slickly as possible, and not come back for a very long time. He wouldn't even send Bethan the bill for his services in this matter. He did it for Davey not her. He owed Davey that much.

Still inside his Pentagon office, Wells digested Coughlin's report. It lined up with one small point his own people's report had mentioned but ignored as insignificant. A quick call to one of his team at Quantico confirmed that a large riverside house was indeed owned by the White House Chief of Staff. It was on a list they'd prepared of all properties fronting the river upstream from where the body was found.

A second call connected him with one of his Druid enforcers. He gave the man Coughlin's name and description. "Find out where he's staying in Washington. Eliminate him." He disconnected and flipped through the papers again.

"Now, Mr. Armitage, what are we going to do with you? And how?" He made some more calls to his enforcers and made plans to meet them in Poughkeepsie. Finally, he called Bethan Price and invited her to attend the Poughkeepsie meeting.

Wells settled back into his office chair to think. Taking care of Armitage would need to be done carefully. He was the President's Chief of Staff. If anything happened to Armitage, all hell would break loose. But it had to be done and in such a way that it couldn't be traced to him. At the same time, he had to satisfy the gods and punish Armitage so it sent a message to other Druids who might waver in obedience.

Rock Springs, Wyoming

Frustration did not begin to describe Wiz's feelings. He'd flown into Sweetwater Country airport physically tired but alert. After two overnights in Gander, Newfoundland and Duluth, Minnesota it had been a relatively easy flight to Rock Springs. But experience taught him to not rush into things quickly in case he missed some small but vital clue. Armed with his new identify and, at Chad's urging, a new look, he spent most of the first afternoon driving around the town, and getting a better feel for the location. Although it was late spring, they were in the mountains and it remained cold with snow still on the ground in some shadowed places.

The next day he wandered the area around the courthouse where Murphy was killed. He walked up the laneway where the shooter fired from, although all signs had been removed. His wool-lined jacket, jeans and boots helped him blend in as he strolled from the courthouse back to the downtown.

A stop in the library, gave him time to thoroughly scrutinize the local newspapers, online as well as hard print. Meticulously he combed them, looking for references to Murphy. He saw nothing prior to the day of the murder which, he admitted, was not surprising because nobody really knew Murphy had been moved to the remote holding quarters.

Once he got into the coverage of the murder itself he particularly focused on photographs taken by the locals and the names and statements of eyewitnesses. Nothing. The eyewitness reports were frazzled, innocuous and generic—much as any eyewitness to a shocking event would provide. The trick, he knew from experience, was to comb those onlookers' statements carefully, gleaning fragments that, together, would paint a bigger picture. The trouble is, he admitted, that only worked when investigators pulled together dozens of statements. A newspaper would not do that. If they got only two or three quotes from bystanders, they were happy. He sighed. Asking for investigators' statement notes was obviously out of the question.

He left the library. It was lunchtime, so he ambled up to the main street, and found a restaurant. Inside, he placed himself at a small table against the wall. Waiting for his order, he sipped the strong coffee served black, the way he liked it.

Idly, he saw a man enter, then take the table next to him. He noticed the man place two cameras on the seat beside him. As the man fussed with his cameras, he looked up at the approaching waitress said simply, "the usual" and turned back to reviewing some of his shots.

Wiz nodded hello and remarked on the cool weather. "Yeah, won't be surprised if we get snow before nightfall," the man said. As they waited for their food, Wiz nonchalantly noted the cameras and found himself chatting with a very talkative reporter-cameraman for the local paper, who introduced himself as Danny Tremont. Wiz let him talk, asking questions about his job and commenting on some of the shots the reporter had just taken of a store opening. Wiz casually asked Tremont about the biggest stories he'd covered.

"That's easy. You probably heard about the murder we had recently, the one where Liam Murphy the presidential candidate was killed." Wiz showed the expected awe and asked the reporter to tell him more.

By the time their food arrived, Tremont had moved across to Wiz's table and was deep in a recital of all he'd seen and done that day. "No question about it, the biggest news story to hit this town in decades. But all of us, police, media, even the mayor and his people, were just shut down by the feds. They treated us like something they'd scrape off their shoes. Thought we were dumb mountain boys, I guess. I'm talking FBI, Homeland Security, probably even the CIA and other agencies I don't even know about. Even the state troopers were pushed aside. Same attitude from the big media guys, CNN, Fox, CBS and the like. Not right. Absolutely not right," he muttered, still spewing his resentment.

As they ate, Wiz probed carefully, particularly when the reporter complained on behalf of a trooper friend of his. "He told the Feds he'd found a guy who saw somebody with a rifle getting out of a car at the rail yards and then being picked up by another vehicle. But did they pay attention? No. They just thanked him like he was a little puppy or something, and then ignored him. Didn't even ask for the witness' name."

Wiz perked up. He had to move slowly and carefully. Sympathetic, he quietly suggested "surely this guy must have been questioned. I mean, he works at the yards right? You said the car was abandoned there."

Tremont shook his head. "That's just it. This guy, Clint Ronson, was born around here. Joined the army and was sent to Afghanistan. Came back with PTSD and never the same afterwards. The minute my cop friend told the Feds he was a drifter who hung around the rail yard, well they just dismissed it. But Clint went to the same high school I did. He's a sharp guy. The war changed him, but if he said he saw something, he did. PTSD or not."

"Hey," said Wiz, smiling and snapping his fingers. "if you could find him and interview him, you just might have a big story to your credit."

"Yeah. Thought of that myself and kinda looked around for Clint, but couldn't find him." He stood up, signaled the waitress and put a ten dollar bill on the table. "Anyway, gotta run buddy. Get these shots back to the newsroom. Good to talk to you." He swung his cameras onto his shoulders and left.

Wiz waited, finishing his meal then headed back to the library. On the way, he drove by the small railroad yard, looking carefully for a man who fit Ronson's description.

He saw nobody. Inside the library he asked for high school yearbooks. The librarian looked suspiciously at him, but he smiled and explained he was doing a magazine article on small town education. It was a faint hope but one that was rewarded. After looking through several years' worth of high school yearbooks, he finally found one with Ronson's grad photo. He took out his phone and quickly took a photo. Then he searched the local data banks for an address or phone number for Ronson's family.

Back at his hotel he scanned the shot onto his laptop and did another internet search, this time based on the local high school. "Bingo!" Wiz smiled and jotted down the name of a man the yearbook had called Ronson's best friend in high school. Ten minutes later he had an address and phone number for the man. He thought it likely the friend would react better to a personal meeting with a stranger rather than speaking on the phone, Wiz jumped in his car and drove twenty miles southwest to the little town of Green River.

As he drove off the interstate and into the town, he noticed a large, railroad yard to his left. Cruising slowly over the bridge, he changed his mind on a whim and, instead of heading for the high school buddy's address, started slowly driving along the roads that paralleled the tracks.

It was getting colder. Wiz looked towards the west across the barren sage brush horizon and saw snow clouds in the distance. He bounced down a rough road between the yards and the river beside him, peering intently in and around the yard.

An hour later, with winds rising and light fading, he saw a quick movement out of the corner of his eye. He made a mental note of the two graffiti-clad box cars where he saw the motion, but continued driving and bouncing at the same pace. When he thought he was safely away from the site, Wiz pulled his vehicle to the side and walked carefully and quietly back. As he approached the box cars he saw a man huddled against the wheels of one, covered in a thin blanket and shivering.

As he approached, the man looked warily at him. Wiz took both hands out of his pockets to show he was not armed. He squinted in the cold, whistling winds but was sure he'd found his man.

"Clint Ronson."

"Who's asking?"

"A friend." Wiz squatted beside the man. Despite his unkempt appearance and threadbare blanket, he could see that Ronson's eyes were clear and sharp. Whatever the man's problems, they didn't include alcohol or drugs. He took off his gloves and offered them to the man. Ronson did not move.

"I asked you a question."

"Yes you did," Wiz replied quietly and thoughtfully. "So, let me answer. My name is Oscar Zanellli though you may not want to remember that name if government agents ever ask. I believe you might be able to help me."

The man sniffed. This was not going to be easy, Wiz realized, but was exactly what he'd anticipated. Wiz slowly and patiently probed. The answers were hesitant at first, then more forthcoming until Wiz had learned all he could about the day of the killing. It was enough. Ronson's military experience raced to the fore after he realized that Wiz was no threat to him and only wanted precise intel crisply delivered. As he talked, Ronson admitted he was scared. "I don't know if the guy saw me, but I saw him. If he did see me, I want to disappear for a while. You don't want to mess with anyone carrying one of them M39 marksman rifles."

Light snow was falling and beginning to accumulate. Before he left, Wiz gave Ronson his heavy wool jacket and a thousand dollars in cash to keep him warm and help him disappear. Ronson refused a drive, "I prefer to be in the open" he confessed. Wiz nodded understanding and shook the man's hand, wishing him luck.

As quietly as he arrived, he left, cautiously scanning in case, on the off chance, he'd been followed. In his car, he shivered in his shirtsleeves until the blasting heater came to a reasonable temperature. The drive back to his hotel was hairy but worth it.

In his room, mentally replayed his interview, jotting down everything the man had told him. He'd trained his precise and ordered mind to remember the tiniest details and it served him well. When he finished, he knew he'd fallen on a major lead. The killer, according to Ronson, not only carried a sniper's weapon but was "definitely military; the way he walked, held himself, handled the weapon, everything screamed military. I even saw a guy that looked remarkably like him at the base in Kandahar once. Could've been his twin."

The most telling was Ronson's casual comment that a black Suburban pulled into the yard and the killer began to approach it, a door opened. "It's funny, but the guy sitting in the back seat looked familiar; kinda like the guy you always see standing next to the President on TV."

It confirmed their suspicions The President's Chief of Staff, Dexter Armitage, was involved in the assassination and, therefore, possibly even the President himself. None of Ronson's information could be used in court, he realized, unless Ronson was willing to testify—assuming they could find him again.

But it was the first break in this convoluted case. Next stop, was back east and a long talk with Tyler.

Chapter Eighteen

Borth, Wales

It was the wildest, scariest, fastest car ride Stone had ever been on.

Nathan drove like a fiend; Stone couldn't be totally sure, but was almost certain they'd sheared more than a few wandering sheep as they tore along the winding road, racing past pastoral farms and through narrow heavily wooded sections. Hedgerows whipped by. As they ripped through the village of Clarach, he was convinced they'd gone into warp speed, the houses went by so fast. One thing was certain; if they met an oncoming vehicle, there was no passing room, and that meant they'd finish themselves off and save the Druids the trouble.

The race to Borth began earlier that morning when Nathan suddenly pounded through the office door breathlessly shouting that ET's house had been burgled. As they drove, he told them Dilys telephoned. She and the baby were fine, but the house was ransacked.

They pulled up at the house in record time. Two constables from the Dyfed-Powys police were talking to Dilys as they approached. She waved to them and sent them into the glass conservatory where ET was sitting. He looked up as they entered and shook his head 'no' as Stone opened his mouth to speak.

He bellowed loud enough for the officers to hear. "Good to see you all. Thanks for rushing over. As I told the Old Bill, it was a bit of a rum do. Arrived back at the house around two this morning after a party down at a friend's house. Came inside and found the place turned upside down. Fortunately, both Dilys and Samantha were at Dilys' mother's place for the night." He held up his bandaged arm in a sling and pointed to a massive bandage on the left side of his head. "Foolishly went inside and found two of the buggers still in the house. One of them clobbered me on the head and I must have smashed me arm against the table, on the way down." He smiled at them, though it seemed more of a wince, willing them to silence even though he knew they were bursting with questions and worry.

A policeman stepped up to the conservatory door. "We're going now, ET. Nothing more we can do for now. Dilys says she'll look after you, if you're sure you don't want a doctor." At ET's nod he moved off, shouting over his shoulder as he left, "Bloody stupid thing, going inside like that *bach*. Should have just backed off and called us."

ET chuckled. "At that time of night Thomas, *bach?* By the time you woke up, dressed and got here, I'd have been murdered, and the whole neighborhood ransacked!" The policemen both hooted and ET eyed them until they'd driven down the road. He crumpled back in the chair. Dilys rushed over, gave him a gentle kiss on the right cheek, then moved into the house. As she did, ET asked for help to get up.

A scene of utter carnage and devastation greeted them. Books and papers littered the floor along with overturned tables, broken vases and other detritus. He took them into the main living room. "Before the police arrived, I did a careful check to see if the intruders left behind any listening devices. Even unhooked the phone. I don't think they were here long enough and, besides, they didn't seem to be the most sophisticated robbers. Look at the mess around you." ET saw the look on their faces. "Before you ask, they were obviously looking for something important." He grinned. "But they didn't get it!"

A collective sigh of relief filled the room and Stone, Mandy and Nathan visibly relaxed as the tension left their bodies.

ET's grin left as quickly as it arrived. "But I did make a translation copy which seems to have disappeared. Help me look for it." He described the folder and Stone, Mandy and Nathan began sifting through the debris, straightening furniture, picking up broken glass, putting books back on shelves and searching for the elusive blue folder.

As they worked, ET softly explained he'd worried about keeping Padraig's book in the house, particularly knowing the Druid's ruthlessness and desire for revenge. He sent Dilys and the baby to her mother's for the time being. Then, when they were gone, he furtively put the book in a plastic Tesco shopping bag. "I wasn't sure if the place was watched, but I took no chances," then casually walked the book down into the village and a friend's house.

"Emlyn's like me, runs a small holiday place. He has a large safe in his place and agreed to keep the book in it." Relaxing, they'd shared a few pints, "well maybe more than a few," ET said sheepishly, before returning home and discovering two men ransacking the house.

"I was furious, look you. Went in there swinging away. In complete black outfits they were. Head to toe. Couldn't see much, but I caught one of them with a good punch in the face before I got thumped on the head. When I came too, they were gone. I did a quick look for the file then called the local bobbies."

None of them spoke any more as they waded through the mess. Finally, with the living room and study back in order, they admitted defeat. No doubt about it, the folder was gone.

ET rested in a comfortable armchair as Dilys fussed around him. "Mam is looking after the baby," she explained, "so I can take care of this great lummox." Stone watched the pair of them, cautious for any sense of anger or resentment that asking them to look after the book had caused this kind of pain and suffering. He told them that he and the BBC would pay for any damage to the property, as well as install security systems on the house, only to be waved off by ET and Dilys both.

"Stuff and nonsense. Only a few broken glass vases and some picture frames and one broken leg on the side table. And that was caused by me dropping on it. Nothing to pay for at all, boyo. Besides, you're already paying us good money for looking after the book."

He winced slightly as he waved his injured arm around. "Anyway, it all makes a big change from the bed and breakfast routine. Takes me back to my rugby days," he laughed, grabbing a biscuit with his good hand and munching down.

Mandy cautiously asked if the book was still safe. With a nod, ET pulled out his mobile phone. Seconds later he was speaking to Emlyn. Without mentioning the break in, he had a quick chat, thanked him again and hung up. "All's well. You can leave the book there if you want, and it'll be safe."

He reached into one of his pants pockets and pulled out a flash drive. "This has the full translation on it. I'd printed off a copy, but that's what those Neanderthals grabbed. You'll have to print off your own now." He picked up another biscuit and chewed away.

"One thing's for sure." He wiped some crumbs away from his lips. "You absolutely have to go to Lundy like I suggested before. It's getting more and more mysterious. Madoc put a small box into a grave. Well, Padraig used some interesting phrases describing that event. Not sure if he was referring to the man who was buried, or Prince Madoc himself."

Stone leaned forward. "Like what?"

"Well, at one point I saw the word *pocillator* and in another, the phrase *qui custodiet ipsos*, closely followed by *sanctum*." Stone could see the old scholar emerging from the B and B operator. It reminded him strongly of Huw as he expounded on some point. "You must realize, this book has been around since the late twelfth century. It's remarkable that we have it at all, let alone in reasonably good shape. But the truth is, there are parts that are hard to decipher. At some points it's illegible. That might be due to the poor quality of ink or paper perhaps, but other times it seems some of the pages got damaged and stained. Anyway, I couldn't make sense of what Padraig was saying in this portion—I suspect a page or two may be missing—but those phrases jumped out at me."

"What do they mean?"

ET looked serious as he scanned each of their faces. "Are you ready for this?"

He took a deep breath. "*Pocillator* means cup bearer. Sometimes it can be translated as butler. The phrase *qui custodiet ipsos*, on the other hand, is a question that simply asks 'who guards' while *sanctum* means holy, or sacred."

The room was hushed as Stone and Mandy sat in stunned silence. Stone brushed his hands through his hair. "So you're saying…"

"I'm not saying anything," ET interrupted gruffly. "I'm telling you what it says in what I'm calling The Chronicles of Madoc. What those phrases mean or how you interpret them…" he let the thought die away, then shrugged. "But it's clear, your next stop is Lundy. It might be there's more to this Templar business and Madoc's secret than we may have realized."

"Holy Mackinaw." Stone, finally breathed. "This is incredible."

Llanidloes, Wales

Mavis showed Badger into the study then withdrew. Smiling, Badger stepped forward, one eye almost swollen shut, and handed Evans a blue file folder.

"What's this? I told you I wanted that book."

Badger shrugged. "We searched but couldn't find it. We did get this. It's an English translation. I went through it quickly on the way here, and it makes very interesting reading."

"Fool! Idiot!" Evans shouted, adding numerous curses and oaths at the bewildered professor. "That means the book is still in Wallace's possession. You told me you followed him to Borth and assumed he gave it to that former professor. All you've done is bring a translation. But we don't have the book itself," he screamed, throwing papers and books at Badger.

"We have nothing. He has everything. Can you get that through your dim brain?" He stormed around the room, shouting and pounding the walls. "We should sacrifice you for incompetence," he frothed.

Badger quaked but held his ground. "It's more than that Dragon Master. It tells us what we're looking for and gives us a hint where to look."

Evans glared at him. Quickly, Badger found the pertinent pages and showed Evans the passages pointing towards Lundy Island and the possibility Madoc's secret might be in a grave. Evans forced himself to calm down. He thought for a long moment. It might yet work, in fact it just might be better than he'd hoped for. He opened the study door and called out. Moments later, Ioan Parry's tall, bald frame loomed in the doorway.

Evans stared at Badger, noticing for the first time the man's large red welts and blackened eye. So, you got hurt in the burglary, he thought. Good. He spoke coldly. "You have one last chance to redeem yourself. Ioan is going back to the Uni with you. You will do one of two things. Put Stone Wallace under surveillance no matter where he goes and keep me informed as to who he sees, where he goes and what he does and, most importantly, by whatever means get your hands on that book." He glared at Badger, forcing him to maintain eye contact and increasing the man's stress level.

"Or, if you fail, your second choice is kill yourself quickly and simply before I do the job for you. And if I do it, it will be a very painful, extended death. That black eye you got last night will be nothing compared to what I will do."

"But my research projects…my classes…"

"No problem there, boyo. You are terminated from the College effectively immediately. A letter will be delivered to your flat and a redundancy payment made, but I want you out of the College before this day is over. Parry will go with you and make sure that is done. He will also help you to follow Wallace and retrieve the book."

A seething Badger began to argue with Evans to no avail, then to beg for his job. Evans pointed him to repeated negative reviews from staff and students. "You've been on thin ground for a while, Badger. Your usefulness as a college professor is done. I only kept you around put of pity. I also thought you might be useful to the movement. You still are for now, but I warn you, it's hanging by a thread. Get the book and bring it to me. Then we'll see what happens."

He turned away, dismissing him with a desultory wave. Parry stepped forward and ushered the flushed and angry man away. As he did, Parry looked back and saw Evans make a slashing gesture across his throat. Nodding, Parry got the message, Badger had a few days at most to get the book. No more.

Evans forced himself to remain calm. He took deep breaths; I must regain control and focus, he scolded himself. Things were spinning out of control.

First, Parry had returned and reported the almost complete breakdown within the American movement. Evans was frantic to know the current status but had never developed contacts there outside Bethan herself. He had a vague idea that an American general of some kind was Serpent Master but didn't know who. Moreover, Parry indicated the finger for young Price's murder was pointing directly at someone not only close to the President, but a Druid. Gods what a mess!

He wondered too, what kind of demonstration was Bethan planning? She never provided details, promising only that she'd let him know once it was finalized. In all, America was a massive chaotic maelstrom.

His own planning was shunted aside, the last few days, with the reports from America and Badger. All week, he'd concentrated on his own demonstration of power. He had to return to it now, in order to calm down.

He scrupulously avoided drawing one major player in. Apart from his hatred, Evans' major concern was that the man's palpable ambition might either sabotage everything or, if it was successful, he might claim credit for it amongst the Druids. Gregory Belmont would not find out anything until it was too late. Since his elevation to Dragon Master, Belmont's name kept popping up as the one who opposed him. Very well, Evans thought, then I will extinguish him.

He picked up his notes. His meticulous, methodical writing laid it all out. On the day in question, the Prince of Wales would be at St. David's Cathedral. There he would participate in a service of commemoration of Welsh writers and poets. It was a recreation of the famed Poet's Corner at Westminster Abbey, except this would be exclusively for Welsh artists and writers. It was the perfect place and opportunity to make a vividly magnificent demonstration that the church would be destroyed and that the old religion would ascend.

'Prince of Wales', he scoffed; heredity, a title, one term at the Old College learning Welsh, and a house in Carmarthenshire for occasional use, did not in any way make him a 'Prince' of Wales or anywhere else for that matter.

The plan was excellent. However, it required careful preparation, running the gamut from purchasing equipment and material to selecting the right candidates to participate in this momentous action.

Then there was this complicating business of Madoc.

He drummed his pen against the desktop. He wanted to ignore it and focus on the attack. But he was intrigued by the Madoc material. He flipped through the translation Badger brought and ran his fingers slowly along the portions regarding Lundy. He ignored the lunch Mavis brought him. Carefully and methodically he examined it, pondering the phrases referring to cup bearer and guard. Obviously, his predecessors knew something and wanted whatever the Templars gave to Madoc for safekeeping and transportation. Therefore, it had value.

It was, he admitted, absorbing. Maybe after all, it was a mission worth pursuing. It would divide his personnel and resources, but if this secret was a sacred thing the Christians thought worth protecting, then getting his hands on it would be a masterstroke.

One thing he knew though. More than ever he needed Parry's muscle and intelligence for both projects.

No weekend retreat, as planned, for the Dragon Master, he told himself. It's back to Aber and start putting things in motion.

Poughkeepsie, New York

Wells was shocked at the change in Bethan Price.

Any time he'd interacted with her before, she was cool, calm, collected and presented herself impeccably. This time she was flushed and angry-looking. Her clothing was slightly more disheveled rather than her normal pristine, glamor look. When she spoke, it was with a clipped, icy fury, even merely asking for a brandy. As it was, she'd spoken barely a word to him since she arrived, demanding only that he brief all of them at once rather than accept an individual briefing. She sat on the edge of the sofa, waiting as Well's operatives gathered.

Wells stood before them, making eye contact with each. Although in civilian clothes, there was no mistaking his military bearing and command presence. Bethan didn't even seem to notice the others, merely nodding to Wells, giving him silent permission to proceed.

Systematically, he went over his meticulously gathered report, detailing times and locations. He linked Price's activities in Washington and the steps leading up to his kidnapping. He detailed the connection of Dex Armitage's personal staff to Price's hotel on the day he disappeared. Wells then followed a carefully confirmed trail of Armitage's disappearances from official Washington on critical days, and subsequent Armitage sightings in and around Hughsville, Maryland later those same days.

Wells felt Bethan's eyes laser focused on him as he pointed out that Armitage owned a house fronting on the banks of the Patuxent River near Hughsville, and that the property in question was only a few miles from where the body was found.

Then he dropped the bombshell.

One of the team—he nodded at a stocky, bearded man sitting in the background—penetrated the unoccupied property two nights ago. Inside, he discovered a large underground chamber that had been used recently. He found stains on the cement floor that were compatible with dried blood. Wells glanced up at Bethan. Her face was immobile; her obsidian eyes dark and brooding. He was proud of the way he'd laid out the case against Armitage as he built up the mountain of circumstantial evidence.

"Raven Master, there can be no doubt. Dex Armitage was responsible for your son's kidnapping and murder."

The was a long, icy silence. She held herself rigid and did not stir. They waited. Finally, she tilted her head up to him. In a frigid voice she asked him to dismiss the others in the room. When they were gone, she stood up and placed herself directly in front of him, staring down at his face. She spoke quietly but forcefully. "I told you I would see the guilty ones destroyed, General Wells. I want Armitage and his accomplices taken."

She spat out her words, eyes unblinking as they penetrated his gaze. "Not harmed—much—but taken. I want them all held in that underground room where Davey died. However you do it, take over that house. Make sure nobody can trace him or link you or your men to his disappearance. And do nothing more until I am there."

He returned her gaze just as steadily. "As you wish, Raven Master. Ta muid anseo—the Master has spoken."

As he turned away she reached out and stopped him. "I told you that I will destroy anyone who stands in my way or who had a part in Davey's death. That includes you Wells. Don't think it doesn't." With that, she spun on her heels and left the room, calling for a driver to return her to New York City.

Wells glared at her in anger and frustration. She'd denigrated him by refusing to use either of his titles and treated him like a recalcitrant schoolboy. In her last words, Bethan Price had declared war on him. So be it, he thought. He was not intimidated. He'd faced enemies more vicious and cruel in Iraq and Afghanistan. She would get her war. She would lose.

The more he thought about it, the more he considered the gods were working in his favor to become the new Raven Master. Taking out the woman would be easy. And Armitage? Well, that was a foregone conclusion.

He poured a whiskey. Full glass in hand, he saluted himself, congratulating himself for his astute handling of the situation. The only fly in the ointment, he conceded, was that the insufferably arrogant Coughlin had escaped his grasp. Wells nursed his drink. If Coughlin ever showed his face in the United States again, he would suffer the same fate as Armitage, he promised.

He took another sip before calling the others back into the room and issuing orders.

Chapter Nineteen

Old College, Aberystwyth

Stone's mind was whirling like a dervish; one shock after another buffeting him. From the high of finding Padraig's book, to the lows of the break-in at Borth and the gut-wrenching discovery that the Druids were still seeking revenge.

Now this.

His mouth gaped as he stormed into the tiny office, closely followed by one of the porters, Mandy and Nathan. As they'd approached the office they'd heard noises inside. Fearing another break-in, Stone had whispered to the others to wait in the hall while he got help. He'd rushed downstairs and grabbed a cricket bat from the porter's cubicle. He swung the door open and charged in, bat at the ready.

He stopped cold and stared at the man sitting in Mandy's chair, facing the door. As he slowly lowered the bat, he heard quiet laughing from behind the door. He spun and saw Freddy Garrett nodding his head. "Yes, it's him. It really is him."

Mandy and Nathan pushed into the now crowded office. The porter, relieved there was no danger, retrieved the bat and left shaking his head, closing the door as he did.

"Chad? You're…. you're alive? What? How?" Stone blurted out the questions as he tried to wrap his head around the grey-haired, bearded, bespectacled apparition in front of him. Mandy just gasped. Nathan looked frantically from one to the other, trying to make sense of what was happening.

There was a sudden clamor of talking, with everyone speaking at the same time. As the explanations poured out, one on top of the other, tears and laughter were intermingled with expressions of concern, fear and puzzlement. By the time it was all sorted out and the emotions exhausted,

Nathan had been introduced to both Freddy and Chad. "Say anything you want in front of Nathan. He's one of the team now. He knows all about the Druids and their attempts against us."

In the excitement of seeing his friend alive and well, Stone momentarily forgot about the manuscript. Instead, both Stone and Mandy listened intently, intrigued by the story of Chad's firing, escape and faked death. "So the President is behind all this?"

Chad shook his head. "Neither Wiz or I are convinced we have the full picture. Frankly, we suspect that we're being used. We're not sure of his motivations but right now he's using us to do his dirty work. If we succeed, he looks good. If we fail, we're the scapegoats." He shrugged his shoulders. "Sorry to be so cynical, but frankly we're suspicious of anyone and everyone right now. I'm simply over here to get as much information as I can from Crown Security and anyone else, in the hopes that it might give us some threads to follow, however thin."

Silence enveloped the room momentarily, then Stone told them he had some intriguing news. He was about to launch into his news when Freddy interrupted.

"Stone. Not right now, please. This is vital. We've got to get you and Mandy away from this place immediately. That's why we're here. The new Dragon Master is the head of one of this university's affiliated college. He's literally right on your doorstep."

Stone grinned. "A man named Evans, perhaps? Figured it might be him. And yes, we know about his cronies in the area as well. One of them in particular, by the name of Morgan but known around here as Badger, or Dai Badger."

Stone filled them on the latest turns in the saga, including their mad dash to Borth earlier that day. Even as Stone spoke, Freddy urged them to pack their files and books. Nathan joined in, examining every item and placing it in an appropriate box. When everything was finished, Stone looked around the cramped office and marveled at how much larger and cleaner it seemed now. "Where are we going?"

"Our thought was to get you back to Greyfell and operate from there."

"But we have responsibilities to the BBC and we still need to finish examining and trying to interpret the Madoc Chronicles."

"And we have to go to Lundy Island," Mandy added.

"Whatever for? a puzzled Freddy looked from one to the other.

"Madoc buried something in a grave on that island. We need to find out if it still exists and, if so, what impact it will have on this documentary. We know the Druids are after it too. They were in the late 1100's and they are now. They've already stolen my notes and broken in to our friend's house trying to get the book. They did get a printed translation or it, so we've got to get to Lundy ahead of them."

Mandy snapped her fingers. "Why not stay with ET? He runs a B and B We could rent the place and you," she turned to Freddy, "could arrange for onsite protection. We'd be away from Aber but still able to examine the book and do our Lundy trip as well."

Before anyone could say anything, Nathan added "and you could tell the Uni your project was complete. Tell them you no longer needed me which will explain my reappearance at the National Library. Then I can do a closer examination of those other boxes."

Freddy protested, arguing Greyfell was the better option, but was soon overwhelmed by Stone and Mandy's obstinance. Finally, he gave in and phoned Sir Giles, bringing him up to date on the latest spiraling developments, including the arguments for and against Greyfell. Half an hour later he closed the connection and looked at the expectant assemblage.

"Okay. The guvnor reluctantly agrees," he held up his hand to stop the sudden burst of cheers and clapping.

"But there are conditions. First, we take over your friend's whole property—every room—and make sure that we have our own people there in case anything goes wrong. Second, the guvnor would like Chad to stay with you, at least until we can assemble all the information he's asked for. Third, he wants Lord Greyfell plugged in so he can work with you and Chad can pick his brains. We were going to send Chad up to Greyfell Abbey anyway."

He scanned each of the faces in front of him to see if there was any argument so far. Seeing none, he continued. "If all this means we must get rooms at another nearby B and B, so be it. Fourth, we clean out both your flats now and we leave on the London train this evening. Very visibly. Say your obvious goodbyes and thanks to people around here. Make it known you're heading for London tonight and won't be back.

"In Birmingham, we'll leave the train where a vehicle will drive us all back to Borth. Hopefully that will throw them off. But you've got to stay away from here at all costs!"

He looked around at the smiling people. "So, what are we waiting for? First things first. Call your friend up there and secure all the necessary rooms."

He turned to Nathan. "And you, young man, can return to the Library but we're providing a minder for you. You've become too closely identified with this horde, and we don't want anything to happen to you."

Freddy looked Nathan squarely in the eyes and held them. He spoke harshly. "They will seize you and harm you, probably kill you, if they can and if they think you either have information or can lead them to Stone and Mandy. If a minder here is not acceptable, then I must insist that you return to London with me and we will arrange for your security there."

At Nathan's nod of agreement, Freddy glanced at the others.

"If we're finished here, I suggest we do your flats then have a bang-up pub lunch to celebrate Madoc, his book and Chad's remarkable resurrection before we leave."

Crown Security offices, London

Adam Carswell looked around his new office.

His quiet pub meeting with Sir Giles went exceedingly well, better than he'd expected. He'd handed over the Belmont information Freddy requested. As they talked and downed their pints, he was surprised when the guvnor asked him bluntly if he'd join Crown Security. "Got the authorization and the budget to increase resources and personnel. Came from Her Majesty direct. Question is, are you interested?"

By the time they'd finished their conversation, Carswell had signed on. At Sir Giles' suggestion, he immediately put in for all the holiday and time owing, then submit his resignation. In return, he'd become a Queen's Agent.

Two days later, he followed Sir Giles' instructions, taking a convoluted path into the office. In the narrow street running parallel behind the Crown Security building, he entered a typically modest brick town house converted to an insurance company's headquarters. As instructed, he asked the receptionist for Suite 1A and was directed downstairs. He entered the suite and found himself in an empty reception room. He stood there and suddenly heard a buzz, as a disconnected voice bid him enter. A door opened silently and Carswell found himself in a tunnel-like corridor. A minute later he emerged through a little-known back door entrance into the Crown Security offices.

Sir Giles told him to enter and leave by this method until further notice. "They're watching us and I don't want them to know about you."

It may have been his first day on the job, but he only had an hour or so to absorb the atmosphere in the offices, find his cubicle, and receive congratulations from the assembled staff, before he was hustled into the guvnor's office for a briefing.

"Glad you're with us. First assignment." With that, Carswell was presented with the clipped curtness of the guvnor's style and found out he was on his way to Wales. Sir Giles handed over photographs of Stone, Mandy, Huw and the new Chad Lawson. "Need your eyes sharp as a tack. Key people in the fight against Druids. Don't introduce yourself. Don't want you seen as part of the group."

He placed two more photographs in front of the ex-DCI. "Your main targets. These men must be watched like hawks. This one," he pointed to Richard Evans "is the new Druid leader. Also, professor at a college in the University there. Has a place in Llanidloes, but I've sent people to keep an eye on that." He indicated the second photo. "Distinctive hair. Can't miss him. Call him Badger, but real name Morgan. Also a professor at the Uni."

Sir Giles made it clear the assignment was to know exactly what both men were doing at all times. To help him, two junior agents would meet him in Birmingham. Sir Giles selected the city because of its accessibility and location as a main hub between London and Aberystwyth. He gave Carswell two mobile numbers, one for Freddy Garrett and his own, so that Carswell could maintain twenty-four-hour contact if necessary. A car, loaded with specialized equipment and weapons, was waiting in Birmingham as well. He could brief his new colleagues on the drive to Aberystwyth.

As he left the office, one thing Carswell was sure of; life would not be dull at Crown Security. If he thought policing was fulfilling and exciting, he'd just upped the level. No more bureaucratic fussing and fuming. *I can really work with this close-knit team*, he acknowledged, *even an eccentric like Sir Giles*.

As he made his way to the railway station, he smiled. *Good move*, he silently congratulated himself.

Tappahannock, Virginia

Wiz was exhausted. The solo flight from Wyoming had been grueling, especially when he hit turbulence over the plains. After landing, Tyler immediately hustled him to a golf course, kitted him out with clubs and embarked on a marathon eighteen-hole game. But I don't play, he'd warned the Chief, only to receive the gruff reply "just pretend the ball is one of those damned Druids and swing away."

If, as in any normal sport, the higher the score the better, Wiz would have won by a huge margin. As it was, the round was an exercise in futility. But it did allow him to fully brief Tyler away from prying ears while they tramped the course.

As Wiz described his Wyoming trip and its results between shots, Tyler kept barking "circumstantial" at him. Patiently, Wiz walked through the evidence. He could see that Tyler was taken aback by the news of Dexter Armitage's presence at the murder. He unveiled more and more evidence linking Armitage to the killer and the killer's apparent military background, Tyler teed the ball and shanked it left into a deep bunker. Instead of letting Wiz wait for him on the green, he insisted that the agent get down into the sand with him. There Tyler spoke softly. "I have a meeting with the President tomorrow afternoon. I'm not going to mention all this to him, but I will probe around, see what I can find out. Meanwhile, you keep working the military angle."

Wiz looked at the Chief, eyebrows raised. "How? Can't contact anyone who could check Armitage's daily schedules over the time in question. Nor can I contact anyone who'll give me military information."

Tyler swung and popped the ball out of the bunker like a cork out of champagne, eyeing it as it rolled to within two feet of the hole. "I still have friends I can call on. Former government officials, Congressional staffers, former federal prosecutors and so on. I'll send you a couple I think might help and I'll let them know you're going to contact them. You take it from there."

Before they left the bunker, Wiz handed Tyler the flash drive with Armitage's picture plus the information he'd collected on Ronson. Tyler pocketed it.

They climbed out of the bunker and strolled down towards the hole. As they walked, Tyler confessed he found it difficult to believe the President was involved. "I've known him for years. Even before he became President. And I've worked closely with him since." He paused and shaded his eyes from the bright sun, "but on the other hand, he is a politician. A very wily one. So, for now, we'll say nothing to him about Armitage or the military connection." He tapped the ball in for par.

By the time they arrived at the bar in the clubhouse, Wiz was ready to curl up on the bar itself and fall asleep instantly. He rubbed his eyes. Tyler downed his beer. "There's a Super 8 down the road. Get a room and get some sleep. Meet me at the diner next door for breakfast tomorrow."

Gratefully, Wiz left the golf course. Fifteen minutes later he was checked in, dumped his bags on the floor and dropped into a sound sleep.

Breakfast was quick and easy. The two men avoided the investigation, preferring to talk about safe topics. As they ate, Tyler slipped over a note with a name and address. By mid-morning, refreshed, Wiz was back in the air heading for Ocean City, New Jersey to meet one of Tyler's old friends, a retired senior officer with the Defense Intelligence Agency.

After listening to Wiz's deliberately vague description of searching for a suspected military sniper, the man quickly stopped Wiz cold. "You're talking about the Liam Murphy killing. Don't know of any other sniper-like attacks in recent months. Most of our shootings are mass murders." He saw Wiz' jaw drop. "Don't take me for a fool. I'm retired, not senile."

Two hours later, armed with the man's promise to dig up what he could on sniper units in Kandahar, Wiz flew back to Winchester and began calling some of the other contacts Tyler given him.

Washington, D.C.

Wells hated cocktail parties. He disliked having to make inane conversations with people. He didn't care about, eating scrawny pieces of food, and watching others down copious amounts of liquor. While he liked his whisky, he made it a strict point of discipline to refuse alcohol at these events. He always wanted to remain sober throughout and if someone under the influence said more than he or she should about topics of interest to him, well so be it. If he had to attend these damned events, he'd make them intelligence gathering forays.

This function, at the Canadian Embassy, was the culmination of the new Canadian Defense Minister's first visit to Washington for joint briefings with his US counterpart. Among the topics up for discussion were joint military exercises and increased security ties. With military interests as an excuse, Wells wangled an invitation for one specific reason. Dex Armitage would be in attendance.

A Navy admiral tried to engage him in conversation, but Wells politely but coolly brushed him off and stationed himself close to the bar, leaning against one of the walls, carefully noting who Armitage spoke with and how the man worked the room. The squat man slid easily from group to group, individual to individual, smiling, talking then moving on. He spent some time with the Canadian Ambassador and his wife, then had a quick, quiet chat with a couple of Congressmen who served on the House Intelligence Committee.

As he moved around the room, Armitage caught Wells' eye, nodded briefly towards the balcony and kept moving and talking. Just as easily, Wells wandered over to the doors that opened out onto the concrete balcony that looked directly at the Capitol Dome.

The General couldn't figure out how or why the Canadians had been allowed to build their embassy on Pennsylvania Avenue overlooking Congress. It was symbolic of the close relationship between two allies, he'd been told earlier. Whatever the diplomats believed, all he knew is that it was the only embassy on the ceremonial route between the Capitol and the White House. Symbolic, to him, was the fact that the balcony, high above street level had a prow-like corner, almost as if it were arrow pointed directly at the Capitol. When the Druids took over, he promised himself, the Canadians would be thrown out of this location.

He passed through the doors onto the balcony and stood, absorbing the view. He sensed, rather than saw, Armitage drift next to him. "Sad business about the Raven Master's son, RG." Armitage drawled. "Hopefully it won't be too long before they catch the perpetrators."

Wells said nothing for a moment or two, then blandly responded. "We're working on that ourselves, Dex. We're not depending on the police or Homeland Security to do it for us."

"Ah." Armitage swirled his drink around his glass and took a swallow. He slurred his words and hiccupped as the liquor impacted him. "Be ver' careful, Serpent Master, so's ya don't cross the official 'vestigation. Seems to me we're flying under the radar now that Tyler and his people have been removed. Wanna keep it that way. Should leave th' vestigation to us."

"Of course. I have no intention of messing things up." Wells continued to stare at the brightly floodlit Capitol dome. "But, as Serpent Master it's my responsibility to investigate all security breaches that impact the movement. Price's death was one." He paused a moment while Armitage's drink-addled brain tried to comprehend.

Wells switched subjects. "Have you spoken to her? He glanced at Armitage who shook his head no.

"Neither have I. It seems to me as the Gorsedd, we should make a formal response to her tragedy, rather than just individual condolences, don't you?"

"Hadn't really thought 'bout it."

Wells turned to face him. "I think it would be a good idea for the leaders of the movement to at least convene and talk about it. Why don't you come to my residence near New York one Sunday soon? I'll get the others together and we'll see what, if anything, we need to do."

Armitage hesitated and began making excuses about schedules and meetings.

"Look, it need not be a long session. Fly up with me on the Saturday and be back in DC Sunday afternoon." He smiled at Armitage. "You haven't seen my house on the Hudson, have you? I'm sure you'll find it comfortable and refreshing away from this place," he waved his hand encompassing Washington. "We can also talk about other things. Like the future. Who knows if she will want to remain Raven Master after this heartbreak. If that's the case, we'll need to find a someone strong to replace her. Think about it and I'll make the arrangements. A week next Saturday would work well for me. How about you?"

The seed planted, he watched Armitage's sodden brain process the information and saw the lust for power begin to take hold. At Armitage's hesitant acceptance, he arranged for a driver to pick him up and transfer him to Andrews Air Force Base on the chosen day at three.

"One thing. Whatever you tell your wife or your staff or put in your appointment book is entirely up to you. But for obvious reasons, as Serpent Master, I must insist that not one word of this meeting is leaked to anyone. No mention of me. No mention of destination. Not even to our own people."

Armitage scoffed at the thought he would break secrecy, then thanked him and muttered he needed another drink and should mingle with the guests.

As he tottered off, an emotionless smile crossed Wells' face. So easy, he thought. So easy. His team had thrown out all manner of plots to kidnap Armitage. All it took was to dangle the possibility of replacing the Raven Master and the man was putty in his hands. The fool's walking into the trap by himself, Wells grinned. I'll wrap his body and, like a boa constrictor, squeeze him until he's got nothing left to give.

To celebrate his easy victory, he decided to allow himself one drink for the road.

Mission one accomplished, he smiled.

Chapter Twenty

Lundy Island, England

It was one place he'd never visited as a travel writer, but Lundy Island surprised and intrigued Stone when he first saw it; a bleak, lonely, green dot in the middle of the Bristol Channel.

From Swansea airport where they'd gathered the team, including geophysics specialists and a few Crown Security agents, it had been a short hop. Lundy itself was only twelve miles off the Devon shore and about twenty-five miles southwest of Swansea and the Gower peninsula in Wales.

It was a sparkling, sunny day. Stone could see various ships heading to or from the major port at Avonmouth, outside Bristol. Below him he saw a smaller boat heading south. In the distance to his right, there was Pembrokeshire in Wales; to his left, Somerset, the Mendip Hills and Devon.

The island loomed on the horizon. At first glance, it looked like a green flat-bottomed boat had capsized and anchored itself to the sea bottom. On all sides, the plains-like island dropped off into the sea dramatically. The cliffs were sharp and rugged in contrast to the relatively smooth island itself. As they got closer, he was surprised at how small and empty Lundy seemed. But, as they hovered in preparation for landing, he realized the island was bouncing with incredibly varied and vibrant wildlife; from puffins, guillemots and shearwaters darting and swooping over the waters, to seals barking along the shore and beneath the lonely cliff faces. As they landed, he saw a small herd of ponies running away from the sound of the descending helicopter while sheep scattered in every direction.

They touched down in a small enclosed field close to an old lighthouse. As Stone looked around he saw the stone shells of abandoned buildings in addition to some that seemed still useable. All the structures seemed to cluster in the south end of the island, not far from, but high above, a stone jetty that protruded out into a small cove.

A Land Rover roared up and they were met by a tall, rake-thin, unhappy man who introduced himself as the Warden, appointed by Landmark Trust that managed the entire island. He made it clear in a very precise order that he did not like visitors he had not expected or planned for, nor their arrival by large helicopter which disturbed the native species and set the larger ones scattering in panic as the noisy aerial monstrosity upset their tranquility. Most especially, he did not like the fact that he'd effectively been shut out of all information about who the visitors were and why they were on his island. All he knew was that he'd been ordered to allow them to land and offer his utmost cooperation.

Fortunately, it was a quiet time on the island. In peak season, apart from day-trippers who came by boat, he'd have almost thirty people accommodated in various structures from a thirteenth century castle, to a Georgian villa and a group of cottages in a village-like cluster close to the jetty at Landing Beach. Now, apart from the Warden and a few permanent farmworkers, there were only two visiting birdwatchers in residence. The Warden assigned cottages to his visitors, all the while reminding them that the accommodations were "fairly primitive compared to the mainland" with no television, radio or telephones and the electricity turned off every night from midnight to six a.m. to save power. He was surprised when they asked to stay at the lighthouse and adjacent keeper's cottage. They didn't tell him they'd brought their own generator, knowing about the nightly power cut.

The Warden expected them to relax and enjoy the island, perhaps even join him in a drink at the Marisco Tavern—center of the island's limited social life—where he hoped to pump them for information. He was disappointed when they gracefully refused and trooped up to the lighthouse cottage. Muttering to himself, the Warden left.

While the Crown Security agents unloaded the helicopter and checked their rooms, Stone, Mandy, and the rest of the team gathered inside the cottage's large reception room.

"Here's the Ordnance Survey map of the island." Freddy spread the map on the table in front of them. "As you can see, it's not very big. Three miles long and only half a mile or so wide." He pointed to a small bay in the south-east corner of the island. "Here's the only landing spot on the entire island. In the summer months there's a ferry from Ilfracombe that brings visitors in. There's also the grass airfield beside where we landed, but that's for any pilot willing to risk a landing what with all the rabbit holes and rough ground. With all of us and our equipment I didn't want to risk it in a Cessna or something like that. Hence the chopper. Not like that other chap," he said, pointing in the direction of a small light aircraft they'd seen at the far east end of the airfield.

Chad ran his fingers along the map. "Even though it's a tiny island, finding our grave will be like finding a needle in a haystack. I mean, where do we even begin?"

Freddy pointed south towards the cluster of buildings and a stone church "That church probably has a graveyard. I guess we start there."

Before he could continue, both Stone and Mandy shook their heads in disagreement. "That's St. Helen's. It wasn't founded until the mid-thirteenth century, almost one hundred years after Madoc." Mandy wrinkled her brow in thought. "There are certainly some burials there, especially from Georgian and Victorian times. But I think we might have more luck in a small burial ground just outside this building. It's why I pushed for us to stay here. It's called Beacon Hill, though I grant you it's not much of a hill." She pointed to a spot north and west of their location.

"This was an old Celtic burial ground. Probably associated with a small chapel. This area was investigated in the late sixties and they found some memorial stones here and they reckoned there might actually be hundreds of graves still untouched and unmarked. If Madoc buried something, I'd wager it was somewhere up here."

"But isn't that churchyard closer to the harbor? Wouldn't it make sense that they'd stick pretty close to their ships and the harbor rather than stray over to this rather desolate terrain?" Freddy interjected.

"Doubt it. If you were burying a secret, would you do so where everyone might see? Not just Madoc's own men, but the De Marisco family and their people, plus the Templars. The island's empty now, but who's to say it wasn't teeming with traders and the like at that time. Remember too, De Marisco was more pirate than landowner. This was his base and that harbor is the only place that boats could come and go. The other coves," she pointed to a number of them around the island, "are too exposed to wild weather with no real landing place, not to mention that the cliffs are too high and rocky above the water.

"Anyway, we have a couple of clues that Nathan and ET pulled out of the book," she glanced over at Stone who'd stood quietly amused while her take-charge persona was on display.

He grinned and opened his laptop. "ET has looked at the original yet again. He was able to really examine some of the words and phrases. Madoc's man was the captain of one of his vessels and would be buried appropriate to his position. Plus, they were Welsh. There's a suggestion that there was indeed an old chapel close to where we are now. It also explains the stone walls that mark the small fields we saw on the way in. In Wales they're called *llans* or en-closures. Most churches were enclosed in a *llan* which is why so many places in Wales start with that word. Remember, we found Excalibur at Llanffyron. Madoc was a devout Christian. Padraig was a monk. St. Helen's did not exist. So, it makes sense for our gravesite to be somewhere around here."

He put the laptop onto the table beside the map. He zoomed in on some of the phrases ET had highlighted. "Padraig says the grave was 'close to the water, facing west where 'he'—I presume the deceased captain—wanted to go.'" He scrolled down. "And here, Padraig says he 'lies in peace with the saints of glory.'" Stone looked around him. "To me, that says Beacon Hill where we are, facing west, in a *llan* and buried with 'saints' or others who are also buried on sacred ground."

There were nods of agreement. "Sure, but where in this area" Chad burst in. "There's still a lot of ground to cover. If indeed there's anything to find at all."

The discussion continued as arguments for and against various stone enclosed fields in the area were thrown around, until Stone finally put his foot down. "Let's cut the crap! This is not an academic exercise. We haven't got time for this. Evans and the Druids have a translation of the book, so it stands to reason they know about Lundy. For all we know, they're getting their own forces together as we speak. We need to get out there now and start finding that blasted grave."

It was the first time many of them had seen Stone so angry. He looked around at them then shrugged and apologized for his outburst.

"All I'm saying is, let's get started. And we'll do it very scientifically."

He reached into his pocket and pulled out a pound coin. "Heads it's the field closest to the cliff, tails it's the one closest to the airfield. He flipped the coin. "Tails," he said dramatically. The laughter eased the tension as they all began gathering their equipment.

Outside, they quickly identified the place where the 1969 excavations took place in the middle field. Three men emerged from the helicopter lugging heavy equipment and laid it out at the chosen location.

Dr. Doug Davis, leader of the geophysical aspect of the investigation, explained they'd be using a new, highly sophisticated version of ground penetrating radar to peer beneath the surface. Davis identified four possible locations in the field, because of their relatively flat terrain, two in the enclosed fields and one larger site outside the north wall. "Easier to bury on flat ground than sloping, but then again, the land contours might have changed in eight hundred plus years." he explained.

As he outlined the areas, his assistants marked each with yellow paint, spraying the aerosol cans carefully. As they did, Freddy ruefully noted that the Warden would have a fit if he saw what they were doing, claiming they were ruining the island's ecology.

The GPR machine looked to Stone like a low-slung lawn mower as it slowly covered the chosen area, controlled remotely by the geophys specialists. Every so often they stopped, sometimes to remove surface stones and rocks, but most of the time so Davis could study the readouts on his laptop. Where the machine indicated a hit on what Davis called "an anomaly", everyone was drafted in to dig. Most of the time they proved to be large buried boulders, nothing more.

Lunch and tea breaks came and went, but still there was no progress. Four graves, complete with skeletons, were found. But no wooden boxes or other artifacts. One hopeful moment occurred in mid-afternoon when the readout showed a smaller object approximately seven feet underground. It took nearly thirty minutes for them to dig out a small, rusted pail that produced more disappointment for the tiring team.

"Is it possible that the *llan* was larger in Madoc's time," Freddy asked. "There are a couple of flat areas just past the lighthouse." He pointed to the area.

"Yes. But it's also possible our grave is underneath the lighthouse or the cottage," Mandy said gloomily. Nevertheless, they decided to follow Freddy's suggestion.

Darkness was setting in. The generator fired up and bright white lights lit the area Freddy indicated. Exhausted and frustrated though they all were, they watched as the geophys unit slowly traversed the grassy area.

Freddy leaned on his shovel next to Stone. "Funny. I would have thought for sure the lights would have brought the Warden rushing up to complain." Stone agreed. "Painting his grass and now massive lights to scare away the animals. Where is he anyway?"

As another target appeared on the geophys readout, Freddy hung back. The non-appearance of the Warden was niggling away at him. While the others dug, buoyed by what Davis called a "good hit", he strolled over to Chad, stood next to him, and whispered his concern. "Think I'll just sidle off and see what's happening back in that little village area." With that, he silently disappeared into the dark.

There was a sudden whoop. Stone, kneeling in the dirt, was now scraping away with a small trowel, quietly telling everyone it seemed to be some kind of wooden item. As they gathered around and shone extra lights into the hole, Chad stayed on the periphery.

Stone began to dig frantically, anxious to unearth his find.

Concerned by Freddy's comments, Chad furtively slipped his jacket on and checked that his pistol was still in place. Thanks to Sir Giles he had a temporary weapons permit in a nation where gun control on civilians was incredibly strict. He put his own shovel down and drifted to the edge of the lit area. In the shadow of a stone wall he made his way towards the cottage and old lighthouse.

Chad turned away from the blazing lights in order to regain his night vision. Keeping the buildings between himself and the lights he slowly made his way across the unfamiliar ground, hoping against hope that he didn't trip and fall or, worse, topple off the edge into the roaring, cliff-pounding seas below.

Rather than follow the dirt footpath that led back to the village, Chad carefully probed his way parallel to it, working his way towards the buildings. His eyes adjusted, and he took advantage of the light from the weak moonlight that occasionally broke through the clouds. He flattened himself against a cottage, squeezing into the shadow, and was just about to enter when he heard a moan.

Quietly following the sound, he saw a body lying slumped against a wall. He looked down and realized with a shock that it was Freddy. He knelt and saw that Freddy was holding his right side tightly. The man opened his eyes when he felt Chad touch him. He smiled faintly. "Druids. On the island.

Warden's throat slashed. Don't know about the other workers. Get back to our people. Warn."

Chad pulled out a handkerchief and could see, even in the dim light leaking out from a cottage window, that Freddy had been slashed badly. He padded the handkerchief onto the wound. From what he could see, while there was a lot of blood, it seemed to have stopped. From his police first aid training, he knew this was a good thing. He slipped the gun out of his pocket then took the jacket off and wrapped it around Freddy. "I'll be back."

Quietly he retraced his steps and began to work his way back to the dig site. As he approached he suddenly heard shots. He raised his gun and was about to break into a run when a shadow leaped out of the dark and pulled him down. Before he could cry out, a hand was slapped over his mouth. He felt two bodies on top of him as he fell, forcing him hard into the ground and trapping his arms. His gun was wrestled from his fingers.

"Stay quiet," one of them whispered. "We're friends sent to protect you." To prove it, they slowly eased the pressure on Chad and returned his gun.

"Who are you? You're not Crown Security. Are you MI6?"

"No talking now. Later," was the whispered response. The two men rose and began creeping towards the lights as Chad reluctantly followed. As they got closer, they could see three armed men covering the assembled group of diggers. The Crown agents were just standing up after following orders—emphasized with shots—to put their weapons on the ground. One agent lay moaning, on the ground.

A burly bald man stood facing the group, rifle raised and aimed at Mandy. "Give me the box. Now!" he shouted. Stone, still on his knees, slowly pulled the box out of the hole. He placed it on the lip and began to rise. "Stop!" The bald man changed his mind. "I don't want you trying anything stupid or heroic. On your hands and knees, crawl away from the box then stand next to the others. Slowly."

Stone obeyed. As he got close to Mandy, the man gestured with his rifle. "Badger. Get over there and open it." Despite the blazing light, Chad had not noticed a smaller man in the shadows. As he moved forward, Chad saw a slash of white hair bright amidst the man's dark mane. So that's the Badger Stone talked about, Chad thought. The bald man bent down and picked up a pistol abandoned by one of the Crown operatives.

The wind had picked up considerably and the noise of the surf smashing against the cliff face below made it difficult to hear the two men's animated conversation as Badger walked towards the hole. The shorter man knelt by the box. It took him a while and he had to use the shovel and an axe lying close at hand, but finally, he pried it open.

"Well. What's in there."

Badger peered in and shouted, "Looks like a hammer and some spikes. There's also some kind of pouch."

"That's it? That's all that's in there?" the bald man screamed.

He fired the pistol and caught Badger in the stomach. The man collapsed, groaning. "Why, Ioan? What are you doing?"

"Regrettably, there was a horrible mass murder on Lundy Island, perpetrated by a frustrated, angry and unbalanced Welsh professor who was fired from his tenured position. Unfortunately, the insane professor was killed before his true motivations could be deciphered and brought to justice."

Badger moaned in pain, clutching his side and shaking as he stood facing his assailant.

Chaos broke out. Chad fired and hit the bald man in the head. His new partners also fired their silenced weapons and dropped the armed guards. As the gunfire began, Mandy and the rest of the team dropped to the ground, hugging it as closely as they could to avoid stray bullets. One of the Druids returned fire briefly, but as he whirled around in pain his shot hit the generator. Sparks and flashes exploded, and the lights suddenly went out.

If it was chaos before, it was unbridled pandemonium now. It was not quite midnight, so amidst the cacophony of noise and shouting, Davis crawled into the nearby cottage and flipped on the interior lights.

As a stunned and silent Stone looked around, he saw Chad and the agents checking out the Druids who were shot in the fire fight. He also saw the two strangers, pistols in hand, coming towards him but their eyes were fixed behind him. He spun and realized they were staring at the spot where Badger and the box had been.

Both were gone.

The outsiders ran up as Chad shouted to the agents to call up medical aid and then sent one of the Crown agents back towards the village to help Freddy.

"Who are you? What's going on?" A puzzled Stone watched as one of the men aimed his gun down, while the other was peering into the darkness behind, weapon at the ready and looking for the missing man. He stepped past Stone and disappeared into the dark.

"Let's just say we're people with a vested interest in this matter. We were sent to watch the island and, if necessary protect you. It seems we were needed." A smile creased the face of the man in front of Stone. He was slightly shorter than Stone but held himself erect and had a dark, neatly-trimmed beard. It might have been the poor light coming from the cottage, but Stone swore he could see a twinkle flitting through the eyes as if the man was amused that he had a secret.

"Military?"

"Of a sort. Your friend asked me that. I'll explain later. Right now, we must find that man and the box. Can't have got far." He stepped around Stone, gun raised and strode into the darkness.

The man's words forced Stone into action. Calling to Mandy to stay where she was, he grabbed his shovel and also moved off into the darkness. One of the strangers, Stone noted, swept his way past the lighthouse west towards the sea cliffs, while the other began searching southwards towards the main cluster of buildings.

Right, Stone decided, I'll look north. It didn't make sense, he considered, because there was nothing to the north of them. Just wild moor like terrain pockmarked with holes, hollows, rugged cliffs and sheep, deer and ponies and other wildlife. But, he argued, Badger was wounded and probably not thinking clearly. Nor did he have a clear understanding of the island's layout.

He walked softly and carefully, listening for the slightest non-natural sounds. He saw a rough dirt path to his left that he knew, from studying the map, ran along the very edge of the cliffs. Lacking a flashlight, he could only rely on the sporadic light from the moon as it broke through the cloud. As his eyes adjusted to the limited light he also trained his ears to penetrate beyond the crashing seas below.

He heard a brief sound ahead of him. A sound like a grunt. Was it some animal or was it human? He slowed his pace even more, stepping softly so as not to make noise himself. As the moon broke through, he saw a figure. It was Badger stumbling along and clutching the box.

He ran up. Badger heard the noise and, in a panic, stopped and turned to face Stone.

"Get away. Leave me alone or I'll throw this chest into the sea. I will. Put that shovel down."

Stone complied. The wind howled even stronger.

"It's over Badger..." Before Stone could continue, the man screamed "don't call me that. I hate it. It's Morgan. Professor Morgan."

"Alright, Professor Morgan, but it's over. Your Druid friends are dead. There's no way off this island and you're badly wounded. Come. Let's get you some help."

Badger, moaning and unstably rocking to stay upright and balance against the wind, shook his head and kept screaming invective and curses at Stone. Imperceptibly Stone edged himself closer and closer. If only he could just grab the man and pull him away from the cliff edge.

In an effort to distract him, Stone kept talking, interchangeably promising help, cajoling and then pointing out the futility of the man's position.

"They've abandoned you, Professor Morgan. Do you hear the roaring in the seas below and the winds above? That's God saying enough is enough." He stepped closer and kept talking, barely aware of what he was saying yet trying to keep Badger distracted.

But Badger wasn't listening. He alternately moaned in pain, wrestled to keep himself upright with a good grasp of the box, while also raging on about his gods and their destiny. "Belmont will help me," he screamed. "You see if he doesn't."

Finally, Stone was as close as he could ever get. It was now or never.

Watching Badger's face as much as he could in the dark, he waited for a moment until Badger shut his eyes momentarily and grunted with pain. Stone lunged forward, grabbed the box and pulled with such force that it flung the box behind him onto the ground. But it also destabilized both men.

Badger spun to his right with the force of the pull. It was enough. With a loud prolonged scream, he disappeared over the cliff edge.

Stone lost his footing and stumbled then fell, rolling towards the edge himself, frantically grasping for something to grip and stop his slide. He shouted as his legs suddenly were kicking in thin air as he slid inevitably in the spray-slicked grass. His legs were over and hanging when his hands grasped a rough-edged rock. Desperately clinging to it, his backwards and downwards slide halted momentarily.

He yelled and screamed for help, hanging bent over the cliff and hearing the waves pounding against the rocky shore hundreds of feet below. His hands were already blistered and raw from the unaccustomed wielding of the shovel. His palm and fingers were bleeding and sweaty, slipping on the rock already dampened by sea spray.

He closed his eyes, prepared for his fingers to give way. Surprisingly, he felt no panic, just a calmness as a sense of the inevitable crept up on him. Now I know what Mandy was talking about. I want to live, but if not, I'm ready. She told me that even if I had a minuscule amount of faith he wouldn't reject me. But, he shouted out loud to himself and the rest of the world, "I'm not going down without a fight."

His feet bashed against the cliff face trying for a toehold but all it seemed to do was break off chips and loose rocks and send them clattering down.

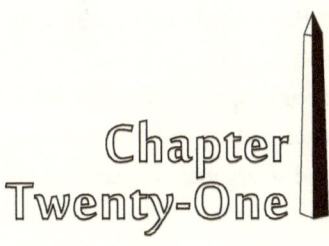

Chapter Twenty-One

Whitehall, London

B elmont was glowering. He told Fiona to cancel his schedule for the rest
of the day, even his long-awaited session with the newly-installed Commissioner of the Metropolitan Police. Fiona raised her eyebrows at this but
refrained from comment as he stalked back into his inner sanctum.

He sat at his desk, pounding it as if it were to blame for the betrayal he
felt. "Gods avenge me. Damn Evans. Damn them all. Let them burn forever
in the twisting netherworld," he fumed.

One phone call was all it had taken. One moment he was patting himself on the back for quickly pulling together a team to go to Lundy Island.
The next, he was shocked as an informant called and told him Badger Morgan and some other Druids were not only already on the island but had been
killed in some kind of fire fight.

He rubbed his forehead aggressively. Whenever he was thwarted, massive headaches ensued. Rubbing hard, he'd been told, mitigated their severity. Calm. He needed to regain a sense of calm. One thing was certain. He
was not going to call Donovan yet. He had to find out what happened first.
Then the remainder of the man's money would be spent destroying Evans.

Just thinking that, helped calm him. What, he mused, if they'd found
nothing on the island? What if Badger had misinformed him or, worse, misunderstood the message in that book. Donovan's money would still be useful. No, the issue now was to find out how were they all killed and who did
it? Was it that damned Sir Giles' mob again? Gods, he needed answers.

His rage mollified, he used his private mobile. Since that weasel Mc
Leod had been dealt with in Southend, he not bothered Martin Bryn. His
protégé had no qualms about bloodshed but now he was needed in another

role. Before the day was out, Bryn would be in Wales infiltrating Evans' organization and disrupting it.

A knock on the office door dragged him out of his haze. Fiona stepped through. "The Commissioner is willing to meet with you some other time, but he's stressing that the need is urgent. He wants to go over plans for the Prince's' tour in Wales. It's less than a fortnight away. He also wondered why the Crown Security Bureau were not invited to this briefing session."

"Tell him, we're going to downgrade their role and give his Protection Command even greater responsibility for the Royal Family. He'll like that." He paused, then just as Fiona was closing the door, shouted "Never mind. I'll tell him myself. Reschedule the Commissioner for first thing tomorrow morning."

The one thing, he admitted to himself, that he was not good at was reading briefing files and documents. He sighed and pulled a red, top-priority file about the tour, toward him.

St. David's Cathedral, Wales

"I must say, Professor Evans, I'm surprised at your request for a meeting. I've heard of your... umm... shall we call them strong condemnations of the Christian church...at your College."

Unfazed, Evans stared the Bishop of St. David's in the eye and shrugged. "We will never agree on spiritual matters, certainly, Bishop Harding. But I heard of the plans for a recognition of Welsh writers, poets, musicians and artists and followed it with interest. I recognize that you have already chosen the first recipients to be honored."

He reached into his shoulder bag and pulled out a large stack of papers. "Although we have religious differences, we can surely agree on the need to promote Welsh cultural identity. That is one of the specialties of IMC. I've taken the liberty of identifying potential worthy recipients for future honors. You will find them listed there along with their qualifications. I thought that in this enterprise at least, we could work with the Church to promote Welsh culture."

Harding reached forward and began flipping through the papers. A smile crossed his face. "Well, Professor Evans. I see you've selected many of the names we're already considering." He continued working through the pile. "I don't think I've seen as much supporting material presented to us before either. I'm very grateful for this information and pleased you're willing to work with us."

The two men went over some of the more prominent names. Evans pointed to a few lesser-known individuals from both history and modern times, arguing for their possible inclusion and pointing out their strong pedigree.

By the end of the meeting, the Bishop was in a good mood. His defensiveness with Evans, he felt, might be justified in terms of religion but he found the man himself quite pleasant and certainly supportive of Welsh culture.

After a quick lunch in the Cathedral's refectory now turned into a café, Bishop Harding escorted Evans out. As they chatted amiably, Evans slipped the upcoming visit and ceremony into the conversation. Proudly, Harding discoursed on the visit, pointing out the location where the Prince and the Duchess would sit during the ceremony and stressing the tight security that would be in place that day. "Because we're in a valley and the city is on top of the hill over there, all the buildings overlooking us will be cleared and secured for the visit."

"I presume this will all be televised so that people like me can see it happen live?"

"Certainly, professor. We'll have BBC and ITV on hand, along with S4C doing the broadcast in Welsh. The service will, of course, be bilingual."

They reached the outer massive wooden doors to the Cathedral. Evans looked around, noting the pristine graveyard and tombstones stretching out and up the steeply sloped green hillside to the Cathedral's bell tower and gateway near the top of the hill. In the other direction he saw the small stream that separated the Cathedral from the ruins of the Bishop's Palace and the narrow stone bridge that connected the two.

"If you don't mind my saying so, Bishop Harding, these telly people have masses of equipment to do live broadcasts. I know. We've had them at the university. How are they going to get all the way down here?"

Harding smiled and pointed over the stream and past the souvenir shop. "They'll be parked over there. Tight fit, right by the old Bishop's Palace—which of course will be closed for the day--but there's enough room and there's a road behind that leads in. I understand they'll run their cables across the bridge and into the church. They'll be fine I'm sure."

With a hearty handshake and thanks, the Bishop strode back inside. Evans wandered over to the small parking area. He scanned the area, noting it's position relative to the Cathedral itself. He frowned. It would require a bit more planning and more equipment than he first considered. But it was doable.

Deep in thought, he walked back to his car.

Lundy Island

Not long now.

The exhaustion from all the digging along with the cuts and blisters, took their toll. He couldn't hold on much more. Stone made one more frantic effort to get a toehold on the cliff face. This time it caught, but he knew he no longer had the strength to leverage it and force his body upwards. He closed his eyes. So many regrets. So many people he'd pushed away. So few he'd drawn close to. And now he couldn't even tell them.

He jerked as an arm grabbed his hand to hold him steady. Another arm reached down and pulled up from his underarm. Other arms grasped and pulled. Slowly he felt himself dragged up and over the rocky lip and away from the edge. Apart from the roar of the waves and the cries of the gulls and seabirds, there was silence.

Exhausted, he raised his head. The two strangers stared back at him. "Did you save the box?"

Stone nodded, unable to speak; barely able to comprehend these two had hauled him away from sure death. "Thank you, but who are you?" he gasped.

"We are a group who care deeply about the secrets contained in the box and the secrets he took away to the west," one whispered close to Stone's ears. "They were given into our care many years ago and we have not relinquished that responsibility."

Stone struggled to sit up. He squinted at the faces before him. Above him, the clouds were blowing away and the moon was casting a thin light. "Are you saying......" he hesitated. "But I thought you were disbanded centuries ago."

The second man smiled slightly. "Yes, we are who you think we are. We survive because we are faithful and obedient." He reached down and helped Stone to stand. "The other one. The one who took the box?"

Stone grimaced and faced the cliff. "He went over when I grabbed at it. I tried to pull both onto the grass, but he lost his balance as he tried to wrench it back. I doubt if he survived." Stone looked at the men, one of whom had retrieved the box. Stone thanked them again for saving his life. "What now?"

"For now, we are content to leave this in your care and protection. We've investigated you, Mr. Wallace and are satisfied you will treat this with the care and concern it deserves. All we ask is that, when we request it, you'll let us know what's happening and what you discover. Further, we may require the return of the things Madoc was tasked to protect, if you find them."

"How? I don't know your names or how to contact you."

"When we need to, we will find you."

With that the two disappeared.

In the distance, Stone heard shouting back and forth, calling his name. He yelled back. Flashlights waved around and he kept shouting as several shadows loomed out of the dark.

"Thank God. You disappeared, and we didn't know where you'd gone." Chad reached out and grabbed him solidly by the shoulder. He flashed his light around. "What happened to those other guys?"

Stone shrugged. Still shaking in shock, he was trying to decipher the horror of Badger's death, his own ordeal, and the sudden appearance of his saviors. He decided until he himself made sense of everything, he'd keep his own counsel. In the morning, perhaps, he'd think more clearly and tell the others what actually happened, but for now, silence.

Chad glanced down and saw the box at Stone's feet. "Fantastic! You got it back. Where's that Badger guy. Did he escape with those other two?" Without giving Stone time to respond, he continued verbally thinking through the situation. "Of course he didn't. They were enemies of some kind. Whoever they were, they sure didn't like the Druids." He stared off into the darkness, turning around in hopes of seeing them. "They saved our bacon, anyway."

As Chad paused, Stone told him that Badger had fallen onto the rocks below the cliff as they wrestled for the box. He didn't mention his own near-death experience. That, he decided, could wait and Mandy would be the first he'd tell.

Two others, including Mandy, ran up panting. There was a cacophony of noise as they fell all over themselves asking questions, answering them, and re-asking; conversations, answers and questions piled on top of each other. Finally, Mandy—who'd flung herself into Stone's armed and almost knocked him over—called a halt. "One at a time. Stone, you first. What happened to you?" Suddenly she too saw the box at his feet. A sigh of relief passed her lips. "You saved it," she breathed.

As Stone hesitatingly began to tell his story, they heard the sudden roar of an engine. Before they could think about reacting, bright lights bore down on them. Mesmerized, they watched as the small aircraft, bounding and bumping along the rough ground, easily and smoothly lifted off, soaring ten feet over their heads and disappearing into the darkness over the sea. Moments later, they saw the aircraft's lights as it banked, gaining altitude and flying south towards Devon.

"Well, that explains where those two guys got to," Chad remarked.

Just as suddenly the cacophony of noise began again. The remainder of the team was already at the helicopter, loading Freddy and the wounded agent on board for evacuation to the hospital in Barnstaple. One agent went with them while the rest trudged back to the cottage.

Surprisingly, the lights suddenly came on even though it was well past midnight. One of the agents explained they'd found the rest of the Landmark Trust employees huddled in one of the barns, scythes and pitchforks in hand ready to repel attacks. Relieved to find out that the attack was over and grieving over the Warden's death, they agreed to turn the power back on. The Warden's body was respectfully covered but the agents wouldn't allow any bodies to be moved, arguing they needed to be left in situ so police could investigate.

None slept well that night. By mutual consent, the box remained in Stone's possession. Examining the contents would be done later. The Trust's workers were on their own in the old Marisco castle, hunkered down on mattresses and sheets, protected by an agent.

As he tossed and turned in his sleeping bag on the cottage floor, Stone wrestled with conflicting thoughts. He was relieved at his own survival and saving their discovery, while, at the same time, horrified by the deaths he'd seen right in front of his eyes.

Not taking any chances, Chad and the lone Crown operative left with the team agreed to share watches. Chad pulled the first shift and sat in a hard-backed chair off to the side of the window, situated so he could see outside towards the door but in the shadows so he, himself, would not be easily seen. The others spread sleeping bags and tried to drop off, but Stone could tell from the slight rustling and muffled noises, that sleep was the furthest thing from any of their minds.

Morning came with bright sun bursting in through the windows and a raucous clattering as the helicopter returned. In short order, a police helicopter also landed. The good news was that Freddy also emerged from the police helicopter. Walking stiffly because, as he said, he was bandaged around the mid-section "tight enough for a mummy", he grinned as he walked into the cottage and saw Stone and Mandy standing alongside the old wooden, battered and damaged chest. The Crown agent was in serious but stable condition and would survive.

As the police started taking statements and reconstructing the previous day's events, they explained more police officers and a 'scene of crime' forensic team were coming on the day-tripper's steamer *MS Oldenburg* which would also remove the bodies for an inquest.

Freddy reassured them that he was, while slightly incapacitated around the middle, quite in order, thank you. The slash wound, while large, had not been deep and apart from loss of blood and a little wooziness, he was fine. "No way I was going to be left out, so I discharged myself and hitched a ride back."

During the flight he'd had a long chat with the DCI leading the investigation, explaining the role of Crown Security and the team on the island as well as invoking the Official Secrets Act. Whatever orders Belmont had given regarding Crown Security, they had not drifted down to West Country, he told Stone. "The DCI was very cooperative. Especially after a brief phone chat with Sir Giles. Very few can stand against the guvnor."

Once Stone and Chad gave their statements, Freddy joined them as they walked north from the cottage along the coastal path. It was far different this bright sunny day. As they left, a Devon constable told them the Druids—all now identified by dragon tattoos on their forearms—arrived late yesterday evening by boat. It was still tied up at the stone pier.

They came to the spot Stone now knew was called Battery Point. Stone stopped and looked around. At the very edge he saw the sharp rock he'd grabbed and that held him for what seemed hours, but was probably no more than ten minutes. He knelt carefully and crept to the edge, finally lying on his belly and peering over. There, more than a hundred feet below him he saw Badger's body tightly wedged between two sharp rocks, the legs still lifting and rising as the waves rolled in. He sensed Chad beside him.

"They'd better get that scum out of there before too long," Chad said matter-of-factly. "Last night's high tide didn't take him out to sea, but we don't want to give the seas another chance."

Nobody spoke as they slithered backwards until it was safe to stand. Stone quietly recounted the night's events to the two men. "You mean they just saved your life and flew off into the night?" an astonished and disbelieving Freddy blurted! "No indication of who they were or why they were on the island? Or why they injected themselves into the situation and were armed?" he continued "Not that that was a bad thing, mind."

As they spoke, a police team moved toward them. The next step would be recovery of Badger's body, hampered as that was by the difficulty of rappelling down the cliff face. The three men watched as the team began setting up.

Stone still had not completely resolved the situation of the strangers in his own mind, so he was reluctant to verbalize it until he had a better handle. To change the subject, he suggested their next move was to get the team off the island. Dr. Davis and his group would be returned to Swansea and normal life. "I think it might be best if we then collect Padraig's chronicle and take the chest and the book up to Greyfell where we can examine it properly and safely."

He took one final look at the rock that helped save his life. As he did, he caught a glint of light flash on a tiny object. He reached down and picked it up. It was part of a small round white lapel pin that must have been dropped by one of the men last night. What stunned him was the small red cross emblazoned on the white background.

Quickly, he pocketed it and joined the others. Another thing to be discussed in the safe haven of Greyfell Abbey.

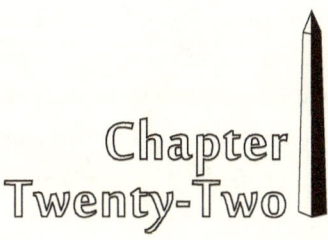

Chapter Twenty-Two

New York City

Bethan Price smiled. Not the cold, icy smirk that had been her too frequent sole expression since Davey's murder. No, this was a genuine smile of satisfaction as she contemplated the view before her.

At just over five thousand feet the small Cessna was flying over Brooklyn. They'd just passed both LaGuardia airport to her right and JFK to her left. Ahead was Governors Island and the lower Hudson River. The Manhattan skyline glistened and sparkled in the sun, but she ignored it. This was not a tourist flight. As they crossed Governors Island, the plane began a gentle bank to the left as the pilot lined up his final approach to the airport in Linden, New Jersey. But her eyes were focused on something else. She asked the pilot to delay the banking for a moment while she drank in the view. Yes, it would work.

So far, the flight from Danbury, Connecticut to the city had been a piece of cake. The pilot assured her that flying VFR or visual flight rules would give her the best view of the Statue of Liberty, and there it was. Her smile grew broader. She leaned back in her seat, eyes still focused on the statue as the plane finished its banking maneuver and crossed over the container docks of Bayonne, New Jersey, skirting the north end of Staten Island as it made final approach to Linden. On the ground she reminded the pilot to be ready to return to Danbury in two hours.

A hired car waited at the Linden terminal and, at her instructions, drove north on I-95 then east on I-78 to Black Tom Road. After a short drive through a non-descript urban industrial landscape flanked by several boat launch areas, they arrived at the small park jutting out into the Hudson. She got out and walked to the end of the park. There she stared at the massive figure sitting on its tiny island just off shore. Boats of all sizes and descriptions flitted across the waters surrounding Liberty Island. A large container ship slogged its way slowly north towards Bayonne, while ferries churned in and out of the island's docks transporting thousands of tourists back and forth to Manhattan. She watched for nearly an hour, then abruptly turned and headed to the car.

The return flight was uneventful. Back in the secluded house she'd rented for the month, she tried again to contact Malcolm Coughlin. And, once again, there was no response. Frustrated, she hung up. Her emails and text messages had also been ignored. Her anger built again. Betrayal on every side, she told herself as she wept in frustration. When Malcolm walked out of her Tahoe house she'd noted his anger but forgotten how stubborn he could be. He'd come crawling back to her when he saw how powerful she'd become, she promised. The only question was, how she'd repay him for ignoring her.

She was mulling the issue when her phone beeped at her. She glanced at the screen, saw it was Wells and responded immediately with an abrupt "Report!"

"We are now in possession of the objects you desired. You may come and inspect at any time."

Without waiting for a response, Wells severed the connection. She knew where he was and how to find him. If she was as keen on participating in the interrogation as she claimed, she would come. As long as she was Raven Master, he would do as she ordered, but there was nothing that said he had to bow before her and make nice.

Bethan didn't even notice the slight. She put the phone down, pleased that her son's killers were now in her hands. Since she couldn't contact Coughlin, she pursued her second option and rang a special number he'd given her many years ago. She didn't even know if it was still valid and would have preferred a more circumspect approach. But time was of the essence.

Half an hour later she sat back delighted. The number was not only valid, but the man she sought was still in business and willing to meet. Furthermore, he was not that far away in Binghamton, New York.

Satisfied, she made arrangements to meet him at his facility at the Tri-City airport near Binghamton the next day. Immediately after that meeting, she'd fly to Maryland and finally face Armitage.

Winchester, VA

Wiz was tired but pleased. He'd interviewed four of the Chief's contacts and gleaned interesting details from them. Each was unknown to the other and each provided information based upon their areas of expertise. But, as studied his notes, it boiled down to one thing. The man he sought was indeed a sniper who'd served in Kandahar. More interestingly, he was an army veteran dishonorably discharged in 2011 for his over-aggressive and brutal actions during a series of operations. Further digging found that the man joined a private security firm shortly after his discharge. Flying solo on this investigation was beginning to overwhelm him. He hoped Chad was getting useful information from the Brits, but the sooner he returned Stateside the better.

Googling the man's name, Lee Schumacher, pulled up little, so penetrating the security firm seemed the next best option. There was very little online about Greystone Security other than an oblique reference to its ownership by Azyx Inc.

Wiz searched again. Azyx was registered in the District of Columbia but its web page was sparse in information other than a generic mission statement along with a street address. Wiz turned to a GPS app and found that the address on Fifteenth Street NW was directly across from the Treasury Building and, more importantly, only a block away from the White House. He whistled and decided an afternoon drive was in order.

As he sped down I-66 to the capital, he phoned a stock broker friend in New York City who'd helped him in other investigations over the years. Briefly Wiz outlined the information he needed.

Wiz strolled the sidewalk alongside the Treasury Building. He looked across the street at the structure Azyx Investments listed as its head office. It was a non-descript twelve story building, with only a discreet entrance in the middle of the block and a small deli-restaurant on the corner breaking up the street façade. The faux marble lobby was empty except for a directory on the wall beside the elevators. He noted that Azyx was on the top floor. As he discreetly scanned the lobby, he saw two CCTV cameras posted inconspicuously against the ceiling in two corners; one covered the elevators, the other covered the main entrance.

He dithered. He was tempted to take the elevator and check out the Azyx offices. On the other hand, he was concerned with the tighter than normal security he could see—which meant it was likely there were other measures in place that he couldn't see. Probably already got my mug on video, he muttered as he mimed scanning the directory, then giving up. He exited.

His mind was whirling. The office's location in the center of Washington with proximity to the White House certainly raised eyebrows, but he still had nothing solid. Questions about the company niggled at him. Why would a financial investment company need such security? Although he watched the main doors for more than an hour, from across the street and other locations, he saw nobody enter or leave the building, which was unusual for an office building in the heart of the city and the middle of a work week. Wiz appraised the situation honestly. He didn't even have circumstantial evidence, just a gut feel, but it bothered him all the way back to Winchester.

In his suite, he chided himself for an amateurish expedition that accomplished nothing. You've been going about this the wrong way, he told himself. You've been trying to tie strings from the back end; from the assassination and Armitage's appearance in Rock Springs. You need to approach it from the other end.

He booted up his laptop and began a search on Dexter Armitage. Page after page popped up, detailing the man's career. As he read the myriad of articles and biographical information about Armitage, a picture developed of a man who was wealthy and thoroughly ruthless. Hidden in the mountain of information Wiz found instances of Armitage's penchant for using and then disposing of people—assistants, colleagues, business partners and even friends—over the years. Armitage was emerging as a doer—a man who let nothing stand in his way, or between him and his goals. Perfect choice for a Presidential Chief of Staff, Wiz supposed.

The evening wore on. Apart from a quick break for food, he plodded away at the search. He was just starting his third cup of coffee when an article caught his eye. It outlined an unsuccessful court case. Armitage was charged with conflict of interest, failing to disclose his business interests as key government officials were expected to. The less than flattering piece noted that a journalist in his home state of Illinois investigated the matter until he was shut down and fired.

Intrigued, Wiz looked up the newspaper and the reporter, Jason Carpenter. In the newspaper's archives he found the pertinent stories. But while there were many other articles by the reporter prior to the investigative series, there was nothing later. Intrigued, Wiz began probing the paper's staff lists then moved to online phone directories searching for an address or phone number for Carpenter. Stymied by finding no one of that exact name in the Mattoon and Charleston areas, he began methodically phoning each Carpenter he had found. He hit gold on the seventeenth attempt.

A woman answered. When asked if she was related to, or knew the whereabouts of, a reporter named Jason Carpenter, he heard her suck her breath sharply. A momentary silence and he heard the woman hiss and whisper away from the phone, "Jimmy, you'd better take this."

Moments later a husky, brusque voice asked who he was and why he was calling. Carefully, Wiz told the man he was a researcher looking into Dexter Armitage's background and that he'd found a series of news stories by a Jason Carpenter. What followed was a volley of swearing. When the man calmed down, he apologized to Wiz. "My father was destroyed by that disgusting excuse for a human being. Armitage got him fired for doing the articles and then he hounded Dad, making sure nobody in Illinois would hire him."

Wiz calmly listened, interjecting sympathetic comments when he deemed it appropriate. Finally, the man told him he still had some of his father's files as well as more information on Armitage that he was not able to publish.

"Armitage wondered if Dad had more stuff on him, which is why I think he made sure Dad could never work again. It broke Dad's heart. Literally. Dad loved writing and reporting and he was damned good at it. That creep put enormous pressure on the paper and they fired Dad—some silly song and dance about fraudulent expense sheets. As if a small town paper in southern Illinois would have unlimited expense funds for reporters to steal from." He swore again. "It sucked the life out of Dad. He died of a heart attack a year later."

As the conversation continued, Wiz broached the idea of dropping in to see the man and look over Carpenter's archives the next afternoon.

Greyfell Abbey

They gathered around the huge table smack in the middle of the dining room. Chairs were pushed aside because nobody wanted to sit down at this critical moment. Apart from Stone and Mandy, Freddy Garrett and Chad Lawson also crowded around the table with Lord and Lady Greyfell. Huw and two others stood by to actually do the honors and reopen the scarred and ancient wooden box. Beside them was the object that had kickstarted the unearthing of the wooden relic, Padraig's leather-bound history of Madoc.

The massive bear of a man, ET, glanced around at the spectators eagerly watching him. "Well, Iechyd da, everyone. Let's do it." Huw, with ET's assistance gently pried open the box. Huw's gloved hands gently pulled out a remarkably well-preserved wooden mallet. He laid it on a clean white sheet in front of him and immediately followed with two rusting iron spike-like pieces about seven inches long. While ET arranged them carefully on the sheet, Huw reached in again and pulled out a well preserved, supple leather pouch.

Huw surveyed the items. "Of course, we'll send everything for forensic analysis. We'll get some carbon dating certainly, and on the box and mallet, some dendrochronology…"

"Dendro what!?" Chad blurted.

"Dendrochronology. It's studying the tree rings in wooden artifacts as well as trees. It's a way we can get accurate dating on this box or any other wooden item such as this hammer or mallet." Before he could launch into a detailed scientific explanation," Chad waved his hands in surrender, "Okay Huw, I believe you. Explain it all later. Right now, let's skip the nerdy business and get to the juicy stuff. What exactly have we got here."

While Huw and Chad were engaged in their discussion, ET carefully inserted a thin knife into the pouch to gently pry it open. As the rest watched, he laid the contents on the sheet.

"It's remarkably preserved," Huw commented. "It's not brittle like I would expect. It's actually quite flexible."

Apart from the sound of the breeze outside and a hall clock ticking away in the background, there was complete silence in the room as he slowly and tenderly unfolded the package. "It's a parchment of some kind. Interesting," he mused, "because it's folded over and very thin. Not rolled. No, wait. It's two separate parchments." He continued thinking out loud as he unfolded the first item. "It seems to be in Latin…very faded…I can make out the first word, *lectorem*, that means reader. It's a very generic form of address; correspondence to nobody in particular, just to a general audience."

Huw adjusted his glasses and gestured ET to join him in trying to read the document. He smiled gratefully when Lord Greyfell appeared a few moments later, magnifying glass in hand. As they passed the glass slowly over the text, Huw suddenly gasped and put his finger on a line and looked up at ET. "Does this say what I think it does?"

ET studied the words and nodded deliberately.

"Well, what does it say?" everyone around the table asked in various tones and volumes.

Huw straightened up. "It seems this is a letter from one special person. A person we know very little about and, indeed, a person who many historians doubt existed."

"Da, please. No lectures. Who is it?" an exasperated Mandy burst out.

"It's from someone named Claudia Procula."

"Who was she, when she was at home," Freddy quipped.

"Claudia Procula is the name the Orthodox church, as well as some historians and theologians, associate with the wife of Pontius Pilate. If she's who I think, she's mentioned only in passing in the gospel of Matthew and no name is given. In the Eastern and Ethiopian Orthodox Churches, she's considered a Saint."

"You mean *THE* Pontius Pilate? The one who condemned Jesus Christ to death?" Freddy's jaw looked like it was inches away from hitting the floor. "What does it say in the Bible about her? I don't recall anything."

"Matthew records that Pilate's wife had a dream and sent a message to him asking him to have nothing to do with the innocent man—meaning Jesus. She's not identified by name, just Pilate's wife. It wasn't until the Middle Ages she got a name. Theologians have argued over that passage for centuries. Some see her dream as coming from God to stop Pilate from proceeding with his judgement, while others see it as a dream given by Satan to try to thwart the redemptive death of Christ and ultimately, therefore, his resurrection."

As Huw walked them through the story, ET kept reading. As he did, he reverently picked up the two iron artifacts and examined them closely. He glanced at the document once again and whistled.

"It's more than a letter, my friends. More than a letter."

Even Huw stopped talking as ET turned the items over and over in his hands, peering intently at first one, then the other. "According to the letter, these are the very spikes that nailed Jesus to the cross. The hammer, what she calls a *malleus*, is what the Romans used to pound the spikes into him."

He put them down thoughtfully and pointed to the letter. "According to my quick read of this, she watched the crucifixion. In the aftermath of the darkness and earthquake she prevailed upon the soldiers to give her both the mallet and the spikes after Jesus' body was removed. She was the Procurator's wife, so they obeyed. She kept them at first out of remorse and, later, out of her newly-found faith in the resurrected Christ." He dropped into a nearby chair, stunned by what he'd just read and shared.

A hush settled over the room. They all stared at the hammer and spikes, awed and afraid to touch them or even speak.

Finally, Huw pulled himself together. "If this letter and these items are indeed authentic, then Claudia Procula most certainly did exist, and has given us extraordinary relics the medieval church would have given a king's ransom for. But why give them to Madoc and why did he bury them in Lundy?"

While they all stood around speechless, processing what they'd just learned, Nathan gestured towards the second document still lying beside the box. "I wonder what's in that, then."

It broke the silence. A buzz of both excitement and skepticism swept around the room. Chad and Freddy, in particular, questioned the legitimacy of the items. Freddy pointed out that forgeries and fake artifacts were a fact of life in modern day Europe, not just the Middle Ages. Which is why, Huw, ET and Mandy all argued, the scientific testing needed to take place.

A glum Stone worried that the find might severely change, perhaps even derail, their documentary. The whole thing is unravelling in front of our eyes, he argued. "It changes the whole tone of the project. It's not a documentary for television anymore, it's become a historical finds investigation. We cannot let this distract us from our original goal—to tell the unheard story of Prince Madoc. And we're now missing a huge chunk of it, because we didn't take a film crew with us to Lundy."

Huw looked at him. "We can film a restaging of the discovery—without mentioning the awful events—and you can continue with the rest of the show. The authenticity or lack thereof of these artifacts would simply be an additional layer that will keep people tuned in to the end."

"Sorry Huw. I don't work that way. I don't do 're-stagings' of anything. We do an honest programme start to finish. Or we stop now."

"May have a problem there, old boy." Freddy jumped in. "The presence of the Druids and the manner of their deaths, slides into the area of national security. Our office is now involved as are the Devon Police and, probably by now MI6 and others. Somehow you're going to have to work around all that as well."

Stone's gloominess pervaded the room, taking away some of the excitement. He admitted he was just as thrilled and intrigued as the rest about the chest and its contents, but it cast a pall over what he considered one of the most exciting television projects he'd ever worked on, and, he added to himself, one that had brought him closer to Mandy than ever.

Mandy lifted her head from staring at the table. "Look. This is a fabulous discovery. If, as Da says, it's legitimate, it's one that will shake Christianity to the core. But Stone is right. We have to push hard on the documentary and just see this as another twist in the crazy tale of Prince Madoc."

Stone considered her words and, a little more cheered, spoke up. "Why don't we work it this way? Freddy, you and your team look after the whole security angle; what we can discuss on the show without compromising things and yet tell a comprehensive story. Huw, you and ET along with Nathan work on authenticating these artifacts and the veracity of this letter. Mandy and I will slug away at the documentary. I already have most of the first episode outlined anyway."

"And what do you want us to do Stone?" Lord Greyfell spoke up quietly. "You track down whatever you can get on Dai Badger—Dafydd Morgan. In particular, who he associated with, what his connections were and so on. What were his ties to Evans? What can you tell us about Evans' next moves? Oh, and provide Chad with as much information as you can about the operation of the Druids and their connections with the United States. I know he's anxious to return home." Lord Greyfell nodded. Freddy added that they also had people watching Evans. If Sir Giles agreed, he'd give Greyfell the contact name and information. "And, as Sir Giles has already requested, any connections between Evans and Gregory Belmont would be icing on the cake."

At that, Stone remembered Badger's final words. "They're connected somehow. Badger said Belmont would help him, just before he went over the cliff." As they discussed their various moves, Lord Greyfell indicated that he'd work on the Evans angle while Nees briefed Chad.

Until now, Nathan had been quiet, feeling unsure of his role in this high-powered assemblage. "Wait! While you're all running off and doing various things, you've forgotten something." They looked at him expectantly.

"We still have this second parchment to open and examine. It might have something interesting to say.

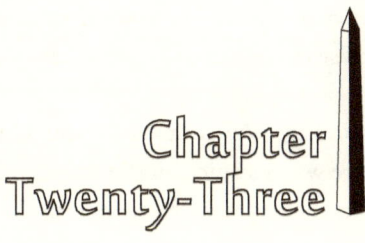

Chapter
Twenty-Three

Winchester, Virginia

When Wiz returned from Illinois, he was more convinced than ever Armitage was behind the Murphy killing.

Carpenters files did it. He saw two piles of the reporter's work, but it was the smaller one with the conflict of interest stories, that drew him. He wasted no time digging into it, asking permission to scan anything he needed into his laptop. He'd not even finished the first story when he hit pay dirt.

Armitage was accused of not declaring his ownership of Azyx which in turn owned several other companies who were bidding on or secured major contracts with the federal government. Prominent among them was a security firm named Greystone. The final article reported the judge decided that while Armitage should have declared his interest in Azyx, it was a technical violation since Azyx itself was not bidding or involved in the management decisions of its subsidiary firms.

He now had a direct connection between the Armitage and Greystone, the company that hired the former army sniper. He was still digesting the stories when his phone buzzed.

"Whatever Azyx is, my friend, you stirred up a hornet's nest. This is way beyond my pay grade. Even with bonuses thrown in." After initiating a research into the company's financial status and dealings, the broker had been called into his boss's office. "He got a call from somebody and it was made abundantly clear, Azyx is off limits." A worried Wiz sighed with relief as the broker told him he'd kept his name out of the discussion. "I told him I had a client looking to invest some funds and who'd seen the company name somewhere." Satisfied, the boss pulled back. "Before I got called on the carpet, I found out that Azyx owns Greystone Securities. Greystone works with the Pentagon, I took a quick peek at Greystone as well. One of the directors of the company is a man named Wells who, it turns out, is a Marine Corps General. Pretty close to conflict of interest, I'd say. Anyway, that's all I've got."

After he thanked the broker, Wiz contacted Tyler immediately and brought him up to date. There was a silence on the on the other end of the connection. Tyler finally broke the stillness. "Keep your phone handy. I'll be back to you as quickly as I can."

The call ended abruptly.

Thirty minutes later, Tyler called. "Be at the Rosslyn Metro station, Fort Myer Drive entrance tomorrow. Hold a copy of the Washington Post in your left hand. Be there precisely at 10:25."

Calvert County, Maryland

"Well, Mr. Armitage. We meet again, albeit under slightly different circumstances."

Armitage glared at the woman, refusing to acknowledge her presence, then turned his face away to look at his captor. "RG, I demand that you release me immediately. Ignore this pathetic woman. We are brothers in the cause. We can accomplish much together. We're on the verge of a major transformation of our nation. Don't throw away this opportunity. Don't let this woman distract us from our goals."

Armitage sat bound to a wooden chair. Might even be the chair young Price had sat on while being tortured, Wells thought, so it was only fitting. The minimal lighting they'd jury-rigged did not disguise the fear in Armitage's face. Wells said nothing.

"And are these the ones who did the actual killing of my boy, Dex?" Bethan swept her arm around the room to include two other men who were gagged and also bound to chairs. "I understand this is the actual room you used to hold him." Her frigid, unemotional voice surprised even Wells. He'd expected vitriol, swearing and full out wrath.

She asked for a chair. When it was brought, she placed it directly in front of Armitage. She looked in his face for a time. "You puzzle me, Dex. You killed my son, yet I see no remorse in you. You defied the Raven Master, and again, no remorse. I can see fear. I can see terror, even. But no regrets, and certainly no pleas for mercy. Not that you would get any, of course."

She sat staring at him for several minutes. Sweat poured out on his chubby face. His eyes darted back and forth between Bethan and Wells. "Ah, I see some pleading for mercy from the Serpent Master, don't I. Regrettably however, that card is not in play. You've been tried by your betters in the movement. Your guilt was a foregone conclusion. The only real question is punishment."

Bethan stood up. "The fact of the matter is, Dex, the gods demand death for the betrayal you have shown. And death in a very painful and terrible manner in front of those you deceived. Did you know, one of the ways our ancestors used was being burned alive," she said casually.

Armitage began to beg and cry. Tears flowed down his cheeks. She was disgusted but let him continue for a few moments. "Relax, Dex. I am not going to authorize or even suggest death by burning alive. No indeed. Instead, I am going to give you an opportunity to do something glorious for the cause."

Wells' head snapped back. She'd never mentioned this to him. Armitage stopped sniveling but remained silent. Bethan turned to Wells and pointed to the two other men in the underground room. "These vermin don't deserve the formality of a trial. Deal with them immediately so nothing is left of their bodies at the end. I want no trace of them to be found. Ever."

"Ta muid anseo. The master has spoken. It will be as you say, Raven Master." While the men struggled and grunted in terror, Wells and Bethan left the room.

As they walked into the house's main quarters, Bethan looked around, seeing it for the first time. "Had a nice little place here, didn't he? Quiet and somewhat remote, yet with a great view of the river and easy reach of Washington itself."

"You surprise me, Raven Master. I did not expect you to show Armitage mercy."

"Who said anything about mercy?"

"But you said you were giving him a chance…"

"I said a chance to do something glorious for the cause. I said nothing about his being left alive." She smiled enigmatically at Wells. "Keep him here until my plans are finished. Make sure he's kept alive. Don't torture him. Stay with him and stay ready for my orders."

"But Raven Master, I can't just drop out of sight. I have a number of top level functions to attend and some major meetings at the Pentagon over the next few days…"

"Cancel them. Develop a horrible flu, or whatever. Remain here until I tell you differently."

She swept out of the room and out the front door to get into her car.

Furious, Wells glared at her departing car. A day of reckoning was coming soon, he promised himself.

He phoned his Pentagon office and told the officer on duty to expect him at seven the next morning.

Broadcast House, London

The entire four hours plus train journey from Greyfell down to London was both relaxing and frustrating. Relaxing because the physical and mental exhaustion of the past few days had been a health setback for Stone. Frustrating because he could do nothing while sitting in the railway carriage.

His mind was abuzz and tumbling around with all sorts of thoughts, wonders, and questions. They'd opened the second parchment and found to their amazement it was written by Madoc himself. The Prince briefly but carefully explained he'd buried the relics out of caution both for himself and the church. He was alarmed at such items being taken out of Europe and away from the Church. Seeing the hammer and spikes and reading Procula's letter had strengthened his own faith, so think what it would do for others, he wrote.

However, he was also practical about his own voyage and wanted these items kept safe in case he or his men never returned. And, if he did return, he hoped they would prove useful to negotiate with the Templars and the Pope should his own family or, worse, the Druids try to kill him. He asked the Grand Master for forgiveness for his disobedience on part of the task he'd been given.

Lord Greyfell summed it up for them. "Well, our lad Madoc was nothing if not pragmatic. Had to be, I suppose, in that family and circumstances. He was keeping an ace in the hole for if and when he returned to Wales."

With renewed academic cautions about veracity and authentication, the group were stunned at the revelations in the chest. They were even more intrigued by Madoc's throwaway comment at the end of his letter that he would still carry with him "the blessed vessel that Christ himself touched" along with Sir Gregory Fitzhenry and ten other Templar knights to establish the church in the new western worlds.

"Is he saying what I think he's saying?" Stone was incredulous.

Huw jumped in. "Now, Bradstone. Let's not jump ahead of ourselves and read into things what we want to read into them. Let's wait and determine their authenticity first. Then try to decipher." He was about to launch into another lecture, but the combined protests silenced him.

Discovery after discovery. Revelation after revelation. Even so, he'd found the opportunity to quietly tell Mandy about his brush with death on the Lundy cliff and his acceptance and peace about the reality of death. She smiled, nodded and softly said "I know", then embraced him in the biggest and wettest hug of his life as she sobbed her relief and happiness on his shoulder.

What had not happened in that tumultuous time, was a discussion regarding the identity of the two men who saved him. Indeed, with the rush of excitement surrounding the chest and its contents, the harrowing events on Lundy itself seemed to be forgotten. With everything else going on, he hadn't found an appropriate moment. Plus, he was still not totally sure who they were or how they fit the total picture.

Once in London, he headed straight for Broadcast House and his planned update with Bob Mello. He had his draft script outline plus suggestions on shooting locations in both the UK and US as well. Hovering in his mind constantly, however, were the cautions from Freddy regarding state security.

He huddled with Marsh for more than two hours, delighted by the producer's response to both his script ideas and shooting locations. Stone mentioned the finds on Lundy Island but cautioned about relying on them too much unless they were verified. Indeed, Stone found himself downplaying the finds as almost minor additions to the overall story.

"Whatever!" Marsh exclaimed. "Even if they're completely bogus, it adds a dramatic impact to the story about the real Prince Madoc." Declaring himself thrilled with the work done so far, he broached the subject of when to begin filming. "I'd want cameras in the field as soon as possible after the first of June. Our weather, while never predictable, is likeliest to be better moving on from that date. I see us wrapping primary shooting in the UK by September and then moving across to America."

They discussed finances and the happy producer approved all Stone's expenses to date, including the amount offered to ET as protector of Padraig's book. Marsh even suggested a bonus for Nathan as the discoverer of Padraig's journal.

As they enjoyed coffee, Marsh made a suggestion. "You and Mandy probably need a bit of a break from Madoc. Huw too. How would you all like to attend the ceremony setting up a Welsh poets' corner at St. David's Cathedral? I can arrange tickets inside the church. We'll be there broadcasting live. The Prince of Wales will be there too." He paused a moment, "or, if you'd prefer, Huw and Mandy can sit inside, and you can join me in the broadcast control lorry we'll have just outside. You can see how we handle all the technical stuff."

Stone grinned and accepted the offer. Mandy and Huw would love to attend and he was sure they wouldn't mind if he was in the control van.

He was outside trying to hail a cab when his cell rang. He answered. There was a short silence before a voice asked, "Stone Wallace?" Stone refused to bite, asking the voice to identify himself.

"We met in a very wet and windy situation on a cliff side, Mr. Wallace. You may remember me holding your arm?" When Stone cautiously agreed, the voice reminded him he'd wanted some answers on that cliff top. "Would it be possible to meet with us? I assure you, you will be completely safe. We just want an hour of your time."

Reluctant, but intrigued, Stone agreed. He was given an address in the chic and expensive financial area on the Isle of Dogs. From his previous visits to London, Stone knew the old docks and warehouse area on the north bank of the Thames was now a luxurious and prestigious housing and office area. He quickly checked the address on his phone's GPS. It was at the far south end, near the Island Gardens, within spitting distance of the Thames itself. He decided to take the Docklands Railway.

Thirty minutes later, Stone turned right out of the Island Gardens station Three blocks later he stopped in front of the address. He chuckled inside as he saw a small, discreet brass sign beside the red door announcing Solomon Brothers Investments. He rang the doorbell and was immediately buzzed inside. As the door closed, the two men who'd saved his life stood before him. "Nice to see you in less hectic circumstances, Mr. Wallace," the taller, bearded man said. "I am Gilbert Fitzsimmons and my colleague is Henry Syme. Do come in and make yourself at home. I promise you'll be on your way within the hour."

He led Stone into an elegant and well-appointed reception room. "Our leader, John Beauchamp will join us."

"Are you sure you don't mean Master? If I'm correct, that would be his title would it not?"

Fitzsimmons smiled. Before he could respond, a side door opened. Beauchamp strode through, hand extended in welcome. His crisply tailored dark blue suit was accented by a dazzlingly white shirt and brilliant red tie. Elegantly framed glasses added credibility and class to his image. After shaking hands, Beauchamp sat, gesturing Stone and the others to sit in the various chairs available.

"I understand that my people were able to pull you out of a scary situation, Mr. Wallace. I also want to thank you for finding the chest and keeping information about it very discreetly quiet." Stone smiled but said nothing, still trying to understand what their game was.

"You seem to have guessed our identity, so let me confirm it. We are indeed Poor Fellow Soldiers of Christ of the Temple of Solomon, whom you know as Knights Templar. History says we were accused of treason and heresy, tortured, killed and our Order disbanded in the reign of King Philip of France. Our Grand Master, Jacques de Molay was burned at the stake in 1314. To all intents and purposes, I suppose the Order did disappear, because it suited us to remain underground. We continued our work and watched carefully all that our predecessors had set in motion."

He crossed his legs and asked Syme to fetch some refreshments while they talked. As he explained the long history of the Templars, he told Stone they still had extensive records of Templar activities. "We know, for example, that while King Henry gave us Lundy Island, it suited our purposes better to remain silent partners, so to speak, with the de Marisco family. We also know several of our brethren approached Prince Madoc and asked him, on behalf of the Grand Master, to remove some sacred relics from dangerous, lustful, evil, hands in Europe. In retrospect, I'm not sure it was the wisest decision, but there we are. We found out later, through some uncorroborated tales, that Madoc might not have fulfilled his pledge and had, in fact, left artifacts behind. We searched of course, but with little information to go on, we resorted to keeping our antennas up, and a careful watch on places associated with Madoc. From Wales to Ireland and yes, to Lundy."

Beauchamp emphasized the charges of heresy and treason lodged against the Templars were false. "It was all about money—vast amounts that Phillip owed us—and the even bigger treasures that we controlled. He'd already seized the assets of the French Jews and the merchants. He simply went after the largest source of funds he knew—the Knights Templar. But we were warned and removed most of our treasure before he acted.

He put a small book in front of Stone. "This is a book that translates and discusses The Chinon Parchment. Are you familiar with this?" At Stone's negative response, Beauchamp continued. "It's an absolution given by Pope Clement V to the Templars. He had a body of clerics commissioned to look over the confessions obtained under torture. The Chinon is his absolution and declaration of Templar innocence given in 1308. But it was kept secret and locked away in the Vatican's archives. It was only discovered in 2001 and made public. Fascinating document, really." It was clear, Beauchamp wanted Stone to realize the Templars were vindicated.

Stone interrupted Beauchamp's tale as Syme entered with a tray. "You say you're real Templars, successors to the originals."

Beauchamp nodded. "A direct line of succession."

"Then what do you do today? How do you survive and pay for what is obviously a very extensive network of people and resources? How've you been able to stay under the radar for so many centuries?"

"By doing today, what we were very good at in the Middle Ages, Mr. Wallace. In addition to our ancient role as guardians for pilgrims—as you have found out--we were and still are, merchant bankers. We underwrite all manner of projects and endeavors and do it very successfully. Solomon Brothers Investments, for example, is a well-respected and successful firm. But our Templar activities are what they always were—to protect the church and its pilgrims. That we continue to do."

For the next hour, Stone was impressed, amazed, dumbfounded, confused and somewhat intimidated as Beauchamp spoke. Stone cautiously walked them through their finding Padraig's book and how it led them to Lundy. When he asked how they knew his team would be on the island and that Druids might attack, he only got an enigmatic response "we have our sources, and they must remain confidential."

As they talked, Beauchamp Syme brought in a laptop and fired it up. "We've been carefully monitoring a man named Richard Evans in Aberystwyth. Our sources indicate he's the new leader of the Druids." When Stone confirmed it, Beauchamp continued. "These are people we know work very closely with Evans. We vetted them carefully after following them around and are convinced they serve Evans and are, in fact, Druid followers."

The screen was filled with a sharply defined photo of Evans. Beauchamp began scrolling. "Burn these faces into your memory and be very careful if you see them." As he scrolled, he came to one shot. "I don't think you need to worry about this one." Stone saw Badger's face staring back. He shuddered. Beauchamp moved on. Many of the faces looked somewhat familiar, including a shot of the shuttle bus driver and others he assumed were students, faculty or staff members.

"This one too, is someone you should be aware of and cautious about." Beauchamp paused. "Martin Bryn. We believe he may have had a role in the killing of another Druid lackey, Hamish McLeod a few months ago. McLeod, we believe, was the man who poisoned you. We suspect he was killed to ensure his silence. Bryn is brutal and not to be crossed."

He smiled at Stone. "And yes, before you ask, you may share all this with the Crown Security Bureau. I have nothing but the highest respect for Sir Giles Broadbent and his team." He handed Stone a flash drive.

As they finished, Stone asked the question that had been burning in his mind the entire time. "You've been very open with me, but you're not just doing it for altruistic reasons. What do you want from us?"

"At this point, we honestly have no ulterior motives. Our goal is to protect the Church and its artifacts. You haven't told us what was in the chest, but I presume your colleagues are even at this moment, examining them and trying to determine their authenticity. We also know that you were contracted to produce a television documentary on Prince Madoc and his voyage to America. We will not interfere with any of that."

Beauchamp removed his glasses. "What we want, is quite simple. We want you to continue your work. If and when your finds are validated, we would appreciate a heads up. I've given you my contact information for that purpose. I am aware that as a good reporter, never mind one working with our excellent Crown Security Bureau, you will want to check both me and Solomon Brothers out. Feel free to do so. But I ask you to be circumspect in describing our activities. We really do wish to remain under the radar."

He leaned forward and dropped to a reverent tone rather than the confident volume he'd used until now. "The thing is, we know that Madoc transported something of inestimable value to the Americas. It's an item beyond understanding in its importance to the faith. If, through your research, you follow and do indeed find the final resting place of this item, I would be eternally grateful to be one of the first informed. I'd like to be given the opportunity to participate in its discovery. In return we will give you what information we currently have. And we will watch carefully in case you ever need our assistance again."

He sat back. "That, Mr. Wallace, quite simply is what we want. To be there when, and if, you find this object."

Chapter
Twenty-Four

Chelsea, London

Gregory Belmont sat in the elegant reception room, unnerved and sweating. He rang a finger around between his neck and shirt, then loosened his tie slightly. Donovan sat opposite, reading a file very carefully. He finally closed the folder and removed his reading glasses. He ran his hand through his sleek silver hair, glaring at Belmont.

"Purely and simply, you failed. And cost me a fair amount of money with nothing in return."

Blustering, Belmont tried to protest. Donovan cut him off. "I told you if you failed, I would bring you down, Belmont, Minister of the Crown or not."

"Sir Michael, please listen to me. I've received reports from the police in Devon. All Evans' men were killed by an unknown group. Wallace and his team, including some Crown Security people, were expecting to be killed, when total strangers suddenly appeared and shot Badger and the Druid team to death. Badger was found at the bottom of a cliff hundreds of yards away." Belmont paused to swallow bile that rose up in his throat. "My police are trying to identify these strangers and I'm confident we'll soon know who they were."

He didn't tell Donovan that a great deal of his money was spent paying off Badger and then, in turn, bribing Ioan Parry to throw his lot in with Belmont instead of Evans. Cold hard cash trumped loyalty any day of the week in his experience.

"Yes, I read all this in your report. It was a senseless idea and a balls up from the start. I should never have let you persuade me to be part of it." He suddenly switched gears. "You've been trying to shut down Crown Security and block its funding—yes, I know all about that; a friend close to the Finance Minister told me—out of some sense of revenge for last year's fiasco.

Then you chased this wild Madoc story. In all this, have you even paid any attention to your nemesis the Dragon Master? Are you aware of what he's up to? Did you know he's apparently planning some kind of attack?"

Shocked, Belmont shook his head, no.

"Didn't think so. I don't have details, just some whispers my own contacts shared. You'd be far better spending time and resources finding out what's going on and either supporting it or shutting it down. One way or the other. I don't particularly care which. I just want a Dragon Master who makes things happen."

Donovan stood and began moving to another room in the townhouse. "You dodged the bullet this time, Belmont. Don't screw up again. You know the way out." He dismissed Belmont with a weak wave of the hand. As he got to the door, he turned. "By the way, you owe me a substantial amount for the funds I poured into your Lundy expedition. I'll expect to be repaid."

Llanidloes, Wales

Evans walked around the vehicle, inspecting it from every angle. It was delivered in the night and hidden around the back, away from prying eyes. This was his first opportunity to examine it in daylight. And he was pleased.

His men gutted the vehicle after stealing it, changed the plates and gave it an all-over white finish. They'd even done body work on the back doors that were showing signs of rust. Inside they'd set up what looked remarkably like a television control room complete with screens—none of which worked and were, in fact scrounged parts from a friendly computer recycler. There was a fake satellite dish ready to set up on the roof. Next up was a paint job and application of vinyls that would transform the vehicle from a simple white van, to a look-alike mobile studio van for the Welsh language S4C network.

Yesterday was maddening, only made better by the final delivery of the van, a critical piece in his plan.

Badger and Parry were supposed to be tracking Wallace and getting that book. Instead, they'd both vanished. Then yesterday, Wallace and Griffiths also disappeared. Ostensibly to return to London. Nobody knew where in London they'd gone. Even that former professor up in Borth had disappeared, as had his family. Gods, did he have to do everything himself to ensure that it was done correctly?

The harsh ringing of his house phone and then the shrill voice of his housekeeper calling to him, dragged his thoughts back to the present. He stumped inside and less than gracefully took the phone from her hands. "What?" he barked as Mavis withdrew. He listened, then swore, pounding the desk repeatedly in frustration. He hung up and slumped into his chair. If indeed Parry and Badger were dead, as his informant indicated, his plans were disturbingly shaken. He could care less about Badger, but Parry was an integral part of his scheme. His loss, was a blow.

He picked up the phone again and dialed. Slowly he worked through his loyalists, gleaning information. Parry and Badger and two other Druids had gone to Lundy, presumably following Wallace. A day later and they were all dead. Obviously, Wallace was not only armed, but dangerous. A day of reckoning was coming, he promised himself. As soon as St. David's is over they would be taken out.

One thing Evans was particularly good at was his ability to compartmentalize aspects of his life and work. He could isolate his role as Dragon Master while at the same time function equally well as Dean of his College. That ability served him now. He locked the problems of Wallace and the Madoc book away in his mind. He would let them simmer and, when the time was right, he'd open that compartment and ideas and solutions would come flooding out.

For now, his concentration would be on St. David's Cathedral.

He made it clear the van had to be completely ready by Monday for transportation to the Cathedral in time for Tuesday's ceremony. The rest of the supplies should be arriving today, he confirmed. They were the final items he needed. Next, he had to bring in the people he'd chosen. They would arrive Sunday for their final instructions.

Then he would unleash the Hounds of Arawn to destroy those who fought against the gods.

There was a brief flicker of annoyance when the phone interrupted his planning yet again. Steeling himself for more bad news he barked into the receiver only to be silenced almost immediately. He listened carefully, a shallow smile growing into a huge grin as he listened. He asked a few questions while confirming his own plans. He cancelled the connection.

The steely voice he'd been talking to was not the Bethan Price he knew. There was a robotic quality to her conversation, but it didn't matter. He rubbed his hands with pleasure knowing his own demonstration would be followed within days by Bethan's audacious attack.

The western democracies would be devastated by the twin attacks. Politicians would wring their hands in shock and horror but no credible strategy to counter him; the media would blast and blame, looking for scapegoats. Belmont, in charge of security would be dismissed and probably the Prime Minister as well. In the dearth of leadership, he, Richard Evans, Dragon Master, would step forward to show them all a way out of the morass that was western society.

He would lead them out of blindness, destroying those who refused to change.

Washington, D.C.

The Metro station rendezvous was surreal in its setup but pedantic in its operation. At precisely 10:25 a.m., Wiz stood in the entrance, Washington Post visible in his left hand. A woman walked up, introduced herself from military intelligence and said her boss wanted her to give him a package. She thrust a thick envelop at him and, before he could speak or react, disappeared into the bowels of the station.

He scanned the area quickly to see if he could spot tails, then moved out of the station and walked slowly down the street. After half an hour scrutinizing to see if he was followed, he collected his car. Minutes later he was westbound on I-66.

He'd resisted peeking at the package. He had no idea what was in it. Nor did he know who the woman's boss was. The Chief had pulled in an old favor.

When he finally arrived, he ripped the envelope open and pulled out the contents, quickly skimming each page before settling down to study it. The first page had a photo attached. A hard visaged man stared at him. Good to finally put a face and a name to the sniper, Wiz breathed, as he deliberated on the army file in front of him. Lee Schumacher was indeed a crack shot—one of the finest—with a string of successful missions on his record. But he also eschewed military discipline, getting into trouble as often as he was commended. His re-deployment to Afghanistan kicked his disdain for orders up another notch. In late 2010 he was court martialed for an incident in Kandahar province where, against orders, he not only killed the Taliban chief in the village, but also took out the man's wife, two daughters and three sons. As Wiz read the file on the court martial he realized Schumacher was a merciless killer. His previous commendations saved him from prison, but he was dishonorably discharged.

As he worked through the package, Wiz found another photo attached to a printout of an internal Pentagon newsletter. This time it was a smiling Schumacher standing with two men. One, he recognized immediately—Dexter Armitage—and the other was identified in the caption as Marine General R.G. Wells. The three were celebrating the completion of a security assessment and restructuring at a Marine base in Japan. Armitage, apparently, was representing the President at the event.

Wiz put the photo aside. Wells intrigued him. He vaguely recalled the name popping up during interrogations of alleged Druids following Murphy's sudden resignation as presidential candidate. He fired off an encrypted email to Tyler.

Two hours later, the Chief was on the phone. Tyler had called the President and asked for back-door access to interrogation transcripts. "The Man says he'll try to forward that information to me, but there's something bigger happening. Armitage is missing. No response to phones or emails. All his wife knows is that he left the house Saturday saying he'd be back Sunday. No indication of where he was going. He hasn't been seen since and that's almost a week ago. They're keeping it under wraps at the White House, just a vague statement that Armitage is under the weather." Do we trust him, Wiz thought silently?

"Interesting!"

"Isn't it? Think he's run to ground because he found out you were still on the job?"

"Did the President tell him Chad and I were still investigating."

"He swore to me he's told nobody, including Armitage. Speaking of Chad, tell him I haven't heard from him for a while. I want updates from him too, not just you."

After a few more minutes, Wiz disconnected. He'd dodged a response to Tyler about Chad's activities, simply saying Chad was pursuing his own lines of inquiry.

Chad, buddy, he silently murmured, you'd better get back soon and with good intel. I can't keep all these balls in the air myself."

Greyfell Abbey

Stone's return to Greyfell was uneventful even if it was a day late. After leaving the Templars he'd called Sir Giles and arranged a quiet meeting with him at his club. There he'd given the guvnor a full briefing on the Templars and the role they'd played in the events on Lundy Island. Sir Giles' eyebrows raised perceptibly as he told of his own harrowing crisis and raised even more perceptibly when Stone told him of the Templar's wishes to be plugged in on any developments. He pushed across the flash drive, explaining about the photos.

Sir Giles excused himself and disappeared into the inner sanctum of the club. Stone enjoyed the quiet relaxing ambience in the very masculine room with its bookcases and deep leather armchairs, sipping the wines elegantly presented by one of the club's liveried waiters. Sir Giles reappeared. He gave the drive back to Stone. "I used the club's equipment to forward the contents to my office and Greyfell. Hopefully, by the time you get there tomorrow, we'll have more information on this lot."

The next morning, Stone took the first available train out of London. Lord Greyfell met him and drove him to the house. On arrival he found Huw, ET and Nathan had already disappeared with the artifacts to visit Huw's expert colleagues at Oxford.

Chad, Mandy and Freddy anxiously awaited him, along with a stranger Freddy introduced as a former policeman, Adam Carswell. "He's new to Crown Security. Stone vaguely recalled the face from the chaotic mess of the Hyde Park attack.

They huddled together in the dining room that was now, by common consent, their operation center. Freddy, also by common consent, led the discussion asking Stone to update them all on the Templar connection.

While the rest of the group was trying to come to grips with the news that Templars were still around and now involved, Freddy showed the photos Sir Giles had sent. He asked Adam to brief them, explaining he'd been undercover in Aberystwyth, forbidden to contact any of them yet part of the protection team.

Adam took over. "The people who provided these were exactly right. Everyone here has had contact with Evans over the past few weeks. In some cases, the contact was quite extensive." Deliberately, he scrolled each photo putting a name to it along with information on where and when that individual had been with Evans. Most were college students or faculty and staff members, each with varying degrees of contact with the Dragon Master.

The last picture was Martin Bryn. "He showed up a few days ago and, so far as we can determine, has not had direct contact with Evans. He has, however, spent time asking questions, about Dafydd Morgan—whom you know as Badger—and a man named Ioan Parry. We don't have Parry's photo, but he was Evans' nominal assistant. From his description, we believe he is the tall bald man on Lundy who shot Badger."

He paused dramatically, still on Bryn's picture. "As soon as I saw this man's face, I contacted Sir Giles immediately. I also told Freddy, here. Martin Bryn is well known to the Met, especially the counter-terrorism branch. He's a thug with a nasty reputation. We pulled him in after Hyde Park. I was part of the interrogation team. We believe he's the one who delivered the RPG's to the Grosvenor Hotel. A doorman positively identified him. After the doorman disappeared, we had nothing solid to hold him. So, he walked."

Adam stopped for a drink of water. "Last month I was part of a police tactical group attending a seminar at New Scotland Yard. One of the bigwigs attending was Gregory Belmont, Minister of Policing. During a break, I ducked out for fresh air and saw the Minister leaving, heading towards his car. Holding the car door open was none other than Martin Bryn."

A murmur swept around the table. "We've since found out Belmont is a Druid. Obviously, Bryn is a close confidant of Belmont and, probably, his enforcer."

"And you say this Bryn has not had contact with Evans, from what you know?" Freddy asked.

"No contact at all. We had enough gear so we could listen in on phone conversations and intercept emails. Nothing."

"I can help here, perhaps." Lord Greyfell spoke up. "When we found out Evans was the new Dragon Master, our contacts said Belmont resented that Evans was chosen and not him. They hate each other. Perhaps Belmont heard about our finds and wanted Bryn to keep an eye on Evans."

Stone broke in. "That explains Badger's comment just before he died. He said a Belmont would take care of him. I didn't know what he meant. So, while we thought he was working for Evans, he was actually Belmont's man."

"Or," Chad interrupted, "he was playing both ends against the middle. Evans found out. Remember, Parry made him open the box and then shot him! Probably done on Evans' orders."

Together they bounced theories and ideas around, not sure where to proceed next. Even when Nees brought in the tray with sandwiches and tea, they kept talking. The phone rang and Lord Greyfell stepped out to answer it. When he returned he had a puzzled look on his face. "That was Anna Grindell, one of my most valuable people inside the Druids. She's been ill recently but recovered enough now to pass along some information."

He stopped as Nees passed the sugar along to him. "Thanks, love. Anyway, Anna says Evans had a visitor some weeks ago. A woman from America. Anna's friend, who acts as a secretary and housekeeper for Evans in Aber, says it was a cordial but very businesslike encounter from what she saw. It also turns out Parry recently returned from a visit to America. Anna has no idea, nor do I, if this is significant. But there you have it."

They all looked at Chad who, frozen with a sandwich almost in his mouth, looked at them and then munched. He shrugged his shoulders and mumbled "don't look at me. No idea who it could be."

Freddy got serious. "If only we had a name to go on, we could check incoming American visitors for the dates in question to see who she was. But we can check out when Parry left and where he flew to. That is, if he used his real name. I'll get on that immediately." He turned to Lord Greyfell. "Eddie. Could you call Anna back and ask her to scour her sources for the woman's name?"

As they continued to talk, Stone leaned over and told Mandy that Marsh loved the way the documentary was progressing. They agreed that she would continue digging for information on Madoc while he began drafting the script."

"And to think I was so naïve to wish the Druids were not involved," she sighed.

Binghamton, New York

Bethan Price was learning a lesson in patience. It was frustrating and hard, but if her plan was to succeed, she had to curb her feelings and wait. Nothing could proceed until this part of the project was done. Everything hinged on it.

Moving from her elaborate theory to a workable approximation required talent, material, equipment, expertise and, most of all, time. Waiting was all she could do, as her latest visit to the airfield showed. The work progress was agonizingly slow.

"It's a very complex design, Mrs. Price. The electronics must be both correct in the air and on the ground. Not to mention, we have to move a lot of the hydraulics and strengthen part of the rear compartment floor." He showed her the stripped-down plane and explained how he planned to make the modifications she wanted.

"A lot depends upon the weight inside; how many passengers you plan to fly if any and how much each one weighs. I'll have to know that before I can accurately place the equipment, so the aircraft is finely balanced to maintain its ability to fly. I'll also need to know the range you want it to have, so I've an idea how much fuel you'll need. That weight too, needs to be factored in." He paused. "I think you should also realize that the plane's range will be shortened considerably. Lengthy flights will require extra fuel capacity and a longer-range transmitter-receiver than we've installed."

She assured him she was only planning short flights and offered him ten thousand dollars extra if he delivered the completed aircraft on the day she selected. He surprised her by refusing the money. "You want this job to be done properly, don't you? It will be done properly, and I will charge what we agreed to. If you want it done quickly, take your business elsewhere." With that, he stalked away.

Bethan was left chagrined and somewhat amused, a feeling she admitted she'd not had for months.

Chapter Twenty-Five

St. David's, Wales

The drive from the Lake District to St. David's was long, but the day was spectacularly warm and sunny. The bulk of the trip entailed winding roads meandering through pleasant and sometimes spectacular scenery, particularly across mid- and west-Wales.

Stone and Mandy enjoyed the drive from the backseat of the car. Mandy, as always with her nose in a book, popping up every so often to see the sights the others pointed out. Stone, had his earphones in, listening to his favorite classical pieces. In the front, Adam Carswell and Huw chatted interminably, with Huw in particular, giving a running commentary on the history of the places they passed.

Adam was with them because Freddy put his foot down, backed up by Sir Giles. None of them were to travel beyond the Greyfell boundaries without protection, no matter how innocent the trip might be. Reluctantly the trio agreed, and Adam joined them.

Chad remained behind, huddled with Nees and Lord Greyfell and sorting through information about the North American arm of the Druids.

They crested a hill on the A487 and the sparkling expanse of Newgale Beach spread before them. As they enjoyed the impressive sight, a white van blasted by them, disregarding speed limits and the danger of oncoming traffic.

"Crikey! If I had lights and sirens on this car, I'd pull the crazy buggers over and give them a ticket, and a right bollocking." Adam muttered, watching the van disappear around the corner and along the roadway that paralleled the beach.

"Probably going the same place we are," Stone commented.

"How do you know?"

"That van was marked for S4C, the Welsh language broadcaster. My guess is he's heading to the Cathedral. You can give the driver a piece of your mind then."

The rest of the trip was uneventful. As they entered the built-up area, Adam whistled. "Wow! This is one small village, isn't it?"

"City," responded Huw. "This is the City of St. David's."

"You're pulling my leg."

"Not at all. Traditionally, any place that has a diocesan cathedral is given the status of city. So, City of St. David's it is even though there's only two thousand or so people living here. Obviously, that makes it the smallest city in Britain."

They were still arguing the merits of calling the village a city, when Stone pointed to a hotel and confirmed it as their destination. "Marsh told me the BBC has taken over the entire place for their staff, so he put us in here." The car crunched over the honey-colored gravel parking lot.

In the cozy lobby, warmed by a roaring fire, Stone was delighted to see Marsh and Maggie Railstone waiting for them. "Already got you all checked in, old man. When you're settled, I thought maybe you and I could trot on down to the church so you can see where our production trailer will be. Unfortunately, it's closed to the public until after the service tomorrow, so Huw and Mandy won't be able to come. Security, you know."

It was past tea time before Stone and Marsh finally wandered down towards the Cathedral. Marsh provided Stone with a lanyard badge identifying him as part of the BBC crew. They strolled down the High Street, past small shops and cafes already adorned with the red dragon flag of Wales along with the Union Jack.

They passed through Cross Square with its war memorial and planted gardens, and made their way down a narrow laneway. They emerged into a small parking lot and a large grey stone gateway tower guarding the Cathedral itself. No matter where they walked, the massive security was very visible, with armed soldiers and police patrolling every aspect of the little town. Stone knew from talking to Adam, the visible presence was only the tip of the iceberg.

As they walked through the gate, the magnificence of the massive stone church with its gothic muted-yellowish metalwork and stained-glass windows, emerged, sitting nestled in the green valley. The main central tower dominated the church with the nave and chapels emanating from it. Beyond, they saw the extensive ruins of the Bishop's Palace. Stone could see the strategic reason the cathedral was sited where it was. Down in the small, protected valley it would indeed have been quite cleverly hidden from marauding Viking raiders, as legend said.

After passing through security, they ambled down the steep stone stairway towards the main Cathedral doors. Gravestones dating back hundreds of years dotted both sides of the verdant green hillside that was sprinkled with bright yellow daffodils. At the bottom of the hill, they followed the path past the massive ancient wooden doors, which themselves were guarded by troops from one of the Welsh regiments. They walked around the west end of the nave and across the bridge to the area where the television vans were located.

The lot was busy with large trailers representing the various broadcasting companies. ITV cozied up to the rival BBC unit. Marsh invited Stone to step inside. Even now the trailer was busy as technicians checked and double-checked equipment, making sure the cameras and sound equipment dotted throughout the church interior worked perfectly.

In the monitors, Stone saw the magnificent dark brooding interior splashed with light from the windows, as workers scurried around setting up the extra seating they'd need. As he watched, the team did their final sound and light checks. It felt good. Stone was happy and in his element as he asked questions of the two directors on hand and was introduced to the news anchor who would act as what the Brits called, the presenter, for the occasion.

Twenty minutes later they emerged from the trailer. A slight cool breeze made Marsh stop and pull his jacket on. As he did, he surveyed the small, crowded parking area. "That's odd." He pointed to a white S4C van dwarfed by an ITV trailer that was backing in beside it. "Normally they have bigger equipment on site at a major event like this."

"You mean like that one?" Stone pointed at a larger white trailer tucked in against the stone wall. As they strolled away, Marsh was still puzzled. "It's still odd. Usually they like to cluster them together. That one's off on its own," he said, pointing to the smaller vehicle dwarfed by the behemoths around it. He shrugged his shoulders. "Could be a prima donna producer I suppose, wanting to separate himself from the plebeians." He laughed. "Not all producers are as amiable and willing to muck in with the masses as me."

By the time they got back up to the war memorial, Stone was feeling peckish, saw Huw and Mandy poking around the shops across the road and soon organized a quick meal at a quaint little pub nearby.

A quiet evening ensued after the meal. Marsh told Stone he had to be ready early because he and Marsh had to be at the trailer before eight the next morning and before the tight security got even tighter. Huw and Mandy had to be seated no later than 10:15 because the Prince arrived precisely at 10:50. The service itself would begin promptly at eleven, although as Marsh pointed out, BBC coverage began at ten, with the arrival of dignitaries and the Prince.

Stone beat Marsh to the lobby the next morning and together they retraced their steps to the hive of activity that was the production trailer. It was a grey morning with patches of early morning fog still around. At the mobile canteen set up to provide snacks and drinks for the television and security crews, they collected enough coffees and teas for the production crew. The canteen was tucked between the omnipresent gift shop and the small stone bridge. It was an ideal spot to view the entire behind the scenes operation in the broadcasters' parking area. As he looked around, he saw Adam who'd been assigned to the security detail, engaged in deep discussion with an army officer.

Drinks in hand they climbed into the trailer. As much as possible, Stone tried to stay out of the way, finding a tiny corner to squeeze himself into. He watched the producer's screens and the organized chaos inside the trailer.

At ten, the broadcast went live. The news anchor and guest experts, ensconced in a side chapel, explained the significance of the event. They walked through the history of Welsh literature and some of the writers and artists being honored that day. Of them all, the only name Stone recognized was the poet Dylan Thomas.

As 10:50 approached, a hush descended over the congregation inside as the Prince and duchess entered and progressed to their seats. The only sound was the choir singing.

Figuring he had a few minutes yet before the actual service began, Stone ducked to bring back more coffee and tea for the crew. There would be no time once the service began.

Adam was also getting a drink. He and Adam walked back towards the trailer, chatting about the service that was about to begin. As they did, Stone jammed to a stop.

"Can't be!" He pointed. Adam turned to see what Stone was looking at. A man was jumping out of the small S4C vehicle walking away as quickly as possible.

"Meldrew! The shuttle bus driver! Druid! Templars gave us his photo. He's connected with Evans." Stone hissed in rapid fire bullets.

Without another word, Adam dropped the drinks he was carrying and sprinted after the man. Meldrew saw them, turned and took off like a rabbit, headed between two trailers for a stone wall. Adam, younger and faster, caught up and grabbed him, toppling over the wall with his arms wrapped around Meldrew and shouting at the top of his voice for help, waving his ID and yelling "Crown Security" as he did.

Two soldiers ran up instantaneously and held Meldrew on the ground at Adam's instructions. Adam looked around for Stone but couldn't see him. Giving orders to hold Meldrew in custody, Adam stood and scanned the parking area just in time to see Stone duck into the S4C van.

Meldrew was still struggling with the two soldiers as police and other troops arrived. Adam was still waving his identity and shouting his affiliation when he looked down and saw a smirking but scared Meldrew look at him. "Too late. You're too late!"

"Hold him," Adam screamed as he raced towards the van. As he closed on it, he saw Stone in the driver's seat, jamming it into gear. He ran up and was able to fling the sliding side door open just as Stone picked up speed. He leaped in as it lurched forward and began racing out of the lot. Stone saw the back road out of the church and realized it was a narrow one-lane road, bordered by high hedgerows and leading out into the farmlands that spread out at the bottom of the Cathedral's small valley.

"Ammonium nitrate. Fertilizer bomb," Stone shouted grimly as he sped up and wrenched the vehicle around a tight corner. The driver side banged and scraped against the stone wall, but kept going. "I think he's set the detonator. Gotta get it away from here."

The strong smell of diesel, one of the main fuels to ignite the bomb, was enough for Adam. He grabbed the back of the passenger seat and roared out the sliding door at the startled bystanders, running towards them. "Get away! Bomb! Evacuate the church."

"Don't know how much time we've got," Stone shouted. "Jump."

"Not without you, mate."

The van bumped and jarred down the lane, picking up speed which exacerbated each and every rut in the lane.

"There!" Adam pointed down the lane to a tight corner. In the middle of the tall hedgerows, a closed wooden gate led to a track into a field. Stone gunned the vehicle, jamming the accelerator as hard as he could and crashing through the gears.

"Give me something hard and heavy." He shouted.

Adam looked frantically around. He saw a cement block ramming one of the fertilizer sacks against the side of the van. He briefly saw other sacks behind it before grabbing the block and trying to hand it to Stone.

"Don't give it to me. Put it down by my right foot." Adam crouched down and struggled to place it where Stone indicated. "When I take my foot off the accelerator, jam it against the pedal and try to wedge it somehow so it holds."

They were bumping and lurching down the lane, rapidly closing on the gate. Adam kept banging his head against the steering wheel as he bent over, jerking and trying to wedge the block. As they approached the gate he yelled, "That's the best I can do."

"When I yell 'NOW' jam it down as hard and fast as possible, then get out the side door. I'm going out the other door." Stone shouted. "The hedgerows. Take cover in the hedgerows!"

Suddenly they were at the gate. The speeding van splintered the gate as it roared through.

"NOW!"

In one quick move, Adam jammed the pedal and leaped out. He smashed into the ground rolling into the ditch at the edge of the hedgerow, covering his head with his hands and hoping Stone also escaped.

Seconds later there was a horrendous bang. Adam dared not look, but he felt the explosion through the ground and the sudden blast of heat. His ears rang but before he could react, fragments from the van, clods of earth and branches ripped from the trees and hedgerow began raining down. The roar of the explosion did not diminish as the debris fell. His body shuddered as some hit his back, legs, and the back of his hands. Dimly he could hear sirens in the distance but little else.

As loud and destructive as the bomb was, it was followed almost immediately by complete and utter silence. Small bits of earth and fragments continued to fall, and then just as quickly, stop.

Painfully, he moved his body and tried to stand. His arms and legs shook as he used part of the hedge to pull himself upright. He called out for Stone, frantically looking around for the American. A vast plume of black smoke hung unmoving over the field and a sickly smell of diesel fuel burned into his nose.

He kept calling Stone's name as he woozily staggered past the now disintegrated gate. Just past the gate, he looked to his right and saw Stone lying still against a small tree trunk that was part of the hedgerow. He was covered with dirt, bits and pieces of wreckage. As Adam staggered up, he saw slight movement. He stumbled over and helped Stone wobble to his knees then, painfully to his feet.

They held each other up, awed and amazed by the enormous crater left in the field. The van's shattered chassis lay crumpled and in bits ten yards from the center of the crater.

Stone heard shouts and running behind him as security forces ran up. His legs suddenly collapsed and he fell against Adam, who grabbed him and held him up. Blood poured down Stone's face. Adam was about to mention it when he too felt something wet running down his arms and face.

They were quickly but gently placed back on the ground until medical assistance arrived. In a daze, Stone was simply grateful the predicted rain had not yet arrived; lying in a wet, muddy field would have been awful.

His only thought as the paramedics treated him, was the safety of the people inside the Cathedral—particularly Mandy. And Huw.

"Bloody remarkable!" The medic treating him kept repeating it as he gently treated Stone's wounds. Stone barely heard him. There was a roaring noise in his head that blocked the sound. Stone could see the lips moving, but only faintly make out the words.

Both Stone and Adam were placed on makeshift stretchers and moved out of the field to the road where an ambulance had just arrived. Back into another bloody hospital, Stone thought despondently. Just when I was beginning to feel better, too.

His partner in the ambulance was in slightly better, though equally battered condition. He prevailed on the attendant to let him use his mobile. In seconds he was briefing Sir Giles, urging an immediate raid on Evans' locations from Aberystwyth to Llanidloes.

By the time they got to the hospital, news of the aborted attack was spreading rapidly. They were relieved to hear the Cathedral was evacuated and nobody hurt, though the blast shattered a number of windows and severely damaged a nearby farmhouse.

From Stone's perspective, the only good news was that his hearing was slowly recovering. He was worried about Mandy, though as Adam kept repeating, nobody else was injured. "Only us and a couple of the soldiers chasing after us when you drove that van out of that place like a maniac. I sent word to let her know you're okay."

Three hours later, they were released and driven back to St. David's where they met up with Mandy, Huw and Marsh at the hotel. The lobby and bar area were jammed and there was loud applause from the BBC crew when they entered. Stone ignored them and had eyes only for Mandy as she rushed into his arms. "Cariad," she whispered.

"Everyone was cleared out of the Cathedral precincts, because it's now a crime scene." Marsh explained. "HRH and the Duchess were whisked away." He looked at Stone, wrapped in Mandy's arms and with a smiling, relieved Huw hovering beside them. Marsh sent the BBC crew away to the bar with a "drinks on me" promise, and then led the rest to a quiet corner of the lobby.

"You're a bloody hero, you know, Stone. How could you possibly know that van was rigged with a bomb?" He shook his head wonderingly, and then a huge grin swept across his face. "Blimey! This is really going to make the Madoc show a hit! Hosted by a bone fide hero who saved one Prince of Wales while preparing a documentary on another." He rubbed his hands with glee. "Can't wait to tell Maggie that angle."

He disappeared into the bar to get drinks for everyone. As he did, a grim Adam Carswell limped in. "He got away. He bloody got away. Meldrew's gone." He slumped into a chair and accepted the drink Marsh handed him. "When the van blew up, the boys guarding him took their eyes and hands off him momentarily. He just jumped up, ran to the stone wall, hopped over it and into the river. Before they could react, he'd scrambled up the other side and disappeared into the palace ruins."

His mobile chirped. After listening, he silently disconnected. "More bad news, I'm afraid. That was the guvnor. They raided IMC as well as Evans' house in Llanidloes and his flat in Aber. Gone. Vanished into thin air."

The double round of bad news stunned them into a morose mood. Adam's mobile chirped again. "We're to return immediately to Greyfell. Sir Giles isn't taking any chances on a road trip either. A helicopter will take you all as soon as you give police your statement, Stone. The guvnor wants you safe and in protective hands. Meanwhile, I have to stay here and help in the investigation."

Mandy, who'd clung hard to Stone since he entered the hotel lobby, suddenly spoke up, tears falling down her face. "I'm grateful to God that Stone and Adam were not badly hurt. And I'm glad that nobody in the

Cathedral was injured. But until this is all sorted out, I think we need to take a step back from the film, Marsh, and think seriously about where we want to go with it."

She looked up at Stone's battered and bloody bandaged face and arms, then down at his filthy, shredded shirt and ripped trousers. "But before you do or say anything else, you really need to get yourself upstairs into your room and get yourself cleaned up a bit better. And put some new, clean clothing on."

Chapter Twenty-Six

Winchester, Virginia

Lots of dots, lots of lines but very few connections as yet. For the frustrated Wiz, the email was a huge relief. Chad was returning and bringing his friend Stone Wallace with him.

The British government was providing a jet and, according to the email, they'd be at Winchester airport in four hours. Further, they had critical information on Druids in North America and Chad forwarded two names for immediate investigation: An American military officer named Ronald Wells who had contacts with Druids in the UK, and a woman named Bethan Price who'd recently been in Wales to meet with the new Dragon Master. Anna, the Greyfell's contact inside the movement, had come through with her name.

Wiz contacted Tyler immediately and passed along the names, reminding him that Wells surfaced in connection with Armitage and the Murphy killing. Price, however, was a name he was not familiar with.

Intrigued, he Googled her name, finding page after page of information and photos. He worked his way through the pages. Most were society notices about the comings and goings of the wealthy oil widow. He also came across recent news articles reporting the murder of her only son in Maryland.

He examined the many photos documenting a very active high society lifestyle--balls, gala dinners, fundraising events, and the like. As he did he began to connect dots.

Many of the faces and names of people with her were the same; her social crowd, Wiz figured. But scattered around amongst the smiling executives and politicians, he saw more and more photos showing her in groupings or twosomes with people like General Wells and Dexter Armitage. Even more telling were shots from years ago showing her at fundraisers for Murphy's campaign.

Everything was linking together. Wiz knew that in investigations, one item led to a second and a third, which in turn led to further pieces of the puzzle. From the dim recesses of his mind, he recalled an old Sherlock Holmes quote: when you've eliminated the impossible, whatever is left—however improbable—must be the truth. The impossibility was that coincidence explained so many contacts and photos involving Druids or suspected Druids. Ergo, he mused, the improbable suggested she was a Druid herself. He printed off the most telling items and shut down the computer. After a quick, late, fast food lunch he headed to the airport to meet Chad's flight.

The reunion was brief, lasting only as long as the drive from the airport to the hotel suite. Once inside the hotel room it was all business. Wiz quickly brought Chad up to date with the investigation highlighting the connections between Armitage, Wells, Murphy and Price, and identifying the corporate connections to Greystone and Azyx.

Chad, similarly, shared his information. Stone was stationed at a large white board using different colored markers to chart the links between the main suspects. "It's pretty damning," Chad said as they sat back and studied the board. "But nothing concrete. So far, it's still circumstantial."

They took a break. Both Chad and Stone were beginning to wilt from jet lag even though they'd grabbed quick naps. As they relaxed, Chad described Stone's documentary project and finds, as well as his exploits at Lundy and St. David's.

When he finished Wiz merely whistled, eyebrows raised. "So you're not just a TV pretty face."

"No he's not." Chad interjected before Stone could respond. "As Sir Giles said, he's a bloody hero. The guvnor has the rest of them under tight security back at Greyfell Abby, but he felt Stone might be a bigger potential target. So, he came with me, mostly I think, to keep the others safer by removing him." Chad grinned at his journalist friend. "Mind you, I don't think Stone was too pleased about leaving Mandy. And she wasn't either!"

Stone had the grace to blush and stuff some more pizza into his mouth before he said something.

Wiz looked puzzled. "Something I don't get. This Cathedral and obviously the Prince as well, were the targets of a Druid bomb? And you prevented death and destruction even though it blew up. So why haven't we heard anything about it in the news over here?"

Stone, rubbing his drooping eyes, spoke up. "Crown Security with the agreement of the Prime Minister's office totally downplayed it. The explosion was passed off as a gas explosion at a nearby house. Since there were no deaths or injuries, the story got quickly buried. It was of importance in Wales, but only middling interest to the rest of Britain because of the Prince."

As they talked, Chad and Stone talked about the Dragon Master tightening the connection between Evans and Bethan Price.

"Crown Security and MI6 now have a trail for both Price and Wells. From the time they entered the country to the moment they left, they've been able to painstakingly track them both. Wells was often there ostensibly for military meetings, but in fact over the past five years he's spent an inordinate amount of time in both Wales and, Ireland. No big military conferences or bases in either place. Price, on the other hand, was only in Wales once. She stayed in London but went down to Aberystwyth for a day-long meeting with Evans. She also, apparently, had a brief lunch meeting with the Minister of Policing and Security, Gregory Belmont then flew back to San Francisco. Why Belmont? She has no policing connections or interests. But, we now know Belmont was an active Druid, right at the heart of Westminster. Draw your own conclusions." He stopped for a moment and yawned.

"Sir Giles had a long private conversation with the Prime Minister and the Home Secretary yesterday evening. He laid out the case against Belmont. When Sir Giles and some of his people went to take Belmont into custody, he'd disappeared. Somebody tipped him off and forces across the UK are now looking for him. Same with the Dragon Master, Evans, Both gone."

While Stone took a shower and had a snack, Chad and Wiz set up a video teleconference with Tyler. It was clear that Tyler, far from staying in retirement, was actively working his lengthy and long-standing network. "The President doesn't know, nor must he find out yet, that I haven't been as meek and retiring as he wanted when he fired me," Tyler said casually. "You boys didn't really think I'd let you flounder all over the place with not a whiff of brilliant guiding assistance from me, did you?"

They brought Chad and Stone up to date on Armitage. "Nobody seems to know where he is. The official line is Armitage is taking medical leave. Meanwhile, they're scouring the city, and now the country, looking for him."

"He's either gone underground because he knows someone's connected him with Murphy. Or, he's fallen afoul of his Druid colleagues—it seems to be a habit of theirs, devouring their own." Chad looked up and saw the others staring at him, suddenly realizing he was musing out loud. "Well," he challenged. "Anyone else got better ideas?"

They began working their way down the laundry list of people Wiz pulled together. "Wells," said Tyler. "Now there's an interesting situation. According to several different people in the military and on the White House staff he's been very busy, zipping all over the place, the last few weeks. None of it on military business or assignments, yet by and large he's been using military aircraft for his flights. I'm getting a list of his destinations passed to me very quietly. I'm also trying to get my hands on Armitage's travel schedule around the time of Murphy's death. One source told me he flew to San Francisco and back around that time. Wanna bet he and Price got together somewhere for some reason?"

With that, they turned to Price. Tyler was unable to contribute much. "We know she's crossed the country several times and been seen in and around Washington, New York and Maryland. Some of that can be attributed to her son's death. For example, she went to the place in Maryland where they found her boy's body. Trouble is, she uses her private jet for most of her trips. We've got her aircraft registration number and I've got a buddy at the FAA trying to track flights. But right now, we've got little. She's the unknown quantity in all this."

"Chief, I know I've been out of the loop on some of this, but I've got a sick feeling about this woman. Her fingerprints are all over this case: regular contact with the bad guys, mysterious comings and goings, that trip to Wales and everything else. I may be putting two and two together and coming up with nine." He paused.

"But I don't think so."

Rhossili, Wales

From the windows of the borrowed cottage, Evans watched the rain approaching. Down on Rhossili Beach, he could see and hear the surf crashing ashore. Off to his left was the unique tourist draw, Worms Head, a rocky headland that was cut off from the mainland every high tide.

He loved the place because, if one used imagination, the striking, enormous mass resembled a sea serpent rearing its head up out of the sea. He relished the fact that, unknown to most of the tourists trekking over to the feature, it got its name from the old Welsh word, *wurm*, meaning 'dragon'. A fitting place for a Dragon Master to hide, he thought despondently.

After the botched job at St. David's, Meldrew escaped and phoned him. After just a few minutes of searing and cursing Meldrew, Badger, Parry and all the others who'd failed him, he suddenly realized he was himself might be in danger. It was possible the authorities knew who he was despite all his efforts to keep it secret. He quickly swept through his office, destroying anything incriminating. He took his robe and sickle and told Ifor to bury them carefully near the oak grove. He seized his laptop, slipped into the car and drove to Worms Head where an old friend allowed him the use of the cottage.

Radio and television news merely reported that the ceremony at St. David's was interrupted by a nearby house gas explosion. There were no casualties reported and only minimal damage to the church structure. It was expected that the ceremony would be rescheduled.

Frustration burned inside him. Gods, he thought he'd organized the perfect attack only to be let down by his minion. Insufferably incompetent traitors to the cause, he fumed.

His mobile rang. He glanced at the screen and saw who was calling. A red rage flooded over him. He considered ignoring it. It kept ringing. Curiosity took hold. He answered with arguing, cursing, listening, then interjecting when necessary, before finally demanding a face to face meeting. It was indeed time to settle this and establish his leadership. He disconnected and continued looking at the rolling storm coming in.

He decided to make a cup of tea. That usually calmed him down and enabled him to think.

Binghamton, New York

Bethan was pleased. She wasn't technically minded, so paid little attention while the man proudly detailed all the technical improvements and innovations he'd made in the aircraft so it would perform the way she wanted. The completion was two frustrating days longer than she originally planned, but nothing would move him along any faster.

"Awesome idea, Mrs. Price. But like I said before, it will have a limited range for now. If you want something greater, we'll need a larger airframe."

The proof was in the pudding, she told him. Ten minutes later, the Cessna took off and circled the field. On the ground, Bethan and the mechanic used the equipment. The set up was quite simple, he explained, showing her how the various toggles worked. "Speed, turns to port and starboard and ascend and descend. Easy as pie."

Following his instructions, she manipulated the controls and watched the plane race down the runway, ascend and turn to starboard. She did three circuits of the airport before bringing the craft down.

With the inspection and trial flight over, they entered his tiny workshop office. She handed over the agreed sum in cash as promised. With the transaction finished, he walked her out to her own jet. "Biggest and best drone I've ever built. Don't know why you want one that size, but I guarantee you've got the best."

"Do I have to be in a plane flying along with it, in order to control it?"

"No. That's what I mean by range. You could be here at the airport in Binghamton and control the plane from the ground. You have a control range of one hundred and fifty miles. Once you input the precise GPS coordinates, all you have to do is control the speed and altitude. I've given this thing the same fly-by-wire technology that keeps the A-380 going. You can watch the flight on your laptop screen thanks to the cameras I mounted, plus you'll get the same technical readings on the computer as well." He paused a moment. "It would be best if you had an experienced pilot by your side while you fly it. Same as if you were learning to fly for real."

She nodded slowly, her mind racing ahead rather than listening to him. "I want it delivered no later than Friday noon, to the airport at Danbury, Connecticut."

He shook hands again, and she climbed the stairs. The engines were already spooling as the door closed and they slowly rolled from the parking pad to the taxiway and onto the runway where it lifted effortlessly into the sky.

Bethan settled back into the comfortable leather seat. As she did, the co-pilot appeared at her elbow with her favorite scotch and a platter of snack food. The short hop was over almost before she finished her drink. The aircraft taxied to the private hangar she'd rented. Before she left, she stopped to give the crew instructions.

"I want this plane reconfigured to carry a stretcher no later than Friday. We'll fly down to Maryland Friday night to pick up the patient Saturday, then come back here. After you drop me, I want you to head for the Long

Island airport. Be prepared for the trip back to San Francisco Saturday afternoon. I'll meet you in Long Island."

She left the hangar and walked over to the airport's business aviation area. It took less than half an hour and she'd arranged for a rental aircraft to carry her on a sightseeing trip Saturday afternoon from Danbury to the Manhattan area, then over to the Long Island airport near West Islip.

She texted Wells to be ready for the transfer. They would leave with Armitage, Saturday morning.

Manassas, Virginia

Chad and Wiz sat patiently in the car along with a detective from Rock Springs, Wyoming the result of a minor breakthrough yesterday morning. Reviewing information about the sniper from one of Tyler's sources, there was a reference to him living in Manassas, although no address was given.

Chad, Stone and Wiz had slowly and systematically gone through online directories and town records. Fortunately it was an unusual name and they soon winnowed it down until they had three potential addresses. Each rented a car that afternoon and staked out the different addresses, with a photo of the target in hand. Chad scored when the man pulled into the driveway of a neat suburban home. As the man got out of his car, Chad had a clear and prolonged look at his face, then compared it with the shot. Yes, he breathed. You're our guy.

By late afternoon Tyler approached the Rock Springs police with his information, then followed up an hour later with a phone call. It didn't take much persuading. Dangling the carrot that the local police would beat federal agencies to the arrest was enough to convince them. It was enough to put a detective on the red-eye flight to Washington.

Working with Chad and Wiz, the deputy painstakingly went over the information Wiz had assembled. "If you provide anonymity and a new identity for Clint Ronson, he'd probably give a positive ID on Schumacher, Ronson's likely still in the Rock Springs area." Wiz suggested.

Stone was already staking out the Schumacher house. The others arrived, Stone joined them and together they waited. "There!" Chad nodded at a car slowing down and pulling into the driveway. Wiz wasted no time, pulling up behind Schumacher as Chad and the Wyoming officer jumped out.

The whole affair was over in minutes. A shocked and subdued Schumacher was handcuffed and sitting beside the detective in the back seat as Wiz drove off. Chad and Stone walked quickly back to Stone's car. They followed Wiz to the Manassas airport where their jet was already gassed up and ready for the flight.

While the detective and Schumacher were placed on board the plane and Schumacher secured, they were surprised to see Tyler and another man approach.

"Good digging gentlemen," Tyler acknowledged. He looked directly at Wiz. "You're planning to deliver this guy back to Wyoming, right?" Wiz nodded.

"Wrong!" Tyler corrected. "I want you here. My gut tells me something big is happening here; bigger than any delivery flight. He pointed to his companion. "Chuck here, is qualified on this type and he'll fly Schumacher and the cop out to Rock Springs then return immediately. Meantime, I need you guys to look over some of this material."

As he handed a pile of documents to Chad and led them back to the airport parking lot, Chuck boarded the aircraft.

Within an hour of Schumacher's arrest, he was in the air.

Winchester, Virginia

After leaving Tyler in the parking lot, Stone drove while Wiz and Chad began combing the material Tyler had turned over. "Some of these are from the FAA. Must be Price's flight records." Wiz was flipping through them quickly. "Hmm. She's been a busy gal these past few weeks. Several cross country flights, some within California, and a lot of short hop flights in the east." He scanned the list again. "Most of the eastern flights seem to be in the greater New York City area, with some as far afield as Washington."

While he reviewed the flight information, Chad was also plowing through his stack. "These are mostly records of Price's donations to political causes and campaigns." He began to list them. "The President, a number of Senators and some Representatives." He continued flipping through the list. He stopped and thought for a moment. "You'd expect her to give to California candidates but most of these are not Californian."

His finger slowly pulled down the list. "Most of them are from the east—Massachusetts, New York, Pennsylvania, New Jersey, Maryland—and huge amounts to Murphy's campaign." He paused a moment, mentally adding the numbers and whistled. "Almost two million in all to Murphy's campaign." He snapped his fingers. "Of course!" Excited, Chad whirled around in the seat as much as he could in the confines of the vehicle. "Each of these campaigns is for sitting politicians or candidates that were taken into custody or questioned when Murphy's campaign collapsed. All of them are either Druids or Druid supporters."

Wiz and Chad smiled at each other. "Gotcha babe!" Wiz shouted.

Back at the hotel, they used the white board again, this time with a map of the eastern United States, and began to chart Bethan Price's flight pattern by deciphering the various airport codes. They eliminated flights to Maryland. "That's where her son was murdered. Probably nothing significant there."

"There's a lot around New York. Look, here's DXR that's..." he looked it up, "Danbury, Connecticut. Then there's SWF, that's Stewart up near West Point academy, and BGM is Binghamton, New York."

As they decoded the airport names, Stone began adding the number of visits beside each. They finally finished and all stepped back to view the results. "Most of the activity seems to be centered on Danbury and Binghamton. Four flights back and forth in the last two and a half weeks."

They cross-checked the donations records but saw no pattern linking either Binghamton or Danbury to the list of supported campaigns. "Obviously political fundraisers or the like." Wiz rubbed his chin in contemplation."

Chad rolled his eyes. "Of course not. It's not an election year, for crying out loud!"

"It's always election year when it comes to raising campaign finances."

They studied the board in silence, each wrapped up in his own thoughts. Finally, Chad spoke. "I spent a long time with Lord and Lady Greyfell drinking in all they could give me about the Druids. Seems to me, these guys are not just ordinary flunky Druids. They wouldn't be flitting around like this. Plus, their high profile civilian profiles and lifestyles mean they're not foot soldiers. Guys, I think this is the American leadership we're looking at."

He stood up and went to the board. "Ninety percent of this activity is post-Murphy. One of them, Price or Wells, is what Lord Greyfell called the Raven Master. That's the leader, answerable only to the Dragon Master himself. The other one would be what he called the Serpent Master. Sort of the Security Chief, if you will. Either way, they're the two top leadership posts."

"So, which is which?"

"Don't know. Could be Wells. He's already a general, so he's a leader and, apparently, a pretty rigid one. On the other hand, that background would make a fearsome security chief too. Price is, from all accounts, a strong, no nonsense person. She takes no guff from anyone, including Senators, the media and fellow CEO's. She has tons of money—which they need—and a reputation as a fundraiser. One article said she could wheedle a million dollars out of Ebenezer Scrooge if she needed to. Plus, the Druids are not hung up on women as leaders."

Chad's suggestions threw a new gallon of gasoline on the fire. "They're not just running around having meetings to plan the future or to rack up frequent flyer points. Something big is in the air. Really big. Murphy was—pardon the pun—the trigger. Wells and Price are planning something, and Armitage is their tool."

The thought sobered them.

As they debated the point, Stone reflected. "Sitting around here talking won't solve it. What say we do a little trip up to Binghamton and Danbury, talk to airport officials and see if we can dig anything up?"

"The plane won't be back until later tomorrow. I suppose I could do a quick turn around, but it would be better if we went Saturday morning, if that's okay with you guys." Wiz drummed his fingers on the coffee table. "Gives us all day tomorrow to work on the rest of these files. And the Chief said more were coming tomorrow."

"Well, that blows my plan!" Chad slumped down in his chair in a fake pout. "Tomorrow is Good Friday and I was looking forward to a quiet Easter weekend."

Chapter Twenty-Seven

Rhossili, Wales

Evans trudged the gravel path out of the village and down towards Worms Head. Even this late in the evening, there were still hikers and tourists, albeit most were headed back towards the village and its small cafes and accommodations.

The path meandered past the old cottages now used as an interpretive center and gift shop, through a gate and along the edge of the cliff. Below, he could hear the thundering surf rolling ashore. It didn't seem to bother the free-running sheep who wandered along the knife edge happily munching on the grass.

He saw his quarry beside some gorse bushes, seated on a small rock outcrop. Evans slowed and looked around. He seemed to be alone, so Evans approached. As he did, Gregory Belmont rose to meet him.

Evans sneered as he approached. "I didn't think the gods had given you the courage to show up."

"I won't mince words. You've buggered it all up Evans. You're a sham as Dragon Master and have dealt the movement a mighty blow."

Evans looked at him calmly. "And you, of course, are more than willing to step in for me, are you?"

Belmont snorted. "Aye. I'd make a right better Dragon Master than you. Here I am sitting in parliament and a cabinet minister to boot, with the power to ensure the success of that botched operation. But ye didnae tell anyone about your cack-handed plans. You had to do it by yourself, keeping it secret from the Gorsedd and everyone else. My people told me what a mess it was. You're a bloody academic. No sense of how to set up operations like that. D'ya ken ye've crippled the movement with that pointless and poorly handled mess. What were you thinking man?"

Anyone on the path would see two men casually chatting and strolling along the uneven ground close to the cliffs, not realizing the blazing intensity of their hatred as they verbally attacked and counter-attacked.

Evans drew himself up and glared at Belmont. "I am the Dragon Master, look you. I have no need to explain to you or anyone else, what my plans are or why."

"Aye, and that fiasco on Lundy Island was another striking success wasn't it?"

As they walked, the uneven ground dropped into a small gully. Scattered gorse bushes and the darkening sky combined to conceal them from anyone on the path. Evans stopped and whirled in fury. "Your thugs raided the island and killed all my men, including Ioan and Badger, so don't talk to me about buggering things up."

Denying his followers played any part in Lundy, Belmont raged again about the aborted attack on St. David's. Knowing the plan, he could have ensured security and police on hand would have looked away, perhaps even help smuggle the weapon inside. Evans fumed silently, a whisper of doubt sparking in his mind that Belmont might be right. Perhaps he should have enlisted the Minister's aid.

It was quickly wiped away, as he saw Belmont smirking. "I've had to clean up your other mess before Crown Security or anyone else could intervene."

He waited, willing Evans to ask him what happened. Evans refused to budge.

He slipped up close and whispered in Evans ear. "Ask me about Meldrew." He stepped back grinning.

Evans balled his fists, a ferocious rage building inside, but said nothing, glowering at Belmont instead. The leader makes the lackey explain to him, not the other way around, he kept telling himself.

Night fell rapidly, aided by dark clouds obscuring the half-moon's light.

The silence grew louder. The only sounds were the rustle of wind in the bushes, crashing waves, and the cries of seagulls returning to their nests. Evans waited. Tension from the devastating twin catastrophes coupled with his loathing of Belmont, built to a volcanic level.

Belmont broke first. "Meldrew got away from the Cathedral, didn't he? Came running home only to find his lord and master, the Dragon Master, scarpered like a scared rat." He straightened his shoulders. "Well, luckily, my man Bryn was on the scene, keeping an eye on things. He saw Meldrew poking around and followed him to your flat. You don't have to worry any more. Bryn took care of everything. Meldrew met with a little 'accident'.

The rage boiled over. With a screech of frustration and fury, Evans lunged at Belmont, fists pummeling the minister. If there had been onlookers, they would have been amused as two overweight, flabby middle-aged men flailed away, missing as many times as they landed hits. They struggled, swinging and pushing, tearing at each other's clothing. Evans wound up with one almighty lunge, ramming both his fists into Belmont's midsection. A grunt of expelled air burst from Belmont. He staggered backwards. Neither realized how close they were to the edge. Belmont suddenly waved his arms about and silently disappeared.

Panting and bent over, Evans rested his arms on his knees. The irony was not lost on him. He straightened, took one last glance and whispered, "Well, Badger. You were useless in life and in death. But you got your sweet revenge."

Still gasping for breath, he turned and walked unsteadily up the gully. He was startled as a shadow rose, striding menacingly towards him. He didn't recognize the man.

"I told him not to meet you alone, but he wouldn't listen. I followed, but he paid the price anyway. He hated you Evans; hated you with a passion. So, you deserve this."

Martin Bryn abruptly sprang at Evans, driving his razor-sharp knife deep into Evans' chest perfectly, penetrating his heart. As Evans gurgled and sank heavily to the ground, Bryn grabbed him, holding him up while he wiped blood off his knife and onto the jacket. Without ceremony he dragged Evans' body to the edge and tipped it over.

He backed away from the cliff, then strode quickly out of the gully, across the grassy verge and onto the gravel path. Five minutes later he slipped behind the wheel of his car and pulled out of Rhossili village.

Winchester, Virginia

It was nearly noon before Tyler's second batch of records arrived. When they did, all three poured over them, Stone stationed at the white board as before.

Armitage's travel history was easy. A government plane delivered him to Salt Lake City the day before Murphy's killing. According to White House records, Armitage was in Utah to do a little arm-twisting with local politicians. The trouble was, Tyler's handwritten scribble in the margins said, neither Utah's congressmen nor Senators recalled any meeting with him. Further digging showed that Armitage flew from Salt Lake to San Francisco the evening of the murder, and then a red-eye back to Washington the next night. No government or White House business was involved.

Information on Wells' travels was more difficult to dig out. Military records were not as easily obtained. The only confirmed flights included one to New York for a UN conference and several to Stewart International airport. Other flights were classified.

Wiz was disappointed. He'd hoped Wells' flight pattern would match Price's and said so.

"Wait a minute though." Chad studied the information carefully. "Both flew into Stewart, right."

"On different days. It's not far from West Point, so it's possible he had meetings with army brass or something."

"Maybe. The records would have said so though."

Chad dug through some of the internet research he'd done the night before. Buried deep in a puffy magazine profile about the free time enjoyed by military leaders, he found what he wanted. "Aha! Here it is. Our man has a swanky little pad by the Hudson, near Poughkeepsie. Stewart is the closest major airport. Who's willing to take a bet Wells was on private, probably Druid, business at the old estate instead of being a good soldier and protecting our nation?"

With grins all round, they began to speculate. "Some kind of Gorsedd meeting, perhaps?" Chad mused. "Or a security type meeting to discuss Murphy's death and their plans going forward?" was Wiz' contribution.

"It may be something simpler." Stone waved his hand at the board where flights and dates were posted. "All this was also after her son's murder, don't forget. It might be them getting together to console her."

"Once, maybe. Not three times." Chad was shaking his head. "No. They're up to something. I feel it."

A cell phone rang. Wiz answered. "That was the Chief. Our wings are scheduled back on the ground in Winchester within the hour. We fly first thing tomorrow."

"Binghamton first. It's further away. Then down to Danbury. And hope to God we get some solid information."

Salisbury, Maryland

Wells drove to the rented hangar Saturday morning, followed by an ambulance. It had been harder than expected to find an airport close enough to Patuxent to deliver Armitage yet capable of handling Bethan's jet. She'd stayed in Salisbury overnight rather than travel to Patuxent, preferring to convey her orders to Wells via phone calls and texts.

Wells' car and the ambulance rounded the corner and parked at the foot of the staircase. Swiftly, the stretcher bearing a drugged Armitage was whisked aboard. Bethan raised an eyebrow as she saw the head and eyes almost completely obscured with bandages. "Unlikely that anyone would get close enough to recognize him," Well said, "but just in case, we covered him."

Wells was smoldering. He resented being treated as mere servant. As Serpent Master and second-in-command, he expected—no, demanded—respect and inclusion in any planning. On this flight, he intended to confront her. She was proving irrational and uncontrollable. Her unfettered anger and hatred caused by the boy's death had, in his opinion, sent her around the bend. Her ability to remain as leader was compromised.

As they flew, she dismissed his concerns flippantly, claiming she wanted the ultimate secrecy so that nobody, not even him, would let slip her plan. Oblivious to his anger, she leaned forward. He saw an unearthly coldness in her eyes as she finally leaned forward. "Now is the time I planned to inform you anyway."

In fifteen minutes she'd outlined her scheme for an attack that was both deadly and symbolic. She also described her plans for Armitage.

"It's a magnified version of a drug that paralyzes the body but leaves the mind fully aware of what's going on." She jerked her head at Armitage. "He'll be sitting in the drone watching it all happen but unable to move or speak. It will be impossible for him to prevent it." She laughed coldly. "He'll know what it was like for my Davey at the end. To know icy fear as the inevitable happens. I did promise him a starring role in doing something glorious. I keep my promises."

Wells shifted uncomfortably in his seat. Death and destruction was not a stranger to him. He'd seen death. He killed combatants himself, in Iraq and Afghanistan. He'd sent men to their deaths. Nor, committed as he was to the Druids, was he overly concerned about collateral damage. But this… his mind struggled with the enormity of what she planned…was beyond his comprehension. He sat silently pondering as she proudly told him of her preparations, the search for and finally procurement of the necessary weaponry. "Went through a number of back channels, I can tell you. From Syria, to South Africa, Indonesia and finally to me. Funny thing is, it fits inside a small suitcase."

Old Stoneface came to the fore. He didn't comment or show reaction as she walked him through the details. "The gods are with us. They will be avenged for thousands of years of suppression. I will be avenged. Out of the chaos we create today, we'll build a new order.

He remained silent for the remainder of the flight, struggling with the enormity of what she'd told him.

Chapter Twenty-Eight

Danbury, Connecticut

Once the jet was on the ground, it taxied to the hangar. As soon as Armitage was off-loaded and moved inside, the doors shut. It left Bethan and Wells alone with the comatose Armitage. The jet left immediately.

"That was a massive tranquilizer you dosed him with." Exasperated, she kept slapping Armitage's face while simultaneously trying to remove the bandages.

Wells walked over to the Cessna and peered inside.

In the center of the hangar, close to the doors, was a small table and chair with laptop and gaming-type equipment, arranged so that once the hangar doors were opened, the entire airfield could be seen. The person operating the controls could sit quietly in the shadows and have a perfect view of taxiing and taking off. He picked up the headset resting on the table beside the control stick.

"That's to talk to Danbury tower for takeoff clearance," Bethan said, dividing her attention between Armitage and Wells. "Come over here and help me rouse him." As he turned to face her, he saw a small tray with a syringe and vials. "Is this what you're going to give him?" he asked idly. She nodded. "Yes. Now get over here."

As he helped, he saw his answer.

Finally, Armitage stirred and opened his eyes. He jerked in surprise and terror when he saw Bethan leaning over and staring into his face. He struggled but suddenly realized he was no longer in the underground room. Instead, he was lying prone, strapped tight. His speech was slurred but they could make out his panic-stricken queries.

"Well here we are Dex. Just like I promised. Your moment of glory."

She left him and walked towards the table, signaling Wells. "We'll wait a half hour or so. I don't want these drugs to conflict with what you gave him. He must be wide awake and cognizant."

She went into the hangar office, rummaged around for a moment then emerged with two cups of coffee. "Sorry, no milk or sugar so it has to be black." She handed him a mug and pulled a second chair close to the table. Armitage's stretcher was hidden behind some packing boxes and tool racks. The Cessna, doors open, was sitting perched ready for flight.

It's bizarre, Wells thought. She's acting like it's some kind of picnic yet in a few hours she will have authored a horrific attack on the United States. He looked over at her. Her eyes were closed, a blithe smile on her face as she sipped her coffee.

Totally surreal, he thought.

Binghamton, New York

It was the right move to fly to Binghamton first.

It took a while to convince the airport's staff to talk to them. Chad finally flashed his old SID credentials. Bethan Price had indeed visited Binghamton several times in the past few weeks. One of the staff mentioned she seemed to spend a lot of time at a small aeronautical company's hangar on the periphery of the airport.

In short order, the three of them walked into the hangar.

The owner wiped his hands on a spotted red handkerchief and stuffed it in his jeans pocket, carefully looking over Chad's SID badge. "So, you guys are not IRS or anything like that?"

"Nope. Not gonna check your financial records or anything like that. Just want to know what business you had with someone named Bethan Price."

The mechanic looked them over carefully before answering. He popped a piece of chewing gum into his mouth, while they waited patiently. Finally, he answered. "She was a customer. I did work for her. That's all."

Wiz stepped up beside him "We know that, sunshine. We want to know exactly what business you had with her."

Twenty minutes later they left, hurrying to their jet.

"A drone? A Cessna turned into a drone? Holy Mackinaw. She's planning something big!"

"Which is why we've got to get to Danbury ASAP. Our friend said that's he delivered it."

Danbury, Connecticut

"So how does this thing work anyway? I wasn't aware our military had anything this sophisticated."

"You don't. It's something I devised myself, with a little help from a brilliant Venezuelan aeronautical engineer. He moved here when he was a young man, but, because he was an immigrant and hadn't attended the 'right' universities, he couldn't find work with the Lockheeds and Boeings who could have used his genius. He opened his own small business. He took my plans and made them reality."

As she spoke she proudly gave Wells a quick overview of the controls and laptop readouts. "I added one other fail-safe option. Once I click this," she pointed to a small green switch on the panel, "everything is engaged. It's all automatic from there. Nothing can stop it. You can unplug the laptop and try to reboot, but it won't work. The autopilot will kick in and the arming mechanism goes live. In other words, push that and it's all over but for the flying. I'm the only one who has the password to cancel it."

Once the laptop booted up, she tested the toggles. "This is so easy," she smiled with satisfaction. "One click on this icon and the engine starts. Then all I have to do is use these headsets, contact the tower for clearance and away we go."

She turned and faced the General. "Well, I guess it's show time, as they say."

She moved to the table and opened the vial, carefully filling the syringe. "This is an improved and much more effective derivative of the drug Zemuron," she casually explained as she drew the plunger up. "It blocks the muscle neurons while leaving the mind fully functional. The brain knows exactly what's going on at all times."

She moved over to Armitage and ripped his sleeve off. His eyes widened in terror and he began to blubber, twisting his head and pleading for mercy as tears streamed down his cheeks.

"Like the mercy you showed my Davey?"

The iceberg coldness of her voice hissed her hatred as she jabbed the needle not too gently into Armitage's bared skin and pushed the plunger with all her might. She and Wells watched as it took effect. Armitage's jaw slackened. No more sounds came out of his mouth. The tears dried up. His head stopped jerking and twisting.

Bethan smiled. "Don't need the straps anymore."

She handed Wells the needle and ordered him to help her move Armitage into the Cessna's pilot seat. Even with the two of them, it was a struggle because he was so heavy. Wells was surprised that while the drugs blocked Armitage's ability to control his muscles, his body was still surprisingly flexible. Once they got him into the seat, they bent his knees into the sitting position and strapped him in.

"Now for the piece de resistance!"

She wandered into the office and pulled out a small suitcase. "The sources who sold it to me, said it's a very dirty little nuclear device. The whole area will be impacted for years after the event. Not to worry though. It's only New York. Never did like the place."

Wells moved swiftly.

As Bethan opened the passenger door, leaned the front seat forward and placed the suitcase carefully on the rear floor of the passenger compartment, he went to the table, grabbed the syringe and filled it as quickly as he could. He approached her, hiding the syringe.

Bethan stepped back to admire her work but kept her eyes on Armitage as she spoke to him. "Well Dex, you really are going to go out with a bang. A glorious blow for our movement. You have the honor of flying a small nuclear device into the Statue of Liberty. It's Saturday of Easter weekend. The place will be jammed with thousands of visitors. We strike a symbolic blow at democracy and, at the same time, create mass horror and hysteria at Christianity's holiest time." A harsh cackling laugh slipped past her lips. "Thank you Dex, for your sacrifice."

As she turned she felt a sudden sting in her arm and felt a surge of icy coldness shoot up her veins. Before she could react, she started to crumple. Wells caught her as he threw the syringe to the corner of the hangar.

He manhandled her into the passenger seat. As he did, he talked to her in the same cold, calculating tone she'd used on Armitage. "You were completely unsuitable and useless as Raven Master. They were fools to choose you simply because you had money. You know squat about leadership and command."

Her eyes flashed back and forth as the reality of her situation seeped into her brain. He could see the fear and pleading in them as he reached around to buckle her in. For the next few minutes while he fussed with her placement, he vented his anger and frustration. Finally, he was satisfied.

"You turned everything into a personal revenge crusade. Good leaders put the movement first, something you never really understood. For all your money, you've done nothing worthwhile. No, Bethan, you may have swanned around living the good life, but your betters did the grunt work. We'll be better off with both of you gone. With a competent leader at the helm, we'll deliver victory out of this assault. You're right Bethan, this will be a double blow against both democracy and the church. Regrettably, however, you were not capable of delivering that victory."

He stepped back and flashed a cold smile at his victims.

"Ladies and gentlemen, please ensure that your seatbelts are securely fastened, your belongings carefully stowed away, and that your seatbacks are in the full and upright position." He slammed the door, laughing diabolically as he did. Who says Old Stoneface has no sense of humor, he sneered to himself.

Wells opened the hangar doors. He studied the control panel and its connections to the laptop again.

Finally, he clicked the mouse. The engine coughed, clouds of blue smoke shot out of the exhaust and just as quickly dissipated. Tentatively he moved the throttle forward and the Cessna moved forward slowly, out of the hangar.

As the engine was still running, he quickly ran out to the plane idling on the ramp. A quick look ensured there was no traffic on the ramp or taxiway. He ran back inside and contacted the tower, asking for clearance.

As he worked the toggles, the view from the cockpit appeared on the laptop's screen. It gave a wide image forward. He guided the plane down the taxiway, coming to a stop at just shy of the end of the runway, as instructed by the tower. From his position, he could see perfectly down the runway to the waiting Cessna.

As he watched, he could see a jet bank to port and begin its final approach.

Washington, D.C.

Tyler was tired of the nonsense. He minced no words with the President.

"Did you or did you not, know that Dexter Armitage was a Druid and the man behind Liam Murphy's killing."

Armed with the information his agents had uncovered and a transcript of Lee Schumacher's confession sent earlier that morning by the Rock Springs police chief, Tyler had demanded an urgent meeting. Inside the secure room they'd used before, Tyler calmly and methodically laid out the evidence for the President. "It all comes down to Armitage and General Wells orchestrating Murphy's death."

He drew himself up and looked the President directly in the eye. "You're the President. I have supported you and worked for this country to the absolute best of my ability and, sadly, to the detriment of my own family life. I do not take any of this lightly, but I have provided a package with all this information to a trusted source. He will not hesitate to release it all to the media if he has not heard from me by this time tomorrow.

"I also have two very good agents out there; very patriotic agents. They are doing the job you asked them to do, even though you humiliated them. They've solved the Murphy case and even now are tracking down Armitage, Wells and others. They need visible support from you right now."

"So, Mr. President, I ask you again. Did you know Armitage was a Druid and that he arranged the killing?"

The President stared unanswering at Tyler. The hum of the air conditioning unit was the only sound except for the President tapping a pen against the table in front of him. He finally broke the silence.

"Cal, this is a very lonely position. You are called upon to hide secrets you know should be shared. You have to make tough decisions, many of which unfortunately, will result in harm and possible death for people." He hunched over the papers in front of him, idly flipping through them once again. "The art of presidency is sometimes speaking out, sometimes remaining silent and hoping to God that you are wise enough to choose the right one at the right time."

He smiled for the first time. "You're a good investigator and, more than that, a good man Cal Tyler. Your boys are good too." He fell silent, still tapping his pen.

"Did I know Dex was a Druid? No. But I had strong suspicions. The thing is, Dex was a doer. He could twist arms, get things done. He was invaluable in pulling that herd of cats they call the Senate, into a somewhat cohesive bunch when I needed them. Dex pushed hard for Murphy's release. So, he went to Wyoming to oversee it."

"Let me understand this," a disgusted Tyler spat, "You knew who had Murphy killed, yet you created the sham of this Committee D, fired us all and then sent them on this wild goose chase!" Tyler's explosion would have been heard in Wyoming if the room wasn't soundproof.

"I had suspicions. No proof. I hoped your guys would come up with something concrete. They have. That's why I bankrolled you; provided the jet."

A new tone entered his voice. "Murphy and the Druids are a cancer on our nation. His removal solved a huge problem. We couldn't prosecute without substantial evidence, especially since key witnesses recanted testimony. And, we had no idea what chaos he would cause once released. Dex solved a problem for us. If, as I suspected, this was an internal fight within the Druids, then your investigation might get the proof we needed to destroy them once and for all.

"Simply put, it was a political necessity that Murphy be removed. I couldn't authorize an illegal move against him. But if it happened, we would certainly be the beneficiaries. Being President means taking the pragmatic route sometimes."

Tyler scoffed. "There are rules of law and order, Mr. President. They're there for a reason. And that reason is not for you to cherry pick which ones you want to follow and which ones you don't."

Tyler's face hardened. "The Druids are planning a major attack against this country. We don't know what. Taking Murphy out didn't solve the problem of treason and violent revolution, it enhanced it. There's a rogue General out there, a missing Chief of Staff and a madwoman all about to cause death and destruction somewhere in the New York area."

"What do you want? What do you need?"

"Mr. President, I need an immediate and very public reversal of Chad and Wiz's firings. You must issue an immediate order to apprehend General Wells and Dexter Armitage on suspicion of treason. Finally, immediate messages to federal, state and local officials in the eastern United States to offer all assistance and resources to Chad and Wiz."

He waited for a response. The President re-read the summary, then looked up.

"Done."

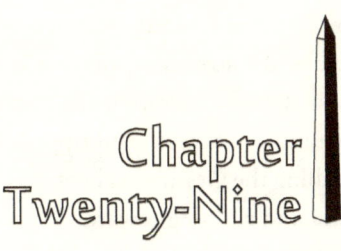

Chapter
Twenty-Nine

Danbury, Connecticut

Wiz handled the jet gentle as a feather, dropping down over the trees that surrounded the airport. Stone was in the co-pilot's seat while Chad was frantically using a satellite phone in the passenger compartment. His first call alerted Tyler to the possibility of a major attack and, second, demanding that Danbury tower tell him Bethan Price's location. He was shocked to learn her jet had already left but relieved she was apparently not on board. Now he was on the phone to Tyler once again. This time it seemed to be good news as both Wiz and Stone heard an excited "yes!" from the rear.

As they neared touchdown, Stone looked out his window. Waiting patiently on the taxiway was a white and red Cessna, revving and waiting for clearance to use the runway after them. As they flashed by, he saw two people in the plane and did a double-take. "My God! Can't be." He craned his head around as hard as he could, but they were long past the Cessna.

While Wiz involved in radio conversation with the tower he fought hard to remain quiet. It wasn't until Wiz pulled off the runway he was able to blurt "Armitage and Price. They're on that Cessna back there."

Wiz began to turn the craft and frantically called the tower, asking them to prevent the Cessna's takeoff, citing his credentials with SID. As he did, Stone peered into the fast-approaching open hangar. "Wells. There's Wells." Chad came charging into the cockpit as Stone pointed.

"Too late. There she goes." The Cessna lurched into the air, wings waggling as it did. "Whoever's flying, is a lousy pilot." Wiz gunned the jet towards the hangar opening

Before the engines could spool down, Chad wrenched the door open and activated the internal staircase, jumping down while it was still extending.

Wells, concentrating on the takeoff, heard a jet approaching but did not look up. He was mesmerized by the streaming video from the cockpit and trying to get the airspeed and stability correct while also gaining altitude. The minute he'd received clearance for takeoff, he'd ripped the earphones off and did not hear the tower calling the Cessna to abort.

Chad was on the ground and running towards the hangar. Stone was right behind him. Wiz was struggling to shut down the aircraft as quickly as possible.

Wells heard the pounding feet and looked up. He didn't recognize the men heading his way but took no chances. He reached over and activated the fail-safe button.

Chad didn't break stride. He bodychecked Wells, bouncing him off the table. The two hit the floor and rolled around, each trying to gain the advantage over the other. Stone jumped into the fray and between the two of them, subdued Wells, dragging him to his feet.

"Whoever you are, you're too late. This will devastate New York with a nuclear bomb and there's nothing you can do to stop it now." Wells snarled.

Chad slugged him. Hard. The General dropped like a stone. With Wells unconscious on the hangar floor, both turned their attention to the electronic array on the table.

Wiz raced in. "What's going on?" He took a look at the screen and quickly scanned the readouts. He saw the video feed and the jerkiness as the plane lurched around. "It's the bloody drone. He's controlling it from here. But what about Price and Armitage? What are they doing in the thing?" He began frantically trying to disable the controls.

Grimly, Stone picked up one of the drug vials lying on the table. "They were drugged. Whatever he's got planned, he put them on it and they're likely going down with the plane."

Wiz struggled with the computer and swore. "It's got some kind of block that's been activated. Can't seem to disable it no matter what I try. Keep getting a screen asking for a password."

Chad pushed in. "Let me try. I can hack pretty good when I want to." While his fingers flew over the keyboard and played the computer like a piano, he shouted "oh yeah, by the way. The President reinstated us. We're legit again!"

Stone grabbed Wiz by the arm. "We need to get in the air. Bring them down."

"Ours is too fast. We can catch up with them, but do damn all when we do. We've got to notify the air force. Shoot them down."

"My God, no!" Chad shouted. "It's got a bomb on board. Big enough to devastate New York, Wells said. Shooting it down might trigger something worse."

As they argued and tried to help Chad break the code, none of them noticed Wells had recovered consciousness. Three against one were too high odds, he decided, and a good military man knows when it's wise to retreat and regroup. Slowly and quietly he moved backwards until he was close enough to the open doors to make a run for it.

Out of the corner of his eye, Wiz saw the movement, swore and started after him. Stone yanked at his arm and stopped him. "Let him go. We'll get him later. We've got to stop that plane."

"Over there! Beechcraft Bonanza." Wiz started running towards a small single-engine, low-winged plane sitting on the tarmac in front of the next hangar down. Stone tore after him. In the background he could hear the siren wails of approaching police. Wiz jumped on the wing and looked in. A man came running out of the neighboring hangar shouting at them. Stone yelled back that they were federal agents and needed the plane. He stopped, stared at them, ran back into the hangar emerging a few seconds later with the ignition keys. He threw the keys up.

Wiz yelled at Stone to get in as he was already inserting himself. With the engine started, he called the tower for immediate take off clearance and began moving even before they answered.

As they rolled, police cars screeched to a halt in front of Price's hangar. Inside, the officers found a frantic Chad trying to break into the computer's program. As the cops ran in he started firing instructions, pulled out his wallet and told them to look for his SID card. He shouted for some of them to chase after Wells. "Short guy. Mouthy. Thinks he's a general or something. He's a terrorist."

Without lifting his eyes from the screen, he warned them about the probability that a nuclear weapon was about to be launched at New York.

He picked up the headset, jammed it on his head and told the tower to patch him through immediately to the aircraft that was just taking off.

As they climbed, Stone and Wiz debated how they were going to find the rogue aircraft. The tower was no help. The filed flight plan merely called for a large circular sightseeing tour of the Danbury area. Before the tower could explain further, Chad broke in.

"I've got an altitude reading and a heading from this contraption. I also have a visual through that video stream."

"Give it to me, big guy."

Armed with the new information, Wiz corrected his course and climbed higher, explaining their own craft was slightly faster and height would enable them to search the skies better. He asked the tower to give them priority clearance and, once they spotted the rogue drone, to clear the airspace around them. Clouds were moving in and the possibility of turbulence surfaced in Wiz's mind.

Fifteen minutes later, Stone strained his eyes ahead, methodically scanning the horizon. In the near distance out his right-hand window, he could see the Manhattan skyline. He leaned forward suddenly as he saw a flash of white. He pointed, and Wiz nodded, banking slightly so that he could approach from above and the rear.

"Seems to be heading more south than straight towards New York." Wiz pointed downwards. "That's Queens down there, just at the end of Long Island Sound."

Carefully he approached from the rear and from a few hundred feet above. He was just going to throw some ideas out, when the drone slowly banked to the right and straightened out.

"Passing between LaGuardia over there and JFK."

Looking ahead, Stone said "If we keep on this heading we'll pass south of Manhattan. What the devil's going on? Where did you program this thing for, lady?" he muttered. He watched the Cessna wobble in the air. "Something's not quite right. It almost looks like it's not balanced properly so it's destabilized."

"Guys. I've tried every Druid word or phrase I could think of. Can't break into this password." Stone could hear the utter frustration and resignation in Chad's voice.

"Keep trying. We can't give up."

"Can't break in. It's a five-space code. If it's a number and symbols, we're screwed."

Frantically, Stone dredged his brain. In the dim recesses he recalled reading some of the articles on Bethan Price. As he tried, he felt the blood drain out of his face.

"Oh crap." He pointed ahead as they approached the lower reaches of the Hudson. "The Statue of Liberty! That's her target."

The drone was now passing over the massive jammed area that was Brooklyn. Another few minutes and it would be too late.

An article abruptly popped into his brain. "Her son's name. The one who was killed. Chad, try David"

There was silence. "No. Not it. David fits, but no."

"Wait. She called him Davey. Try that."

"With an 'ey' or 'ie'?"

"Try both."

The brief silence was shattered by a whoop. "We're in." Seconds later, Chad whooped again. "The device is deactivated."

"But the plane is still going. It will still hit."

"Yeah," Wiz said, "it's dropped down to three thousand feet and adjusted course, so it will hit smack on the statue."

They saw another ferry sail into the island's dock. "There's got to be hundreds of people there. My God. It will be catastrophic even without the bomb."

"Air force jets are rolling towards you," Chad reported. "They going to try and down it."

"Not enough time," Stone shouted. "Getting too close.

The could see the disaster looming and were powerless to stop it.

"Can you drop down beside them and fly parallel?"

Wiz looked strangely at him. "You gonna open the door and step across and try to turn off the engine?" he asked incredulously.

"No. Something they used to do in World War Two against the flying bombs the Nazis sent over London. Spitfire pilots would get their wings underneath the bomb's wings and try to flip it over. You said the thing is destabilized already. If we do it hard enough and fast enough, it might just throw the Cessna out of its trajectory. Crash the sucker."

As he spoke, Wiz had already brought them alongside. Both Druids stared straight ahead, seemingly oblivious to the imminent disaster. Even as Wiz encroached on their airspace, they didn't move. Cripes, the drug must have paralyzed them, Stone thought.

"Only going to get one shot at this, Stone. Hope you're right."

The drone aircraft suddenly pitched down, aiming itself directly at the base of the statue.

Without waiting, Wiz tucked his low wing just under the drone's higher one. He eased up. The wings touched. Then he banked right sharply and suddenly.

Stone was suddenly looking down at the fast approaching river, as Wiz picked up speed and circled.

"Yee haw!" He straightened out and the watched the Cessna pitch down, wobbling, struggling to regain its programmed flight path, then suddenly smash into the river. Before they could grasp the enormity of what just happened, an air force jet buzzed them and called them up.

"Sir. Land immediately at Linden airport. You are cleared to make a direct approach. And congratulations, sir. We hear you averted a major disaster."

They circled again as Chad cheered over the radio. Below them, craft of all kinds, including police boats were converging on the crash site. The enormous plume of water had dissipated. Only debris floated on top.

One police boat started to pick up wreckage while others stopped rubberneck boaters. They circled over the Statue one final time. Stone could see hundreds of people looking up and pointing. If they only knew, he thought as they banked away.

He was still in shock as they made their final approach to Linden.

Epilogue

Stone had no eyes or words for anyone other than her when he arrived back at Greyfell Abbey. They held onto each other, kissing, embracing and kissing again, oblivious to the furor his arrival created. Lord Greyfell stepped up to welcome him back, but Nees gripped his elbow and pulled him away. "Later," she said. She turned and shooed the rest out of the room, closing the door quietly behind her.

Mandy was crying, tears streaking her cheeks. "Are you sad, or happy?" She smacked him on the shoulder. "Both, you great big lummox," she hiccupped as she tried to switch from crying to laughing. "When I heard what you did, it scared me to death. I don't ever want to lose you. What actually happened over there?"

Between the tears and questions, it was half an hour before the pair, holding hands tightly, walked into the dining room where the others were starting their meal. Cheers, questions, and exuberant joy permeated the meal as Stone once again recited his story. It was, he figured, the fifth or sixth time he'd recounted it, including local police and state officials and then a more intensive debriefing in front of Tyler and assorted federal law enforcement and intelligence officials.

Tyler had taken Stone, Chad and Wiz to the massive hotel suite he'd reserved for them, close to the White House. "Enjoy. Order whatever you want. It's on the government tab." He'd heard their stories numerous times and already congratulated them. It was now their time to question him.

"How come the Pres suddenly gave us our jobs back and cleared us with the police?"

Tyler grimaced then filled them in on his meeting and its aftermath.

Wiz was succinct as usual. "The bastard! I told you we were being set up. All he really cared about was making sure his butt was covered, no matter what." He threw the couch pillow across the room.

"Did he reinstate you too, Chief? You gonna work for him again?" Chad looked quizzically at Tyler.

"Yes. And no." The enigmatic answer puzzled them all. "Yes, he reinstated me and gave me my old job back. No, I will not work for him and told him so. Too much water under the bridge. He's going to offer you the job, Chad. What you do is up to you."

Chad was still pondering the situation when Stone left, struggling to reconcile his anger and feeling of betrayal, with his innate desire to serve his country and finish the work they'd all set out to do. After all, he'd told Stone privately, Wells is still on the loose. We've got to bring him in.

While they were enjoying the celebration lunch at Greyfell Abbey, Freddy told Stone Belmont's body was found jammed on a rocky ledge some fifteen feet above the sea. Evans had not yet been found. "The Prime Minister announced Belmont's death yesterday. They're putting it down to suicide, brought about by the stress of his position. By the way, the guvnor got the information he needed from Colin Maddox's investigations in Glasgow. Seems Belmont had a sugar daddy who funded his various activities. Inland Revenue has been looking at Michael Donovan for some time. A lot of his financial deals were shady to say the least. Colin tied him to Belmont. He's in custody right now and squealing like a stuck pig. Has a tattoo on his right forearm as well. Need I say more."

Adam added more news. "Meldrew was murdered near Evans' flat. We found enough evidence to charge Martin Bryn. Now we've nailed him, we can squeeze him and clear a number of suspicious deaths off the dockets."

Mandy, meanwhile, couldn't wait to fill them in on the phone call she'd had from Huw just as Stone arrived. "Da will be back in a couple of days. But as it stands now, everything looks authentic. The artifacts date from the first century and the parchments are good for the period from 1100 to 1300. They're still running tests, but it's all looking good. We have a monumental find on our hands."

Lunch finished, they all reluctantly left Stone to himself, recognizing he was shaky after two narrow brushes with death in the past ten days, not to mention jet lag. He made his way into the small snug and settled into his favorite leather armchair. It was deep, warm, comfortable and just what he needed, especially if he wanted to doze off. He was asleep when his cellphone vibrated. He checked the caller ID and, reluctantly, answered.

"John Beauchamp here. My heartiest congratulations on your heroic efforts in Wales and in America."

"How did you know?"

"Sources, dear boy. Sources. You are a true warrior, worthy of Madoc. Who better indeed to tell his story? I'm also told the Lundy material you found is authentic. What are you planning to do with it?"

"Frankly, I've no idea. Anyway, it's not my decision to make."

"On the contrary. You, of all men, have earned the right to say how and when the information is released. If I might make a suggestion I'm sure would go down well with the BBC. Reveal it as part of your program. You are continuing, are you not?"

Stone thought for a moment, then confessed the show had been the furthest thing from his mind in recent days. They continued talking about it, with Beauchamp mounting strong arguments for its continuation. "Madoc's story is still untold, Mr. Wallace. You've only explored the Welsh half. What about the rest? He went to America with a very precious item, then disappeared. Don't you want to know what happened? May I remind you, we are counting on you to follow that journey through and perhaps learn what happened to that object?"

By the time he hung up, Stone was wide awake. He patrolled the house until he found Mandy, took her hand and suggested a walk on the fells. They climbed the hill behind the house, enjoying the brilliant sunshine of the day and the stunning scenery across to Skiddaw. At a rocky outcrop overlooking the valley, they sat down.

He broached the subject first. "The Templars called me just now. Wanted to know if we're going to continue with the show."

"Are we?"

He thought for a moment, weighing his words carefully. "Frankly, after everything, I just want to run away and find a rock somewhere. I'd dig a hole under it and stay there for the rest of my life, away from Druids, death, destruction, terror and everything else." He grinned. "Take you with me, of course."

He got serious again. "But the Templars are right. It's a cracking good story, as you Welsh say. History, intrigue linking two nations and crossing centuries of time." He twirled a blade of grass in his fingers. "We've only uncovered half the story. What about those legends of Welsh-speaking Indians, Thomas Jefferson and those European-style stone fortifications?" He twiddled the grass some more. "A good journalist doesn't leave a story un-done or half-baked. We pursue to the end, no matter where it leads."

"So, you're saying we should continue."

He reached over and pulled her close, hugging her hard. "I guess I am. Who knows what we'll find. But for sure, it will be an amazing program when we're finished."

She looked up at him and smiled. "I was hoping you'd say that. I agree. We go on."

He smiled and kissed her. "We go on as a team. Permanently."

She nodded.

ठ

Two hikers struggling to cross back to the mainland before the tide turned, saw it first. It was tossing against the rocks well below them, close to the massive blowhole carved by the sea into the headland. It was too dangerous for them to try and find out what it was. Besides, the tide was rushing in and they needed to get off Worms Head.

As they scrambled onto the mainland, they used their mobile to alert the Coast Guard. Within the hour, the lifeboat from Tenby was on scene as were lifesaving crews who rappelled down the rockface to retrieve what they found to be a body.

The boated corpse was bobbing, trapped in a small tidal pool area.

The first man on scene flipped it over. The face was gone; battered by the rocks and devoured by fishes. They struggled to secure it. Hoisting it up the rock face was an impossibility. They had to swing it across to the waiting, bobbing lifeboat,

It nudged as close as possible to the rocks. One of the lifeboat men threw a line across that was adeptly caught by one of the rappelers. Swift-ly, they rigged up a harness and lifted the body as high as they could then swung it gently over to the waiting boat.

The crew hauled it in, released the ropes and the boat began to back off into calmer, safer water. They laid the body on deck and the boat's coxswain looked down. "Poor blighter."

As they pulled the body by the arms and into a body bag, the sleeve slipped up, revealing a black dragon tattoo.

www.ingramcontent.com/pod-product-compliance
Lightning Source LLC
Chambersburg PA
CBHW020434030726
47495CB00006B/1801